HARDBALL DIPLOMACY

The Yill circled the floor, sabre twirling. Then suddenly he was towering before Retief. The heavy sabre whipped down with an explosive concussion that cleaved the table. The Yill's eyes held on Retief as he pushed back his stool and stood, the huge gray-skinned Yill topping his six-foot-three by an inch.

In a motion too quick to follow Retief reached for the sabre, twitched it from the Yill's grasp, swung it in a whistling arc. His opponent ducked, sprang back and snatched up a sabre from a table. Retief pressed the Yill, fending off vicious cuts, chopping back relentlessly.

Now the two stood toe to toe, weapons clashing in a furious exchange. The Yill gave a step, then rallied, drove Retief back, back. . . .

Also by Keith Laumer:

RETIEF AT LARGE

from ACE Science Fiction

SF

Retief Unbound

Keith Laumer

SF
ace books

A Division of Charter Communications Inc.
A GROSSET & DUNLAP COMPANY
360 Park Avenue South
New York, New York 10010

RETIEF UNBOUND

An ACE Book

Cover art by Bob Adragna

First Ace printing: May 1979
Second Ace printing: January 1980

Printed in U.S.A.

Table of Contents

PROTOCOL   3

SEALED ORDERS   25

AIDE MEMOIRE   47

POLICY   75

PALACE REVOLUTION   113

RETIEF'S RANSOM   147

". . . into the chaotic Galactic political scene of the post-Concordiat era, the CDT emerged to carry forward the ancient diplomatic tradition as a great supra-national organization dedicated to the contravention of war.[1] As mediators of disputes among Terrestrial-settled worlds and advocates of Terrestrial interests in contacts with alien cultures, Corps diplomats, trained in the chanceries of innumerable defunct bureaucracies, displayed an encyclopedic grasp of the nuances of Estra-Terrestrial mores as set against the labyrinthine socio-politico-economic Galactic context. Never was the virtuosity of a senior Corps diplomat more brilliantly displayed than in Ambassador Spradley's negotiation of the awkward Sirenian Question. . . ."

—extract from the *Official History of the Corps Diplomatique*, Vol I, reel 2. Solarian Press, New New York, 479 A. E. (AD 2940)

PROTOCOL

IN THE GLOOM of the squat, mud-colored reception building, the Counselor, two First Secretaries, and the senior Attachés gathered around the plump figure of Ambassador Spradley, their ornate diplomatic uniforms bright in the vast gloomy room. The Ambassador glanced at his finger watch impatiently.

1) Cf. the original colorful language: "maintenance of a state of tension short of actual conflict." See CDT File 178/b/491, col. VII, spool 12: 745mm (code 2g).

"Ben, are you quite certain our arrival time was made clear?"

Second Secretary Magnan nodded emphatically. "I stressed the point, Mr. Ambassador. I communicated with Mr. T'Cai-Cai just before the lighter broke orbit, and I specifically emphasized—"

"I hope you didn't appear truculent, Mr. Magnan," the Ambassador cut in sharply.

"No indeed, Mr. Ambassador. I merely—"

"You're sure there's no VIP room here?" The Ambassador glanced around the cavernous room. "Curious that not even chairs have been provided."

"If you'd care to sit on one of those crates, I'll use my hanky—"

"Certainly not." The Ambassador looked at his watch again and cleared his throat.

"I may as well make use of these few moments to outline our approach for the more junior members of the staff. It's vital that the entire mission work in harmony in the presentation of the image. We Terrestrials are a kindly, peace-loving race." The Ambassador smiled in a kindly, peace-loving way.

"We seek only reasonable division of spheres of influence with the Yill." He spread his hands, looking reasonable.

"We are a people of high culture, ethical, sincere."

The smile was replaced abruptly by pursed lips. "We'll start by asking for the entire Sirenian System, and settle for half. We'll establish a foothold on all the choicer worlds and, with shrewd handling in a decade we'll be in a position to assert a wider claim.'' The Ambassador glanced around. "If there are no questions . . ."

Jame Retief, Vice-Consul and Third Secretary in the Corps Diplomatique and junior member of the Terrestrial Embassy to Yill, stepped forward.

"Since we hold the prior claim to the system, why don't we put all our cards on the table to start with? Perhaps if we dealt frankly with the Yill, it would pay us in the long run.''

Ambassador Spradley blinked up at the younger man. Beside him, Magnan cleared his throat in the silence.

"Vice-Consul Retief merely means—''

"I'm capable of interpreting Mr. Retief's remark,'' Spradley snapped. He assumed a fatherly expression.

"Young man, you're new to the service. You haven't yet learned the team play, the give-and-take of diplomacy. I shall expect you to observe closely the work of the experienced negotiators of the mission, learn the importance of subtlety. Excessive reliance on direct methods might tend in time to attenuate the rôle of the professional diplomat. I shudder to contemplate the consequences.''

Spradley turned back to his senior staff members. Retief strolled across to a glass-panelled door and glanced into the room beyond. Several dozen tall grey-skinned Yill lounged in deep couches, sipping lavender drinks from slender glass tubes. Black-tunicked servants moved about inconspicuously, offering trays. Retief watched as a party of brightly-dressed Yill moved toward a wide entrance door. One of the party, a tall male, made to step before another, who raised a hand languidly, fist clenched. The first Yill stepped back and placed his hands on top of his head with a nod. Both Yill continued to smile and chatter as they passed through the door.

Retief rejoined the Terrestrial delegation, grouped around a mound of rough crates stacked on the bare concrete floor, as a small leather-skinned Yill came up.

"I am P'Toi. Come thiss way . . ." He motioned. The Terrestrials moved off, Ambassador Spradley in the lead. As the portly diplomat reached the door, the Yill guide darted ahead, shouldering him aside, then hesitated, waiting. The Ambassador almost glared, then remembered the image. He smiled, beckoning the Yill ahead. The Yill muttered in the native language, stared about, then passed through the door. The Terran party followed.

"I'd like to know what that fellow was saying," Magnan said, overtaking the Ambassador. "The way he jostled your Excellency was disgraceful."

A number of Yill waited on the pavement outside the building. As Spradley approached the luxurious open car waiting at the curb, they closed ranks, blocking his way. He drew himself up, opened his mouth—then closed it with a snap.

"The very idea," Magnan said, trotting at Spradley's heels as he stalked back to rejoin the staff, now looking around uncertainly. "One would think these persons weren't aware of the courtesies due a Chief of Mission."

"They're not aware of the courtesies due an apprentice sloat skinner!" Spradley snapped. Around the Terrestrials, the Yill milled nervously, muttering in the native tongue.

"Where has our confounded interpreter be-taken himself?" The Ambassador barked. "I daresay they're plotting openly. . . ."

"A pity we have to rely on a native interpreter."

"Had I known we'd meet this rather uncouth reception," the Ambassador said stiffly, "I would have audited the language personally, of course, during the voyage out."

"Oh, no criticism intended, of course, Mr. Ambassador," Magnan said hastily. "Heavens, who would have thought—"

Retief stepped up beside the Ambassador.

"Mr. Ambassador," he said. "I—"

"Later, young man," the Ambassador snapped. He beckoned to the Counselor, and the two moved off, heads together.

A bluish sun gleamed in a dark sky. Retief watched his breath form a frosty cloud in the chill air. A broad hard-wheeled vehicle pulled up to the platform. The Yill gestured the Terran party to the gaping door at the rear, then stood back, wait-ing.

Retief looked curiously at the grey-painted van. The legend written on its side in alien symbols seemed to read 'egg nog.' Unfortunately he hadn't had time to learn the script too, on the trip out. Perhaps later he would have a chance to tell the Ambassador he could interpret for the mission.

The Ambassador entered the vehicle, the other Terrestrials following. It was as bare of seats as the Terminal building. What appeared to be a defunct electronic chassis lay in the center of the floor, amid a litter of paper and a purple and yellow sock designed for a broad Yill foot. Retief glanced back. The Yill were talking excitedly. None of them entered the car. The door was closed, and the

Terrans braced themselves under the low roof as
the engine started up with a whine of worn turbos,
and the van moved off.

It was an uncomfortable ride. The unsprung
wheels hammered uneven cobblestones. Retief
put out an arm as the vehicle rounded a corner,
caught the Ambassador as he staggered off-
balance. The Ambassador glared at him, settled
his heavy tri-corner hat, and stood stiffly until the
car lurched again.

Retief stooped, trying to see out through the
single dusty window. They seemed to be in a wide
street lined with low buildings. They passed
through a massive gate, up a ramp, and stopped.
The door opened. Retief looked out at a blank grey
facade, broken by tiny windows at irregular intervals. A scarlet vehicle was drawn up ahead, the
Yill reception committee emerging from it.
Through its wide windows Retief saw rich up-
holstery and caught a glimpse of glasses clamped
to a tiny bar.

P'Toi, the Yill interpreter, came forward, gestur-
ing to a small door in the grey wall. Magnan scur-
ried ahead to open it and held it for the Ambassador. As he stepped to it a Yill thrust himself
ahead and hesitated. Ambassador Spradley drew
himself up, glaring. Then he twisted his mouth
into a frozen smile and stepped aside. The Yill
looked at each other, then filed through the door.

Retief was the last to enter. As he stepped inside
a black-clad servant slipped past him, pulled the
lid from a large box by the door and dropped in a
paper tray heaped with refuse. There were alien
symbols in flaking paint on the box. They seemed,
Retief noticed, to spell 'egg nog'.

* * *

The shrill pipes and whining reeds had been warming up for an hour when Retief emerged from his cubicle and descended the stairs to the banquet hall. Standing by the open doors he lit a slender cigar and watched through narrowed eyes as obsequious servants in black flitted along the low wide corridor, carrying laden trays into the broad room, arranging setttings on a great four-sided table forming a hollow square that almost filled the room. Rich brocades were spread across the center of the side nearest the door, flanked by heavily decorated white cloths. Beyond, plain white extended down the two sides to the far board, where metal dishes were arranged on the bare table top. A richly dressed Yill approached, stepped aside to allow a servant to pass and entered the room.

Retief turned at the sound of Terran voices behind him. The Ambassador came up, trailed by two diplomats. He glanced at Retief, adjusted his ruff and looked into the banquet hall.

"Apparently we're to be kept waiting again," he snapped. "After having been informed at the outset that the Yill have no intention of yielding an inch, one almost wonders . . ."

"Mr. Ambassador," Retief said. "Have you noticed—"

"However," Ambassador Spradley said, eyeing Retief, "a seasoned diplomatist must take these little snubs in stride. In the end—ah there, Magnan . . ." He turned away, talking.

Somewhere a gong clanged. In a moment the corridor was filled with chattering Yill who moved past the group of Terrestrials into the banquet hall. P'Toi, the Yill interpreter, came up, raised a hand.

"Waitt heere . . ."

More Yill filed into the dining room, taking their places. A pair of helmeted guards approached and waved the Terrestrials back. An immense grey-jowled Yill waddled to the doors, ropes of jewels clashing softly, and passed through, followed by more guards.

"The Chief of State," Retief heard Magnan say. "The Admirable F'Kau-Kau-Kau."

"I have yet to present my credentials," Ambassador Spradley said. "One expects some latitude in the observances of protocol, but I confess . . ." He wagged his head.

The Yill interpreter spoke up.

"You now whill lhie on yourr intesstinss and creep to fesstive board there." He pointed across the room.

"Intestines?" Ambassador Spradley looked about wildly.

"Mr. P'Toi means our stomachs, I wouldn't wonder," Magnan said. "He just wants us to lie down and crawl to our seats, Mr. Ambassador."

"What the devil are you grinning at, you idiot?" the Ambassador snapped.

Magnan's face fell.

Spradley glanced down at the medals across his paunch.

"This is . . . I've never . . ."

"Homage to godss," the interpreter said.

"Oh-oh—religion," someone said.

"Well, if it's a matter of religious beliefs . . ." The Ambassador looked around dubiously.

"Actually, it's only a couple of hundred feet," Magnan said.

Retief stepped up to P'Toi.

"His Excellency, the Terrestrial Ambassador, will not crawl," he said clearly.

"Here, young man, I said nothing—"

"Not to crawl?" The interpreter wore an unreadable Yill expression.

"It is against our religion," Retief said.

"Againsst?"

"We are votaries of the Snake Goddess," Retief said. "It is a sacrilege to crawl." He brushed past the interpreter and marched toward the distant table. The others followed.

Puffing, the Ambassador came to Retief's side as they approached the dozen empty stools on the far side of the square opposite the brocaded position of the Admirable F'Kau-Kau-Kau.

"Mr. Retief, kindly see me after this affair," he hissed. "In the meantime, I hope you will restrain any further rash impulses. Let me remind you I am Chief of Mission here."

Magnan came up from behind.

"Let me add my congratulations, Retief," he said. "That was fast thinking."

"Are you out of your mind, Magnan?" the Ambassador barked. "I am extremely displeased."

"Why," Magnan stuttered, "I was speaking sarcastically, of course, Mr. Ambassador. Naturally I, too, was taken aback by his presumption."

The Terrestrials took their place, Retief at the end. The table before them was of bare green wood, with an array of shallow pewter dishes upon it.

The Yill at the table, some in plain grey, others in black, eyed them silently. There was a constant stir among them as one or another rose and disappeared and others sat down. The pipes and reeds of the orchestra were shrilling furiously and the susurration of Yillian conversation from the other tables rose ever higher in competition. A tall Yill in black was at the Ambassador's side now. The nearby Yill all fell silent as the servant ladled a whitish soup into the largest of the bowls before the Terrestrial envoy. The interpreter hovered, watching.

"That's quite enough," Ambassador Spradley said, as the bowl overflowed. The Yill servant dribbled more of the soup into the bowl. It welled out across the table top.

"Kindly serve the other members of my staff," the Ambassador commanded. The interpreter said something in a low voice. The servant moved hesitantly to the next stool and ladled more soup.

Retief watched, listening to the whispers around him. The Yill at the table were craning now to watch. The servant was ladling the soup rapidly, rolling his eyes sideways. He came to Retief and reached out with the full ladle for the bowl.

"No," Retief said.

The servant hesitated.

"None for me," Retief said.

The interpreter came up, motioned to the servant, who reached again, ladle brimming.

"I don't want any!" Retief said, his voice distinct in the sudden hush. He stared at the interpreter, who stared back for a moment, then waved the servant away and moved on.

"Mr. Retief," a voice hissed. Retief looked down the table. The Ambassador was leaning forward, glaring at him, his face a mottled crimson.

"I'm warning you, Mr. Retief," he said hoarsely. "I've eaten sheep's eyes in the Sudan, *ka swe* in Burma, hundred-year *cug* on Mars, and everything else that has been placed before me in the course of my diplomatic career, and by the holy relics of Saint Ignatz, you'll do the same!" He snatched up a spoon-like utensil and dipped it into his bowl.

"Don't eat that, Mr. Ambassador," Retief said.

The Ambassador stared, eyes wide. He opened his mouth, guiding the spoon toward it.

Retief stood, gripped the table under its edge, and heaved. The immense wooden slab rose and tilted; dishes crashed to the floor. The table followed with a ponderous slam. Milky soup splattered across the terrazzo; a couple of odd bowls rolled clattering across the room. Cries rang out from the Yill, mingling with a strangled yell from Ambassador Spradley.

Retief walked past the wild-eyed members of the mission to the sputtering chief. "Mr. Ambassador," he said. "I'd like—"

"You'd like! I'll break you, you young hoodlum! Do you realize—"

"Pleass . . ." The interpreter stood at Retief's side.

"My apologies," Ambassador Spradley said, mopping his forehead. "My profound—"

"Be quiet," Retief said.

"Wh-what?!"

"Don't apologize," Retief said.

P'Toi was beckoning. "Pleasse, arll come."

Retief turned and followed him.

The portion of the table they were ushered to was covered with an embroidered white cloth, set with thin porcelain dishes. The Yill already seated there rose, amid babbling, and moved down to make room for the Terrestrials. The black-clad Yill at the end table closed ranks to fill the vacant seats. Retief sat down, finding Magnan at his side.

"What's going on here?" the Second Secretary said.

"They were giving us dog food," Retief said. "I overheard a Yill. They seated us at the servants' section of the table."

"You mean you understand the language?"

"I learned it on the way out—enough, at least—"

The music burst out with a clangorous fanfare, and a throng of jugglers, dancers, and acrobats poured into the center of the hollow square, frantically juggling, dancing, and back-flipping. Servants swarmed, heaping mounds of fragrant food on the plates of Yill and Terrestrials alike, pouring pale purple liquor into slender glasses. Retief sampled the Yill food. It was delicious. Conversation was impossible in the din. He watched the gaudy display and ate heartily.

Retief leaned back, grateful for the lull in the music. The last of the dishes were whisked away, and more glasses filled. The exhausted entertainers stopped to pick up the thick square coins the diners threw. Retief sighed. It had been a rare feast.

"Retief," Magnan said in the comparative quiet. "What were you saying about dog food as the music came up?"

Retief looked at him. "Haven't you noticed the pattern, Mr. Magnan? The series of deliberate affronts?"

"Deliberate affronts! Just a minute, Retief. They're uncouth, yes, crowding into doorways and that sort of thing. But . . ." He looked at Retief uncertainly.

"They herded us into a baggage warehouse at the terminal. Then they hauled us here in a garbage truck."

"Garbage truck!"

"Only symbolic, of course. They ushered us in the tradesmen's entrance, and assigned us cubicles in the servants' wing. Then we were seated with the coolie-class sweepers at the bottom of the table."

"You must be mistaken! I mean, after all, we're the Terrestrial delegation; surely these Yill must realize our power."

"Precisely, Mr. Magnan. But—"

With a clang of cymbals, the musicians launched a renewed assault. Six tall, helmeted Yill sprang into the center of the floor, paired off in a wild performance, half dance, half combat. Magnan pulled at Retief's sleeve, his mouth moving. Retief shook his head. No one could talk against a Yill orchestra in full cry. Retief sampled a bright red wine and watched the show.

There was a flurry of action, and two of the dancers stumbled and collapsed, their partner-opponents whirling away to pair off again, describe the elaborate pre-combat ritual, and abruptly set to, dulled sabres clashing—and two more Yill were down, stunned. It was a violent dance. Retief watched, the drink forgotten.

The last two Yill approached and retreated, whirled, bobbed, and spun, feinted and postured. And then one was slipping, going down, helmet awry, and the other, a giant, muscular Yill, spun away, whirled in a mad skirl of pipes as coins showered—then froze before a gaudy table, raised the sabre, and slammed it down in a resounding blow across the gay cloth before a lace-and-bow-bedecked Yill. The music stopped with a ringing clash of cymbals.

In utter silence the dancer-fighter stared across the table. With a shout the seated Yill leaped up and raised a clenched fist. The dancer bowed his head, spread his hands on his helmet and resumed his dance as the music blared anew. The beribboned Yill waved a hand negligently, flung a handful of coins across the floor, and sat down.

Now the dancer stood rigid before the brocaded table—and the music chopped off short as the sabre slammed down before a heavy Yill in ornate metallic coils. The challenged Yill rose, raised a fist, and the other ducked his head, putting his hands on his helmet. Coins rolled, and the dancer moved on.

He circled the broad floor, sabre twirling, arms darting in an intricate symbolism. Then suddenly he was towering before Retief, sabre above his head. The music cut, and in the startling instantaneous silence, the heavy sabre whipped over and down with an explosive concussion that set dishes dancing on the table-top.

The Yill's eyes held on Retief's. In the silence Magnan tittered drunkenly. Retief pushed back his stool.

"Steady, my boy," Ambassador Spradly called. Retief stood, the Yill topping his six-foot-three by an inch. In a motion too quick to follow Retief reached for the sabre, twitched it from the Yill's grasp, swung it in a whistling arc. The Yill ducked, sprang back and snatched up a sabre dropped by another dancer.

"Someone stop the madman!" Spradley howled.

Retief leaped across the table, sending fragile dishes spinning.

The other danced back, and only then did the orchestra spring to life with a screech and a mad tattoo of high-pitched drums.

Making no attempt to follow the weaving pattern of the Yill bolero, Retief pressed the Yill, fending off vicious cuts with the blunt weapon, chopping back relentlessly. Left hand on hip, Retief matched blow for blow, driving the other back.

Abruptly the Yill abandoned the double role. Dancing forgotten, he settled down in earnest, cutting, thrusting, parrying. Now the two stood toe to toe, sabres clashing in a lightning exchange. The Yill gave a step, two, then rallied, drove Retief back, back—

Retief feinted, laid a hearty whack across the grey skull. The Yill stumbled, his sabre clattered to the floor. Retief stepped aside as the Yill wavered past him and crashed to the floor.

The orchestra fell silent in a descending wail of reeds. Retief drew a deep breath and wiped his forehead.

"Come back here, you young fool!" Spradley called hoarsely.

Retief hefted the sabre, turned, eyed the brocade-draped table. He started across the floor. The Yill sat as if paralyzed.

"Retief, no!" Spradley yelped.

Retief walked directly to the Admirable

F'Kau-Kau-Kau, stopped, raised the sabre.

"Not the Chief of State," someone in the Terrestrial Mission groaned.

Retief whipped the sabre down. The dull blade split the heavy brocade and cleaved the hardwood table. There was utter silence.

The Admirable F'Kau-Kau-Kau rose, seven feet of obese grey Yill. His broad face expressionless to the Terran eye, he raised a fist like a jewel-studded ham.

Retief stood rigid for a long moment. Then, gracefully, he inclined his head and placed his finger tips on his temples. Behind him there was a clatter as Ambassador Spradley collapsed. Then the Admirable F'Kau-Kau-Kau cried out, reached across the table to embrace the Terrestrial, and the orchestra went mad. Grey hands helped Retief across the table, stools were pushed aside to make room at F'Kau-Kau-Kau's side. Retief sat, took a tall flagon of coal-black brandy pressed on him by his neighbor, clashed glasses with The Admirable, and drank.

"The feast ends," F'Kau-Kau-Kau said. "Now you and I, Retief, must straddle the Council Stool."

"I'll be honored, Your Admirableness," Retief said. "I must inform my colleagues."

"Colleagues?" F'Kau-Kau-Kau said. "It is for chiefs to parley. Who shall speak for a king while he yet has tongue for talk?"

"The Yill way is wise," Retief said.

F'Kau-Kau-Kau emptied a squat tumbler of pink beer. "I'll treat with you, Retief, as viceroy, since as you say your king is old and the space between worlds is far. But there shall be no scheming underlings privy to our dealings." He grinned a Yill grin. "Afterwards we shall carouse, Retief. The Council Stool is hard, and the waiting handmaidens delectable; this makes for quick agreement."

Retief smiled. "The Admirable speaks wisdom."

"Of course, a being prefers wenches of his own kind," F'Kau-Kau-Kau said. He belched. "The Ministry of Culture has imported several Terrestrial joy-girls, said to be top-notch specimens. As least they have very fat watchamacallits."

"Your Admirableness is most considerate," Retief said.

"Let us to it then, Retief. I may hazard a tumble with one of your Terries, myself. I fancy an occasional perversion." F'Kau-Kau-Kau dug an elbow into Retief's side and bellowed with laughter.

As Retief crossed to the door at F'Kau-Kau-Kau's side, Ambassador Spradley glowered from behind the plain tablecloth. "Retief," he called, "kindly excuse yourself. I wish a word with you." His voice was icy. Magnan stood behind him, goggling.

"Forgive my apparent rudeness, Mr. Ambassador," said Retief. "I don't have time to explain now—"

"Rudeness!" Spradley yipped. "Don't have time, eh? Let me tell you—"

"Please lower your voice, Mr. Ambassador," Retief said. "The situation is still delicate."

Spradley quivered, his mouth open. He found his voice, "You—you—"

"Silence!" Retief snapped. Spradley looked up

at Retief's face, staring for a moment into Retief's grey eyes. He closed his mouth and swallowed.

"The Yill seem to have gotten the impression I'm in charge," Retief said. "We'll have to maintain the deception."

"But—but—" Spradley stuttered. Then he straightened. "That is the last straw," he whispered hoarsely. "I am the Terrestrial Ambassador Extraordinary and Minister Plenipotentiary. Magnan has told me that we've been studiedly and repeatedly insulted, since the moment of our arrival; kept waiting in baggage rooms, transported in refuse lorries, herded about with servants, offered swill at the table. Now I, and my senior staff, are left cooling our heels, without so much as an audience, while this—this multiple Kau person hobnobs with—with—"

Spradley's voice broke. "I may have been a trifle hasty, Retief, in attempting to restrain you. Slighting the native gods and dumping the banquet table are rather extreme measures, but your resentment was perhaps partially justified. I am prepared to be lenient with you." He fixed a choleric eye on Retief.

"I am walking out of this meeting, Mr. Retief. I'll take no more of these personal—"

"That's enough," Retief said sharply. "We're keeping The Admirable waiting."

Spradley's face purpled.

Magnan found his voice. "What are you going to do, Retief?"

"I'm going to handle the negotiation," Retief said. He handed Magnan his empty glass. "Now go sit down and work on the Image."

* * *

At his desk in the VIP suite aboard the orbiting Corps vessel, Ambassador Spradley pursed his lips and looked severely at Vice-Consul Retief.

"Further," he said, "you have displayed a complete lack of understanding of Corps discipline, the respect due a senior officer, even the basic courtesies. Your aggravated displays of temper, ill-timed outbursts of violence, and almost incredible arrogance in the assumption of authority make your further retention as an Officer-Agent of the Corps Diplomatique Terrestrienne impossible. It will therefore be my unhappy duty to recommend your immediate—"

There was a muted buzz from the communicator. The Ambassador cleared his throat.

"Well?"

"A signal from Sector HQ, Mr. Ambassador," a voice said.

"Well, read it," Spradley snapped. "Skip the preliminaries . . ."

"Congratulations on the unprecedented success of your mission. The articles of agreement transmitted by you embody a most favorable resolution of the difficult Sirenian situation, and will form the basis of continued amicable relations between the Terrestrial States and the Yill Empire. To you and your staff, full credit is due for a job well done. Signed, Deputy Assistant Secretary Sternwheeler."

Spradley cut off the voice impatiently. He shuffled papers, then eyed Retief sharply.

"Superficially, of course, an uninitiated observer might leap to the conclusion that the ah . . . results that were produced in spite of these . . . ah . . . irregularities justify the latter." The Ambassador smiled a sad, wise smile. "This is far from the case," he said. "I—"

The communicator burped softly.

"Confound it." Spradley muttered. "Yes?"

"Mr. T'Cai-Cai has arrived," the voice said. "Shall I—"

"Send him in, at once." Spradley glanced at Retief. "Only a two-syllable man, but I shall attempt to correct these false impressions, make some amends . . ."

The two Terrestrials waited silently until the Yill Protocol chief tapped at the door.

"I hope," the Ambassador said, "that you will resist the impulse to take advantage of your unusual position." He looked at the door. "Come in."

T'Cai-Cai stepped into the room, glanced at Spradley, then turned to greet Retief in voluble Yill. He rounded the desk to the Ambassador's chair, motioned him from it, and sat down.

"I have a surprise for you, Retief," he said in Terran. "I myself have made use of the teaching machine you so kindly lent us."

"That's good," Retief said. "I'm sure Mr. Spradley will be interested in hearing what we have to say."

"Never mind," the Yill said. "I am here only socially." He looked around the room.

"So plainly you decorate your chamber; but it has a certain austere charm." He laughed a Yill laugh.

"Oh, you are a strange breed, you Terrestrials. You surprised us all. You know, one hears such outlandish stories. I tell you in confidence, we had expected you to be overpushes."

"Pushovers," Spradley said tonelessly.

"Such restraint! What pleasure you gave to those of us, like myself of course, who appreciated your grasp of protocol. Such finesse! How subtly you appeared to ignore each overture, while neatly avoiding actual contamination. I can tell you, there were those who thought—poor fools—that you had no grasp of etiquette. How gratified we were, we professionals, who could appreciate your virtuosity—when you placed matters on a comfortable basis by spurning the cats'-meat. It was sheer pleasure then, waiting, to see what form your compliment would take."

The Yill offered orange cigars, then stuffed one in his nostril.

"I confess even I had not hoped that you would honor our Admirable so signally. Oh, it is a pleasure to deal with fellow professionals, who understand the meaning of protocol."

Ambassador Spradley make a choking sound.

"This fellow has caught a chill," T'Cai-Cai said. He eyed Spradley dubiously. "Step back, my man, I am highly susceptible.

"There is one bit of business I shall take pleasure in attending to, my dear Retief," T'Cai-Cai went on. He drew a large paper from his reticule. "His Admirableness is determined that none other than yourself shall be accredited here. I have here my government's exequatur confirming you as Terrestrial Consul-General to Yill. We shall look forward to your prompt return."

Retief looked at Spradley.

"I'm sure the Corps will agree," he said.

"Then I shall be going," T'Cai-Cai said. He stood up. "Hurry back to us, Retief. There is much that I would show you of the great Empire of Yill."

He winked a Yill wink.

"Together, Retief, we shall see many high and splendid things."

... In the face of the multitudinous threats to the peace arising naturally from the complex Galactic situation, the polished techniques devised by Corps theoreticians proved their worth in a thousand difficult confrontations. Even anonymous junior officers, armed with briefcases containing detailed instructions, were able to soothe troubled waters with the skill of experienced negotiators. A case in point was Consul Passwyn's incisive handling of the Jaq-Terrestrial contretemps at Adobe . . .

Vol. II, reel 91 480 A. E. (AD 2941)

SEALED ORDERS

"IT'S TRUE," Consul Passwyn said, "I requested assignment as Principle Officer at a small post. But I had in mind one of those charming resort worlds, with only an occasional visa problem, or perhaps a distressed spaceman or two a year. Instead, I'm zoo-keeper to these confounded settlers, and not for one world, mind you, but eight." He stared glumly at Vice-Consul Retief.

"Still," Retief said, "it gives an opportunity for travel."

"Travel!" the Consul barked. "I hate travel.

Here in this backwater system particularly. . . ."
He paused, blinked at Retief, and cleared his
throat. "Not that a bit of travel isn't an excellent
thing for a junior officer. Marvelous experience."

He turned to the wall-screen and pressed a button. A system triagram appeared: eight luminous
green dots arranged around a larger disc repre-
senting the primary. Passwyn picked up a
pointer, indicating the innermost planet.

"The situation on Adobe is nearing crisis. The
confounded settlers—a mere handful of them—
have managed, as usual, to stir up trouble with an
intelligent indigenous life form, the Jaq. I can't
think why they bother, merely for a few oases
among the endless deserts. However, I have, at
last, received authorization from Sector Headquarters to take certain action."

He swung back to face Retief. "I'm sending you
in to handle the situation, Retief—under sealed
orders." He picked up a fat, buff envelope. "A pity
they didn't see fit to order the Terrestrial settlers
out weeks ago, as I suggested. Now it's too late. I'm
expected to produce a miracle—a rapprochement
between Terrestrial and Jaq and a division of territory. It's idiotic. However, failure would look very
bad in my record, so I shall expect results." He
passed the buff envelope across to Retief.

"I understood that Adobe was uninhabited,"
Retief said, "until the Terrestrial settlers arrived."

"Apparently that was an erroneous impression.
The Jaq are there." Passwyn fixed Retief with a
watery eye. "You'll follow your instructions to the
letter. In a delicate situation such as this, there
must be no impulsive, impromptu element introduced. This approach has been worked out in

detail at Sector; you need merely implement it. Is that entirely clear?"

"Has anyone at Headquarters ever visited Adobe?"

"Of course not. They all hate travel too. If there are no other questions, you'd best be on your way. The mail run departs the dome in less than an hour."

"What's this native life form like?" Retief asked, getting to his feet.

"When you get back," said Passwyn, "you tell me."

The mail pilot, a leathery veteran with quarter-inch whiskers, spat toward a stained corner of the compartment, and leaned close to the screen.

"They's shootin' goin' on down there," he said. "Them white puffs over the edge of the desert."

"I'm supposed to be preventing the war," said Retief. "It looks like I'm a little late."

The pilot's head snapped around. "War?" he yelped. "Nobody told me they was a war goin' on on 'Dobe. If that's what that is, I'm gettin' out of here."

"Hold on," said Retief. "I've got to get down. They won't shoot at you."

"They shore won't, sonny. I ain't givin' 'em the chance." He reached for the console and started punching keys. Retief reached out, catching his wrist.

"Maybe you didn't hear me. I said I've got to get down."

The pilot plunged against the restraint and swung a punch that Retief blocked casually. "Are you nuts?" the pilot screeched. "They's plenty shootin' goin' on fer me to see it fifty miles out."

"The mails must go through, you know."

"I ain't no consarned postman. If you're so dead set on gettin' killed—take the skiff. I'll tell 'em to pick up the remains next trip—if the shootin's over."

"You're a pal. I'll take your offer."

The pilot jumped to the lifeboat hatch and cycled it open. "Get in. We're closin' fast. Them birds might take it into their heads to lob one this way."

Retief crawled into the narrow cockpit of the skiff. The pilot ducked out of sight, came back, and handed Retief a heavy old-fashioned power pistol. "Long as you're goin' in, might as well take this."

"Thanks." Retief shoved the pistol in his belt. "I hope you're wrong."

"I'll see they pick you up when the shootin's over—one way or another."

The hatch clanked shut; a moment later there was a jar as the skiff dropped away, followed by heavy buffeting in the backwash from the departing mail boat. Retief watched the tiny screen, his hands on the manual controls. He was dropping rapidly: forty miles, thirty-nine . . .

At five miles, Retief threw the light skiff into maximum deceleration. Crushed back in the padded seat, he watched the screen and corrected the course minutely. The planetary surface was rushing up with frightening speed. Retief shook his head and kicked in the emergency retro-drive. Points of light arced up from the planet face below. If they were ordinary chemical warheads the skiff's meteor screens should handle them. The screen on the instrument panel flashed brilliant white, then went dark. The skiff leaped and flipped on its back, smoke filling the tiny compartment. There was a series of shocks, a final bone-shaking concussion, then stillness, broken by the ping of hot metal contracting.

Coughing, Retief disengaged himself from the shock-webbing, groped underfoot for the hatch, and wrenched it open. A wave of hot jungle air struck him. He lowered himself to a bed of shattered foliage, got to his feet . . . and dropped flat as a bullet whined past his ear.

He lay listening. Stealthy movements were audible from the left. He inched his way forward and made the shelter of a broad-boled dwarf tree. Somewhere a song lizard burbled. Whining insects circled, scented alien life, and buzzed off. There was another rustle of foliage from the underbrush five yards away. A bush quivered, then a low bough dipped. Retief edged back around the trunk and eased down behind a fallen log. A stocky man in a grimy leather shirt and shorts appeared, moving cautiously, a pistol in his hand.

As he passed, Retief rose, leaped the log, and tackled him. They went down together. The man gave one short yell, then struggled in silence. Retief flipped him onto his back, raised a fist—

"Hey!" the settler yelled. "You're as human as I am!"

"Maybe I'll look better after a shave," said Retief. "What's the idea of shooting at me?"

"Lemme up—my name's Potter. Sorry 'bout that. I figured it was a Flap-jack boat; looks just like 'em. I took a shot when I saw something move; didn't know it was a Terrestrial. Who are you?

What you doin' here? We're pretty close to the edge of the oasis. That's Flap-jack country over there." He waved a hand toward the north, where the desert lay.

"I'm glad you're a poor shot. Some of those missiles were too close for comfort."

"Missiles, eh? Must be Flap-jack artillery. We got nothin' like that."

"I heard there was a full-fledged war brewing," said Retief. "I didn't expect—"

"Good!" Potter said. "We figured a few of you boys from Ivory would be joining up when you heard. You from Ivory?"

"Yes. I'm—"

"Hey, you must be Lemuel's cousin. Good night! I pretty near made a bad mistake. Lemuel's a tough man to explain anything to."

"I'm—"

"Keep your head down. These damn Flap-jacks have got some wicked hand weapons. Come on . . ." He began crawling through the brush. Retief followed. They crossed two hundred yards of rough country before Potter got to his feet, took out a soggy bandanna, and mopped his face.

"You move good for a city man. I thought you folks on Ivory just sat down under those domes and read dials. But I guess bein' Lemuel's cousin—"

"As a matter of fact—"

"Have to get you some real clothes, though. Those city duds don't stand up on 'Dobe."

Retief looked down at his charred, torn, sweat-soaked powder-blue blazer and slacks, the informal uniform of a Third Secretary and Vice-Consul in the Corps Diplomatique Terrestrienne.

"This outfit seemed pretty rough-and-ready back home," he said. "But I guess leather has its points."

"Let's get on back to camp. We'll just about make it by sundown. And look, don't say nothin' to Lemuel about me thinkin' you were a Flap-jack."

"I won't; but—"

Potter was on his way, loping off up a gentle slope. Retief pulled off the sodden blazer, dropped it over a bush, added his string tie, and followed Potter.

"We're damn glad you're here, mister," said a fat man with two revolvers belted across his paunch. "We can use every man. We're in bad shape. We ran into the Flap-jacks three months ago and we haven't made a smart move since. First, we thought they were a native form we hadn't run into before. Fact is, one of the boys shot one, thinkin' it was fair game. I guess that was the start of it." He paused to stir the fire.

"And then a bunch of 'em hit Swazey's farm here. Killed two of his cattle, and pulled back," he said.

"We figure they thought the cows were people," said Swazey. "They were out for revenge."

"How could anybody think a cow was folks," another man put in. "They don't look nothin' like—"

"Don't be so dumb, Bert," said Swazey. "They'd never seen Terries before; they know better now."

Bert chuckled. "Sure do. We showed 'em the next time, didn't we, Potter? Got four—"

"They walked right up to my place a couple

days after the first time," Swazey said. "We were ready for 'em. Peppered 'em good. They cut and run—"

"Flopped, you mean. Ugliest-lookin' critters you ever saw. Look just like a old piece of dirty blanket humpin' around."

"It's been goin' on this way ever since. They raid and then we raid. But lately they've been bringin' some big stuff into it. They've got some kind of pint-sized airships and automatic rifles. We've lost four men now and a dozen more in the freezer, waiting for the med ship. We can't afford it. The colony's got less than three hundred able-bodied men."

"But we're hangin' onto our farms," said Potter. "All these oases are old sea-beds—a mile deep, solid topsoil. And there's a couple of hundred others we haven't touched yet. The Flap-jacks won't get 'em while there's a man alive."

"The whole system needs the food we can raise," Bert said. "These farms we're tryin' to start won't be enough but they'll help."

"We been yellin' for help to the CDT, over on Ivory," said Potter. "But you know these Embassy stooges."

"We heard they were sendin' some kind of bureaucrat in here to tell us to get out and give the oasis to the Flap-jacks," said Swazey. He tightened his mouth. "We're waitin' for him. . . ."

"Meanwhile we got reinforcements comin' up. We put out the word back home; we all got relatives on Ivory and Verde—"

"Shut up, you damn fool!" a deep voice grated.

"Lemuel!" Potter said. "Nobody else could sneak up on us like that—"

"If I'd a been a Flap-jack, I'd of et you alive," the newcomer said, moving into the ring of the fire. He was a tall, broad-faced man in grimy leather. He eyed Retief.

"Who's that?"

"What do ya mean?" Potter spoke in the silence. "He's your cousin."

"He ain't no cousin of mine," Lemuel said. He stepped to Retief.

"Who you spyin' for, stranger?" he rasped.

Retief got to his feet. "I think I should explain—"

A short-nosed automatic appeared in Lemuel's hand, a clashing note against his fringed buckskins.

"Skip the talk. I know a fink when I see one."

"Just for a change, I'd like to finish a sentence," Retief said. "And I suggest you put your courage back in your pocket before it bites you."

"You talk too damned fancy to suit me."

"You're wrong. I talk to suit me. Now, for the last time: put it away."

Lemuel stared at Retief. "You givin' me orders . . . ?"

Retief's left fist shot out and smacked Lemuel's face dead center. The raw-boned settler stumbled back, blood starting from his nose. The pistol fired into the dirt as he dropped it. He caught himself, jumped for Retief . . . and met a straight right that snapped him onto his back—out cold.

"Wow!" said Potter. "The stranger took Lem . . . in two punches . . ."

"One," said Swazey. "That first one was just a love tap."

Bert froze. "Quiet, boys," he whispered. In the

sudden silence a night lizard called. Retief
strained, heard nothing. He narrowed his eyes,
peering past the fire.

With a swift lunge he seized up the bucket of
drinking water, dashed it over the fire, and threw
himself flat. He heard the others hit the dirt a split
second after him.

"You move fast for a city man," breathed
Swazey beside him. "You see pretty good too.
We'll split and take 'em from two sides. You and
Bert from the left, me and Potter from the right."

"No," said Retief. "You wait here. I'm going out
alone."

"What's the idea . . . ?"

"Later. Sit tight and keep your eyes open." Retief took a bearing on a treetop faintly visible
against the sky and started forward.

Five minutes' cautious progress brought Retief
to a slight rise of ground. With infinite caution he
raised himself and risked a glance over an out-
cropping of rock. The stunted trees ended just
ahead. Beyond, he could make out the dim con-
tour of rolling desert: Flap-jack country. He got to
his feet, clambered over the stone, still hot after a
day of tropical heat, and moved forward twenty
yards. Around him he saw nothing but drifted
sand, palely visible in the starlight, and the occasional shadow of jutting shale slabs. Behind him
the jungle was still. He sat down on the ground to
wait.

It was ten minutes before a movement caught
his eye; something had separated itself from a
dark mass of stone, and glided across a few yards
of open ground to another shelter. Retief watched.
Minutes passed. The shape moved again, slipped

into a shadow ten feet distant. Retief felt the butt of the power pistol with his elbow. His guess had better be right. . . .

There was a sudden rasp, like leather against concrete, and a flurry of sand as the Flap-jack charged. Retief rolled aside, then lunged, throwing his weight on the flopping Flap-jack—a yard square, three inches thick at the center, and all muscle. The ray-like creature heaved up, curled backward, its edge rippling, to stand on the flattened rim of its encircling sphincter. It scrabbled with its prehensile fringe-tentacles for a grip on Retief's shoulders. Retief wrapped his arms around the creature and struggled to his feet. The thing was heavy, a hundred pounds at least; fighting as it was, it seemed more like five hundred.

The Flap-jack reversed its tactics, becoming limp. Retief grabbed and felt a thumb slip into an orifice.

The creature went wild. Retief hung on, dug the thumb in deeper.

"Sorry, fellow," he muttered between his clenched teeth. "Eye-gouging isn't gentlemanly, but it's effective. . . ."

The Flap-jack fell still; only its fringes rippling slowly. Retief relaxed the pressure of his thumb. The creature gave a tentative jerk; the thumb dug in. The Flap-jack went limp again, waiting.

"Now that we understand each other," said Retief, "lead me to your headquarters."

Twenty minutes' walk into the desert brought Retief to a low rampart of thorn branches: the Flap-jacks' outer defensive line against Terry forays. It would be as good a place as any to wait for the next move by the Flap-jacks. He sat down, eased the weight of his captive off his back, keeping a firm thumb in place. If his analysis of the situation was correct, a Flap-jack picket should be along before too long. . . .

A penetrating beam of red light struck Retief in the face, then blinked off. He got to his feet. The captive Flap-jack rippled its fringe in an agitated way. Retief tensed his thumb.

"Sit tight," he said. "Don't try to do anything hasty. . . ." His remarks were falling on deaf ears—or no ears at all—but the thumb spoke as loudly as words.

There was a slither of sand, then another. Retief became aware of a ring of presences drawing closer.

Retief tightened his grip on the creature. He could see a dark shape now, looming up almost to his own six-three. It appeared that the Flap-jacks came in all sizes.

A low rumble sounded, like a deep-throated growl. It strummed on, then faded out. Retief cocked his head, frowning.

"Try it two octaves higher," he said.

"Awwrrp! Sorry. Is that better?" a clear voice came from the darkness.

"That's fine," Retief said. "I'm here to arrange an exchange of prisoners."

"Prisoners? But we have no prisoners."

"Sure you have. Me. Is it a deal?"

"Ah, yes, of course. Quite equitable. What guarantees do you require?"

"The word of a gentleman is sufficient." Retief released his captive. It flopped once and disappeared into the darkness.

"If you'd care to accompany me to our head-quarters," the voice said, "we can discuss our mutual concerns in comfort."

"Delighted."

Red lights blinked briefly. Retief, glimpsing a gap in the thorny barrier, stepped through it. He followed dim shapes across warm sand to a low cave-like entry, faintly lit with a reddish glow.

"I must apologize for the awkward design of our comfort-dome," said the voice. "Had we known we would be honored by a visit. . . ."

"Think nothing of it," Retief said. "We diplomats are trained to crawl."

Inside, with knees bent and head ducked under the five-foot ceiling, Retief looked around at the walls of pink-toned nacre, a floor like burgundy-colored glass spread with silken rugs, and a low table of polished red granite set out with silver dishes and rose-crystal drinking tubes.

"Let me congratulate you," the voice said. Retief turned. An immense Flap-jack, hung with crimson trappings, rippled at his side. The voice issued from a disk strapped to its back. "Your skirmish-forms fight well. I think we will find in each other worthy adversaries."

"Thanks. I'm sure the test would be interesting, but I'm hoping we can avoid it."

"Avoid it?" Retief heard a low humming coming from the speaker in the silence. "Well, let us dine," the mighty Flap-jack said at last, "we can resolve these matters later. I am called Hoshick of the Mosaic of the Two Dawns."

"I'm Retief." Hoshick waited expectantly. ". . . of the Mountain of Red Tape," Retief added.

"Take your place, Retief," said Hoshick. "I hope

you won't find our rude couches uncomfortable."
Two other large Flap-jacks came into the room
and communed silently with Hoshick. "Pray forgive our lack of translating devices," he said to
Retief. "Permit me to introduce my colleagues."

A small Flap-jack rippled into the chamber
bearing on its back a silver tray, laden with aromatic food. The waiter served the diners and filled
the drinking tubes with yellow wine.

"I trust you'll find these dishes palatable,"
Hoshick said. "Our metabolisms are much alike, I
believe." Retief tried the food; it had a delicious
nut-like flavor. The wine was indistinguishable
from Chateau d'Yquem.

"It was an unexpected pleasure to encounter
your party here," Hoshick said. "I confess at first
we took you for an indigenous earth-grubbing
form, but we were soon disabused of that notion."
He raised a tube, manipulating it deftly with his
fringe tentacles. Retief returned the salute and
drank.

"Of course," Hoshick continued, "as soon as we
realized that you were sportsmen like ourselves,
we attempted to make amends by providing a bit
of activity for you. We've ordered out our heavier
equipment and a few trained skirmishers and
soon we'll be able to give you an adequate show,
or so I hope."

"Additional skirmishers?" said Retief. "How
many, if you don't mind my asking?"

"For the moment, perhaps only a few hundred.
Thereafter . . . well, I'm sure we can arrange that
between us. Personally I would prefer a contest of
limited scope—no nuclear or radiation-effect
weapons. Such a bore, screening the spawn for

deviations. Though I confess we've come upon some remarkably useful sports: the ranger-form such as you made captive, for example. Simple-minded, of course, but a fantastically keen tracker."

"Oh, by all means," Retief said. "No atomics. As you pointed out, spawn-sorting is a nuisance, and then too, it's wasteful of troops."

"Ah, well, they are after all expendable. But we agree, no atomics. Have you tried the ground-gwack eggs? Rather a speciality of my Mosaic . . ."

"Delicious," said Retief. "I wonder if you've considered eliminating weapons altogether?"

A scratchy sound issued from the disk. "Pardon my laughter," Hoshick said, "but surely you jest?"

"As a matter of fact," said Retief, "we ourselves try to avoid the use of weapons."

"I seem to recall that our first contact of skirmish-forms involved the use of a weapon by one of your units."

"My apologies," said Reitef. "The—ah—skirmish-form failed to recognize that he was dealing with a sportsman."

"Still, now that we have commenced so merrily with weapons . . ." Hoshick signaled and the servant refilled the drinking tubes.

"There is an aspect I haven't yet mentioned," Retief went on. "I hope you won't take this personally, but the fact is, our skirmish-forms think of weapons as something one employs only in dealing with certain specific life-forms."

"Oh? Curious. What forms are those?"

"Vermin. Deadly antagonists, but lacking in caste. I don't want our skirmish-forms thinking of such worthy adversaries as yourself as vermin."

"Dear me! I hadn't realized, of course. Most considerate of you to point it out." Hoshick clucked in dismay. "I see that skirmish-forms are much the same among you as with us: lacking in perception." He laughed scratchily.

"Which brings us to the crux of the matter," Retief said. "You see, we're up against a serious problem with regard to skirmish-forms: a low birth rate. Therefore we've reluctantly taken to substitutes for the mass actions so dear to the heart of the sportsman. We've attempted to put an end to these contests altogether . . ."

Hoshick coughed explosively, sending a spray of wine into the air. "What are you saying?" he gasped. "Are you proposing that Hoshick of the Mosaic of the Two Dawns abandon honor?"

"Sir!" said Retief sternly. "You forget yourself. I, Retief of the Red Tape, merely make an alternate proposal more in keeping with the newest sporting principles."

"New?" cried Hoshick. "My dear Retief, what a pleasant surprise! I'm enthralled with novel modes. One gets so out of touch. Do elaborate."

"It's quite simple, really. Each side selects a representative and the two individuals settle the issue between them."

"I . . . um . . . I'm afraid I don't understand. What possible significance could one attach to the activities of a couple of random skirmish-forms?"

"I haven't made myself clear," Retief said. He took a sip of wine. "We don't involve the skirmish-forms at all; that's quite passé."

"You don't mean . . . ?"

"That's right. You and me."

* * *

Outside the starlit sand Retief tossed aside the power pistol and followed it with the leather shirt Swazey had lent him. By the faint light he could just make out the towering figure of the Flap-jack rearing up before him, his trappings gone. A silent rank of Flap-jack retainers were grouped behind him.

"I fear I must lay aside the translator now, Retief," said Hoshick. He sighed and rippled his fringe tentacles. "My spawn-fellows will never credit this. Such a curious turn fashion has taken. How much more pleasant it is to observe the action from a distance."

"I suggest we use Tennessee rules," said Retief. "They're very liberal: biting, gouging, stomping, kneeling, and, of course, choking, as well as the usual punching, shoving, and kicking."

"Hmmm. These gambits seem geared to forms employing rigid endo-skeletons; I fear I shall be at a disadvantage."

"Of course," Retief said, "if you'd prefer a more plebeian type of contest . . ."

"By no means. But perhaps we could rule out tentacle-twisting, just to even the balance."

"Very well. Shall we begin?"

With a rush Hoshick threw himself at Retief, who ducked, whirled, and leaped on the Flap-jack's back—and felt himself flipped clear by a mighty ripple of the alien's slab-like body. Retief rolled aside as Hoshick turned on him, jumped to his feet, and threw a punch to Hoshick's mid-section. The alien whipped his left fringe around in an arc that connected with Retief's jaw, spinning onto his back. Hoshick's weight struck Retief like a dumptruck-load of concrete. Retief twisted, trying to roll. The flat body of the creature blanketed him. He worked an arm free and drummed blows on the leathery back. Hoshick nestled closer.

Retief's air was running out. He heaved up against the smothering weight; nothing budged. He was wasting his strength.

He remembered the ranger-form he had captured. The sensitive orifice had been placed ventrally, in what would be the thoracic area. . . .

He groped, feeling tough hide set with horny granules. He would be missing skin tomorrow—if there was a tomorrow. His thumb found the orifice, and he probed.

The Flap-jack recoiled. Retief held fast, probed deeper, groping with the other hand. If the creature were bilaterally symmetrical there would be a set of ready-made handholds. . . .

There were. Retief dug in and the Flap-jack writhed and pulled away. Retief held on, scrambled to his feet, threw his weight against Hoshick, and fell on top of him, still gouging. Hoshick rippled his fringe wildly, flopped in distress, then went limp. Retief relaxed, released his hold, and got to his feet, breathing hard. Hoshick humped himself over onto his ventral side, lifted, and moved gingerly over to the sidelines. His retainers came forward, assisted him into his trappings, and strapped on the translator. He sighed heavily, adjusting the volume.

"There is much to be said for the old system," he said. "What a burden one's sportsmanship places on one at times."

"Great fun, wasn't it?" said Retief. "Now, I

know you'll be eager to continue. If you'll just wait while I run back and fetch some of our gouger-forms—"

"May hide-ticks devour the gouger-forms!" Hoshick bellowed. "You've given me such a sprong-ache as I'll remember each spawning-time for a year."

"Speaking of hide-ticks," said Retief, "we've developed a biter-form—"

"Enough!" Hoshick roared so loudly that the translator bounced on his hide. "Suddenly I yearn for the crowded yellow sands of Jag. I had hoped . . . " He broke off, drawing a rasping breath. "I had hoped, Retief," he said, speaking sadly now, "to find a new land here where I might plan my own Mosaic, till these alien sands and bring forth such a crop of paradise-lichen as should glut the markets of a hundred worlds. But my spirit is not equal to the prospect of biter-forms and gouger-forms without end. I am shamed before you."

"To tell you the truth, I'm old-fashioned myself," said Retief. "I'd rather watch the action from a distance too."

"But surely your spawn-fellows would never condone such an attitude."

"My spawn-fellows aren't here. And besides, didn't I mention it? No one who's really in the know would think of engaging in competition by mere combat if there were any other way. Now, you mentioned tilling the sand, raising lichens—"

"That on which we dined," said Hoshick, "and from which the wine is made."

"The big trend in fashionable diplomacy today

is farming competition. Now, if you'd like to take
these deserts and raise lichen, we'll promise to
stick to the oases and raise vegetables."

Hoshick curled his back in attention. "Retief,
you're quite serious? You would leave all the fair
sand hills to us?"

"The whole works, Hoshick. I'll take the oases."

Hoshick rippled his fringes ecstatically. "Once
again you have outdone me, Retief," he cried,
"this time, in generosity."

"We'll talk over the details later. I'm sure we can
establish a set of rules that will satisfy all parties.
Now I've got to get back. I think some of the
gouger-forms are waiting to see me."

It was nearly dawn when Retief gave the whistled signal he had agreed on with Potter, then rose
and walked into the camp circle. Swazey stood
up.

"There you are," he said. "We been wonderin'
whether to go out after you."

Lemuel came forward, one eye black to the
cheekbone. He held out a raw-boned hand. "Sorry
I jumped you, stranger. Tell you the truth, I
thought you was some kind of stool-pigeon from
the CDT."

Bert came up behind Lemuel. "How do you
know he ain't, Lemuel?" he said. "Maybe he—"

Lemuel floored Bert with a backward sweep of
his arm. "Next cotton-picker says some embassy
Johnny can cool me gets worse'n that."

"Tell me," said Retief. "How are you boys fixed
for wine?"

"Wine? Mister, we been livin' on stump water
for a year now. 'Dobe's fatal to the kind of bacteria
it takes to ferment liquor."

"Try this." Retief handed over a squat jug. Swazey drew the cork, sniffed, drank, and passed it to Lemuel.

"Mister, where'd you get that?"

"The Flap-jacks made it. Here's another question for you: would you concede a share in this planet to the Flap-jacks in return for a peace guarantee?"

At the end of a half hour of heated debate Lemuel turned to Retief. "We'll make any reasonable deal," he said. "I guess they got as much right here as we have. I think we'd agree to a fifty-fifty split. That'd give about a hundred and fifty oases to each side."

"What would you say to keeping all the oases and giving them the desert?"

Lemuel reached for the wine jug, his eyes on Retief. "Keep talkin', mister," he said. "I think you got yourself a deal."

Consul Passwyn glanced up as Retief entered the office.

"Sit down, Retief," he said absently. "I thought you were over on Pueblo, or Mud-flat, or whatever they call that desert."

"I'm back."

Passwyn eyed him sharply. "Well, well, what is it you need, man? Speak up. Don't expect me to request any military assistance."

Retief passed a bundle of documents across the desk. "Here's the Treaty. And a Mutual Assistance Pact and a Trade Agreement."

"Eh?" Passwyn picked up the papers and riffled through them. He leaned back in his chair, beaming.

"Well, Retief, expeditiously handled." He

stopped and blinked at the Vice-Consul. "You seem to have a bruise on your jaw. I hope you've been conducting yourself as befits a member of the Consulate staff."

"I attended a sporting event. One of the players got a little excited."

"Well . . . it's one of the hazards of the profession. One must pretend an interest in such matters." Passwyn rose and extended a hand. "You've done well, my boy. Let this teach you the value of following instructions to the letter."

Outside, by the hall incinerator drop, Retief paused long enough to take from his briefcase a large buff envelope, still sealed, and drop it in the slot.

. . . Supplementing broad knowledge of affairs with such shrewd gambits as identification with significant local groups, and the consequent deft manipulating of inter-group rivalries, Corps officials on the scene played decisive roles in the preservation of domestic tranquility on many a far-flung world. At Fust, Ambassador Magnan forged to the van in the exercise of the technique . . .

Vol VII, reel 43. 487 A.E. (AD 2948)

AIDE MEMOIRE

ACROSS THE TABLE from Retief, Ambassador Magnan, rustling a stiff sheet of parchment, looked grave.

"This aide memoire," he said, "was just handed to me by the Cultural Attaché. It's the third on the subject this week. It refers to the matter of sponsorship of Youth groups."

"Some youths," Retief said. "Average age: seventy-five."

"The Fustians are a long-lived people," Magnan snapped. "These matters are relative. At seventy-five, a male Fustian is at a trying age."

"That's right; he'll try anything in the hope it will maim somebody."

"Precisely the problem," Magnan replied. "But the Youth Movement is the important news in today's political situation here on Fust, and sponsorship of Youth groups is a shrewd stroke on the part of the Terrestrial Embassy. At my suggestion, well nigh every member of the mission has leaped at the opportunity to score a few p— that is, to cement relations with this emergent power group: the leaders of the future. You, Retief, as Counselor, are the outstanding exception."

"I'm not convinced these hoodlums need my help in organizing their rumbles," Retief said. "Now, if you have a proposal for a pest control group—"

"To the Fustians, this is no jesting matter," Magnan cut in. "This group," he glanced at the paper, "known as the Sexual, Cultural and Athletic Recreational Society, or SCARS, for short, has been awaiting sponsorship for a matter of weeks now."

"Meaning they want someone to buy them a clubhouse, uniforms, equipment, and anything else they need to plot against the peace in style," Retief said.

"If we don't act promptly, the Groaci embassy may well anticipate us. They're very active here."

"That's an idea," said Retief, "let 'em. After a while they'll be broke—instead of us."

"Nonsense. The group requires a sponsor. I can't actually order you to step forward. However . . ." Magnan let the sentence hang in the air. Retief raised one eyebrow.

"For a minute there," he said, "I thought you were going to make a positive statement."

Magnan leaned back, lacing his fingers over his

stomach. "I don't think you'll find a diplomat of my experience doing anything so naive," he said.

"I like the adult Fustians," said Retief. "Too bad they have to lug half a ton of horn around on their backs. I wonder if surgery—"

"Great heavens, Retief," Magnan spluttered. "I'm amazed that even you would bring up a matter of such delicacy. A race's unfortunate physical characteristics are hardly a fit matter for Terrestrial curiosity."

"Well, I've only been here a month. But it's been my experience, Mr. Ambassador, that few people are above improving on nature; otherwise you, for example, would be tripping over your beard."

Magnan shuddered. "Please—never mention the idea to a Fustian."

Retief stood. "'My own program for the day includes going over to the dockyards. There are some features of this new passenger liner the Fustians are putting together that I want to look into. With your permission, Mr. Ambassador. . . ?"

Magnan snorted. "Your preoccupation with the trivial disturbs me, Retief. More interest in substantive matters—such as working with youth groups—would create a far better impression."

"Before getting too involved with these groups, it might be a good idea to find out a little more about them," Retief said. "Who organizes them? There are three strong political parties here on Fust; what's the alignment of this SCARS organization?"

"You forget, these are merely teen-agers, so to speak," Magnan said. "Politics mean nothing to them . . . yet."

"Then there are the Groaci. Why their passion-

ate interest in a two-horse world like Fust? Normally they're concerned with nothing but business; and what has Fust got that they could
use?"

"You may rule out the commercial aspect in this
instance," said Magnan. "Fust possesses a vigorous steel-age manufacturing economy. The
Groaci are barely ahead of them."

"Barely," said Retief. "Just over the line into
crude atomics . . . like giga-megaton bombs."

Magnan, shaking his head, turned back to his
papers. "What market exists for such devices on a
world at peace?" he said. "I suggest you address
your attention to the less spectacular but more
rewarding work of insinuating yourself into the
social patterns of the local youth."

"I've considered the matter," Retief said, "and
before I meet any of the local youth socially I want
to get myself a good blackjack."

Retief left the sprawling bungalow-type building that housed the chancery of the Terrestrial
Embassy, hailed one of the ponderous slow-
moving Fustian flat-cars, and leaned back against
the wooden guard rail as the heavy vehicle trundled through the city toward the looming gantries
of the shipyards. It was a cool morning with a
light breeze carrying the fish odor of Fustian
dwellings across the broad cobbled avenue. A few
mature Fustians lumbered heavily along in the
shade of the low buildings, audibly wheezing
under the burden of their immense carapaces.
Among them, shell-less youths trotted briskly on
scaly stub legs. The driver of the flat-car, a labor-
caste Fustian with his guild colors emblazoned on

his back, heaved at the tiller, swung the unwieldy conveyance through the shipyard gates, and creaked to a halt.

"Thus I come to the shipyard with frightful speed," he said in Fustian. "Well I know the way of the naked-backs, who move always in haste."

Retief, climbing down, handed him a coin. "You should take up professional racing," he said. "Dare-devil."

Retief crossed the littered yard and tapped at the door of a rambling shed. Boards creaked inside, then the door swung back. A gnarled ancient with tarnished facial scales and a weathered carapace peered out at Retief.

"Long may you sleep," Retief said. "I'd like to take a look around, if you don't mind. I understand you're laying the bed-plate for your new liner today."

"May you dream of the deeps," the old fellow mumbled. He waved a stumpy arm toward a group of shell-less Fustians standing by a massive hoist. "The youths know more of bed-plates than do I, who but tend the place of papers."

"I know how you feel, old-timer," Retief said. "That sounds like the story of my life. Among your papers do you have a set of plans for the vessel? I understand it's to be a passenger liner."

The oldster nodded. He shuffled to a drawing file, rummaged, pulled out a sheaf of curled prints, and spread them on the table. Retief stood silently, running a finger over the uppermost drawing, tracing lines . . .

"What does the naked-back here?" a deep voice barked behind Retief. He turned. A heavy-faced Fustian youth, wrapped in a mantle, stood at the open door. Beady yellow eyes set among fine scales bored into Retief.

"I came to take a look at your new liner," said Retief.

"We need no prying foreigners here," the youth snapped. His eye fell on the drawings; he hissed in anger.

"Doddering hulk!" he snapped at the ancient, moving toward them. "May you toss in nightmares! Put aside the plans!"

"My mistake," Retief said. "I didn't know this was a secret project."

The youth hesitated. "It is not a secret," he muttered. "Why should it be a secret?"

"You tell me."

The youth worked his jaws and rocked his head from side to side in the Fustian gesture of uncertainty. "There is nothing to conceal," he said. "We merely construct a passenger liner."

"Then you don't mind if I look over the drawings," Retief said. "Who knows, maybe some day I'll want to reserve a suite for the trip out."

The youth turned and disappeared. Retief grinned at the oldster. "Went for his big brother, I guess," he said. "I have a feeling I won't get to study these in peace here. Mind if I copy them?"

"Willingly, light-footed one," said the old Fustian. "And mine is the shame for the discourtesy of youth."

Retief took out a tiny camera, flipped a copying lens in place, leafed through the drawings, clicking the shutter.

"A plague on these youths," said the oldster. "They grow more virulent day by day."

"Why don't you elders clamp down?"

"Agile are they and we are slow of foot. And this unrest is new; unknown in my youth was such insolence."

"The police—"

"Bah," the ancient rumbled. "None have we worthy of the name, nor have we needed them before now."

"What's behind it?"

"They have found leaders. The spiv, Slock, is one. And I fear they plot mischief." He pointed to the window. "They come, and a soft-one with them."

Retief, pocketing the camera, glanced out the window. A pale-featured Groacian with an ornately decorated crest stood with the youths, who eyed the hut, then started toward it.

"That's the military attaché of the Groaci Embassy," Retief said. "I wonder what he and the boys are cooking up together?"

"Naught that augurs well for the dignity of Fust," the oldster rumbled. "Flee, agile one, while I engage their attentions."

"I was just leaving," Retief said. "Which way out?"

"The rear door," the Fustian gestured with a stubby member. "Rest well, stranger on these shores," he said, moving to the entrance.

"Same to you, pop," said Retief. "And thanks."

He eased through the narrow back entrance, waited until voices were raised at the front of the shed, then strolled off toward the gate.

It was an hour along in the second dark of the third cycle when Retief left the Embassy technical library and crossed the corridor to his office. He flipped on a light and found a note tucked under a paperweight:

"*Retief: I shall expect your attendance at the IAS dinner at first dark of the fourth cycle. There will be a brief but, I hope, impressive sponsorship ceremony for the SCARS group, with full press coverage, arrangements for which I have managed to complete in spite of your intransigence.*"

Retief snorted and glanced at his watch: less than three hours. Just time to creep home by flatcar, dress in ceremonial uniform, and creep back.

Outside he flagged a lumbering bus, stationed himself in a corner of it, and watched the yellow sun, Beta, rise above the low skyline. The nearby sea was at high tide now, under the pull of the major sun and the three moons, and the stiff breeze carried a mist of salt spray. Retief turned up his collar against the dampness. In half an hour he would be perspiring under the vertical rays of a first-noon sun, but the thought failed to keep the chill off.

Two youths clambered up on the moving platform and walked purposefully toward Retief. He moved off the rail, watching them, his weight balanced.

"That's close enough, kids," he said. "Plenty of room on this scow; no need to crowd up."

"There are certain films," the lead Fustian muttered. His voice was unusually deep for a Youth. He was wrapped in a heavy cloak and moved awkwardly. His adolescence was nearly at an end, Retief guessed.

"I told you once," Retief said. "Don't crowd me."

The two stepped close, their slit mouths snapping in anger. Retief put out a foot, hooked it behind the scaly leg of the over-age juvenile, and threw his weight against the cloaked chest. The clumsy Fustian tottered, then fell heavily. Retief was past him and off the flat-car before the other youth had completed his vain lunge toward the spot Retief had occupied. The Terrestrial waved cheerfully at the pair, hopped aboard another vehicle, and watched his would-be assailants lumber down off their car and move heavily off, their tiny heads twisted to follow his retreating figure.

So they wanted the film? Retief reflected, thumbing a cigar alight. They were a little late. He had already filed it in the Embassy vault, after running a copy for the reference files. And a comparison of the drawings with those of the obsolete Mark XXXV battle cruiser used two hundred years earlier by the Concordiat Naval Arm showed them to be almost identical—gun emplacements and all. And the term obsolete was a relative one. A ship which had been outmoded in the armories of the Galactic Powers could still be king of the walk in the Eastern Arm.

But how had these two known of the film? There had been no one present but himself and the old-timer—and Retief was willing to bet the elderly Fustian hadn't told them anything.

At least not willingly . . .

Retief frowned, dropped the cigar over the side, waited until the flat-car negotiated a mud-wallow, then swung down and headed for the shipyard.

* * *

The door, hinges torn loose, had been propped loosely back in position. Retief looked around at the battered interior of the shed. The old fellow had put up a struggle.

There were deep drag-marks in the dust behind the building. Retief followed them across the yard. They disappeared under the steel door of a warehouse.

Retief glanced around. Now, at the mid-hour of the fourth cycle, the workmen were heaped along the edge of the refreshment pond, deep in their siesta. Taking a multi-bladed tool from his pocket, Retief tried various fittings in the lock; it snicked open and he eased the door aside far enough to enter.

Heaped bales loomed before him. Snapping on the tiny lamp in the handle of the combination tool, Retief looked over the pile. One stack seemed out of alignment—and the dust had been scraped from the floor before it. He pocketed the light, climbed up on the bales, and looked over into a ring of bundles. The aged Fustian lay inside the ring, a heavy sack tied over his head. Retief dropped down beside him, sawed at the tough twine, and pulled the sack free.

"It's me, old fellow," he said, "the nosy stranger. Sorry I got you into this."

The oldster threshed his gnarled legs, rocked slightly, then fell back. "A curse on the cradle that rocked their infant slumbers," he rumbled. "But place me back on my feet and I hunt down the youth Slock though he flee to the bottom-most muck of the Sea of Torments."

"How am I going to get you out of here? Maybe I'd better get some help."

"Nay. The perfidious youths abound here," said the old Fustian. "It would be your life."

"I doubt if they'd go that far."

"Would they not?" The Fustian stretched his neck. "Cast your light here. But for the toughness of my hide . . ."

Retief put the beam of the light on the leathery neck. A great smear of thick purplish blood welled from a ragged cut. The oldster chuckled: a sound like a seal coughing.

"Traitor they called me. For long they sawed at me—in vain. Then they trussed me and dumped me here. They think to return with weapons to complete the task."

"Weapons? I thought it was illegal—"

"Their evil genius, the Soft One," the Fustian said, "he would provide fuel to the Fire-Devil."

"The Groaci again," Retief said. "I wonder what their angle is."

"And I must confess: I told them of you, ere I knew their full intentions. Much can I tell you of their doings. But first, I pray: the block and tackle."

Retief found the hoist where the Fustian directed him, maneuvered it into position, hooked onto the edge of the carapace, and hauled away. The immense Fustian rose slowly, teetered . . . then flopped on his chest. Slowly he got to his feet.

"My name is Whonk, fleet one," he said. "My cows are yours."

"Thanks. I'm Retief. I'd like to meet the girls some time. But right now, let's get out of here."

Whonk leaned his bulk against the ponderous stacks of baled kelp, bull-dozing them aside. "Slow am I to anger," he said, "but implacable in my wrath. Slock, beware . . ."

"Hold it," said Retief suddenly. He sniffed. "What's that odor?" He flashed the light around, playing it over a dry stain on the floor. He knelt and sniffed at the spot.

"What kind of cargo was stacked here, Whonk? And where is it now?"

Whonk considered. "There were drums," he said. "Four of them, quite small, painted an evil green—the property of the Soft Ones, the Groaci. They lay here a day and a night. At full dark of the first period they came with stevedores and loaded them aboard the barge *Moss Rock*."

"The VIP boat. Who's scheduled to use it?"

"I know not. But what matters this? Let us discuss cargo movements after I have settled a score with certain youths."

"We'd better follow this up first, Whonk. There's only one substance I know of that's transported in drums and smells like that blot on the floor. That's titanite: the hottest explosive this side of a uranium pile."

Beta was setting as Retief, with Whonk puffing at his heels, came up to the sentry box beside the gangway leading to the plush interior of the Official Barge *Moss Rock*.

"A sign of the times," Whonk said, glancing inside the empty shelter. "A guard should stand here, but I see him not. Doubtless he crept away to sleep."

"Let's go aboard, and take a look around."

They entered the ship. Soft lights glowed in utter silence. A rough box stood on the floor, rollers and pry-bars beside it—a discordant note in the muted luxury of the setting. Whonk rummaged through its contents.

"Curious," he said. "What means this?" He held up a stained Fustian cloak of orange and green, a metal bracelet, and a stack of papers.

"Orange and green," Retief muttered. "Whose colors are those?"

"I know not. . . ." Whonk glanced at the armband. "But this is lettered." He passed the metal band to Retief.

"SCARS," Retief read. He looked at Whonk. "It seems to me I've heard the name before," he murmured. "Let's get back to the Embassy—fast."

Back on the ramp Retief heard a sound . . . and turned in time to duck the charge of a hulking Fustian youth who thundered past him, and fetched up against the broad chest of Whonk, who locked him in a warm embrace.

"Nice catch, Whonk. Where'd he sneak out of?"

"The lout hid there by the storage bin," Whonk rumbled. The captive youth thumped his fists and toes futilely against the oldster's carapace.

"Hang on to him," Retief said. "He looks like the biting kind."

"No fear. Clumsy I am, yet I am not without strength."

"Ask him where the titanite is tucked away."

"Speak, witless grub," Whonk growled, "lest I tweak you in two."

The youth gurgled.

"Better let up before you make a mess of him," Retief said.

Whonk lifted the youth clear of the floor, then flung him down with a thump that made the ground quiver. The younger Fustian glared up at the elder, his mouth snapping.

"This one was among those who trussed me and hid me away for the killing," said Whonk. "In his repentance he will tell all to his elder."

"He's the same one that tried to strike up an acquaintance with me on the bus," Retief said. "He gets around."

The youth, scrambling to his hands and knees, scuttled for freedom. Retief planted a foot on the dragging cloak; it ripped free. He stared at the bare back of the Fustian.

"By the Great Egg!" Whonk exclaimed, tripping the captive as he tried to rise. "This is no youth! His carapace has been taken from him."

Retief looked at the scarred back. "I thought he looked a little old. But I thought—"

"This is not possible," Whonk said wonderingly. "The great nerve trunks are deeply involved; not even the cleverest surgeon could excise the carapace and leave the patient living."

"It looks like somebody did the trick. But let's take this boy with us and get out of here. His folks may come home."

"Too late," said Whonk. Retief turned. Three youths came from behind the sheds.

"Well," Retief said. "It looks like the SCARS are out in force tonight. Where's your pal?" he said to the advancing trio, "the sticky little bird with the eye-stalks? Back at his Embassy, leaving you suckers holding the bag, I'll bet."

"Shelter behind me, Retief," said Whonk.

"Go get 'em, old-timer." Retief stooped and picked up one of the pry-bars. "I'll jump around and distract them."

Whonk let out a whistling roar and charged for

the immature Fustians. They fanned out . . . one tripped, sprawling on his face. Retief, whirling the metal bar that he had thrust between the Fustian's legs, slammed it against the skull of another, who shook his head, then turned on Retief . . . and bounced off the steel hull of the *Moss Rock* as Whonk took him in full charge.

Retief used the bar on another head; his third blow laid the Fustian on the pavement, oozing purple. The other two club members departed hastily, dented but still mobile.

Retief leaned on his club, breathing hard. "Tough heads these kids have got. I'm tempted to chase those two lads down, but I've got another errand to run. I don't know who the Groaci intended to blast, but I have a suspicion somebody of importance was scheduled for a boatride in the next few hours, and three drums of titanite is enough to vaporize this tub and everyone aboard her."

"The plot is foiled," said Whonk. "But what reason did they have?"

"The Groaci are behind it. I have an idea the SCARS didn't know about this gambit."

"Which of these is the leader?" asked Whonk. He prodded a fallen youth. "Arise, dreaming one."

"Never mind him, Whonk. We'll tie these two up and leave them here. I know where to find the boss."

A stolid-looking crowd filled the low-ceilinged banquet hall. Retief scanned the tables for the pale blobs of Terrestrial faces, dwarfed by the giant armored bodies of the Fustians. Across the room

Magnan fluttered a hand. Retief headed toward him. A low-pitched vibration filled the air, the rumble of sub-sonic Fustian music.

Retief slid into his place beside Magnan. "Sorry to be late, Mr. Ambassador."

"I'm honored that you chose to appear at all," Magnan said coldly. He turned back to the Fustian on his left.

"Ah, yes, Mr. Minister," he said. "Charming, most charming. So joyous."

The Fustian looked at him, beady-eyed. "It is the Lament of Hatching," he said, "our National Dirge."

"Oh," said Magnan. "how interesting. Such a pleasing balance of instruments."

"It is a droon solo," said the Fustian, eyeing the Terrestrial Ambassador suspiciously.

"Why don't you just admit you can't hear it," Retief whispered loudly. "And if I may interrupt a moment—"

Magnan cleared his throat. "Now that our Mr. Retief has arrived, perhaps we could rush right along to the sponsorship ceremonies . . ."

"This group," said Retief, leaning across Magnan to speak to the Fustian, "the SCARS . . . how much do you know about them, Mr. Minister?"

"Nothing at all," the huge Fustian elder rumbled. "For my taste, all youths should be kept penned with the livestock until they grow a carapace to tame their irresponsibility."

"We mustn't lose sight of the importance of channeling youthful energies," said Magnan.

"Labor gangs," said the minister. "In my youth we were indentured to the dredge-masters. I myself drew a muck-sledge."

"But in these modern times," put in Retief, "surely it's incumbent on us to make happy these golden hours."

The minister snorted. "Last week I had a golden hour: they set upon me and pelted me with over-ripe dung-fruit."

"But this was merely a manifestation of normal youthful frustrations," cried Magnan. "Their essential tenderness—"

"You'd not find a tender spot on that lout yonder," the minister said, pointing with a fork at a newly arrived youth, "if you drilled boreholes and blasted."

"Why, that's our guest of honor," said Magnan, "a fine young fellow, Slop I believe his name is—"

"Slock," said Retief. "Nine feet of armor-plated orneriness. And—"

Magnan rose, tapping on his glass. The Fustians winced at the, to them, supersonic vibrations, and looked at each other muttering. Magnan tapped louder. The minister drew in his head, his eyes closed. Some of the Fustians rose and tottered for the doors; the noise level rose. Magnan redoubled his efforts. The glass broke with a clatter, and green wine gushed on the tablecloth.

"What in the name of the Great Egg," the minister muttered. He blinked, breathing deeply.

"Oh, forgive me," Magnan blurted, dabbing at the wine.

"Too bad the glass gave out," Retief said. "In another minute you'd have cleared the hall—and then maybe I could have gotten a word in. You see, Mr. Minister," he said, turning to the Fustian, "there is a matter you should know about. . . ."

"Your attention, please," Magnan said, rising.

"I see that our fine young guest of honor has arrived, and I hope that the remainder of his committee will be along in a moment. It is my pleasure to announce that our Mr. Retief has had the good fortune to win out in the keen bidding for the pleasure of sponsoring this lovely group, and—"

Retief tugged at Magnan's sleeve. "Don't introduce me yet," he said. "I want to appear suddenly—more dramatic, you know."

"Well," Magnan murmured, glancing down at Retief, "I'm gratified to see you entering into the spirit of the event at last." He turned his attention back to the assembled guests. "If our honored guest will join me on the rostrum . . ." he said. "The gentlemen of the press may want to catch a few shots of the presentation."

Magnan moved from his place, made his way forward, stepped up on the low platform at the center of the wide room, took his place beside the robed Fustian youth, and beamed at the cameras.

"How gratifying it is to take this opportunity to express once more the great pleasure we have in sponsoring SCARS," Magnan said, talking slowly for the benefit of the scribbling reporters. "We'd like to think that in our modest way we're to be a part of all that the SCARS achieve during the years ahead. . . ."

Magnan paused as a huge Fustian elder heaved his bulk up the two low steps to the rostrum and approached the guest of honor. He watched as the newcomer paused behind Slock, who was busy returning the stares of the spectators and did not notice the new arrival.

Retief pushed through the crowd and stepped

up to face the Fustian youth. Slock stared at him, drawing back.

"You know me, Slock," Retief said loudly. "An old fellow named Whonk told you about me, just before you tried to saw off his head, remember? It was when I came out to take a look at that battle cruiser you're building."

With a bellow Slock reached for Retief—and choked off in mid-cry as Whonk pinioned him from behind, lifting the youth clear of the floor.

"Glad you reporters happened along," Retief said to the gaping newsmen. "Slock here had a deal with a sharp operator from the Groaci Embassy. The Groaci were to supply the necessary hardware and Slock, as foreman at the shipyards, was to see that everything was properly installed. The next step, I assume, would have been a local take-over, followed by a little interplanetary war on Flamenco or one of the other nearby worlds . . . for which the Groaci would be glad to supply plenty of ammo."

Magnan found his tongue. "Are you mad, Retief?" he screeched. "This group was vouched for by the Ministry of Youth."

"That Ministry's overdue for a purge," Retief said. He turned back to Slock. "I wonder if you were in on the little diversion that was planned for today. When the *Moss Rock* blew, a variety of clues were to be planted where they'd be easy to find . . . with SCARS written all over them. The Groaci would thus have neatly laid the whole affair squarely at the door of the Terrestrial Embassy . . . whose sponsorship of the SCARS had received plenty of publicity."

"The *Moss Rock*?" Magnan said. "But that

was—Retief! This is idiotic. The SCARS themselves were scheduled to go on a cruise tomorrow."

Slock roared suddenly, twisting violently. Whonk teetered, his grip loosened . . . and Slock pulled free and was off the platform, butting his way through the milling oldsters on the dining room floor. Magnan watched, openmouthed.

"The Groaci were playing a double game, as usual," Retief said. "They intended to dispose of these lads after they got things under way."

"Well, don't stand there," Magnan yelped. "Do something! If Slop is the ringleader of a delinquent gang—" He moved to give chase himself.

Retief grabbed his arm. "Don't jump down there," he called above the babble of talk. "You'd have as much chance of getting through there as a jack rabbit through a threshing contest. Where's a phone?"

Ten minutes later the crowd had thinned slightly. "We can get through now," Whonk called. "This way." He lowered himself to the floor and bulled through to the exit. Flash bulbs popped. Retief and Magnan followed in Whonk's wake.

In the lounge Retief grabbed the phone, waited for the operator, and gave a code letter. No reply. He tried another.

"No good," he said after a full minute had passed. He slammed the phone back in its niche. "Let's grab a cab."

In the street the blue sun, Alpha, peered like an arc light under a low cloud layer. Flat shadows lay across the mud of the avenue. The three mounted a passing flat-car. Whonk squatted, resting the weight of his immense shell on the heavy plank flooring.

"Would that I, too, could lose this burden, as has the false youth we bludgeoned aboard the *Moss Rock*," he sighed. "Soon will I be forced into retirement; and a mere keeper of a place of papers such as I will rate no more than a slab on the public strand, with once-daily feedings. Even for a man of high position retirement is no pleasure. A slab in the Park of Monuments is little better. A dismal outlook for one's next thousand years."

"You two continue on to the police station," Retief said. "I want to play a hunch. But don't take too long. I may be painfully right."

"What—?" Magnan started.

"As you wish, Retief," Whonk said.

The flat-car trundled past the gate to the shipyard and Retief jumped down and headed at a run for the VIP boat. The guard post still stood vacant. The two youths whom he and Whonk had left trussed were gone.

"That's the trouble with a peaceful world," Retief muttered. "No police protection." Stepping down from the lighted entry, he took up a position behind the sentry box. Alpha rose higher, shedding a glaring white light without heat. Retief shivered.

There was a sound in the near entrance like two elephants colliding. Retief looked toward the gate. His giant acquaintance, Whonk, had reappeared and was grappling with a hardly less massive opponent. A small figure became visible in the melee, scuttled for the gate, was headed off by the battling titans, turned and made for the opposite side of the shipyard. Retief waited, jumped out and gathered in the fleeing Groacian.

"Well, Yith," he said, "how's tricks. . . ? you should pardon the expression."

"Release me, Retief!" the pale-featured creature lisped, his throat bladder pulsating in agitation. "The behemoths vie for the privilege of dismembering me."

"I know how they feel. I'll see what I can do . . . for a price."

"I appeal to you," Yith whispered hoarsely, "as a fellow diplomat, a fellow alien, a fellow soft-back."

"Why don't you appeal to Slock, as a fellow conspirator?" Retief said. "Now keep quiet . . . and you may get out of this alive."

The heavier of the two struggling Fustians threw the other to the ground. The smaller Fustian lay on its back, helpless.

"That's Whonk, still on his feet," Retief said. "I wonder who he's caught—and why."

Whonk came toward the *Moss Rock* dragging the supine Fustian. Retief thrust Yith down well out of sight behind the sentry box. "Better sit tight, Yith. Don't try to sneak off; I can outrun you. Stay here and I'll see what I can do." Stepping out, he hailed Whonk.

Puffing like a steam engine, Whonk pulled up before him. "Hail, Retief!" he panted. "You followed a hunch; I did the same. I saw something strange in this one when we passed him on the avenue. I watched, followed him here. Look! It is Slock, strapped into a dead carapace! Now many things become clear."

Retief whistled. "So the youths aren't all as young as they look. Somebody's been holding out on the rest of you Fustians."

"The soft one," Whonk said. "You laid him by the heels, Retief. I saw. Produce him now."

"Hold on a minute, Whonk. It won't do you any good to—"

Whonk winked broadly. "I must take my revenge!" he roared. "I shall test the texture of the Soft One! His pulped remains will be scoured up by the ramp-washers and mailed home in bottles."

Retief whirled at a sound, caught up with the scuttling Yith fifty feet away, and hauled him back to Whonk.

"It's up to you, Whonk," he said. "I know how important ceremonial revenge is to you Fustians."

"Mercy!" Yith hissed, his eye-stalks whipping in distress. "I claim diplomatic immunity."

"No diplomat am I," Whonk rumbled. "Let me see; suppose I start with one of those obscenely active eyes." He reached . . .

"I have an idea," Retief said brightly. "Do you suppose—just this once—you could forego the ceremonial revenge if Yith promised to arrange for a Groacian Surgical Mission to de-carapace you elders?"

"But," Whonk protested, "those eyes; what a pleasure to pluck them, one by one—"

"Yess," Yith hissed, "I swear it; our most expert surgeons . . . platoons of them, with the finest of equipment."

"I have dreamed of how it would be to sit on this one, to feel him squash beneath my bulk. . . ."

"Light as a whissle feather shall you dance," Yith whispered. "Shell-less shall you spring in the joy of renewed youth. . . ."

"Maybe just one eye," Whonk said. "That would leave him four. . . ."

"Be a sport," said Retief.

"Well."

"It's a deal then," Retief said. "Yith, on your word as a diplomat, an alien and a soft-back, you'll set up the mission. Groaci surgical skill is an export that will net you more than armaments. It will be a whissle feather in your cap—if you bring it off. And in return, Whonk won't sit on you. In addition, I won't prefer charges against you of interference in the internal affairs of a free world."

Behind Whonk there was a movement. Slock, wriggling free of the borrowed carapace, struggled to his feet . . . in time for Whonk to seize him, lift him high, and head for the entry to the *Moss Rock.*

"Hey," Retief called. "Where are you going?"

"I would not deny this one his reward," Whonk called. "He hoped to cruise in luxury; so be it."

"Hold on," Retief said. "That tub is loaded with titanite!"

"Stand not in my way, Retief. For this one in truth owes me a vengeance."

Retief watched as the immense Fustian bore his giant burden up the ramp and disappeared within the ship.

"I guess Whonk means business," he said to Yith, who hung in his grasp, all five eyes goggling. "And he's a little too big for me to stop, once he sets his mind on something. But maybe he's just throwing a scare into him."

Whonk reappeared, alone, and climbed down.

"What did you do with him?" Retief said.

"We had best withdraw," Whonk said. "The killing radius of the drive is fifty yards."

"You mean—"

"The controls are set for Groac. Long may he sleep."

"It was quite a bang," Retief said, "but I guess you saw it too."

"No, confound it," Magnan said. "When I remonstrated with Hulk, or Whelk—"

"Whonk."

"—the ruffian thrust me into an alley, bound in my own cloak. I'll most certainly mention the indignity in a note to the Minister." He jotted on a pad.

"How about the surgical mission?"

"A most generous offer," Magnan said. "Frankly, I was astonished. I think perhaps we've judged the Groaci too harshly."

"I hear the Ministry of Youth has had a rough morning of it," Retief said. "And a lot of rumors are flying to the effect that Youth Groups are on the way out."

Magnan cleared his throat and shuffled papers. "I—ah—have explained to the press that last night's ahh . . ."

"Fiasco."

"—affair was necessary in order to place the culprits in an untenable position. Of course, as to the destruction of the VIP vessel and the presumed death of the fellow, Slop—"

"The Fustians understand," Retief said.

"Whonk wasn't kidding about ceremonial vengeance. Yith was lucky: he hadn't actually drawn blood. Then no amount of dickering would have saved him."

"The Groaci have been guilty of gross misuse of diplomatic privilege," Magnan said. "I think that a note—or perhaps an *aide memoire;* less formal. . . ."

"'The *Moss Rock* was bound for Groac," Retief said. "She was already in her transit orbit when she blew. The major fragments should arrive on schedule in a month or so. It should provide quite a meteorite display. I think that should be all the aid the Groaci's *memoires* will need to keep their tentacles off Fust."

"But diplomatic usage—"

"Then, too, the less that's put in writing, the less they can blame you for, if anything goes wrong."

"There's that, of course," Magnan said, his lips pursed. "Now you're thinking constructively, Retief. We may make a diplomat of you yet." He smiled expansively.

"Maybe. But I refuse to let it depress me." Retief stood up. "I'm taking a few weeks off . . . if you have no objections, Mr. Ambassador. My pal Whonk wants to show me an island down south where the fishing is good."

"But there are some extremely important matters coming up," Magnan said. "We're planning to sponsor Senior Citizen Groups."

"Count me out. Groups give me an itch."

"Why, what an astonishing remark, Retief. After all, we diplomats are ourselves a group."

"Uh, huh," Retief said.

Magnan sat quietly, his mouth open, and watched as Retief stepped into the hall and closed the door gently behind him.

. . . No jackstraws to be swayed by superficial appearances, dedicated career field personnel of the Corps unflaggingly administered the enlightened concepts evolved at Corps HQ by high-level deep-think teams toiling unceasingly in underground caverns to weld the spirit of Inter-Being amity. Never has the efficacy of close cultural rapport, coupled with Mission teamwork, been better displayed than in the loyal performance of Administrative Assistant Yolanda Meuhl, Acting Consul at Groac, in maintaining the Corps posture laid down by her predecessor, Consul Whaffle . . .

Vol VII, reel 98. 488 A. E. (AD 2949)

POLICY

"THE CONSUL for the Terrestrial States," Retief said, "presents his compliments, et cetera, to the Ministry of Culture of the Groacian Autonomy, and, with reference to the Ministry's invitation to attend a recital of interpretive grimacing, has the honor to express regret that he will be unable—"

"You can't turn down this invitation," Administrative Assistant Meuhl said flatly. "I'll make that 'accepts with pleasure.' "

Retief exhaled a plume of cigar smoke.

"Miss Meuhl," he said, "in the past couple of weeks I've sat through six light concerts, four attempts at chamber music, and God knows how many assorted folk-art festivals. I've been tied up every off-duty hour since I got here."

"You can't offend the Groaci," Miss Meuhl said sharply. "Consul Whaffle would never have—"

"Whaffle left here three months ago," Retief said, "leaving me in charge."

"Well," Miss Muehl said, snapping off the dic-typer. "I'm sure I don't know what excuse I can give the Minister."

"Never mind the excuses. Just tell him I won't be there." He stood up.

"Are you leaving the office?" Miss Meuhl adjusted her glasses. "I have some important letters here for your signature."

"I don't recall dictating any letters today, Miss Meuhl," Retief said, pulling on a light cape.

"I wrote them for you. They're just as Consul Whaffle would have wanted them."

"Did you write all Whaffle's letters for him, Miss Meuhl?"

"Consul Whaffle was an extremely busy man," Miss Meuhl said stiffly. "He had complete confidence in me."

"Since I'm cutting out the culture from now on, I won't be so busy."

"Well! May I ask where you'll be if something comes up?"

"I'm going over to the Foreign Office Archives."

Miss Meuhl blinked behind thick lenses. "Whatever for?"

Retief looked at her thoughtfully. "You've been here on Groac for four years, Miss Meuhl. What was behind the coup d'état that put the present government in power?"

"I'm sure I haven't pried into—"

"What about that Terrestrial cruiser, the one that disappeared out this way about ten years back?"

"Mr. Retief, those are just the sort of questions we avoid with the Groaci. I certainly hope you're not thinking of openly intruding—"

"Why?"

"The Groaci are a very sensitive race. They don't welcome outworlders raking up things. They've been gracious enough to let us live down the fact that Terrestrials subjected them to deep humiliation on one occasion."

"You mean when we came looking for the cruiser?"

"I, for one, am ashamed of the high-handed tactics that were employed, grilling these innocent people as though they were criminals. We try never to reopen that wound, Mr. Retief."

"They never found the cruiser, did they?"

"Certainly not on Groac."

Retief nodded. "Thanks, Miss Meuhl," he said. "I'll be back before you close the office." Miss Meuhl's thin face was set in lines of grim disapproval as he closed the door.

Peering through the small grilled window, the pale-featured Groacian vibrated his throat-bladder in a distressed bleat.

"Not to enter the Archives," he said in his faint voice. "The denial of permission. The deep regret of the Archivist."

"The importance of my task here," Retief said,

enunciating the glottal language with difficulty.
"My interest in local history."

"The impossibility of access to outworlders. To
depart quietly."

"The necessity that I enter."

"The specific instructions of the Archivist."
The Groacian's voice rose to a whisper. "To insist
no longer. To give up this idea!"

"Okay, skinny, I know when I'm licked," Retief
said in Terran. "To keep your nose clean."

Outside, Retief stood for a moment looking
across at the deeply carved windowless stucco
facades lining the street, then started off in the
direction of the Terrestrial Consulate General. The
few Groacians on the street eyed him furtively,
and veered to avoid him as he passed. Flimsy
high-wheeled ground cars puffed silently along
the resilient pavement. The air was clean and
cool. At the office Miss Meuhl would be waiting
with another list of complaints. Retief studied the
carving over the open doorways along the street.
An elaborate one picked out in pinkish paint
seemed to indicate the Groacian equivalent of a
bar. Retief went in.

A Groacian bartender dispensing clay pots of
alcoholic drink from the bar-pit at the center of the
room looked at Retief, then froze in mid-motion, a
metal tube poised over a waiting pot.

"A cooling drink," Retief said in Grocian,
squatting down at the edge of the pit. "To sample a
true Groacian beverage."

"Not to enjoy my poor offerings," the Groacian
mumbled. "A pain in the digestive sacs. To express regret."

"Not to worry," Retief replied. "To pour it out

and let me decide whether I like it."

"To be grappled in by peace-keepers for poisoning of . . . foreigners." The barkeep looked around for support, but found none. The Groaci customers, eyes elsewhere, were drifting out.

"To get the lead out," Retief said, placing a thick gold-piece in the dish provided. "To shake a tentacle."

"To procure a cage," a thin voice called from the sidelines. "To display the freak."

Retief turned. A tall Groacian vibrated his mandibles in a gesture of contempt. From his bluish throat coloration it was apparent the creature was drunk.

"To choke in your upper sac," the bartender hissed, extending his eyes toward the drunk. "To keep silent, litter-mate of drones."

"To swallow your own poison, dispenser of vileness," the drunk whispered. "To find a proper cage for this zoo-piece." He wavered toward Retief. "To show this one in the streets, like all freaks."

"Seen a lot of freaks like me, have you?" Retief asked interestedly.

"To speak intelligibly, malodorous outworlder," the drunk said. The barkeep whispered something and two customers came up to the drunk, took his arms, and helped him to the door.

"To get a cage," the drunk shrilled. "To keep the animals in their place . . ."

"I've changed my mind," Retief said to the bartender. "To be grateful as hell, but to have to hurry off now." He followed the drunk out the door. The other Groaci, releasing the heckler, hurried back inside. Retief looked at the weaving creature.

"To begone, freak," the Groacian whispered.

"To be pals," Retief said. "To be kind to dumb animals."

"To have you hauled away to a stockyard, ill-odored foreign livestock."

"Not to be angry, fragrant native," Retief said. "To permit me to chum with you."

"To flee before I take a cane to you!"

"To have a drink together."

"Not to endure such insolence." The Groacian advanced toward Retief. Retief backed away.

"To hold hands," he said. "To be buddies—"

The Groacian reached for him, but missed. A passer-by stepped around him, head down, and scuttled away. Retief, backing into the opening to a narrow cross-way, offered further verbal familiarities to the drunken local, who followed, furious. Retief stepped around him, seized his collar and yanked. The Groacian fell on his back. Retief stood over him. The downed native half rose; Retief put a foot against his chest and pushed.

"Not to be going anywhere for a few minutes," he said. "To stay right here and have a nice long talk."

"There you are!" Miss Meuhl said, eyeing Retief over her lenses. "There are two gentlemen waiting to see you. Groacian gentlemen."

"Government men, I imagine. Word travels fast." Retief pulled off his cape. "This saves me the trouble of paying another call at the Foreign Ministry."

"What have you been doing? They seem very upset, I don't mind telling you."

"I'm sure you don't. Come along—and bring an official recorder."

Two Groaci, wearing heavy eye-shields and elaborate crest ornaments indicative of rank, rose as Retief entered the room. Neither offered a courteous snap of the mandibles, Retief noted; they were mad, all right.

"I am Fith, of the Terrestrial Desk, Ministry of Foreign Affairs," the taller Groacian said, in lisping Terran. "May I present Shluh, of the Internal Police."

"Sit down, gentlemen," Retief said. They resumed their seats. Miss Meuhl hovered nervously, then sat down on the edge of a chair.

"Oh, it's such a pleasure—" she began.

"Never mind that," Retief said. "These gentlemen didn't come here to sip tea today."

"True," Fith rasped. "Frankly, I have had a most disturbing report, Mr. Consul. I shall ask Shluh to recount it." He nodded to the police chief.

"One hour ago," Shluh said, "a Groacian national was brought to hospital suffering from serious contusions. Questioning of this individual revealed that he had been set upon and beaten by a foreigner; a Terrestrial, to be precise. Investigation by my Department indicates that the description of the culprit closely matches that of the Terrestrial Consul. . . ."

Miss Meuhl gasped audibly.

"Have you ever heard," Retief said, looking steadily at Fith, "of a Terrestrial cruiser, the ISV Terrific, which dropped from sight in this sector nine years ago?"

"Really!" Miss Meuhl exclaimed, rising, "I wash my hands—"

"Just keep that recorder going," Retief snapped.

"I'll not be a party—"

"You'll do as you're told, Miss Meuhl," Retief said quietly. "I'm telling you to make an official sealed record of this conversation."

Miss Meuhl sat down.

Fith puffed out his throat indignantly. "You re-open an old wound, Mr. Consul. It reminds us of certain illegal treatment at Terrestrial hands."

"Hogwash," Retief said. "That tune went over with my predecessors, but it hits a sour note with me."

"All our efforts," Miss Meuhl said, "to live down that terrible episode; and you—"

"Terrible? I understand that a Terrestrial Peace Enforcer stood off Groac and sent a delegation down to ask questions. They got some funny answers and stayed on to dig around a little. After a week, they left. Somewhat annoying to you Groaci, if you were innocent—"

"*If!*" Miss Meuhl burst out.

"If, indeed," Fith said, his weak voice trembling. "I must protest your—"

"Save your protests, Fith. You have some explaining to do, and I don't think your story will be good enough."

"It is for you to explain; this person who was beaten—"

"Not beaten; just rapped a few times to loosen his memory."

"Then you admit—"

"It worked, too. He remembered lots of things, once he put his mind to it."

Fith rose; Shluh followed suit.

"I shall ask for your immediate recall, Mr. Consul. Were it not for your diplomatic immunity, I should—"

"Why did the Government fall, Fith, just after the Task Force paid its visit, and before the arrival of the first Terrestrial diplomatic mission?"

"This is an internal matter," Fith cried, in his faint Groacian voice. "The new regime has shown itself most amiable to you Terrestrials; it has outdone itself—"

"—to keep the Terrestrial Consul and his staff in the dark," Retief said, "and the same goes for the few Terrestrial businessmen you've given visas. This continual round of culture; no social contacts outside the diplomatic circle; no travel permits to visit outlying districts or your satellite—"

"Enough!" Fith's mandibles quivered in distress. "I can talk no more of this matter."

"You'll talk to me, or there'll be a squadron of Peace Enforcers here in five days to do the talking," Retief said.

"You can't—" Miss Meuhl gasped.

Retief turned a steady look on Miss Meuhl. She closed her mouth. The Groaci sat down.

"Answer me this one," Retief said, looking at Shluh. "A few years back—nine, to be exact—there was a little parade held here. Some curious-looking creatures were captured, and after being securely caged, were exhibited to the gentle Groacian public. Hauled through the streets. Very educational, no doubt. A highly cultural show.

"Funny thing about these animals: they wore clothes, seemed to communicate with each other. Altogether a very amusing exhibit.

"Tell me, Shluh, what happened to those six Terrestrials after the parade was over?"

Fith made a choked noise, then spoke rapidly to Shluh in Groacian. Shluh, retracting his eyes, shrank down in his chair. Miss Meuhl opened her mouth, then closed it.

"How did they die?" Retief snapped. "Did you cut their throats, shoot them, bury them alive? What amusing end did you figure out for them? Research, maybe. Cut them open to see what made them yell. . . ."

"No," Fith gasped. "I must correct this terrible false impression at once."

"False impression, hell," Retief said. "They were Terrans; a simple narco-interrogation would get that out of any Groacian who saw the parade."

"Yes," Fith said weakly. "It is true, they were Terrestrials. But there was no killing—"

"They're alive?"

"Alas, no. They . . . died."

"I see," Retief said. "They died."

"We tried to keep them alive, of course; but we did not know what foods—"

"Didn't take the trouble to find out."

"They fell ill," Fith said. "One by one . . ."

"We'll deal with that question later," Retief said. "Right now, I want more information. Where did you get them? Where did you hide the ship? What happened to the rest of the crew? Did they 'fall ill' before the big parade?"

"There were no more! Absolutely, I assure you!"

"Killed in the crash landing?"

"No crash landing. The ship descended intact, east of the city. The . . . Terrestrials . . . were unharmed. Naturally, we feared them; they were strange to us. We had never before seen such beings."

"Stepped off the ship with guns blazing, did they?"

"Guns? No, no guns—"

"They raised their hands, didn't they, asked for help? You helped them; helped them to death."

"How could we know?" Fith moaned.

"How could you know a flotilla would show up in a few months looking for them, you mean? That was a shock, wasn't it? I'll bet you had a brisk time of it hiding the ship, and shutting everybody up. A close call, eh?"

"We were afraid," Shluh said. "We are a simple people. We feared the strange creatures from the alien craft. We did not kill them, but we felt it was as well that they . . . did not survive. Then, when the warships came, we realized our error, but we feared to speak. We purged our guilty leaders, concealed what had happened, and . . . offered our friendship. We invited the opening of diplomatic relations. We made a blunder, it is true, a great blunder. But we have tried to make amends . . ."

"Where is the ship?"

"The ship?"

"What did you do with it? It was too big to just walk off and forget. Where is it?"

The two Groacians exchanged looks.

"We wish to show our contrition," Fith said. "We will show you the ship."

"Miss Meuhl," Retief said. "If I don't come back in a reasonable length of time, transmit that recording to Sector Headquarters, sealed." He stood and looked at the Groaci.

"Let's go," he said.

*   *   *

Retief stooped under the heavy timbers shoring the entry to the cavern and peered into the gloom at the curving flank of the space-burned hull.

"Any lights in here?" he asked.

A Groacian threw a switch and a weak bluish glow sprang up. Retief walked along the raised wooden catwalk, studying the ship. Empty emplacements gaped below lenseless scanner eyes. Littered decking was visible within the half-open entry port. Near the bow the words 'IVS *Terrific B7 New Terra*' were lettered in bright chrome duralloy.

"How did you get it in here?" Retief asked.

"It was hauled here from the landing point, some nine miles distant," Fith said, his voice thinner than ever. "This is a natural crevasse; the vessel was lowered into it and roofed over."

"How did you shield it so the detectors didn't pick it up?"

"All here is a high-grade iron-ore," Fith said, waving a member. "Great veins of almost pure metal."

"Let's go inside."

Shluh came forward with a hand-lamp. The party entered the ship. Retief clambered up a narrow companionway and glanced around the interior of the control compartment. Dust was thick on the deck, the stanchions where acceleration couches had been mounted, the empty instrument panels, the litter of sheared bolts, and on scraps of wire and paper. A thin frosting of rust dulled the exposed metal where cutting torches had sliced away heavy shielding. There was a faint odor of stale bedding.

"The cargo compartment—" Shluh began.

"I've seen enough," Retief said. Silently, the Groacians led the way back out through the tunnel and into the late afternoon sunshine. As they climbed the slope to the steam car, Fith came to Retief's side.

"Indeed I hope that this will be the end of this unfortunate affair," he said. "Now that all has been fully and honestly shown."

"You can skip all that," Retief said. "You're nine years late. The crew was still alive when the Task Force called, I imagine. You killed them—or let them die—rather than take the chance of admitting what you'd done."

"We were at fault," Fith said abjectly. "Now we wish only friendship."

"The *Terrific* was a heavy cruiser, about twenty thousand tons." Retief looked grimly at the slender Foreign Office official. "Where is she, Fith? I won't settle for a hundred-ton lifeboat."

Fith erected his eye stalks so violently that one eye-shield fell off.

"I know nothing of . . . of . . ." He stopped. His throat vibrated rapidly as he struggled for calm.

"My government can entertain no further accusations, Mr. Consul," he said at last. "I have been completely candid with you, I have overlooked your probing into matters not properly within your sphere of responsibility. My patience is at an end."

"Where is that ship?" Retief rapped out. "You never learn, do you? You're still convinced you can hide the whole thing and forget it. I'm telling you you can't."

"We return to the city now," Fith said. "I can do no more."

"You can and you will, Fith," Retief said. "I intend to get to the truth of this matter."

Fith spoke to Shluh in rapid Groacian. The police chief gestured to his four armed constables. They moved to ring Retief in.

Retief eyed Fith. "Don't try it," he said. "You'll just get yourself in deeper."

Fith clacked his mandibles angrily, his eye stalks canted aggressively toward the Terrestrial.

"Out of deference to your diplomatic status, Terrestrial, I shall ignore your insulting implications," Fith said in his reedy voice. "We will now return to the city."

Retief looked at the four policemen. "Sure," he said. "We'll cover the details later."

Fith followed him into the car and sat rigidly at the far end of the seat.

"I advise you to remain very close to your Consulate," Fith said. "I advise you to dismiss these fancies from your mind, and to enjoy the cultural aspects of life at Groac. Especially, I should not venture out of the city, or appear overly curious about matters of concern only to the Groacian government."

In the front seat, Shluh looked straight ahead. The loosely-sprung vehicle bobbed and swayed along the narrow highway. Retief listened to the rhythmic puffing of the motor and said nothing.

"Miss Meuhl," Retief said, "I want you to listen carefully to what I'm going to tell you. I have to move rapidly now, to catch the Groaci off guard."

"I'm sure I don't know what you're talking about," Miss Meuhl snapped, her eyes sharp behind the heavy lenses.

"If you'll listen, you may find out," Retief said. "I have no time to waste, Miss Meuhl. They won't be expecting an immediate move—I hope—and that may give me the latitude I need."

"You're still determined to make an issue of that incident." Miss Meuhl snorted. "I really can hardly blame the Groaci; they are not a sophisticated race; they had never before met aliens."

"You're ready to forgive a great deal, Miss Meuhl. But it's not what happened nine years ago I'm concerned with. It's what's happening now. I've told you that it was only a lifeboat the Groaci have hidden out. Don't you understand the implication? That vessel couldn't have come far; the cruiser itself must be somewhere nearby. I want to know where."

"The Groaci don't know. They're a very cultured, gentle people. You can do irreparable harm to the Terrestrial image if you insist—"

"We're wasting time," Retief said, as he crossed the room to his desk, opened a drawer, and took out a slim-barreled needler.

"This office is being watched; not very efficiently, if I know the Groaci. I think I can get past them all right."

"Where are you going with . . . that?" Miss Meuhl stared at the needler. "What in the world—"

"The Groaci won't waste any time destroying every piece of paper in their files relating to this affair. I have to get what I need before it's too late. If I wait for an official Enquiry Commission, they'll find nothing but blank smiles."

"You're out of your mind!" Miss Meuhl stood up, quivering with indignation. "You're like a . . . a . . ."

"You and I are in a tight spot, Miss Meuhl. The logical next move for the Groaci is to dispose of both of us. We're the only ones who know what happened. Fith almost did the job this afternoon, but I bluffed him out—for the moment."

Miss Meuhl emitted a shrill laugh. "Your fantasies are getting the better of you," she gasped. "In danger, indeed! Disposing of me! I've never heard anything so ridiculous."

"Stay in this office. Close and safe-lock the door. You've got food and water in the dispenser. I suggest you stock up, before they shut the supply down. Don't let anyone in, on any pretext whatever. I'll keep in touch with you via handphone."

"What are you planning to do?"

"If I don't make it back here, transmit the sealed record of this afternoon's conversation, along with the information I've given you. Beam it through on a Mayday priority. Then tell the Groaci what you've done and sit tight. I think you'll be all right. It won't be easy to blast in here and anyway, they won't make things worse by killing you in an obvious way. A Force can be here in a week."

"I'll do nothing of the sort! The Groaci are very fond of me! You . . . Johnny-come-lately! Roughneck! Setting out to destroy—"

"Blame it on me if it will make you feel any better," Retief said, "but don't be fool enough to trust them." He pulled on a cape, and opened the door.

"I'll be back in a couple of hours," he said. Miss Meuhl stared after him silently as he closed the door.

* * *

It was an hour before dawn when Retief keyed the combination to the safe-lock and stepped into the darkened Consular office. Miss Meuhl, dozing in a chair, awoke with a start. She looked at Retief, rose, snapped on a light, and turned to stare.

"What in the world—Where have you been? What's happened to your clothing?"

"I got a little dirty—don't worry about it." Retief went to his desk, opened a drawer, and replaced the needler.

"Where have you been?" Miss Meuhl demanded. "I stayed here."

"I'm glad you did," Retief said. "I hope you piled up a supply of food and water from the dispenser, too. We'll be holed up here for a week, at least." He jotted figures on a pad. "Warm up the official sender. I have a long transmission for Sector Headquarters."

"Are you going to tell me where you've been?"

"I have a message to get off first, Miss Meuhl," Retief said sharply. "I've been to the Foreign Ministry," he added. "I'll tell you all about it later."

"At this hour? There's no one there."

"Exactly."

Miss Meuhl gasped. "You mean you broke in? You burgled the Foreign Office?"

"That's right," Retief said calmly. "Now—"

"This is absolutely the end," Miss Meuhl said. "Thank heaven I've already—"

"Get that sender going, woman! This is important."

"I've already done so, Mr. Retief!" Miss Meuhl said harshly. "I've been waiting for you to come back here." She turned to the communicator and flipped levers. The screen snapped aglow, and a wavering long-distance image appeared.

"He's here now," Miss Meuhl said to the screen. She looked at Retief triumphantly.

"That's good," said Retief. "I don't think the Groaci can knock us off the air, but—"

"I have done my duty, Mr. Retief; I made a full report of your activities to Sector Headquarters last night, as soon as you left this office. Any doubts I may have had as to the rightness of my decision have been completely dispelled by what you've just told me."

Retief looked at her levelly. "You've been a busy girl, Miss Meuhl. Did you mention the six Terrestrials who were killed here?"

"That had no bearing on the matter of your wild behavior. I must say, in all my years in the Corps, I've never encountered a personality less suited to diplomatic work."

The screen crackled, the ten-second transmission lag having elapsed. "Mr. Retief," the face on the screen said sternly, "I am Counselor Nitworth, DSO-1, Deputy Under-Secretary for the Sector. I have received a report on your conduct which makes it mandatory for me to relieve you administratively. Pending the findings of a Board of Inquiry, you will—"

Retief reached out and snapped off the communicator. The triumphant look faded from Miss Meuhl's face.

"Why, what is the meaning—"

"If I'd listened any longer, I might have heard something I couldn't ignore. I can't afford that, at this moment. Listen, Miss Meuhl," Retief went on earnestly, "I've found the missing cruiser. It's—"

"You heard him relieve you!"

"I heard him say he was going to, Miss Meuhl.
But until I've heard and acknowledged a verbal
order, it has no force. If I'm wrong, he'll get my
resignation. If I'm right, that suspension would be
embarrassing all around."

"You're defying lawful authority. I'm in charge
here now." Miss Meuhl stepped to the local communicator.

"I'm going to report this terrible thing to the
Groaci at once, and offer my profound—"

"Don't touch that screen," Retief said. "You go
sit in that corner where I can keep an eye on you.
I'm going to make a sealed tape for transmission to
Headquarters, along with a call for an armed Task
Force. Then we'll settle down to wait."

Retief, ignoring Miss Meuhl's fury, spoke into
the recorder.

The local communicator chimed. Miss Meuhl
jumped up and stared at it.

"Go ahead," Retief said. "Answer it."

A Groacian official appeared on the screen.

"Yolanda Meuhl," he said without preamble,
"for the Foreign Minister of the Groacian Autonomy, I herewith accredit you as Terrestrial
Consul to Groac, in accordance with the advices
transmitted to my Government direct from the
Terrestrial Headquarters. As Consul, you are requested to make available for questioning Mr. J.
Retief, former Consul, in connection with the assault on two Peace Keepers, and illegal entry into
the offices of the Ministry of Foreign Affairs."

"Why . . . why," Miss Meuhl stammered. "Yes,
of course, and I do want to express my deepest
regrets—"

Retief rose, went to the communicator, and assisted Miss Meuhl aside.

"Listen carefully, Fith," he said. "Your bluff has been called. You don't come in and we don't come out. Your camouflage worked for nine years, but it's all over now. I suggest you keep your heads and resist the temptation to make matters worse."

"Miss Meuhl," Fith replied, "a Peace Squad waits outside your Consulate. It is clear you are in the hands of a dangerous lunatic. As always, the Groaci wish only friendship with the Terrestrials, but—"

"Don't bother," Retief cut in. "You know what was in those files I looked over this morning."

Retief turned at a sound behind him. Miss Meuhl was at the door reaching for the safe-lock release.

"Don't!" Retief jumped . . . too late. The door burst inward, a crowd of crested Groaci pressed into the room, pushed Miss Meuhl back, and aimed scatter guns at Retief. Police Chief Shluh pushed forward.

"Attempt no violence, Terrestrial," he said. "I cannot promise to restrain my men."

"You're violating Terrestrial territory, Shluh," Retief said steadily. "I suggest you move back out the same way you came in."

"I invited them here," Miss Meuhl spoke up. "They are here at my express wish."

"Are they? Are you sure you meant to go this far, Miss Meuhl? A squad of armed Groaci in the Consulate?"

"You are the Consul, Miss Yolanda Meuhl," Shluh said. "Would it not be best if we removed this deranged person to a place of safety?"

"Yes," Miss Meuhl said. "You're quite right, Mr. Shluh. Please escort Mr. Retief to his quarters in this building."

"I don't advise you to violate my diplomatic immunity, Fith," Retief said.

"As Chief of Mission," Miss Meuhl said quickly, "I hereby waive immunity in the case of Mr. Retief."

Shluh produced a hand recorder. "Kindly repeat your statement, Madam, officially," he said. "I wish no question—"

"Don't be a fool, woman," Retief said. "Don't you see what you're letting yourself in for? This would be a hell of a good time for you to figure out whose side you're on."

"I'm on the side of common decency!"

"You've been taken in. These people are concealing—"

"You think all women are fools, don't you, Mr. Retief?" She turned to the police chief and spoke into the microphone he held up.

"That's an illegal waiver," Retief said. "I'm Consul here, whatever rumors you've heard. This thing's coming out into the open, in spite of anything you can do; don't add violation of the Consulate to the list of Groacian atrocities."

"Take the man," Shluh said. Two tall Groaci came to Retief's side, guns aimed at his chest.

"Determined to hang yourselves, aren't you?" Retief said. "I hope you have sense enough not to lay a hand on this poor fool here." He jerked a thumb at Miss Meuhl. "She doesn't know anything. I hadn't had time to tell her yet. She thinks you're a band of angels."

The cop at Retief's side swung the butt of his

scatter gun and connected solidly with Retief's
jaw. Retief staggered against a Groacian, was
caught and thrust upright, blood running down
onto his shirt. Miss Meuhl yelped. Shluh barked
at the guard in shrill Groacian, then turned to
stare at Miss Meuhl.

"What has this man told you?"

"I—nothing. I refused to listen to his ravings."

"He said nothing to you of . . . some alleged . . .
involvement."

"I've told you," Miss Meuhl said sharply. She
looked at the expressionless Groaci, then back at
the blood on Retief's shirt.

"He told me nothing," she whispered. "I swear
it."

"Let it lie, boys," Retief said, "before you spoil
that good impression."

Shluh looked at Miss Meuhl for a long moment.
Then he turned.

"Let us go," he said. He turned back to Miss
Meuhl. "Do not leave this building until further
advice."

"But . . . I am the Terrestrial Consul."

"For your safety, madam. The people are
aroused at the beating of Groacian nationals by
an . . . alien."

"So long, Meuhlsie," Retief said. "You played it
real foxy."

"You'll . . . lock him in his quarters?" Miss
Meuhl said.

"What is done with him now is a Groacian affair, Miss Meuhl. You yourself have withdrawn
the protection of your government."

"I didn't mean—"

"Don't start having second thoughts," Retief

said. "They can make you miserable."

"I had no choice. I had to consider the best interests of the Service."

"My mistake, I guess. I was thinking of the best interests of a Terrestrial cruiser with three hundred men aboard."

"Enough," Shluh said. "Remove this criminal." He gestured to the Peace Keepers.

"Move along," he said to Retief. He turned to Miss Meuhl.

"A pleasure to deal with you, Madam."

The police car started up and pulled away. The Peace Keeper in the front seat turned to look at Retief.

"To have some sport with it, and then to kill it," he said.

"To have a fair trial first," Shluh said. The car rocked and jounced, rounded a corner, and puffed along between ornamented pastel facades.

"To have a trial and then to have a bit of sport," the Peace Keeper said.

"To suck the eggs in your own hill," Retief said. "To make another stupid mistake."

Shluh raised his short ceremonial club and cracked Retief across the head. Retief shook his head, tensed—

The Peace Keeper in the front seat beside the driver turned and rammed the barrel of his scatter gun against Retief's ribs.

"To make no move, outworlder," he said. Shluh raised his club and carefully struck Retief again. He slumped.

The car, swaying rounded another corner. Retief slid over against the police chief.

"To fend this animal—" Shluh began. His weak voice was cut off short as Retief's hand shot out, took him by the throat, and snapped him down onto the floor. As the guard on Retief's left lunged, Retief uppercut him, slamming his head against the door post. Retief grabbed the guard's scatter gun as it fell, and pushed it into the mandibles of the Groacian in the front seat.

"To put your pop-gun over the seat—carefully—and drop it," he said.

The driver slammed on his brakes, then whirled to raise his gun. Retief cracked a gun barrel against the head of the Groacian.

"To keep your eye-stalks on the road," he said. The driver grabbed at the tiller and shrank against the window, watching Retief with one eye, driving with another.

"To gun this thing," Retief said. "To keep moving."

Shluh stirred on the floor. Retief put a foot on him, pressing him back. The Peace Keeper beside Retief moved. Retief pushed him off the seat onto the floor. He held the scatter gun with one hand and mopped at the blood on his face with the other. The car bounded over the irregular surface of the road, puffing furiously.

"Your death will not be an easy one, Terrestrial," Shluh said in Terran.

"No easier than I can help," Retief said. "Shut up for now, I want to think."

The car, passing the last of the relief-encrusted mounds, sped along between tilled fields.

"Slow down," Retief said. The driver obeyed.

"Turn down this side road."

The car bumped off onto an unpaved surface,

then threaded its way back among tall stalks.

"Stop here." The car stopped, blew off steam, and sat trembling as the hot engine idled.

Retief opened the door, taking his foot off Shluh.

"Sit up," he ordered. "You two in front listen carefully." Shluh sat up, rubbing his throat.

"Three of you are getting out here. Good old Shluh is going to stick around to drive for me. If I get that nervous feeling that you're after me, I'll toss him out. That will be pretty messy, at high speed. Shluh, tell them to sit tight until dark and forget about sounding any alarms. I'd hate to see you split open and spill all over the pavement."

"To burst your throat sac, evil-smelling beast!" Shluh hissed in Groacian.

"Sorry, I haven't got one." Retief put the gun under Shluh's ear. "Tell them, Shluh; I can drive myself, in a pinch."

"To do as the foreign one says; to stay hidden until dark," Shluh said.

"Everybody out," Retief said. "And take this with you." He nudged the unconscious Groacian. "Shluh, you get in the driver's seat. You others stay where I can see you."

Retief watched as the Groaci silently followed instructions.

"All right, Shluh," Retief said softly. "Let's go. Take me to Groac Spaceport by the shortest route that doesn't go through the city, and be very careful about making any sudden movements."

Forty minutes later Shluh steered the car up to the sentry-guarded gate in the security fence surrounding the military enclosure at Groac Spaceport.

"Don't yield to any rash impulses," Retief whispered as a crested Groacian soldier came up. Shluh grated his mandibles in helpless fury.

"Drone-master Shluh, Internal Security," he croaked. The guard tilted his eyes toward Retief.

"The guest of the Autonomy," Shluh added.

"To let me pass or rot in this spot, fool?"

"To pass, Drone-master," the sentry mumbled. He was still staring at Retief as the car moved jerkily away.

"You are as good as pegged-out on the hill in the pleasure pits now, Terrestrial," Shluh said in Terran. "Why do you venture here?"

"Pull over there in the shadow of the tower and stop," Retief said.

Shluh complied. Retief studied a row of four slender ships silhouetted against the early dawn colors of the sky.

"Which of those boats are ready to lift?"' Retief demanded.

Shluh swivelled a choleric eye.

"All of them are shuttles; they have no range. They will not help you."

"To answer the question, Shluh, or to get another crack on the head."

"You are not like other Terrestrials, you are a mad dog."

"We'll rough out a character sketch of me later. Are they fueled up? You know the procedures here. Did those shuttles just get in, or is that the ready line?"

"Yes. All are fueled and ready for take-off."

"I hope you're right, Shluh. You and I are going to drive over and get in one; if it doesn't lift, I'll kill you and try the next one. Let's go."

"You are mad. I have told you: these boats have
not more than ten thousand ton-seconds capacity;
they are useful only for satellite runs."

"Never mind the details. Let's try the first in
line."

Shluh let in the clutch and the steam car
clanked and heaved, rolling off toward the line of
boats.

"Not the first in line," Shluh said suddenly.
"The last is the most likely to be fueled. But—"

"Smart grasshopper," Retief said. "Pull up to
the entry port, hop out, and go right up. I'll be
right behind you."

"The gangway guard. The challenging of—"

"More details. Just give him a dirty look and say
what's necessary. You know the technique."

The car passed under the stern of the first boat,
then the second. There was no alarm. It rounded
the third and shuddered to a stop by the open port
of the last vessel.

"Out," Retief said. "To make it snappy."

Shluh stepped from the car, hesitated as the
guard came to attention, then hissed at him and
mounted the steps. The guard looked wonderingly at Retief, mandibles slack.

"An outworlder!" he said. He unlimbered his
scatter gun. "To stop here, meat-faced one."

Up ahead, Shluh turned.

"To snap to attention, litter-mate of drones,"
Retief rasped in Groacian. The guard jumped,
waved his eye stalks, and came to attention.

"About face!" Retief hissed. "To hell out of
here—march!"

The guard tramped off across the ramp. Retief took the steps two at a time, slammed the port shut behind himself.

"I'm glad your boys have a little discipline, Shluh," Retief said. "What did you say to him?"

"I but—"

"Never mind. We're in. Get up to the control compartment."

"What do you know of Groacian Naval vessels?"

"Plenty. This is a straight copy from the life boat you lads hijacked. I can run it. Get going."

Retief followed Shluh up the companionway into the cramped control room.

"Tie in, Shluh," Retief ordered.

"This is insane. We have only fuel enough for a one-way transit to the satellite; we cannot enter orbit, nor can we land again! To lift this boat is death. Release me. I promise you immunity."

"If I have to tie you in myself, I might bend your head in the process."

Shluh crawled onto the couch, and strapped in.

"Give it up," he said. "I will see that you are re-instated—with honor. I will guarantee a safe-conduct—"

"Count-down," Retief said. He threw in the autopilot.

"It is death!" Shluh screeched.

The gyros hummed, timers ticked, relays closed. Retief lay relaxed on the acceleration pad. Shluh breathed noisily, his mandibles clicking rapidly.

"That I had fled in time," he said in a hoarse whisper. "This is not a good death."

"No death is a good death," Retief said, "not for a while yet." The red light flashed on in the center of the panel, and sound roared out into the breaking day. The ship trembled, then lifted. Retief could hear Shluh's whimpering even through the roar of the drive.

"Perihelion," Shluh said dully. "To begin now the long fall back."

"Not quite," Retief said. "I figure eight-five seconds to go." He scanned the instruments, frowning.

"We will not reach the surface, of course," Shluh said. "The pips on the screen are missiles. We have a rendezvous in space, Retief. In your madness, may you be content."

"They're fifteen minutes behind us, Shluh. Your defenses are sluggish."

"Nevermore to burrow in the grey sands of Groac," Shluh mourned.

Retief's eyes were fixed on a dial face.

"Any time now," he said softly. Shluh canted his eye stalks.

"What do you seek?"

Retief stiffened. "Look at the screen," he said. Shluh looked. A glowing point, off-center, moving rapidly across the grid . . .

"What—?"

"Later—"

Shluh watched as Retief's eyes darted from one needle to another.

"How . . ."

"For your own neck's sake, Shluh, you'd better hope this works." He flipped the sending key.

"2396 TR-42 G, this is the Terrestrial Consul at Groac, aboard Groac 902, vectoring on you at an MP fix of 91/54/942. Can you read me? Over."

"What forlorn gesture is this?" Shluh whispered. "You cry in the night to emptiness."

"Button your mandibles," Retief snapped, listening. There was a faint hum of stellar background noise. Retief repeated his call.

"Maybe they hear but can't answer," he muttered. He flipped the key.

"2396, you've got forty seconds to lock a tractor beam on me, before I shoot past you."

"To call into the void," said Shluh. "To—"

"Look at the DV screen."

Shluh twisted his head and looked. Against the background mist of stars, a shape loomed, dark and inert.

"It is . . . a ship," he said, "a monster ship . . ."

"That's her," Retief said. "Nine years and a few months out of New Terra on a routine mapping mission; the missing cruiser, *IVS Terrific*."

"Impossible," Shluh hissed. "The hulk swings in a deep cometary orbit."

"Right, and now it's making its close swing past Groac."

"You think to match orbits with the derelict? Without power? Our meeting will be a violent one, if that is your intent."

"We won't hit; we'll make our pass at about five thousand yards."

"To what end, Terrestrial? You have found your lost ship; what then? Is this glimpse worth the death we die?"

"Maybe they're not dead," Retief said.

"Not dead?" Shluh lapsed into Groacian. "To have died in the burrow of one's youth. To have burst my throat sac before I embarked with a mad alien to call up the dead."

"2396, make it snappy," Retief called. The

speaker crackled heedlessly. The dark image on the screen drifted past, dwindling now.

"Nine years, and the mad one speaking as to friends," Shluh raved. "Nine years dead, and still to seek them."

"Another ten seconds," Retief said softly, "and we're out of range. Look alive, boys."

"Was this your plan, Retief?" Shluh reverted to Terran. "Did you flee Groac and risk all on this slender thread?"

"How long would I have lasted in a Groaci prison?"

"Long and long, my Retief," Shluh hissed, "under the blade of an artist."

Abruptly the ship trembled, seemed to drag, rolling the two passengers in their couches. Shluh hissed as the restraining harness cut into him. The shuttle boat was pivoting heavily, up-ending. Crushing acceleration forces built. Shluh gasped, crying out shrilly.

"What . . . is . . . it. . . ?"

"It looks," said Retief, "like we've had a little bit of luck."

"On our second pass," the gaunt-faced officer said, "they let fly with something. I don't know how it got past our screens. It socked home in the stern and put the main pipe off the air. I threw full power to the emergency shields, and broadcast our identification on a scatter that should have hit every receiver within a parsec; nothing. Then the transmitter blew. I was a fool to send the boat down, but I couldn't believe, somehow . . ."

"In a way it's lucky you did, captain. That was my only lead."

"They tried to finish us after that. But, with full

power to the screens, nothing they had could get through. Then they called on us to surrender."

Retief nodded. "I take it you weren't tempted?"

"More than you know. It was a long swing out on our first circuit. Then coming back in, we figured we'd hit. As a last resort I would have pulled back power from the screens and tried to adjust the orbit with the steering jets, but the bombardment was pretty heavy. I don't think we'd have made it. Then we swung past and headed out again. We've got a three-year period. Don't think I didn't consider throwing in the towel."

"Why didn't you?"

"The information we have is important. We've got plenty of stores aboard, enough for another ten years, if necessary. Sooner or later I knew a Corps search vessel would find us."

Retief cleared his throat. "I'm glad you stuck with it, Captain. Even a backwater world like Groac can kill a lot of people when it runs amok."

"What I didn't know," the captain went on, "was that we're not in a stable orbit. We're going to graze atmosphere pretty deeply this pass, and in another sixty days we'd be back to stay. I guess the Groaci would be ready for us."

"No wonder they were sitting on this so tight. They were almost in the clear."

"And you're here now," the captain said. "Nine years, and we weren't forgotten. I knew we could count on—"

"It's over now, captain. That's what counts."

"Home . . . After nine years . . ."

"I'd like to take a look at the films you mentioned," Retief said. "The ones showing the installations on the satellite."

The captain complied. Retief watched as the scene unrolled, showing the bleak surface of the tiny moon as the *Terrific* had seen it, nine years before. In harsh black and white, row on row of identical hulls cast long shadows across the pitted metallic surface of the satellite.

"They had quite a little surprise planned; your visit must have panicked them," Retief said.

"They should be about ready to go, by now. Nine years . . ."

"Hold that picture," Retief said suddenly. "What's that ragged black line across the plain there?"

"I think it's a fissure. The crystalline structure—"

"I've got what may be an idea," Retief said. "I had a look at some classified files last night, at the Foreign Office. One was a progress report on a fissionable stock-pile. It didn't make much sense at the time. Now I get the picture. Which is the north end of that crevasse?"

"At the top of the picture."

"Unless I'm badly mistaken, that's the bomb dump. The Groaci like to tuck things underground. I wonder what a direct hit with a 50 megaton missile would do to it?"

"If that's an ordnance storage dump," the captain said, "it's an experiment I'd like to try."

"Can you hit it?"

"I've got fifty heavy missiles aboard. If I fire

them in direct sequence, it should saturate the defenses. Yes, I can hit it."

"The range isn't too great?"

"These are the deluxe models." The captain smiled balefully. "Video guidance. We could steer them into a bar and park 'em on a stool."

"What do you say we try it?"

"I've been wanting a solid target for a long time," the captain said.

Half an hour later, Retief propelled Shluh into a seat before the screen.

"That expanding dust cloud used to be the satellite of Groac, Shluh," he said. "Looks like something happened to it."

The police chief stared at the picture.

"Too bad," Retief said. "But then it wasn't of any importance, was it, Shluh?"

Shluh muttered incomprehensibly.

"Just a bare hunk of iron, Shluh, as the Foreign Office assured me when I asked for information."

"I wish you'd keep your prisoner out of sight," the captain said. "I have a hard time keeping my hands off him."

"Shluh wants to help, captain. He's been a bad boy and I have a feeling he'd like to co-operate with us now, especially in view of the eminent arrival of a Terrestrial ship, and the dust cloud out there," Retief said.

"What do you mean?"

"Captain, you can ride it out for another week, contact the ship when it arrives, get a tow in, and your troubles are over. When your films are shown in the proper quarter, a Peace Force will come out

here and reduce Groac to a subtechnical cultural
level and set up a monitor system to insure she
doesn't get any more expansionist ideas—not that
she can do much now, with her handy iron mine
in the sky gone."

"That's right, and—"

"On the other hand, there's what I might call the
diplomatic approach . . ."

He explained at length. The captain looked at
him thoughtfully.

"I'll go along," he said. "What about this fellow?"

Retief turned to Shluh. The Groacian shuddered, retracting his eye stalks.

"I will do it," he said faintly.

"Right," Retief said. "Captain, if you'll have
your men bring in the transmitter from the shuttle, I'll place a call to a fellow named Fith at the
Foreign Office." He turned to Shluh. "And when I
get him, Shluh, you'll do everything exactly as
I've told you—or have Terrestrial monitors dictating in Groac City."

"Quite candidly, Retief," Counselor Nitworth
said, "I'm rather nonplussed. Mr. Fith of the
Foreign Office seemed almost painfully lavish in
your praise. He seems most eager to please you. In
the light of some of the evidence I've turned up
of highly irregular behavior on your part, it's
difficult to understand."

"Fith and I have been through a lot together,"
Retief said. "We understand each other."

"You have no cause for complacency, Retief,"
Nitworth said. "Miss Meuhl was quite justified in
reporting your case. Of course, had she known

that you were assisting Mr. Fith in his marvelous work, she would have modified her report somewhat, no doubt. You should have confided in her."

"Fith wanted to keep it secret, in case it didn't work out. You know how it is."

"Of course. And as soon as Miss Meuhl recovers from her nervous breakdown, there'll be a nice promotion awaiting her. The girl more than deserves it for her years of unswerving devotion to Corps policy."

"Unswerving," Retief said. "I'll go along with that."

"As well you may, Retief. You've not acquitted yourself well in this assignment. I'm arranging for a transfer; you've alienated too many of the local people."

"But as you said, Fith speaks highly of me . . ."

"True. It's the cultural intelligentsia I'm referring to. Miss Meuhl's records show that you deliberately affronted a number of influential groups by boycotting—"

"Tone deaf," Retief said. "To me a Groacian blowing a nose-whistle sounds like a Groacian blowing a nose-whistle."

"You have to come to terms with local aesthetic values. Learn to know the people as they really are. It's apparent from some of the remarks Miss Meuhl quoted in her report that you held the Groaci in rather low esteem. But how wrong you were. All the while they were working unceasingly to rescue those brave lads marooned aboard our cruiser. They pressed on, even after we ourselves had abandoned the search. And when they discovered that it had been a collision with their satellite which disabled the craft, they made that magnificent gesture—unprecedented. One hundred thousand credits in gold to each crew member, as a token of Groacian sympathy."

"A handsome gesture," Retief murmured.

"I hope, Retief, that you've learned from this incident. In view of the helpful part you played in advising Mr. Fith in matters of procedure to assist in his search, I'm not recommending a reduction in grade. We'll overlook the affair, give you a clean slate. But in the future, I'll be watching you closely."

"You can't win 'em all," Retief said.

"You'd better pack up; you'll be coming along with us in the morning." Nitworth shuffled his papers together. "I'm sorry that I can't file a more flattering report on you. I would have liked to recommend your promotion, along with Miss Meuhl's."

"That's okay," Retief said. "I have my memories."

... Ofttimes, the expertise displayed by experienced Terrestrial Chiefs of Mission in the analysis of local political currents enabled these dedicated senior officers to secure acceptance of Corps commercial programs under seemingly insurmountable conditions of adversity. Ambassador Crodfoller's virtuoso performance in the reconciliation of rival elements at Petreac added new lustre to Corps prestige ...
Vol VIII, reel 8. 489 A. E. (AD 2950)

PALACE REVOLUTION

RETIEF PAUSED before a tall mirror to check the overlap of the four sets of lapels that ornamented the vermilion cut-away of a First Secretary and Consul.

"Come along, Retief," Magnan said. "The ambassador has a word to say to the staff before we go in."

"I hope he isn't going to change the spontaneous speech he plans to make when the Potentate impulsively suggests a trade agreement along the lines they've been discussing for the last two months."

"Your derisive attitude is uncalled for, Retief," Magnan said sharply. "I think you realize it's delayed your promotion in the Corps."

Retief took a last glance in the mirror. "I'm not sure I want a promotion. It would mean more lapels."

Ambassador Crodfoller pursed his lips, waiting until Retief and Magnan took places in the ring of Terrestrial diplomats around him.

"A word of caution only, gentlemen. Keep always foremost in your minds the necessity for our identification with the Nenni Caste. Even a hint of familiarity with lower echelons could mean the failure of the mission. Let us remember: the Nenni represent authority here on Petreac; their traditions must be observed, whatever our personal preferences. Let's go along now; the Potentate will be making his entrance any moment."

Magnan came to Retief's side as they moved toward the salon.

"The ambassador's remarks were addressed chiefly to you, Retief," he said. "Your laxness in these matters is notorious. Naturally, I believe firmly in democratic principles myself."

"Have you ever had a feeling, Mr. Magnan, that there's a lot going on here that we don't know about?"

Magnan nodded. "Quite so; Ambassador Crodfoller's point exactly. Matters which are not of concern to the Nenni are of no concern to us."

"Another feeling I get is that the Nenni aren't very bright. Now suppose—"

"I'm not given to suppositions, Retief. We're here to implement the policies of the Chief of Mission. And I should dislike to be in the shoes of a member of the Staff whose conduct jeopardized the agreement that's to be concluded here tonight."

A bearer with a tray of drinks rounded a fluted column, shied as he confronted the diplomats, fumbled the tray, grabbed, and sent a glass crashing to the floor. Magnan leaped back, slapping at the purple cloth of his pants leg. Retief's hand shot out and steadied the tray. The servant rolled his terrified eyes.

"I'll take one of those, now that you're here," Retief said easily, lifting a glass from the tray. "No harm done. Mr. Magnan's just warming up for the big dance."

A Nenni major-domo bustled up, rubbing his hands politely.

"Some trouble here? What happened, Honorables, what, what . . ."

"The blundering idiot," Magnan spluttered. "How dare—"

"You're quite an actor, Mr. Magnan," Retief said. "If I didn't know about your democratic principles, I'd think you were really angry."

The servant ducked his head and scuttled away.

"Has this fellow given dissatisfaction. . . ?" The major-domo eyed the retreating bearer.

"I dropped my glass," Retief said. "Mr. Magnan's upset because he hates to see liquor wasted."

Retief turned and found himself face-to-face with Ambassador Crodfoller.

"I witnessed that," the ambassador hissed. "By the goodness of Providence the Potentate and his retinue haven't appeared yet, but I can assure you the servants saw it. A more un-Nenni-like display

I would find it difficult to imagine."

Retief arranged his features in an expression of deep interest. "More un-Nenni-like, sir? I'm not sure I—"

"Bah!" The ambassador glared at Retief. "Your reputation has preceded you, sir. Your name is associated with a number of the most bizarre incidents in Corps history. I'm warning you; I'll tolerate nothing." He turned and stalked away.

"Ambassador-baiting is a dangerous sport, Retief," Magnan said.

Retief took a swallow of his drink. "Still, it's better than no sport at all."

"Your time would be better spent observing the Nenni mannerisms; frankly, Retief, you're not fitting into the group at all well."

"I'll be candid with you, Mr. Magnan; the group gives me the willies."

"Oh, the Nenni are a trifle frivolous, I'll concede. But it's with them that we must deal. And you'd be making a contribution to the overall mission if you abandoned that rather arrogant manner of yours." Magnan looked at Retief critically. "You can't help your height, of course, but couldn't you curve your back just a bit—and possibly assume a more placating expression? Just act a little more . . ."

"Girlish?"

"Exactly." Magnan nodded, then looked sharply at Retief.

Retief drained his glass and put it on a passing tray.

"I'm better at acting girlish when I'm well juiced," he said. "But I can't face another sorghum and soda. I suppose it would be un-Nenni-like to slip one of the servants a credit and ask for a Scotch and water."

"Decidedly." Magnan glanced toward a sound across the room.

"Ah, here's the Potentate now . . ." He hurried off.

Retief watched the bearers coming and going, bringing trays laden with drinks, carrying off empties. There was a lull in the drinking now, as the diplomats gathered around the periwigged chief of state and his courtiers. Bearers loitered near the service door, eyeing the notables. Retief strolled over to the service door and pushed through it into a narrow white-tiled hall filled with kitchen odors. Silent servants gaped as he passed and watched him as he moved along to the kitchen door and stepped inside.

A dozen or more low-caste Petreacans, gathered around a long table in the center of the room, looked up, startled. A heap of long-bladed bread knives, carving knives and cleavers lay in the center of the table. Other knives were thrust into belts or held in the hands of the men. A fat man in the yellow sarong of a cook stood frozen in the act of handing a twelve-inch cheese-knife to a tall one-eyed sweeper.

Retief took one glance, then let his eyes wander to a far corner of the room. Humming a careless little tune, he sauntered across to the open liquor shelves, selected a garish green bottle, then turned unhurriedly back toward the door. The group of servants watched him, transfixed.

As Retief reached the door, it swung inward. Magnan stood in the doorway, looking at him.

"I had a premonition," he said.

"I'll bet it was a dandy. You must tell me all about it—in the salon."

"We'll have this out right here," Magnan snapped. "I've warned you—" His voice trailed off as he took in the scene around the table.

"After you," Retief said, nudging Magnan toward the door.

"What's going on here?" Magnan barked. He stared at the men and started around Retief. A hand stopped him.

"Let's be going," Retief said, propelling Magnan toward the hall.

"Those knives!" Magnan yelped. "Take your hands off me, Retief! What are you men—"

Retief glanced back. The fat cook gestured suddenly, and the men faded back. The cook stood, arm cocked, a knife across his palm.

"Close the door and make no sound," he said softly.

Magnan pressed back against Retief. "Let's . . . r-run . . ." he faltered.

Retief turned slowly, put his hands up.

"I don't run very well with a knife in my back," he said. "Stand very still, Mr. Magnan, and do just what he tells you."

"Take them out through the back," the cook said.

"What does he mean," Magnan spluttered. "Here, you—"

"Silence," the cook said, almost casually. Magnan gaped at him, then closed his mouth.

Two of the men with knives came to Retief's side, gestured, grinning broadly.

"Let's go, peacocks," said one.

Retief and Magnan silently crossed the kitchen,

went out the back door, stopped on command, and stood waiting. The sky was brilliant with stars and a gentle breeze stirred the tree-tops beyond the garden. Behind them the servants talked in low voices.

"You go too, Illy," the cook was saying.

"Do it here," said another.

"And carry them down?"

"Pitch 'em behind the hedge."

"I said the river. Three of you is plenty for a couple of Nenni dandies."

"They're foreigners, not Nenni. We don't know—"

"So they're foreign Nenni. Makes no difference. I've seen them. I need every man here; now get going."

"What about the big guy?"

"Him? He waltzed into the room and didn't notice a thing. But watch the other one."

At a prod from a knife point, Retief moved off down the walk, two of the escort behind him and Magnan, another going ahead to scout the way.

Magnan moved closer to Retief.

"Say," he said in a whisper, "that fellow in the lead—isn't he the one who spilled the drink? The one you took the blame for?"

"That's him, all right. He doesn't seem nervous any more, I notice."

"You saved him from serious punishment," Magnan said. "He'll be grateful; he'll let us go. . . ."

"Better check with the fellows with the knives before you act on that."

"Say something to him," Magnan hissed, "remind him."

The lead man fell back in line with Retief and Magnan.

"These two are scared of you," he said, grinning and jerking a thumb toward the knife-handlers. "They haven't worked around the Nenni like me; they don't know you."

"Don't you recognize this gentleman?" Magnan said. "He's—"

"He did me a favor," the man said. "I remember."

"What's it all about?" Retief asked.

"The revolution. We're taking over now."

"Who's 'we'? "

"The People's Anti-Fascist Freedom League."

"What are all the knives for?"

"For the Nenni; and for you foreigners."

"What do you mean?" gasped Magnan.

"We'll slit all the throats at one time; saves a lot of running around."

"When will that be?"

"Just at dawn—and dawn comes early, this time of year. By full daylight the PAFFL will be in charge."

"You'll never succeed," Magnan said. "A few servants with knives; you'll all be caught and executed."

"By who; the Nenni?" The man laughed. "You Nenni are a caution."

"But we're not Nenni—"

"We've watched you; you're the same. You're part of the same blood-sucking class."

"There are better ways," Magnan said. "This killing won't help you. I'll personally see to it that your grievances are heard in the Corps Courts. I can assure you that the plight of the downtrodden workers will be alleviated. Equal rights for all."

"Threats won't help you," the man said. "You don't scare me."

"Threats? I'm promising relief to the exploited classes of Petreac."

"You must be nuts. You trying to upset the system or something?"

"Isn't that the purpose of your revolution?"

"Look, Nenni, we're tired of you Nenni getting all the graft. We want our turn. What good it do us to run Petreac if there's no loot?"

"You mean you intend to oppress the people? But they're your own group."

"Group, schmoop. We're taking all the chances; we're doing the work. We deserve the pay-off. You think we're throwing up good jobs for the fun of it?"

"You're basing a revolt on these cynical premises?"

"Wise up, Nenni; there's never been a revolution for any other reason."

"Who's in charge of this?" Retief said.

"Shoke, the head chef."

"I mean the big boss; who tells Shoke what to do?"

"Oh, that's Zorn. Look out, here's where we start down the slope. It's slippery."

"Look," Magnan said. "You. This—"

"My name's Illy."

"Mr. Illy, this man showed you mercy when he could have had you beaten."

"Keep moving. Yeah, I said I was grateful."

"Yes," Magnan said, swallowing hard. "A noble emotion, gratitude."

"I always try to pay back a good turn," Illy said. "Watch your step now on this sea-wall."

"You'll never regret it."

"This is far enough." Illy motioned to one of the knife men. "Give me your knife, Vug."

The man passed his knife to Illy. There was an odor of sea-mud and kelp. Small waves slapped against the stones of the sea-wall. The wind was stronger here.

"I know a neat stroke," Illy said. "Practically painless. Who's first?"

"What do you mean?" Magnan quavered.

"I said I was grateful; I'll do it myself, give you a nice clean job. You know these amateurs: botch it up and have a guy floppin' around, yellin' and splatterin' everybody up."

"I'm first," Retief said. He pushed past Magnan, stopped suddenly, and drove a straight punch at Illy's mouth.

The long blade flicked harmlessly over Retief's shoulder as Illy fell. Retief took the unarmed servant by the throat and belt, lifted him, and slammed him against the third man. Both screamed as they tumbled from the sea-wall into the water with a mighty splash. Retief turned back to Illy, pulled off the man's belt, and strapped his hands together.

Magnan found his voice. "You . . . we . . . they . . ."

"I know."

"We've got to get back," Magnan said. "Warn them."

"We'd never get through the rebel cordon around the palace. And if we did, trying to give an alarm would only set the assassinations off early."

"We can't just . . ."

"We've got to go to the source: this fellow Zorn. Get him to call it off."

"We'd be killed. At least we're safe here."

Illy groaned and opened his eyes. He sat up.

"On your feet, Illy," Retief said.

Illy looked around. "I'm sick."

"The damp air is bad for you. Let's be going." Retief pulled the man to his feet. "Where does Zorn stay when he's in town?"

"What happened? Where's Vug . . ."

"They had an accident. Fell in the pond."

Illy gazed down at the restless black water.

"I guess I had you Nenni figured wrong."

"We Nenni have hidden qualities. Let's get moving before Vug and Slug make it to shore and start it all over again."

"No hurry," Illy said. "They can't swim." He spat into the water. "So long, Vug. So long, Toscin. Take a pull at the Hell Horn for me." He started off along the sea wall toward the sound of the surf.

"You want to see Zorn, I'll take you see Zorn. I can't swim either."

"I take it," Retief said, "that the casino is a front for his political activities."

"He makes plenty off it. This PAFFL is a new kick. I never heard about it until maybe a couple months ago."

Retief motioned toward a dark shed with an open door.

"We'll stop here," he said, "long enough to strip the gadgets off these uniforms."

Illy, hands strapped behind his back, stood by

and watched as Retief and Magnan removed medals, ribbons, orders, and insignia from the formal diplomatic garments.

"This may help some," Retief said, "if the word is out that two diplomats are loose."

"It's a breeze," Illy said. "We see cats in purple and orange tailcoats all the time."

"I hope you're right," Retief said. "But if we're called, you'll be the first to go, Illy."

"You're a funny kind of Nenni," Illy said, eyeing Retief. "Toscin and Vug must be wonderin' what happened to 'em."

"If you think I'm good at drowning people, you ought to see with a knife. Let's get going."

"It's only a little way now. But you better untie me. Somebody's liable to notice it and start askin' questions and get me killed."

"I'll take the chance. How do we get to the casino?"

"We follow this street. When we get to the Drunkard's Stairs we go up and it's right in front of us. A pink front with a sign like a big luck wheel."

"Give me your belt, Magnan," Retief said.

Magnan handed it over.

"Lie down, Illy."

The servant looked at Retief.

"Vug and Toscin will be glad to see me. But they'll never believe me." He lay down. Retief strapped his feet together and stuffed a handkerchief in his mouth.

"Why are you doing that?" Magnan asked. "We need him."

"We know the way now and we don't need anyone to announce our arrival." Magnan looked at the man. "Maybe you'd better—ah, cut his throat."

Illy rolled his eyes.

"That's a very un-Nenni-like suggestion, Mr. Magnan," Retief said. "But if we have any trouble finding the casino following his directions, I'll give it serious thought."

There were few people in the narrow street. Shops were shuttered, windows dark.

"Maybe they heard about the coup," Magnan said. "They're lying low."

"More likely they're at the palace checking out knives."

They rounded a corner, stepped over a man curled in the gutter snoring heavily, and found themselves at the foot of a long flight of littered stone steps.

"The Drunkard's Stairs are plainly marked," Magnan sniffed.

"I hear sounds up there . . . sounds of merry-making."

"Maybe we'd better go back."

"Merrymaking doesn't scare me. Come to think of it, I don't know what the word means." Retief started up, Magnan behind him.

At the top of the long stair a dense throng milled in the alley-like street.

A giant illuminated roulette wheel revolved slowly above them. A loud-speaker blared the chant of the croupiers from the tables inside. Magnan and Retief moved through the crowd toward the wide-open doors.

Magnan plucked at Retief's sleeve. "Are you sure we ought to push right in like this? Maybe we ought to wait a bit, look around."

"When you're where you have no business be-ing," Retief said, "always stride along purpose-fully. If you loiter, people begin to get curious."

Inside, a mob packed the wide low-ceilinged room and clustered around gambling devices in the form of towers, tables, and basins.

"What do we do now?" Magnan asked.

"We gamble. How much money do you have in your pockets?"

"Why . . . a few credits . . ." Magnan handed the money to Retief. "But what about the man Zorn?"

"A purple cutaway is conspicuous enough, without ignoring the tables. We'll get to Zorn in due course."

"Your pleasure, gents," a bullet-headed man said, eyeing the colorful evening clothes of the diplomats. "You'll be wantin' to try your luck at the Zoop tower, I'd guess. A game for real sporting gents."

"Why . . . ah . . ." Magnan said.

"What's a Zoop tower?" Retief asked.

"Out-of-towners, hey?" The bullet-headed man shifted his dope-stick to the other corner of his mouth. "Zoop is a great little game. Two teams of players buy into the pot; each player takes a lever; the object is to make the ball drop from the top of the tower into your net. Okay?"

"What's the ante?"

"I got a hundred-credit pot workin' now, gents."

Retief nodded. "We'll try it."

The shill led the way to an eight-foot tower mounted on gimbals. Two perspiring men in trade-class pullovers gripped two of the levers that controlled the tilt of the tower. A white ball lay in a hollow in the thick glass platform at the top. From the center an intricate pattern of grooves led out to the edge of the glass. Retief and Magnan took chairs before the two free levers.

"When the light goes on, gents, work the lever to jack the tower. You got three gears; takes a good arm to work top gear. That's this button here. The little little knob controls what way you're goin'. May the best team win. I'll take the hundred credits now."

Retief handed over the money. A red light flashed on, and Retief tried the lever. It moved easily, with a ratcheting sound. The tower trembled, slowly tilted toward the two perspiring workmen pumping frantically at their levers. Magnan started slowly, accelerating as he saw the direction the tower was taking.

"Faster, Retief," he said. "They're winning."

"This is against the clock, gents," the bullet-headed man said. "If nobody wins when the light goes off, the house takes all."

"Crank it over to the left," Retief said.

"I'm getting tired."

"Shift to a lower gear."

The tower leaned. The ball stirred and rolled into a concentric channel. Retief shifted to middle gear and worked the lever. The tower, creaking to a stop, started back upright.

"There isn't any lower gear," Magnan gasped. One of the two on the other side of the tower shifted to middle gear; the other followed suit. They worked harder now, heaving against the stiff levers. The tower quivered, then moved slowly toward their side.

"I'm exhausted," Magnan gasped. Dropping the lever, he lolled back in the chair, gulping air. Retief, shifting position, took Magnan's lever with his left hand.

"Shift it to middle gear," he said. Magnan gulped, punched the button and slumped back, panting.

"My arm," he said. "I've injured myself."

The two men in pullovers conferred hurriedly as they cranked their levers; then one punched a button, and the other reached across, using his left arm to help.

"They've shifted to high," Magnan said. "Give up, it's hopeless."

"Shift me to high. Both buttons."

Magnan complied. Retief's shoulders bulged. He brought one lever down, then the other, alternately, slowly at first, then faster. The tower jerked, tilted toward him, farther. . . . The ball rolled in the channel, found an outlet—

Abruptly, both Retief's levers froze. The tower trembled, wavered, and moved back. Retief heaved. One lever folded at the base, bent down, and snapped off short. Retief braced his feet, gripped the other lever with both hands and pulled. There was a squeal of metal, a loud twang. The lever came free, a length of broken cable flopping into view. The tower fell over as the two on the other side scrambled aside.

"Hey!" the croupier yelled, appearing from the crowd. "You wrecked my equipment!"

Retief got up and faced him.

"Does Zorn know you've got your tower rigged for suckers?"

"You tryin' to call me a cheat?"

The crowd had fallen back, ringing the two men. The croupier glanced around. With a lightning motion he pulled out a knife.

"That'll be five hundred credits for the equipment," he said. "Nobody calls Kippy a cheat."

Retief picked up the broken lever.

"Don't make me hit you with this, Kippy."

Kippy looked at the bar.

"Comin' in here," he said indignantly, looking to the crowd for support, "bustin' up my rig, threatenin' me . . ."

"I want a hundred credits," Retief said. "Now."

"Highway robbery!" Kippy yelled.

"Better pay up," somebody said.

"Hit him, mister," another in the crowd yelled.

A broad-shouldered man with greying hair pushed through the crowd and looked around. "You heard him, Kippy. Give."

The shill growled, tucked his knife away, reluctantly peeled a bill from a fat roll and handed it over.

The newcomer looked from Retief to Magnan.

"Pick another game, strangers," he said. "Kippy made a little mistake."

"This is small-time stuff," Retief said. "I'm interested in something big."

The broad-shouldered man lit a perfumed dope stick, then sniffed at it.

"What would you call big?" he said softly.

"What's the biggest you've got?"

The man narrowed his eyes, smiling. "Maybe you'd like to try Slam."

"Tell me about it."

"Over here." The crowd opened up and made a path. Retief and Magnan followed across the room to a brightly-lit glass-walled box. There was an arm-sized opening at waist height, and inside was a hand grip. A four-foot clear plastic globe a quarter full of chips hung in the center. Apparatus was mounted at the top of the box.

"Slam pays good odds," the man said. "You can go as high as you like. Chips cost you a hundred credits. You start it up by dropping a chip in here." He indicated a slot.

"You take the hand grip. When you squeeze, it unlocks and starts to turn. Takes a pretty good grip to start the globe turning. You can see, it's full of chips. There's a hole at the top. As long as you hold the grip, the bowl turns. The harder you squeeze, the faster it turns. Eventually it'll turn over to where the hole is down, and chips fall out. If you let up and the bowl stops, you're all through.

"Just to make it interesting, there's contact plates spotted around the bowl; when one of 'em lines up with a live contact, you get a little jolt—guaranteed non-lethal. But if you let go, you lose. All you've got to do is hold on long enough, and you'll get the pay-off."

"How often does this random pattern put the hole down?"

"Anywhere from three minutes to fifteen, with the average grip. Oh, by the way, one more thing. That lead block up there . . ." The man motioned with his head toward a one-foot cube suspended by a thick cable. "It's rigged to drop every now and then: averages five minutes. A warning light flashes first. You can set the clock back on it by dropping another chip—or you can let go the grip. Or you can take a chance; sometime's the light's a bluff."

Retief looked at the massive block of metal.

"That would mess up a man's dealing hand, wouldn't it?"

"The last two jokers who were too cheap to feed the machine had to have 'em off; their arm, I mean. That lead's heavy stuff."

"I don't suppose your machine has a habit of getting stuck, like Kippy's?"

The broad-shouldered man frowned.

"You're a stranger," he said. "You don't know any better."

"It's a fair game, mister," someone called.

"Where do I buy the chips?"

The man smiled. "I'll fix you up. How many?"

"One."

"A big spender, eh?" The man snickered and handed over a large plastic chip.

Retief stepped to the machine and dropped the coin.

"If you want to change your mind," the man said, "you can back out now. All it'll cost you is the chip you dropped."

Retief, reaching through the hole, took the grip. It was leather-padded, hand-filling. He squeezed it. There was a click and bright lights sprang up. The globe began to twirl lazily. The four-inch hole at its top was plainly visible.

"If ever the hole gets in position, it will empty very quickly," Magnan said.

Suddenly, a brilliant white light flooded the glass cage. A sound went up from the spectators.

"Quick, drop a chip," someone yelled.

"You've only got ten seconds . . ."

"Let go!" Magnan pleaded.

Retief sat silent, holding the grip, frowning up

at the weight. The globe twirled faster now. Then the bright white light winked off.

"A bluff!" Magnan gasped.

"That's risky, stranger," the grey-templed man said.

The globe was turning rapidly now, oscillating from side to side. The hole seemed to travel in a wavering loop, dipping lower, swinging up high, then down again.

"It has to move to the bottom soon," Magnan said. "Slow it down, so it doesn't shoot past."

"The slower it goes, the longer it takes to get to the bottom," someone said.

There was a crackle, and Retief stiffened. Magnan heard a sharp intake of breath. The globe slowed, and Retief shook his head, blinking.

The broad-shouldered man glanced at a meter.

"You took pretty near a full jolt, that time," he said.

The hole in the globe was tracing an oblique course now, swinging to the center, then below.

"A little longer," Magnan said.

"That's the best speed I ever seen on the Slam ball," someone said. "How much longer can he hold it?"

Magnan looked at Retief's knuckles. They showed white against the grip. The globe tilted farther, swung around, then down; two chips fell out, clattered down a chute and into a box.

"We're ahead," Magnan said. "Let's quit."

Retief shook his head. The globe rotated, dipped again; three chips fell.

"She's ready," someone called.

"It's bound to hit soon," another voice added

excitedly. "Come on, mister!"

"Slow down," Magnan said. "So it won't move past too quickly."

"Speed it up, before that lead block gets you," someone called.

The hole swung high, over the top, then down the side. Chips rained out, six, eight . . .

"Next pass," a voice called.

The white warning light flooded the cage. The globe whirled; the hole slid over the top, down down . . . a chip fell, two more . . .

Retief half rose, clamped his jaw, and crushed the grip. Sparks flew, and the globe slowed, chips spewing. It stopped and swung back. Weighted by the mass of chips at the bottom, it stopped again with the hole centered. Chips cascaded down the chute, filled the box and spilled on the floor. The crowd yelled.

Retief released the grip and withdrew his arm at the same instant that the lead block slammed down.

"Good lord," Magnan said. "I felt that through the floor."

Retief turned to the broad-shouldered man.

"This game's all right for beginners," he said. "But I'd like to take a really big gamble. Why don't we go to your office, Mr. Zorn?"

"Your proposition interests me," Zorn said, an hour later. "But there's some angles to this I haven't mentioned yet."

"You're a gambler, Zorn, not a suicide," Retief said. "Take what I've offered. Your dream of revolution was fancier, I agree, but it won't work."

"How do I know you birds aren't lying?" Zorn snarled. He stood up and strode up and down the room. "You walk in here and tell me I'll have a squadron of Corps Peace Enforcers on my neck, that the Corps won't recognize my regime. Maybe you're right; but I've got other contacts. They say different." Whirling, he stared at Retief.

"I have pretty good assurance that once I put it over, the Corps will have to recognize me as the legal de facto government of Petreac. They won't meddle in internal affairs."

"Nonsense," Magnan spoke up, "the Corps will never deal with a pack of criminals calling themselves—"

"Watch your language, you!" Zorn rasped.

"I'll admit Mr. Magnan's point is a little weak," Retief said. "But you're overlooking something. You plan to murder a dozen or so officers of the Corps Diplomatique Terrestrienne along with the local wheels. The Corps won't overlook that. It can't."

"Their tough luck they're in the middle," Zorn muttered.

"Our offer is extremely generous, Mr. Zorn," Magnan said. "The post you'll get will pay you very well indeed; as against certain failure of your coup, the choice should be simple."

Zorn eyed Magnan. "I thought you diplomats weren't the type to go around making deals under the table. Offering me a job—it sounds phony as hell."

"It's time you knew," Retief said. "There's no phonier business in the galaxy than diplomacy."

"You'd better take it, Mr. Zorn," Magnan said.

"Don't push me," Zorn said. "You two walk into

my headquarters empty-handed and big-mouthed. I don't know what I'm talking to you for. The answer is no. N-i-x, no!"

"Who are you afraid of?" Retief said softly.

Zorn glared at him.

"Where do you get that 'afraid' routine? I'm top man here. What have I got to be afraid of?"

"Don't kid around, Zorn. Somebody's got you under his thumb. I can see you squirming from here."

"What if I let your boys alone?" Zorn said suddenly. "The Corps won't have anything to say then, huh?"

"The Corps has plans for Petreac, Zorn. You aren't part of them. A revolution right now isn't part of them. Having the Potentate and the whole Nenni caste slaughtered isn't part of them. Do I make myself clear?"

"Listen," Zorn said urgently, "I'll tell you guys a few things. You ever heard of a world they call Rotune?"

"Certainly," Magnan said. "It's a near neighbor of yours, another backward—that is emergent."

"Okay," Zorn said. "You guys think I'm a piker, do you? Well, let me wise you up. The Federal Junta on Rotune is backing my play. I'll be recognized by Rotune, and the Rotune fleet will stand by in case I need any help. I'll present the CDT with what you call a *fait accompli*."

"What does Rotune get out of this? I thought they were your traditional enemies."

"Don't get me wrong. I've got no use for Rotune; but our interests happen to coincide right now."

"Do they?" Retief smiled grimly. "You can spot a sucker as soon as he comes through that door out there—but you go for a deal like this."

"What do you mean?" Zorn looked angrily at Retief. "It's fool-proof."

"After you get in power, you'll be fast friends with Rotune, is that it?"

"Friends, hell. Just give me time to get set, and I'll square a few things with that—"

"Exactly. And what do you suppose they have in mind for you?"

"What are you getting at?"

"Why is Rotune interested in your take-over?"

Zorn studied Retief's face. "I'll tell you why," he said. "It's you birds; you and your trade agreement. You're here to tie Petreac into some kind of trade combine. That cuts Rotune out. They don't like that. And anyway, we're doing all right out here; we don't need any commitments to a lot of fancypants on the other side of the galaxy."

"That's what Rotune has sold you, eh?" Retief said, smiling.

"Sold, nothing—" Zorn ground out his dope stick, then lit another. He snorted angrily.

"Okay—what's your idea?"

"You know what Petreac is getting in the way of imports as a result of the trade agreement?"

"Sure, a lot of junk. Clothes washer, tape projectors, all that kind of stuff."

"To be specific," Retief said, "there'll be 50,000 Tatone B-3 dry washers; 100,000 Glo-float motile lamps; 100,000 Earthworm Minor garden cultivators; 25,000 Veco space heaters; and 75,000 replacement elements for Ford Monomeg drives."

"Like I said: a lot of junk," Zorn said.

Retief leaned back, looking sardonically at Zorn. "Here's the gimmick, Zorn," he said. "The

Corps is getting a little tired of Petreac and Rotune carrying on their two-penny war out here. Your privateers have a nasty habit of picking on innocent bystanders. After studying both sides, the Corps has decided Petreac would be a little easier to do business with; so this trade agreement was worked out. The Corps can't openly sponsor an arms shipment to a belligerent; but personal appliances are another story."

"So what do we do—plow 'em under with back-yard cultivators?" Zorn looked at Retief, puzzled. "What's the point?"

"You take the sealed monitor unit from the washer, the repeller field generator from the lamp, the converter control from the cultivator, et cetera, et cetera. You fit these together according to some very simple instructions; presto! you have one hundred thousand Standard-class Y hand blasters; just the thing to turn the tide in a stalemated war fought with obsolete arms."

"Good Lord," Magnan said. "Retief, are you—"

"I have to tell him. He has to know what he's putting his neck into."

"Weapons, hey?" Zorn said. "And Rotune knows about it . . . ?"

"Sure they know about it; it's not too hard to figure out. And there's more. They want the CDT delegation included in the massacre for a reason; it will put Petreac out of the picture; the trade agreement will go to Rotune; and you and your new regime will find yourselves looking down the muzzles of your own blasters."

Zorn threw his dope-stick to the floor with a snarl.

"I should have smelled something when that

Rotune agent made his pitch." Zorn looked at the clock on the wall.

"I've got two hundred armed men in the palace. We've got about forty minutes to get over there before the rocket goes up."

In the shadows of the palace terrace, Zorn turned to Retief. "You'd better stay here out of the way until I've spread the word. Just in case."

"Let me caution you against any . . . ah . . . slip-ups, Mr. Zorn," Magnan said. "The Nenni are not to be molested."

Zorn looked at Retief. "Your friend talks too much. I'll keep my end of it; he'd better keep his."

"Nothing's happened yet, you're sure?" Magnan said.

"I'm sure," Zorn said. "Ten minutes to go; plenty of time."

"I'll just step into the salon to assure myself that all is well," Magnan said.

"Suit yourself. Just stay clear of the kitchen, or you'll get your throat cut." Zorn sniffed at his dope-stick. "I sent the word for Shoke," he muttered. "Wonder what's keeping him?"

Magnan stepped to a tall glass door, eased it open, and poked his head through the heavy draperies. As he moved to draw back, a voice was faintly audible. Magnan paused, his head still through the drapes.

"What's going on there?" Zorn rasped. He and Retief stepped up behind Magnan.

". . . breath of air," Magnan was saying.

"Well, come along, Magnan!" Ambassador Crodfoller's voice snapped.

Magnan shifted from one foot to the other, then

pushed through the drapes.

"Where've you been, Mr. Magnan?" The ambassador's voice was sharp.

"Oh . . . ah . . . a slight accident, Mr. Ambassador."

"What's happened to your shoes? Where are your insignia and decorations?"

"I—ah—spilled a drink on them. Maybe I'd better nip up to my room and slip into some fresh medals."

The ambassador snorted. "A professional diplomat never shows his liquor, Magnan. It's one of his primary professional skills. I'll speak to you about this later. I had expected your attendance at the signing ceremony, but under the circumstances I'll dispense with that. You'd better depart quietly through the kitchen."

"The kitchen? But it's crowded . . . I mean . . ."

"A little loss of caste won't hurt at this point, Mr. Magnan. Now kindly move along before you attract attention. The agreement isn't signed yet."

"The agreement . . ." Magnan babbled, sparring for time, "very clever, Mr. Ambassador. A very neat solution,"

The sound of an orchestra came up suddenly, blaring a fanfare.

Zorn shifted restlessly, his ear against the glass. "What's your friend pulling?" he rasped. "I don't like this."

"Keep cool, Zorn. Mr. Magnan is doing a little emergency salvage on his career."

The music died away with a clatter.

". . . my God." Ambassador Crodfoller's voice was faint. "Magnan, you'll be knighted for this. Thank God you reached me. Thank God it's not too late. I'll find some excuse. I'll get off a gram at once."

"But you—"

"It's all right, Magnan. You were in time. Another ten minutes and the agreement would have been signed and transmitted. The wheels would have been put in motion. My career would have been ruined. . . ."

Retief felt a prod at his back. He turned.

"Double-crossed," Zorn said softly. "So much for the word of a diplomat."

Retief looked at the short-barreled needler in Zorn's hand.

"I see you hedge your bets, Zorn."

"We'll wait here until the excitement's over inside. I wouldn't want to attract any attention right now."

"Your politics are still lousy, Zorn. The picture hasn't changed. Your coup hasn't got a chance."

"Skip it. I'll take up one problem at a time."

"Magnan's mouth has a habit of falling open at the wrong time."

"That's my good luck I heard it. So there'll be no agreement, no guns, no fat job for Tammany Zorn, hey? Well, I can still play it the other way. What have I got to lose?"

With a movement too quick to follow, Retief's hand chopped down across Zorn's wrist. The needler clattered to the ground as Retief's hand clamped on Zorn's arm, whirling him around.

"In answer to your last question," Retief said, "your neck."

"You haven't got a chance, double-crosser," Zorn gasped.

"Shoke will be here in a minute. Tell him it's all off."

"Twist harder, mister. Break it off at the shoulder. I'm telling him nothing."

"The kidding's over, Zorn. Call it off or I'll kill you."

"I believe you. But you won't have long to remember it."

"All the killing will be for nothing. You'll be dead and the Rotunes will step into the power vaccum."

"So what? When I die, the world ends."

"Suppose I make you another offer, Zorn?"

"Why would it be any better than the last one?"

Retief released Zorn's arm, pushed him away, stooped and picked up the needler.

"I could kill you, Zorn; you know that."

"Go ahead."

Retief reversed the needler and held it out.

"I'm a gambler too, Zorn. I'm gambling you'll listen to what I have to say."

Zorn snatched the gun and stepped back. He looked at Retief. "That wasn't the smartest bet you ever made, but go ahead. You've got maybe ten seconds."

"Nobody double-crossed you, Zorn. Magnan put his foot in it; too bad. Is that a reason to kill yourself and a lot of other people who've bet their lives on you?"

"They gambled and lost. Tough."

"Maybe they haven't lost yet—if you don't quit."

"Get to the point."

Retief spoke earnestly for a minute and a half. Zorn stood, gun aimed, listening. Then both men

turned as footsteps approached along the terrace.
A fat man in a yellow sarong padded up to Zorn.

Zorn tucked the needler in his waistband.

"Hold everything, Shoke," he said. "Tell the
boys to put the knives away; spread the word fast:
it's all off."

"I want to commend you, Retief," Ambassador
Crodfoller said expansively. "You mixed very
well at last night's affair; actually, I was hardly
aware of your presence."

"I've been studying Mr. Magnan's work," Retief
said.

"A good man, Magnan. In a crowd, he's virtu-
ally invisible."

"He knows when to disappear, all right."

"This has been in many ways a model operation, Retief." The ambassador patted his paunch
contentedly. "By observing local social customs
and blending harmoniously with the court, I've
succeeded in establishing a fine, friendly, working relationship with the Potentate."

"I understand the agreement has been post-
poned a few days."

The Ambassador chuckled. "The Potentate's a
crafty one. Through . . . ah . . . a special study I
have been conducting, I learned last night that he
had hoped to, shall I say, 'put one over' on the
Corps."

"Great Heavens," Retief said.

"Naturally, this placed me in a difficult position. It was my task to quash this gambit, without
giving any indication that I was aware of its existence."

"A hairy position indeed."

"Quite casually, I informed the Potentate that certain items which had been included in the terms of the agreement had been deleted and others substituted. I admired him at that moment, Retief. He took it coolly—appearing completely indifferent—perfectly dissembling his very serious disappointment. Of course, he could hardly do otherwise without in effect admitting his plot."

"I noticed him dancing with three girls each wearing a bunch of grapes; he's very agile for a man of his bulk."

"You mustn't discount the Potentate. Remember, beneath that mask of frivolity, he had absorbed a bitter blow."

"He had me fooled." Retief said.

"Don't feel badly; I confess at first I, too, failed to sense his shrewdness." The ambassador nodded and moved off along the corridor.

Retief turned and went into an office. Magnan looked up from his desk.

"Ah, Retief," he said. "I've been meaning to ask you. About the . . . ah . . . blasters; are you—"

Retief leaned on Magnan's desk and looked at him. "I thought that was to be our little secret."

"Well, naturally I—" Magnan closed his mouth and swallowed. "How is it, Retief," he said sharply, "that you were aware of this blaster business, when the ambassador himself wasn't?"

"Easy," Retief said. "I made it up."

"You what!" Magnan looked wild. "But the agreement—it's been revised. Ambassador Crodfoller has gone on record."

"Too bad. Glad I didn't tell him about it."

Magnan leaned back and closed his eyes.

"It was big of you to take all the . . . blame," Retief said, "when the ambassador was talking about knighting people."

Magnan opened his eyes. "What about that gambler, Zorn? Won't he be upset when he learns the agreement is off? After all, I . . . that is, we, or you, had more or less promised him—"

"It's all right. I made another arrangement. The business about making blasters out of common components wasn't completely imaginary. You can actually do it, using parts from an old-fashioned disposal unit."

"What good will that do him?" Magnan whispered, looking nervous. "We're not shipping in any old-fashioned disposal units."

"We don't need to. They're already installed in the palace kitchen—and in a few thousand other places, Zorn tells me."

"If this ever leaks . . ." Magnan put a hand to his forehead.

"I have his word on it that the Nenni slaughter is out. This place is ripe for a change; maybe Zorn is what it needs."

"But how can we know?" Magnan said. "How can we be sure?"

"We can't. But it's not up to the Corps to meddle in Petreac's internal affairs." He leaned over, picked up Magnan's desk lighter, and lit a cigar. He blew a cloud of smoke toward the ceiling.

"Right?" he said.

Magnan looked at him and nodded weakly. "Right."

"I'd better be getting along to my desk," Retief said. "Now that the ambassador feels that I'm settling down at last."

"Retief," Magnan said, "tonight, I implore you: stay out of the kitchen—no matter what."

Retief raised his eyebrows.

"I know," Magnan said. "If you hadn't interfered, we'd all have had our throats cut. But at least . . ." He paused—"we'd have died in accordance with regulations."

RETIEF'S RANSOM

"MONSTERS?" SAID FIRST Secretary Magnan of the Terrestrial delegation to the planetary Peace Conference at Lumbaga. "Where?" He gazed searchingly around the crowded bazaar, thronged with gaily garbed pedestrians. A nine-foot, orange-skinned local jostled past humming a tune through a nose set in the middle of his forehead; a three-legged native with pink and purple spots haggled vigorously with a stallkeeper distinguished by a red- and green-striped epidermis, seven eyes arranged in random fashion on a lumpy head further adorned with a handsome spread of mismatched antlers.

"I see no monsters," Magnan said stuffily. "Only ordinary Lumbagans. I fear you've been listening to rumors, my dear colonel."

"I'm not talking about these fellows," the military attaché muttered, "I'm referring to the recurring reports of meat-eating magicians, carnivorous cadavers, and ferocious freaks swarming from the swamps."

"Nonsense." Magnan dismissed the thought, pausing to admire a merchant's display of chest wigs, plastic trideos tuned loudly to competing channels, prosthetic tentacles (the all-purpose appendage, suitable for sports or formal wear), native mudwork, and murky carboys of mummified glimp eggs for the luxury trade. "I concede that only six years ago the locals were little better than Neolithic savages; but today, thanks to the enlightened policies of the *Corps diplomatique terrestrienne,* they're already well into their Medieval period."

"An acute observation," Second Secretary Retief acknowledged. "Too bad it's so hard to distinguish between Neolithic savagery and the Medieval variety."

"The problem," Colonel Warbutton said, "is that no two of these ruddy natives look alike! Everyone on the planet's a member of a minority of one—and none of the minorities can stand the sight of another!"

"Pish-tush, Colonel," Magnan chided. "I confess that what with the multiplicity of native racial strains the problem of prejudice does pose something of a riddle for our Togetherness Teams, but I'm sure we'll soon turn up a solution satisfactory to Sector HQ."

"I'm hardly the chap to spook easily," Colonel Warbutton persisted. "A few riots in front of the embassy are nothing to get excited about, and the mud-and-ragweeding of the odd diplomat is par for the course. But when they run ads in the daily paper offering bounties for alien heads in good condition, it's time to start barricading the chancery."

"Mere campaign rhetoric," Magnan dismissed the objection. "After all, when a people as diverse as the Lumbagans—with their hallowed traditions of mutual genocide—set out to choose a ruler acceptable to all, there's bound to be a modicum of unrest among dissident elements."

"Especially when the dissident elements outnumber the population," Retief agreed. "I have a feeling that Ambassador Pouncetrifle's decision to

sponsor a planetary government was a trifle over-
zealous."

"A gross understatement," Colonel Warbutton
grunted. "Inasmuch as no two Lumbagans can
agree on so much as the correct time, I suspect
they'll have some difficulty in agreeing on who's
going to tell them what to do."

"Your remarks reflect scant confidence in the
process of democracy, as implemented by Corps
peace enforcers," Magnan said rather sharply.
"You'd do well to recall that firepower outweighs
flowerpower, and a vote in the hand is worth two
in the offing."

"But what more can we do?" the colonel inquired plaintively. "We've already fired our big
guns, pacificationwise: saturation leaflet bombing, nonstop armistice propoals, uni-, bi-, and
multilateral   cease-fires,   interlocking   de-
militarized zones—the works. And they go right
on headhunting—to say nothing of leg-, arm-, and
haunchhunting!" Warbutton's remark was interrupted by the impact of a clay pot against the wall
three feet from his head, accompanied by a sharp
rise in the decibel output of the crowd.

"Maybe we'd better start back," Retief said,
"unless we want to get a closer view of the Saturday riot than usual."

"Ridiculous, Retief," the first secretary said a
trifle uneasily. "Merely a display of high spirits.
My analysis of the trends, local unrestwise, indicates today will be utterly peaceful."

Retief glanced across the cobbles toward the
low, irregular buildings at the far side of the plaza,
between which greenish sunlight glinted on a
stretch of open sea dotted with sails, and gleamed

chartreuse and orange on the adjacent island of the equatorial archipelago which constituted the sole land masses of the world.

"You may be right," he said, "but there seem to be a remarkable number of spears, spikes, pitchforks, swords, and carving knives in evidence."

"Purely decorative, Retief. In spite of splendid progress toward civilization, the locals seem to feel more comfy with a symbolic weapon in hand."

"No doubt—but there's a note in the crowd noises that reminds me of a beehive just after it's been poked with a stick."

"They're merely taking a childlike pleasure in their bargaining, Retief. Heavens, I've heard shriller haggling in Macy's." Magnan glanced up severely at his junior. "It's hardly like you to display such timidity, Retief. I suggest you buck up now; I don't intend to return until I've secured the beaded tea cozy I promised Aunt Ninny—"

"Duck!" Retief snapped, and swept Magnan aside as a broad-headed assegai clanged against the rough-hewn stone wall behind them. He caught it on the rebound, grabbed Magnan's arm and thrust him into a doorway as, with a mass screech, the mob surging through the narrow way erupted into violence. Robed locals of wildly varied skin coloration and wart distribution brandished suddenly produced weapons in hands numbering from one to six, and charged each other with bloodcurdling yells. Glass shattered nearby; smoke boiled from an overturned toasted-nidnut cart. A tall, blue-faced Lumbagan with four staring eyes, three pendulous ears, and a mouth capable of encompassing a tripleburger in

one gulp rushed toward the Terrans, swinging up
a five-foot steelwood cutlass edged with broken
glass. Retief dropped the spearpoint to chest level
and grounded the butt against the plank door
behind him. The alien braked, too late; the
spearhead took him square in the midriff. Magnan
made a squeaking noise as the victim dropped his
sword and grasped the shaft of the spear with
three of four hands, and with a powerful surge,
withdrew it.

"Hey, you loused up a perfectly good
duodenum that time or I miss my guess, Terry,"
the warty local said in a rather barbaric dialect of
the local tongue, fingering the bloodless entry.
"What's the idea? The word was, you Terries don't
fight back."

"Sorry, fellow," Retief said, "Sometimes the
word gets distorted in transmission. How about
passing the new version along to your compat-
riots; it may save wear and tear all around."

"Yeah, I'll do that." The alien turned and was
swept away by the crowd.

"I can't think what went wrong with my
analysis," Magnan wailed as a brass-tipped arrow
chipped the lintel above him. "I must have mis-
judged the intensity of the xenophobic
coefficient—or possibly read the seasonal hostility index from the wrong column!"

"Get the door open!" Warbutton yelled behind
Retief as he parried a thrust by a passerby pausing
to take a slash at the target of opportunity.

"But that would be illegal entry!"

"Getting killed in public without a death permit is a felony punishable by decapitation plus a
year in the local Bastille, according to the local

penal code," Retief pointed out. "Take your choice."

There were rattling sounds behind Retief, followed by the creak of rusty hinges. At that moment, a large Lumbagan burst from the crowd, whipped a rusty but effective-looking power gun from under his doublet, took aim at Retief's head—

A small local sprang at the gunner, entangling the latter's legs in several of his own, and with a hearty shove sent him sprawling while the shot burned harmlessly across the pavement. With a yell of fury, the fallen assassin leaped up. Retief felt the draft on his back from the open door behind him.

"This way," he called in the local patois; the diminutive Lumbagan dived past him through the opening; Retief jumped through behind him, slammed the heavy panel. Missiles clattered against it as he shot the massive bolt. Angry fists hammered, angry voices screeched threats. Magnan uttered a yelp as he noted the presence of the alien.

"Help! One of them got in!"

"He's with us," Retief said. "Thanks for the assist, Mr. . . . ?"

"Ignarp's the handle. Glad to oblige, Terry. Some of the boys got no use for Terries, but what do those slobs know? A bunch of Blue-spots and Four-eyes and Shaggy-feet and War-heads—"

"Corps policy frowns on the use of racial epithets, Mr. Ignarp," Magnan remonstrated. "Besides which," he added surveying the Lumbagan, "unless I'm very much mistaken you seem to have a number of warts of your own."

"Oh, yeah; I forgot. I just picked those up on sale last week."

"It must be confusing," Magnan said sympathetically. "With so many minorities to choose from, I suppose one hardly knows whom to discriminate against."

"Yeah—you Terries have got the best system; just check a couple minor details like how many eyes or what color spots a guy's got, and you know who your friends are. A lot easier than trying to pick 'em one at a time."

"What made you pick us?" Retief asked.

"I got a soft spot in my head for foreigners," the local said. "Come on, I'll show you the way out of here." He waved them toward the dark, stone-floored passage leading back into the gloomy recesses of the monolithic structure.

"Well, how lucky you happened along, Mr. Ignarp," Colonel Warbutton said, falling in behind their guide. "By the way, where are we going?"

"You Terries are housed right in the Castle complex, along with the other foreigners, right? You're practically there now."

"Heavens, I hope we're not late for the Joint Staff meeting." Magnan said, glancing at his thumb watch. "Who'd have thought when we set out for a short constitutional we'd end threading a maze with a pack of rabid racists at our figurative heels?"

"Think of the impact on the ambassador when you give your eye-witness report," Retief encouraged his superior.

"That's a thought," Magnan agreed. "Ah—just what was it I eye-witnessed?"

"The initiation of the Spring Hostility Rites,"

the local called over his shoulder. "The boys certainly started things off with a bang."

"The spring rites?" Warbutton queried. "I was under the impression the Winter Mayhem Festival was still on."

"So it is; along with the Ritual of Revolution, the Symbolic Sacrament of Savagery, and o' course the Perennial Violence Cycle. With a crowded schedule, we get a certain amount of overlap."

"Why—the situation is deteriorating into total anarchy!" Magnan gasped.

"Not so, Terry," their guide demurred. "We got rules. Like we always give warning before we change sides."

"What sort of warning?" Magnan queried.

"Well, a kick in the right spot usually gets the message across," the Lumbagan confided. "But we're not particular. A sharp blow on the head will do in a pinch."

"Or. a spear between the ankles?" Retief suggested.

"I hope Gumrong sees it that way. He's not a bad fellow; in fact he was my sidekick and loyal comrade-in-arms. But he holds a slot as my mortal hereditary enemy for the rites—so naturally when he jumped you Terries, I stepped in. Lucky you got that door open, or my component parts would be strewn all over the jungle by now, rooting for acorns."

"Which side are *they* on?" Warbutton inquired dazedly.

"Luckily, Lumbagan vegetable life is neutral," Retief said. "Otherwise the prospects for planetary pacification would be even dimmer than they are."

"They couldn't be," Magnan groaned. "How in the world are we going to bring racial tolerance to a world whose only recreation is mutual mass murder?"

"If you come up with the answer to that one, Mr. Magnan, I predict a sharp upward turn in your career prospects."

"Watch your step, gents," the Lumbagan said, indicating a narrow stone stair leading down into pitch darkness. "Just a little farther and there we are."

As Magnan hesitated, Retief stepped past him.

"You must be a little confused, Ignarp," he said. "Mr. Magnan doesn't have time right now to explore any abandoned mine shafts."

"Who's leading this parade, you or me, Terry?" the Lumbagan said truculently. "I'm the guy that just saved your necks, remember?"

"Just between us," Retief said, "Why did you decoy us here?"

Magnan gasped.

"Wh—where'd you get an idea like that?" The Lumbagan edged sideways, but was restrained by Retief's quick grab.

"Hey—leggo my neck," he yelped. "I already told you—"

"Uh-huh. But I happen to know spring rites don't start for another two days. Somebody went to a lot of trouble to set up the whole charade, including the conveniently unlocked door. Why, Ignarp?"

"No fair, Retief," the local grunted. "I heard you Terries didn't know a mob killing from a quiet little domestic knifing—"

"Some of these impressions die hard." Retief

gave the local's collar another half-twist. "Come on, give, Ignarp."

"Retief," Magnan demurred, "are you sure? After all, if anyone had wanted to do us an injury they could have done it as well in the street. . . ."

"Wrong," the Lumbagan contradicted. "This was a hush-hush deal. And besides, the orders were to bring you in whole."

"You admit your duplicity?" Warbutton barked.

"With your chum's knuckles digging into my medulla oblongata, I got no choice," Ignarp said aggrievedly.

"Whose orders?"

"The ones that hired me," Ignarp muttered. "They wanted a Terry in good condition, that's all I can tell you. I'm just a legman—"

"Hold it," Retief said. From the dark stairwell came faint sounds as of stealthy feet approaching.

"We'll have to defer our talk until later, Ignarp," Retief said. "Lead the way out of here—and this time get it right."

"I might as well; if the boys see me with your thumb under my ear, my rep as a slick conniver is shot anyway. Come on. . . ." He led the Terrans back along the passage, took a branching corridor—hardly more than a damp-walled tunnel cut through the massive masonry pile—and in five minutes halted at the foot of a narrow stone stair leading upward.

"It comes out in the embassy commissary," he said glumly. "Just don't let on I told you about the gap in your security. There's a couple dozen families living high on imported caviar and pâté who'd hate to go back to pulverized nidnuts and dehydrated frinkfruit."

"Stealing from embassy stores?" Magnan gasped.

"Relax," the local advised. "It's costing you a lot less than if we applied for disaster-area status and welfare handouts. As we see it a self-respecting life-form ought to make its own way."

"What shall we do with the beggar?" Warbutton said. "No good turning him over to the local constabulary. Pity we can't do him in out of hand, but that sort of thing doesn't look at all good when the yellow press gets hold of it."

"Lemme go now, pal," Ignarp said. "I admit it was a lousy idea. And to clinch the deal, I'll throw in a tip for free: Look out when Summer Slaughter time comes rolling around. I'm assigned to a Terry-Go-Home team, and those babies play rough."

"Come along, Retief," Magnan said, starting up the stairs. "There's no point in escaping death at the hands of a mob only to face an irate Chief of Mission."

Retief released his grip on the Lumbagan. "We'll call it even for now, Ignarp. Go back and tell your employers that we Terries like a chance to RSVP our invitations."

"You foreigners are full of surprises," the local muttered, and darted away.

"Here, Retief," Warbutton remonstrated, "we should have held the blighter up by the heels until he'd divulged all the details of the conspiracy."

"I have a feeling he'll talk more freely on his home ground," Retief said, and glanced at the finger-marked card he had lifted from the Lumbagan's coat pocket. "The Stake and Kidney Tavern, number twelve Dacoit Street," he read.

"I know the spot," Warbutton said. "An unsavory dive across from the scalpfields where the hair is short."

"It's a date," Retief said.

2

MAGNAN AND RETIEF were among the last to take seats at the long table in the conference room, netting a baleful glance from the protuberant eye of Ambassador Pouncetrifle, seated at the head of the table beside Jith, his diminutive Groacian opposite number and Joint Chairman of the Lumbagan Peace Commission.

"Now, if we're quite ready," his Excellency began in an ominous tone, "I—"

"A moment, if you please, Harvey," Jith spoke up in his breathy whisper. "It happens to be my turn to chair the meeting, so if you don't mind—"

"What's this, one of your little jokes?" Pouncetrifle barked. "Most amusing, Mr. Ambassador. Now, as I was saying—"

"Just hand me the gavel, there's a good chap, and we'll get on with the meeting." Jith plucked the microphone from before the Terran dignitary. "Fellow beings—" he started.

"Look here, Jith," the Terran said sharply, "you know perfectly well you took precedence in the elevator this morning—and at breakfast, I distinctly noted the bearer handing you your menu before so much as whisking the crumbs off my chair—"

"Doesn't count," Jith cut in tersely, and keyed the microphone. "This afternoon, I should like to review our progress in bringing racial equality to Lumbaga." His amplified voice crackled through the room.

"—to say nothing of your subtle maneuver in bribing the chief of the motor pool to repaint your parking space upwind of mine!" Pouncetrifle's remonstrance rose above the PA system.

"And in bringing the blessings of noncombatant status to the unhappy natives of this benighted world," Jith continued, "no offense to our native guests intended, of course." The Groaci inclined three of his five eyestalks in a perfunctory salute to the latter—a pair of observers squatting silently on a bench by the far wall, both bulky, multilimbed, and heavily swathed in beaded robes. They returned the gesture with stony expressions.

"Now, the past six years during which the Interplanetary Peace Tribunal has exercised its good offices in the search for an avenue of racial rapprochement have not been unmarked by progress," Pouncetrifle stated, leaning across to address the microphone. "To date, we've completed forty-two VIP villas for Class One personnel and above, a hundred-table billiardium, and a forty-bed fun house—"

"Frivolities aside," Jith breathed, recommandeering the mike, "I direct your attention to the recent consecration of a hundred-stall cybernetic confessional, featuring coin-operated holy sand dispensers, a scourgomat capable of processing one gross of penitents per hour, and a most ingenious mechanized collection plate, employing 1000-Gauss magnets—"

"On the substantive side," Pouncetrifle's voice boomed out amid a vicious feedback howl as he ripped the mike from his rival's grasp, "pacification efforts proceed apace. In reply to certain critics I can report that close statistical analyses by departmental teams skilled in the detection of obscure phenomena report that the percentage of casualties among unemployed frume-leaf gatherers between the ages of eighteen and forty-nine during the daylight hours in alternate months are down a big, big .0046 percent over a similar period last year."

Jith ducked under Pouncetrifle's arm to clutch the microphone.

"While it's quite true that the basis of the racial conflicts here on Lumbaga have not yet been isolated," he stated breathily, "nor have the precise ideological battle lines been delimited, nor the values involved definitely identified, some progress has been made in the study of native beadwork, a circumstance which lends substance to the hope that in the near future—say the next half-dozen years—we may meet with limited success in determining who is fighting whom—or should I say whom is fighting who—if not why."

"Come to the point," the assistant military attaché muttered. "What it boils down to is that with all these rival cliques, factions, races, mobs, unions, congregations, bands, platoons, crews, and clans constantly involved in squabbles, bickerings, pitched battles, bombings, disagreements, feuds, wrangles, wars, altercations, misunderstandings, ruptures, brawls, rows, sit-ins, shoot-ins, and assorted Donnybrooks, with the participants changing sides at irregular intervals according to no known scheme, our chances of unifying the planet under a single flag are on a par with the likelihood of my making Light Colonel by Voom Festival."

"Alas, I fear we're actually losing ground," the Groaci functionary seated beside him whispered in tones of deepest pessimism. "Not content with strewing each other's members in the public ways, the aborigines now widen the scope of their hostilities to include us selfless diplomats. Only yesterday I was savaged by a seeing-eye leg—"

"Heavens, what about me?" Magnan cut in. "Only minutes ago I was forced to deal sharply with a chap intent on an audacious diplomat-napping."

"You didn't lend substance to any potential charges of Terran intellectual brutality, I trust, Magnan?" a sharp-eyed cultural attaché said.

"Naturally not," Warbutton spoke up. "I was present, luckily, and smoothed the incident over."

"Pah!" the Groaci whispered. "There are plots afoot here, I feel it in my cartilaginous members!"

"Poppycock," Warbutton snorted. "The natives may appear to detest our internal integuments, but down deep they like us."

"About six feet down, preferably," someone muttered.

"Now, before we can set about establishing one-world rule on Lumbaga," Pouncetrifle cut through the chatter, the smooth flow of his diction somewhat marred by the silent scuffle in which he was engaged for possession of the floor, "it's clear that until we devise some means of discriminating—pray pardon the expression—between the wildlife and the population, certain problems will inevitably crop up in categorization of life forms as to vermin, livestock, and constituents. I now call on Mr. Lunchbun, our xenoecologist, for a brief report on the complexities of Lumbagan biology." The ambassador favored his Grocian colleague with a frosty smile and subsided. From his place near the foot of the table, a sad-faced chap with thinning hair rose, rattled papers, and cleared his throat.

"As his Excellency so discerningly pointed out," he began in a nasal drone, "the ecological situation here on Lumbaga is hardly susceptible to analysis by conventional means. To begin with, we've so far identified over two hundred thousand distinct phyla of basic wild life running loose on the islands, a circumstance which has sent our ecological computer into catatonic withdrawal—"

"Yes, yes, Mr. Lunchbun," Jith prompted impatiently. "If you have nothing further to report—"

". . . we deduce from paleontological evidence," Lunchbun bored on, "that life has spontaneously arisen from the primordial Lumbagan mud on at least a hundred thousand separate occasions—"

"Fascinating, no doubt," Jith said sibilantly. "Now to other matters, such as provisions for a rest and recreational camp for Groaci ladies and their lovable grubs—"

"While all of the surviving life forms are mutually infertile," Lunchbun droned on, "—in fact, reproduction in the conventional sense is not practiced by Lumbagan life—it seems that symbiotic relationships provide the necessary proliferation of ecological niche-holders necessary for the full exploitation of the environment—"

"Yes, yes, quite so," Jith piped faintly. "Now as for my proposal for a gift to the Lumbagan masses of a Bolshoi-type ballet theatre—"

"Now, as for the VH—vital hierarchy, a term referring to the ascending order of complexity of competing and cooperating species—it appears we're faced here with a regular gradation from the mindless free-living gall bladder and/or medulla oblongata through the *pneumopteryx,* or flying lung, the night-blooming liver, or *Hepaticus noctens*—"

"Kindly speak either Terran or Groaci," a representative of the latter species whispered irritably, "as a courtesy to those of us who are not specialists in arcane linguistic lore."

"—to the subcultural forms such as the Gliding Leg, *Pedis volens,* and the Bounding Rib Cage, *Os leapifrons*—"

"Splendid," Pouncetrifle said heartily, "I'm sure we all enjoyed Mr. Lunchbun's most lucid rundown on the subject on which he has just presented his briefing. Now, the next item on the agenda—"

"To continue," Lunchbun cut through the rising conversation level, "I've recently achieved a breakthrough, classificationwise." He turned to pull down a wall chart. "The basic building blocks of Lumbagan life, which I've designated here with Chinese ideographs for convenience, are capable of a large but finite number of cross-

combinations, indicated by Egyptian hiero-
glyphics, which compounded forms in turn are
capable of further linkages to create still more
complex entities, shown on the accompanying
schematic by Greek letters, Norse runes, and the
letters A thru Q inclusive. The chart represents
schematically the theoretical relationships of
biological subgroups and groups within the
hyper- or super-groups, in light of the presumed
intergroup taboo structure, the affinity-schemes
implicit in observed pro- and counter-indications
social-mobilitywise, and the mutual interdepen-
dency pattern as deduced from a careful sifting of
rumors from the interior. Naturally, it's only ap-
proximate."

"Yes, yes, we all know the woods are full of
tongues, elbows and less mentionable members,"
Pouncetrifle prompted the speaker. "Get to the
point, man!"

"Well, I'm skipping over the most fascinating
part—but as it happens, Mr. Ambassador, I have a
few slides for you this afternoon," Lunchbun said
hastily. "Freddy . . . ?" He signaled to a local
employee hidden in the wings; the lights dimmed
and a pair of vivid trideo images flickered into
existence above the ornamental fungus cen-
terpiece adorning the long board. One of the beings represented was a seven-foot creature with
an oversized head crowded with sensory appendages in no particular arrangement, surmounting
a cluster of arms of varying lengths, which sprang
directly from a flattened pelvic girdle to which
were attached three long, skinny legs, each ending in a pair of multitoed feet, the whole encased
in a warty hide of a mottled purplish hue. The

other was some four feet in height, with a lumpy head adorned by antlers, fangs, tusks, eyestalks, and a bushy magenta crest matching a ruff springing from the base of a long, limber neck. The remainder of the creature consisted largely of a penduluous, leathery paunch of a peculiarly objectionable yellowish shade, featuring stubby wings, tentacles, pincers, and a clump of noodlelike appendages presumably designed for locomotion.

"Here we have lab mock-ups of a pair of hypothetical composites, embodying what appear to be the most popular elements of what I term the ABCD and WXYZ forms," Lunchbun stated in a proprietary tone.

"On the whole," Colonel Warbutton commented, "I think the chap on the left has the more wholesome look about him. True, he's gone a bit overboard frequency-of-occurrencewise, but those are recognizable arms, legs, and the like—"

"I assume the simulacrum on the right represents the higher form," Ambassador Jith spoke up, "inasmuch as it has tastefully selected handsome stalked oculars, efficient grasping chelae, and a most soothing pigmentation, reminiscent of my own."

"Hold it right there," a reedy voice interrupted the proceedings. One of the local observers was on his feet—six in number—waving several arms. "I object! You foreigners are profaning the arcane mysteries by exhibiting undraped bodies without throwing in some redeeming entertainment value. What do those fellows do? Dance? Sing? Nonstop pray? Juggle zingfruit? No! They just stand there!"

"Why, how remarkable," Magnan whispered to Retief. "I didn't know the observers spoke Terran. Heavens, I wonder if we've uttered any indiscretions, racial-prejudicewise. . . ."

"They're full of surprises," Retief agreed. "Not the least of which is the fact that they've stayed awake through Lunchbun's lecture."

"Curious," Magnan mused. "I would have sworn that yesterday the one with the six feet had three eyes and a half a dozen snoof-organs; today he's down to two of the latter and only one of the former."

"Now, now, ah, sir or madam," Pouncetrifle was soothing the aroused local, "I'm sure no offense to your local mores was intended. I'll see that it doesn't happen again—"

"Don't do that, sport," the Lumbagan said in a more expansive tone, producing a tambourine from beneath his robes. "Just drop a little something in the old collection box, and on with the show."

"Why, yes, of course, I suppose a small contribution to a worthy charity would be quite in order," the ambassador agreed hastily.

"Small, nothing, sport! A couple thousand standard creds would be about right—and don't try to tell me how to spend it. I'm not in business for my health. And while I've got the floor, maybe I can interest some of you gents, Terry and Five-Eyes alike, in a snappy line of musical spud peelers for which I happen to be sole agent in this end of the archipelago—"

"What's this? Mercantile endeavor in the midst of solemn diplomatic proceedings?" Ambassador Jith whispered. "And a competing line, at that!"

"Look here—you can't conduct yourself as a peddler," Pouncetrifle said sternly.

"Why not? Anything shameful about honest merchandising, sport?"

"You were accredited here as an official observer, not a purveyor of novelty items!"

"Nix, sport. That was another fellow entirely—or almost entirely; I picked up a nice used clavicle from him on the way out."

"Where did he go?"

"He had to get back home and see to his liver and lights, you know how it is."

"He was in need of surgery?" Pouncetrifle gasped.

"Are you kidding? The guy runs a small giblet ranch two islands over."

"Then—what are you doing here?"

"I came in to get out of the cold wind. Why?"

"What about your, ah, the other one?" Pouncetrifle demanded, indicating the second local, who had not stirred during the exchange.

"Him? That's my sidekick, name of Difnog. I kind of look out for him, you know, since he lost his wits."

"In an accident?" the press attaché inquired with morbid interest, craning his neck for a better look at the victim.

"Nope, in a game of nine-handed *splung*. Difnog was a shrewd player, but he was outclassed; he only had seven hands at a time."

"Well, I'm sure that's all very interesting, Mr., er—"

"Gnudf. Yeah, but I got to be going. If you'll hand over the cash, I might still be able to make it down to the body shop before closing time."

"The effrontery of the fellow," Magnan sniffed as the ambassador and the budget-and-fiscal officer went into a huddle. "It's a well-established principle that the CDT only gives handouts to *bona fide* enemies."

"Maybe he's hoping to qualify," Retief suggested.

"It's a status much sought after, of course," Magnan conceded. "But a seasoned diplomat like Pouncetrifle will require proof of authentic hostility, not mere aspiration to the role."

"Maybe Gnudf can establish that he was part of the gang that broke all the windows out the Information Service Library yesterday."

"Nonsense, Retief, that was merely an expression of youthful impatience with established social forms."

"What about the mob that invaded the chancery at gunpoint last week and threw the classified files out the window along with the code clerk?"

"A student prank, nothing more."

"And I suppose the fellows who slipped the stink bombs into the ambassador's kitchen during the banquet were actually only expressing legitimate minority aspirations."

"Doubtless—although the matter nearly got out of hand. The ambassador didn't wish to offend the cook by complaining of what he assumed was the aroma of native cookery, and the guests were equally hesitant to appear critical of the ambassadorial cuisine. We might have all stifled in silence if Ambassador Jith hadn't chosen to take it as a direct affront to the Groacian state."

"Golly, I wish I'd been there," the assistant military attaché commented. "Old Jith didn't care for the smell, eh?"

"On the contrary, it seems that the effluvium of burning hot-water bottles closely resembles that of sacred Groacian incense. Pouncetrifle had to promise to book a troop of Groaci ritual grimacers for the next culturefest before he could placate him."

"I see your point, Mr. Magnan," Retief conceded. "It's not easy to qualify for enemy status these days."

"Precisely. It's one of the hopeful signs I like to point out to those who complain that our culture is going downhill."

The B-and-F officer having departed with the two locals to work out a settlement, the ambassador gaveled the meeting back to order.

"Gentlemen," he said firmly, "my predecessors waged pacification on Lumbaga for six years with no visible result. The native passion for mutual mayhem rages unabated. The confounded locals appear to like to fight! Now, then, it's vital at this juncture in my career—vital, that is, to the success of our mission—that we produce a breakthrough, racial-tolerancewise, without further delay. Naturally, I have a vastly effective plan all ready for implementation, but still, I'd be willing to listen to suggestions from the floor. Now, who's first?"

"I propose saturation bombing of the entire planet," a Groaci attaché proposed in a crisp whisper, "followed by mop-up squads armed with flamethrowers, fragmentation grenades, and other pesticides."

"Why—how brutal!" Magnan blurted.

"But effective," the Groaci pointed out. "One cannot deny: No population—no popular unrest!"

"Heavens," Magnan confided to Retief, "it wouldn't do to say so for the record, but one must concede there is a certain directness about Groaci methods."

"Possibly someone can offer a less spectacular alternative," Pouncetrifle said grimly. "Perhaps one designed to preserve an electorate for the new world government to govern!"

"Ah—what about a contest, sir?" Magnan piped up. "Cash prizes for snappy integration jingles, say."

"I know," the assistant military attaché cried, "cash rewards for defectors, deserters, scabs, AWOLS and turncoats!"

"What about straight cash grants to all who'll come and stand in line for them?" the senior economic attaché proposed grumpily. "If they're standing in line they can't be out participating in raids."

"Splendid notion, Godfrey," Colonel Warbutton spoke up. "We can stall them along until we have the majority of the able-bodied personnel queued up. Then—a lightning swoop, and we round up all the troublemakers at a stroke!"

"Don't we run the risk of accidentally scooping up a percentage of innocent noncombatants?" the press attaché said doubtfully.

"You can't break eggs without dropping a few on the floor, or however the old saying goes," Warbutton stated curtly. "In any event, since the majority of the population are activists, part-time guerillas, undercover commandos, and/or weekend warriors, the risk is statistically negligible."

"But—what do we do with them, once we've clapped them all in concentration camps?"

"Pension 'em off," Warbutton stated firmly.

"There appears, gentlemen," Pouncetrifle cut in coldly, "to be an emphasis on the materialistic in your proposals. While I recognize that massive handouts—monetary aid to the deserving, that is to say—have long been a staple of Terran policy, I feel in this instance an approach on a loftier level is in order."

"Oh-oh," the commercial attaché muttered. "That sounds like budget-cut to me."

"Gentlemen. . . ." The chief of the Terran delegation looked bleakly along the table. "Unless we achieve a discernible advance toward planetary unification within the next thirty days, I suspect a number of promising diplomatic careers will be nipped in the bud."

"Frankly, Mr. Ambassador," Magnan spoke up, "unless the local anti-Terran prejudices can be overcome in the near future, we may be nipped before we can be fired. Why, only today—"

"Anti-Terran prejudice? Nonsense, Magnan! Mere rumor! I've already pointed out how popular we Terrestrials are—"

With a loud crash, the window on the ambassadorial left burst inward, scattering a shower of glass chips over the table, while a paper-wrapped brick thudded to the floor. An eager vice-consul retrieved the latter.

"Why—it's a message," he exclaimed. "It says: A GOOD TERRY IS A DEAD TERRY!"

"You see?" Pouncetrifle said heartily. "Only a dear friend would feel free to perpetrate such a broad practical joke. And now"—he rose hastily—"we'll adjourn and make ready for tonight's reception."

"Good idea," Warbutton said sourly as the meeting broke up. "Before our unknown prankster decides to lob a grenade through and really bring down the house."

3

STANDING BEFORE THE mirror in his apartment in the Terran wing, Retief flicked a speck of dust from the chrome-plated lapel of his celery-top-green, midevening, hyperformal cutaway and checked the effect in the rippled surface.

"Wow, Mr. Retief, quel splendor," his valet commented with an envious sigh. "Jeeze, youse don't happen to have a old suit like this one you don't need any more, I guess?"

Retief surveyed the five-foot figure of the local youth, vaguely humanoid except for the unusual number and variety of eyes, ears, and snoof-organs adorning his cranium, plus the circumstance that his shoulders seemed to spring directly from his hips without the intervention of a torso.

"Not precisely, Fnud," the diplomat replied, opening the closet door. "But how about a

banana-yellow, demi-informal jumpsuit, appropriate for croquet, mah jong, and ouija board ses-
sions during the hours twelve noon to three pee
em inclusive?"

"Gangbusters, Mr. Retief," Fnud fondled the
gleaming garment. "I'll get my tailor to stitch the
sleeves right onto the waistband, and then watch
me shine at the neighborhood booze-and-knife
bust tonight!" He snapped two of the nine fingers
on his right hand. "Say—why don't you drop
around, Mr. Retief? Plenty of straight grain for-
maldehyde and bloodshed—all the markings for a
memorable night on the town. What do you say?"

"Sorry, Fnud. The joint ambassadors are stag-
ing the annual Victory Ball tonight, and I'll have
to be there to keep an eye on the silverware.
Maybe next week."

"It's a date." Fnud studied his employer's six-
foot three-inch physique, wagging his asymmetrical head admiringly. "You know, that's kind of a
neat arrangement you Terries use at that, Mr. Retief. A nifty idea, having just the two of everything, like eyes and ears and all. But how come
only one nose?"

"Just for contrast. You can overdo a good thing,
you know."

"Yeah. You know, a nose ain't a bad idea at that.
Maybe I'll invest in one when I get my next step
increase. What does a deluxe job like the ambassador's run?"

"I see you have an eye for a noble organ, Fnud.
I'd say the cost in brandy alone would be well up
into three figures.

"I guess it's outa my reach then. Oh, well—I'll
settle for a more modest shnozz and maybe install

a spare kidney. A fellow can't have too many kidneys, they say."

The valet seemed suddenly to recollect himself. "But Jeez, Mr. Retief, I don't guess you got time to waste talking about my development program. The shindig starts in a few minutes, and I'm due in the kitchen."

"You go ahead, Fnud. I'll make it on time."

When the door had closed behind the local, Retief opened the casement window and lifted a potted jelly-flower from the planting box on the sill, extracted from beneath it a flat 2mm needler which he tucked under his gold-satin cummerbund. As he turned away, something caught his eye, dangling just beyond the window. It was a heavy-gauge rope ladder, swaying slightly in the breeze. At that moment there was a soft sound from the direction of the hall door, as of stealthy fingers examining the latch. Retief turned swiftly to the open closet, lifted a formal black coverall from the rod and crossed the room to hang the garment from the curtain rail above the open window. He switched off the light and stepped silently behind the bathroom door as the outer door swung open soundlessly.

A small, spindle-legged Groaci in a drab-colored hip cloak and plain eye shields slipped into the room, pushed the door shut, and headed directly for the closet. He was halfway there when the wind stirred the empty suit hanging in the window. The intruder snatched a bulky power gun from his tunic and aimed it at the grament.

"So—to have mistakenly judged your chambers to be unoccupied, Soft One," the alien hissed in his native tongue. "To place your manual ex-

tremities above your organ cluster and to prepare
to go quietly!"

The hanging garment stirred. The Groaci
jumped backward. "One more move, Soft One,
and *jsssp!* to join your forebears in the Happy
Burrowing Ground!"

The suit seemed to edge sideways as the breeze
thrust at it.

"To make no move to escape!" the Groaci
keened. "To turn slowly and mount the ladder
thoughtfully provided by a trusted lackey. . . ."
The alien's faint voice faded out as he apparently
noted something amiss with the supposed target.
"Retief . . . ?" he whispered, advancing cautiously. A yard from the window, he uttered a hiss
of annoyance and lowered the gun.

"Not bad technique, Lilth," Retief said, emerging from concealment, the needler leveled at the
Groaci. "Except that your draw was a little on the
slow side—"

With a soft cry, the startled intruder whirled,
leaped to the window, thrust aside the hanging
coverall and lunged, checked himself too late. For
a moment, he teetered on the sill; then with a
despairing cry he toppled outward and dropped
from view. Retief arrived at the window in time to
observe the splashdown in the moat five stories
below, marked by an imposing column of stag-
nant water and fruit rinds fountaining upward.
The rope ladder, he noted, was gone.

"Too bad," he murmured. "It's getting so you
just can't trust a lackey anymore."

There was a stealthy rap at the door; Retief went
to it, swung it open. The visage of the Groaci
counselor appeared, all five eyes canted alertly to

scan the interior of the room.

"Neatly executed, Lilth," he started—and froze at the sight of Retief, casually puffing a dope stick alight.

"Evening, Nish," the Terran greeted his informal caller. "Looking for your code clerk? I'm afraid he just stepped out."

"You? What—that is, how—I mean to say— murderer!" Nish rushed to the window to stare down in dismay at his *landsman* floundering among the imported carp. "Mayhem! A wanton attack on the person of a diplomatic member of His Groacian Excellency's staff! Seize the miscreant!"

A number of persons, both Terran and Groaci, attracted by the cries of the deputy chief of the Groaci Mission, were now thrusting their heads into Retief's apartment. The choleric features of the Terran counsellor, Career Minister Biteworse, appeared amid the press.

"What seems to be the trouble here?" the plump senior officer demanded in a penetrating nasal tenor.

"I demand the instant arrest of this . . . this ruffian!" Nish whispered, his feeble voice shaking with emotion.

"Why, er, certainly," Biteworse agreed. "That is to say, ah, what's he done this time?"

"This time he's gone too far! His reputation for the flaunting of the niceties of diplomatic usage is notorious—but the defenestration of my colleague, junior rank notwithstanding, is the final anvil!"

"You mean—he threw someone out the window?" Biteworse looked disconcerted.

"Even now the unhappy chap sinks for the third
time!" Nish declaimed.

"Hadn't we better, er, throw him a rope?" Colonel Warbutton suggested from the window, craning to observe the still-struggling figure far below.

"Don't seek to alleviate the gravity of the offense by ill-timed salvage efforts!" Nish hissed.
"Clap the criminal in irons! In fact, Biteworse, I
suggest you declare your entire staff under arrest
until a properly constituted Groaci Board of Inquiry has sifted the matter to the bottom!"

"Now, now, let's not be hasty," Biteworse demurred. "Why don't you just settle for Retief for
now, and hold off on the mass incarceration until
our respective chiefs of mission have had time to
review the matter—"

'No quibbling! I'll settle for half the Terran Mission in durance vile and the remainder stripped of
diplomatic privilege and confined to quarters!"

"Why, that's generous of you, Nish." Biteworse
pursed his lips judiciously. "But I'm not prepared
to go farther than Retief plus a couple of third
secretaries, and the revoking of snack-bar
privileges for all personnel below Class Three
rank—"

"Before you commit yourself, sir," Retief spoke
up casually, "I'd like to point out that Mr. Nish
seems to be laboring under a false impression."

"What?" The Groaci whirled, his throat sac vi-
brating in expression of total indignation. "You
suggest that the spectacle of my underling even
now perishing in the moat is a nonobjective
phenomenon?"

"Oh, he's down there, all right," Retief confirmed. "But he couldn't have fallen from *this*

window, as I'm sure you'll agree."

"Indeed? And why could he not?"

"It's my apartment. And my *Do Not Disturb* sign is lit. So, obviously, Lilth couldn't have been in my room—unless, of course, you'd like to stipulate that he was guilty of trespass, unauthorized entry, burglary, and a number of other irregularities."

"Why—the very idea," Nish said weakly.

"Clearly a simple case of mistaken identity," Biteworse announced briskly. "Now, if it had been Retief who fell, it would be logical to assume he had effected egress through this window. . . ." His voice trailed off. "By the way, Nish—just how did it happen that you were on the spot so soon after Lilth was pushed—fell, that is—out of, ah, some other window, I mean to say?"

"I but nipped up to borrow a book," the discomfited Groaci snapped.

"Indeed?" Biteworse purred, back in command. "I wasn't aware Terran literature was a fancy of yours, my dear Nish. You must drop by and browse over my modest collection some evening—when you're not engaged in, ah, other duties, here in the Terry wing."

"Meanwhile, don't forget your book," Retief said, offering a fat volume titled *How To Tell Your Friends from Your Enemies with Virtual Ninety-Percent Accuracy.*

"Bah!" Nish muttered, spurning the proffered tome. "We'll all be late for the gala." He shouldered his way through the crowd.

"Just between us, Retief," Second Secretary Magnan inquired confidentially, after the others had left, "What was that little sneak Lilth after?"

"I didn't get a chance to ask him," Retief said. "However, he left this as a momento of his visit." He held up a small disk-shaped object dangling from a strap of imitation alligator hide. "I found it by the window."

"It looks like an ordinary Mickey Mouse watch," Magnan said doubtfully. "However, I assume from your enigmatic expression it's something more arcane. Dare I ask what?"

"That's what I propose to find out, Mr. Magnan, at the first opportunity."

4

"I DON'T LIKE it, Retief," Magnan said behind his hand, half an hour later, surveying the gala crowd of Terran and alien diplomats thronging the ballroom from his position near the hundred-gallon punchbowl, cut from a single crystal of red quartz mined in the interior.

"It could stand a little more gin," Retief agreed judiciously.

"Not the punch—the atmosphere!" Magnan corrected. "And I don't refer to the air conditioning; I mean the ominous feeling that something dreadful is about to happen."

"Relax, Mr. Magnan," Retief said soothingly. "The ambassador won't be making his speech for half an hour yet."

"Kindly spare me your ill-timed japes, Retief! As you know, I'm extremely sensitive to extrasensory vibrations of all sorts—a trick I fancy I inherited from my Aunt Prudelia—"

"That *is* a neat trick," Retief acknowledged, raising his glass en *passant* to a well-shaped stenographer waltzing past in the grip of Colonel Warbutton.

"Retief! Kindly attend to my remarks! After all, a diplomat learns to rely on his hunches—"

"A telling point, Mr. Magnan," Retief said, and deposited his glass on a passing tray. "And I have a hunch Miss Braswell would be grateful for a few civilian anecdotes, after two and a half waltzes' worth of military reminiscences."

"Quite possibly," Magnan said icily. "However, I suggest you defer your mission of mercy until we've dealt with the more substantive problem of incipient skulduggery in the air!"

"If you're referring to the fact that Ambassador Nith has been in a huddle with his military attaché for the past twenty minutes, I agree it bodes no good for joint peacemaking efforts," Retief conceded.

"It's not only that—I've observed that Counselor Lilth seems to be exceptionally clubby with the Bogan military observer."

"So he does. While Ambassador Pouncetrifle has been cornered for the past forty minutes by three of our guests from the Dames Auxiliary for Militant Pacifism."

"I doubt that the dowagers have any fell intent," Magnan said. "However, that sneaky little Groaci cultural attaché—Fink, or Sneak or whatever his name is—"

"Snink; he seems unusually absorbed in whatever it is that Counselor Biteworse is holding forth on. He's had him backed in among the potted frogfronds for the past half hour."

"Ever since the arrival of the provisional Minister of Illegal Activities, to be precise," Magnan pointed out. "And at the same time, the pro tem Chief of Police has been huddling with Captain Thilth—even among the Groaci, not one whom one would care to entrust with assisting one's grand-mère across the street."

"Not if she were carrying more than jelly-bean money," Retief concurred. "All of which suggests that there are plans afoot that have nothing to do with the tranquillity of Lumbaga."

"In that case, how can you stand there ogling the female clerical help?" Magnan demanded indignantly. "It's perfectly obvious that the Groaci and their toadies are up to no good!"

"Very probably, Mr. Magnan. However, if we stand here with our heads together, looking gloomy, they're likely to deduce that we're onto them—"

"And a good thing, too! The very idea, plotting right under our noses!"

"Better there than in some place less easy to observe," Retief suggested.

"The gall of the scoundrels! Come, Retief— let's report our suspicions to His Excellency at once—"

"I suggest we wait a few more minutes, Mr. Magnan. There are a pair of Groaci administrative aides edging past the Marine guards over by the French doors; let's give them time to get in the clear."

"Whatever for?" Magnan gasped. "So they can rifle the chancery safe?"

"We won't let them get that far. But it would be interesting to know what they've got in mind."

"But—what if they plant a bomb—or set fire to the building—or insinuate a set of falsified documents into the voucher files?"

"That last item is pretty scary," Retief conceded. "Still, maybe we can stop them before any real damage is done—" He broke off as the drapes twitched shut behind the aliens whom he had been observing. "Shall we trail along and see what they're up to, Mr. Magnan?"

"Well—we really ought to refer the matter to the appropriate authorities . . . still, they'd hardly dare anything really drastic right here in the complex—and it *would* be rather a coup to lay them by the heels unassisted." Magnan twitched the multiple lapels of his grapejuice-colored, early midevening, hyperformal cut-away into line, assumed a stern expression, and followed Retief as he made his way through the crowd.

On the terrace, they caught a glimpse of their quarry just disappearing over the balustrade into the shrubbery below.

"Just as I thought!" Magnan gasped. "And there's a *Keep Off the Grass* sign in plain view! I'll report them at once, and—"

"Wait." Retief motioned Magnan back. There were sounds of threshing in the bushes, then soft footfalls along a flagstoned path. Suddenly a brilliant beam of greenish light sprang up, shining vertically up through the foliage. It blinked once, twice, three times. There was a pause; then the signal was repeated.

"The plot thickens," Retief said softly as Magnan clutched his arm. "Let's see what's next."

Again they heard footfalls, this time approaching. The shrubbery rustled. A pale Groaci visage appeared over the balustrade. A moment later the two aliens had regained the terrace and were sauntering casually back toward the French doors, puffing dope sticks in an insouciant manner.

"Why, the very idea," Magnan whispered from the shadow of the pilaster where he and Retief were concealed. "They're rejoining the party just as though nothing at all had happened!"

"You'd hardly expect them to skulk back in just because they skulked out," Retief pointed out. "Also, nothing much *has* happened—yet."

"You mean—you think there'll be more?"

"I suspect that what we saw was a modulated light signaler. They could have conveyed an unabridged set of Corps regulations in the time they had."

"But—whatever would they want with a set of CDT regs?"

"A figure of speech, Mr. Magnan—" Retief broke off as a faint *Bee-beep!* sounded from his wrist. He turned back his cuff; the tiny figure of Mickey was glowing softly in the dark; his arms whirled against the disc, semaphoring frantically.

"Come in, Lilth!" a tiny, harsh voice rasped in badly accented Lumbagan. "Why haven't you reported in as scheduled?"

Retief brought the device close to his face. "Alas," he whispered in a passable imitation of the Groaci's breathy tones, "I was detained by certain unscheduled natatorial exertions—"

"You've been advised how important split-second timing is! Where are you now?"

"On the south terrace, catching a breath of re-vivifying night air from the rigors of the receiving line," Retief hissed.

"Cretin! To the roof at once! It's now M-minute minus four! Get going!"

"Roger and out," Retief breathed.

"Just a minute! You're not Lilth!" The glow died from the watch face. Mickey's hands came to rest at twenty fifty-six.

"It was useful while it lasted," Retief said, and tossed the deactivated communicator aside. "Let's go, Mr. Magnan. It looks like we're running late for a hot date."

Two and a half minutes later, after a dizzying run up a tight spiral stair cut into the thick stone of the keep walls, Retief and Magnan stepped silently out onto the complex roof. The bright pink light of the two moons cast double shadows across the rough, tarred planks.

"Looks like we're first on the scene," Retief noted. "Let's pick an inconspicuous spot and wait for developments."

"Retief," Magnan gasped, breathing hard from his exertions. "What in the world do you suppose . . . ?"

"This afternoon someone hired Ignarp to gather us in. Later on, Lilth seemed to have the same idea. Somebody seems to have an urgent desire to own a Terry."

"But—if that's true—aren't we playing into their hands?"

"Sometimes it's the only way to get a look at the other fellow's cards."

"But what if they catch us here! I suggest we go back at once and file a written report—"

"Too late now," Retief said softly as the door through which they had emerged was thrust rudely open. A short, plump figure emerged, sputtering, closely accompanied by a trio of hefty individuals in floppy hats and trailing hemlines.

"Why—it's the ambassador—and the ladies from DAMP!" Magnan chirped. "Gracious, what a relief—" As he started to step out, Retief pulled him back.

"One more sound out of you, Terry, and we deliver you in do-it-yourself-kit form," one of Pouncetrifle's escorts barked at the Chief of Mission in the native tongue.

"Why—they're not DAMP members at all!" Magnan whispered. "They're not even ladies! In fact"—he gulped as one of the trio tossed aside a voluminous frock and followed it with the hat—"they're not even human!"

"Sit tight, Mr. Magnan," Retief said, "the party's not complete yet. . . ."

Overhead a soft whap-whap-whap became audible, grew swiftly louder. A dark shadow floated across the lesser moon; dust swirled up as a small copter settled gently in at the far side of the roof.

"No navigation lights!" Magnan blurted. "That's a violation of the provisional traffic code!"

As the bogus pacifists hustled the ambassador toward the copter there was a clatter from the door, accompanied by a clink of medals. Colonel Warbutton appeared, turned back to assist a slighter figure through.

"Remarkable view from up here, my dear," the military attaché said expansively. "Just savor a lungful of that fresh air!"

"It smells like turbo fumes to me," Miss Braswell's voice replied. "But I thought you said we were going up to your office for some emergency dictation. . . ." Her voice trailed off into a yelp as two dark shapes loomed suddenly beside her and her escort.

"Here, what's the meaning of this!" Warbutton boomed, struggling in the grip of what appeared to be a portly matron. "Are you ladies out of your minds? Attacking a military man is no way to wage pacifism!"

"It's an ambush," a Lumbagan voice yelled. "Over the side with the both of 'em!"

"Don't shoot, Retief!" Magnan blurted as Retief stood and snapped his needler into his hand. "You'll hit His Excellency!"

As the kidnappers thrust Warbutton toward the parapet, Retief jumped toward the lone alien manhandling the ambassador toward the copter. The ersatz dowager whirled to intercept him; he palmed the gun and rammed a right hook into the local's midsection, grabbed the ambassador's arm and spun him toward the open door. One of Warbutton's captors whirled with a yell and dived after the escaping dignitary, only to trip over Magnan's outthrust foot. Warbutton wrenched himself from the grasp of the other, dived for the door, bulldozing Miss Braswell aside into the embrace of the first of the three thugs, now back on his feet; he lifted her, sprang toward the parapet as the second Lumbagan caught Warbutton's ankle, bringing the military man down with a resounding crash. Retief reached the parapet in the same instant that Miss Braswell's captor, with a hearty heave, tossed her over the side. He dived, caught her hand as she fell, her weight dragging him half across the parapet. Instantly, horny hands seized his ankles, lifted, and shoved. As he went over, Retief grabbed for the coping, hooked his fingers over the edge. With a bone-wrenching shock, he was brought up short, the girl dangling below him. The Lumbagan appeared above him, fist raised to smash at his fingers; then Magnan's narrow features were visible over the alien's shoulder as he brought an elevator shoe down on the local's skull.

As the Lumbagan crumpled, Retief pulled himself up, hauling Miss Braswell over the parapet beside him, to see the other two Lumbagans wrestling Warbutton toward the copter. He charged them, hurled one aside—and collided with Warbutton as the colonel tore free and dashed for freedom.

"Help!" Warbutton yelled, grappling Retief. "I demand protection!

Retief thrust him aside, lunged for the copter as it lifted suddenly, rotors beating furiously. He was too late; the machine rose swiftly, bore away to the west across the dark rooftops. As he turned back, the two still-present Lumbagans plunged through the door a scant inch in advance of Warbutton. Retief caught the colonel by the collar and dragged him back, too late. The fugitives were gone.

"I'll have you court-martialed for this, you whippersnapper!" Warbutton yelled.

"Oh, Mr. Retief, you were wonderful!" Miss Braswell sighed, and sagged against him.

"I'd have nabbed the lot of them if you hadn't interfered with my pursuit just now!" Warbutton ranted. "Actually, I've been well aware of the ruffians' plans for some weeks now—"

"In that case, maybe you know where they're taking him," Retief cut in.

"Taking who?" the colonel snorted.

"Magnan," Retief said. "They got him."

5

"OUT OF THE question, Mr. Retief," Ambassador Pouncetrifle snorted, yanking his rumpled lapels into line. "No one leaves the embassy until the present crisis is past! Having lost one diplomat, through no fault of my own, I have no intention of blotting my copybook further!"

"Why, even while I was manning the barricades on the roof," Warbutton stated indignantly, "a coup, by the way, which would have succeeded brilliantly but for the interference of Retief—even as I manned the barricades, I say, a mob of irresponsibles invaded the courtyard and pelted the chancery's north façade with overripe frinkfruit!"

"It would be as much as our lives were worth to sally forth in the midst of the disorders," an Information Service man spoke up. "I say let's acknowledge the failure of the mission and get busy concocting an alibi—"

"Conducting an analysis in depth of the unforeseen factors necessitating a rethinking of Corps policy anent the timetable for Lumbagan unification, I presume you mean," Biteworse amended.

"Make a note of that phrase, Miss Braswell. It will do nicely as a title for my report."

"I'll handle the report end, Fenwick," Pouncetrifle snapped. "I hereby assign you the chairmanship of a task force to turn up evidence proving me blameless in the fiasco."

"I think you're all mean," Miss Braswell spoke up, netting shocked stares from the great men present. "Poor Mr. Magnan was just marvelous when he conked that big, ugly brute over the head—"

"He assaulted Colonel Warbutton?" Pouncetrifle barked. "Obviously the man's in the pay of the enemy!"

"How perfectly silly!" Miss Braswell exclaimed. "Those big bullies dragged him into that copter and took off while Mr. Retief was trying to unglue the colonel from his neck! He—"

"That will do, Miss Braswell!" Pouncetrifle barked. "The situation is deteriorating hourly, gentlemen." He turned a choleric gaze on his staff. "And if Mr. Retief's to be believed, the Groaci are back of the skulduggery, as usual—"

"Don't believe a word of it," Warbutton snapped. "The fellow's making a transparent attempt to cover up—"

"Be that as it may, Colonel—I decree no further contact with our Groaci colleagues. Also, no contact with Lumbagans. In addition, no contact with offworld representatives of any stripe!"

"W-will it be all right if I cable Sector?" the communications officer inquired diffidently. "Just to keep them informed?"

"Better not," Warbutton said. "We don't know how far the rot has spread."

"I'm not certain I'd go *that* far," Pouncetrifle
said sternly. "However, I see no point in unduly
alarming the department with premature reports
which my critics might distort so as to imply some
culpability on my part. We'll wait for cheerier
tidings."

"B-but if the embassy is surrounded by hostile
mobs . . . and under air attack by native commandos . . . and threatened from within by fifth col-
umnists . . . and we can't even tell anyone . . . how
in the world are we going to get any cheery
tidings—to say nothing of getting ourselves out of
this pickle?" the political officer queried.

"We'll employ a wait-and-see strategy,"
Pouncetrifle decreed. "We'll retire to the air-raid
shelters and wait a few days, and see if they'll go
away. Possibly not the most dynamic program
open to us"—he forestalled objections with a
plump palm—"but one hallowed by centuries of
bureaucratic tradition. Now. . . ." He favored the
assembled staff with a frosty twinkle. "I've decided to advance the schedule for the checkers
tournament so as to fully occupy our time underground. And as an added fillip, I personally will
make available to the winner an autographed
photo of myself admiring my plastic doily collection for a modest charge barely covering ex-
penses." He fixed Retief with an icy glare. "And as
for you, sir—you may regard yourself as under
close house arrest pending a full investigation by
Colonel Warbutton into your conduct during the
raid."

"The old meany," Miss Braswell commiserated
with Retief after the meeting had dispersed. "He's
going to let poor Mr. Magnan fend for himself

without lifting one of his pudgy little fingers to help him—and blaming it all on you!"

"His Excellency is a bit distraught at the moment," Retief soothed the girl. "I suspect he'll revise this morning's pronouncements in his dispatch to Sector after this is all over."

"But—what good will that do Mr. Magnan?"

"I agree something needs to be done in the meantime to lend substance to his retrospections. Actually, I have one or two errands to run in that connection. Will you convey my regrets to the checker team?"

"But—he put you under house arrest! Doesn't that mean you can't leave the complex?"

"Not quite; it just gives him grounds to disavow me in case things don't work out."

"You mean—he *expects* you to go AWOL?"

"Let's just say he's prepared to risk it."

"But you—you're risking your life, going out there! You can hear the mob howling around the front entrance!"

"I'll use another route to avoid the autograph fans."

"Mr. Retief—take care," Miss Braswell whispered; she kissed him quickly on the cheek and fled.

Five minutes later, wrapped in a dark cloak, Retief opened the hidden door behind the dumbwaiter and descended into the catacombs.

6

DACOIT STREET WAS deserted. The yells of the demonstrators gathered before the grand entrance to the Castle complex were a dull surf-roar here. The shops were shuttered and dark; scattered brickbats and broken spears attested to the activities of the day, but only a few candy wrappers and old newspapers blowing across the oily cobbles lent movement to the scene, pitch dark but for a weak glow from a spluttering flambeau at the next corner.

Retief made his way unmolested through the narrow ways; five minutes' brisk walk brought him to a corner half a block from a rough-hewn door under a swinging signboard adorned with a lumpy purplish shape pierced by a pointed length of wood. Yellow light leaked from a small leaded-glass window. As Retief took up his post under the spreading branches of a music tree, a gust stirred the leaves, evoking a rippling arpeggio of crystalline sound that mingled mournfully with the fluting of the night wind.

A small wild creature resembling a disembodied blue eyeball with tiny bird feet hopped along a twig overhead, goggling at the Terran with an appearance of intentness heightened by the absence of an eyelid. A second free-lance ocular appeared, peeping from among glassy, needle-shaped leaves. Nearer at hand, another variety of the local fauna—this one a convoluted three-inch ellipsoid bearing a remarkable resemblance to an oversized ear—perched in a froomble bush, pivoting slowly from left to right and back again as if tuning in on a faint sound in the distance.

"You boys ought to get together with a nose and form a corporation," Retief murmured. "You'd be a dynamite vaudeville act."

Both eyeballs whipped out of sight; the ear

jerked and began to crawl hastily down the stem. A faint footfall sounded from the direction of the nearby alley mouth. Retief faded back against the bole of the ancient tree and eased his 2mm gun into his hand. A furtive five-foot figure wrapped in an ankle-length djellaba emerged into view.

"Ignarp," Retief called softly. The newcomer jumped and emitted a sharp yelp.

"Galloping gastropods!" he hissed. "You nearly scared me out of my epidermis!" He advanced another step to peer closely at Retief with three large, watery eyes not unlike those concealed in the foliage above.

"Aren't you the Terry I did the big favor for this afternoon?" he queried. "Frankly, all you foreigners look alike to me."

"An accusation I can't level against you, Ignarp," Retief said. "Didn't you have four eyes and a purple hide this afternoon?"

"Yeah; I stopped by my place for a shower and change." Ignarp gave his rattling sigh. "I didn't know it was going to be such a rough evening. What are you doing out in the streets? The rallying cry of the mob is 'Get Terry.' "

"It does seem the incidence of violence is escalating since the peace talks have been under way. Any idea why?"

"We got a few ideas—but maybe it's not time to spill 'em."

"Who's 'we'? "

"I guess it won't hurt to tell you; I'm a member of an undercover organization known as the Goody Redistribution Action Bunch. But why pump me? I'm just an average citizen, trying to get along—"

"Don't kid me, Ignarp. Conditions have changed since this afternoon. They got Magnan."

"Why, the lousy, sneaky, double-crossing—"

"Don't take it so hard; you can still earn a nice fee. Just tell me who hired you and why."

"Well—that sounds like a gracious offer. But let's get out of sight. I've got the feeling unfriendly eyes are upon us."

"After you, Ignarp."

"Come on," he said. "The Stake and Kidney's a discreet bistro, if not too clean. All the regulars will be out rioting, so we'll have a modicum of privacy."

The local led the way past the shuttered fronts of darkened shops to the heavy door, rapped a complicated tattoo, shifting from one of his six large feet to another and casting worried glances along the avenue until the door rattled and swung inward with a lugubrious creak. An undersized cranium adorned with an odd assortment of sensory organs poked out at belt level to look the callers up and down.

"For Greep's sake, Fudsot, let us in before the City Guard sees us," Ignarp hissed. "This Terry's got diplomatic immunity, but those dupes of the power structure would like nothing better than to rearrange my internal components along more conventional lines."

Grumbling, the landlord ushered them down three crooked steps into a long, low-ceilinged room smelling of fried zintx patties and sour wine. He locked the door behind them, and indicated a five-legged table in the corner.

"Too conspicuous," Ignarp demurred. "How about the back room?"

"That'll run you an extra five xots."

"Five xots? You're as bad as the entrenched exploiters!"

"Except they'd charge you ten—and then report you. Pay up or get out, you and your offworld chum. It's all the same to me."

"OK. OK. The Bunch will get around to you, you tool of the establishment!" Ignarp extracted a small-mouthed purse from beneath his voluminous robes and handed over a triangular coin of green plastic. Fudsot subjected it to close examination under what seemed to be an olfactory organ before using a six-inch key to unlock the small door at the back.

"It's all yours, gents," he grunted. "For the next half hour, anyways. After that it'll cost you another five xots."

"Bring us wine," Ignarp ordered as he dusted off a three-legged stool.

"Sure. Four xots for a quarter-zub o' the house brew. Six xots for bottled-in-bond. And I can give you a special deal on some aged Pepsi; I happened to get aholt of a small consignment through a special contact down south. Five xots the flask, uncut."

"Smuggler," Ignarp snapped. "Profiteer! Robber! We'll take the Pepsi—in sealed bottles, mind you!"

"Sure—whatta you think I am, one o' these chiselers?"

Ignarp waited in glowering silence until the landlord had delivered the refreshments and withdrawn.

"That's what we're up against," he said gloomily. "You'd think Fudsot would be a loyal supporter of the movement—but no, he's out for the fast xot!''

"What's this movement all about?" Retief asked.

"I should think it was obvious," Ignarp said sharply. "Even a foreigner can see that the entire planet's in the grip of an elite corps of self-serving reactionaries!''

"Curious," Retief said, puffing a Chanel dope stick alight. "I had the impression that anarchy was complete. In fact, that's why we Terries are here—"

"I know all about your so-called Peace Commission, Retief. You Terries and those main-chance Groaci are all spinning your wheels. Sure, we fight a lot—we have ever since the dawn of recorded history, six years ago. And even before, if the old tribal legends mean anything. And that's jake—except lately it's taken a nasty turn. The old system of you break my back, I'll break yours, is falling apart!''

"Uh huh." Retief sampled his drink. "And where does your Bunch come into the picture?"

"We've formed a third force to combat the special privilege groups. Of course, we're just getting started—only thirteen members at present—but we won't stop until the gross inequities of the system have been corrected!''

"You intend to divide up the wealth, an equal share for everyone?"

"You think we're out of our brainpans? We'll keep the loot for ourselves, naturally!''

"That's your idea of an equitable arrangement?" Retief inquired mildly.

"Of couse not!" Ignarp looked puzzled. "It's just

simple, old-fashioned greed, the noblest of emotions."

"Sounds like a highly realistic program," Retief said. "And what about the rest of the population?"

"We're planning on selling them into slavery, naturally. And say—maybe you Terries would like a slice of the action!"

"What makes you think so?"

"Well—aside from the fact that the mob is out to get both of us—I've heard you Terries get your jollies out of taking things away from the original owners and handing them over to new management. I could never figure out why, but we members of GRAB are perfectly willing to get in on the redistribution."

"That's a fair assessment of our foreign-aid policy, Ignarp; but sometimes it's a little difficult to determine who the deserving parties are."

"Simple enough: Possession is *prima facie* evidence of moral leprosy; have-nots are pure in heart by definition."

"But if we hand the planet over to you fellows, then *you'll* be the haves—"

"That's different," Ignarp stated crisply. "Now, when can we expect the first consignment of guns, tanks, bombers, zip guns, poisoned bodkins and the rest?"

"Well, there may be a few administrative delays, Ignarp. Even a bureaucrat as dedicated to the spread of enlightenment as Ambassador Pouncetrifle may have some difficulty picturing a baker's dozen of malcontents as the authentic inheritors of the mantle of planetary dictatorship."

"I had an idea you might try to stall," Ignarp

said accusingly. "Fortunately, we have a telling ideological point in reserve." He leaned toward Retief confidentially. "The situation," he stated solemnly, "has a very nasty—are you ready?—racial angle."

"Tell me about it."

"You don't sound very excited." Ignarp said in tones reflecting disappointment. "I heard all a fellow had to do was mention the word and you Terries automatically started writing checks."

"A mild exaggeration. In any event, the syndrome hardly applies to Lumbaga. You fellows don't have any races."

"Hey, what kind of a crack is that?"

"I've noticed," Retief said, "that the eyeballs and lower lips hopping around in the underbrush don't look much different than the ones you and your fellow citizens employ in your daily activities—"

"Now, hold it right there, Retief! I don't like the turn the conversation's taking—"

"In fact," Retief went on unperturbed, "it seems that the higher forms of Lumbagan life are all evolved from the lower forms by combination—"

"Don't come preaching your godless evolutionary doctrines around here!" Ignarp snapped.

"Don't worry, I'm just making it up as I go along," Retief said soothingly. "If my theory is correct, you, for example, represent the end product of a whole series of combinations—"

"Let's not get personal, Terry!"

"Just getting a few facts straight, Ignarp, no offense intended. Tell me, how old are you?"

"That's none of your blasted business, Retief!"

"I thought you wanted Terran backing in your scheme to take over the world."

"Yeah, that's right, but—"

"Then it's my business."

"Well . . . I don't know exactly," Ignarp muttered. "But the best theories give a figure around a quarter of a million. That's average, of course. After all, by the time you go back a couple of centuries, things get kind of vague." The Lumbagan looked embarrassed, as attested by the purplish tinge mounting his wattles.

"I think I understand," Retief said. "When a Lumbagan has a bad heart or a broken arm, he trades the injured member in on a new one. In time, he's completely replaced. Is that it?"

"That covers most of it," Ignarp said hastily. "Now, back to practical politics—"

"So in effect, a Lumbagan never dies. The question is, how does he get started?"

"Cripes, Retief, is nothing sacred to you foreigners?"

"My interest is purely scientific, Ignarp."

"This racy conversation gets me all stirred up," the local said. "However, I guess it's for the cause. You've got it right as it goes, but there's a few points you missed. Like the fact that the Singletons—you know, the free-living eyeballs and pituitary glands and the like—can only get together in bunches of up to ten. An ear might team up with a tentacle for mutual security, you know, and then later add on an esophagus—strictly by instinct, natch. Not all these teams work out, of course. Evolutionary dead ends, you might say. They break up again, no hard feelings, and maybe later the different parts join another accretion. In the end, after a few million years, you get quite a large number of working accretions swinging through the jungle or creeping around in the underbrush, as happy as clams. So OK. A tenner Singleton can't add any more free units—but what *can* happen is that two Singletons can link up to form a Dubb. Got it?"

"I'm trying, Ignarp. Pray continue."

"Right. Now, that's not the end of the trail. Two well-established Dubbs can get together, and make up a Trip. Now, a Trip's a pretty complicated life-form; most of 'em don't work out, but with up to forty basic units to play around with, you *can* come up with some pretty successful combos. But Trips are a lot rarer than Dubbs, naturally."

"Naturally. And I suppose two congenial Trips can join forces, to continue the process?"

"Right! And when that happens, you get a Quad." Ignard looked at Retief expectantly.

"And two Quads can combine to make a still more complicated creature?"

"Huh? Where'd you get an obscene idea like that!" Ignarp looked shocked, an effect achieved by rotating his eyeballs rapidly. "A four-decker is the ultimate produce of evolution—a Lumbagan—like me!"

"I won't say it's clear, Ignarp, but it's not quite as opaque as it was. But you still haven't explained why you Furtheronians spend so much time disassembling each other—or just how you decide who's against whom."

"That's where the racial angle comes in. Now it's perfectly natural and wholesome when everybody is out to get everybody else; but when discrimination rears its ugly head—that's different. And even that wouldn't bother me," Ignarp added, "except I happen to be a member of the persecuted minority."

"A minority usually implies at least two people

with a few characteristics in common," Retief pointed out. "Since every Lumbagan is unique—"

"Except my kind," Ignarp said gloomily. "Somehow, due to a component nobody's isolated yet, we've got something nobody else has got."

"A disability?"

"Heck, no, Retief! They'd forgive us that! We're vastly superior, that's what gravels 'em! Just a hint of our special skill, and the witch-hunt is on!"

"And just what is this trait that gives you the advantage—"

"Aha! That's our big secret! You see—"

There was a sudden sound of disturbance in the outer room: a dull clatter, a yelp, a thump that rattled the cups on the table. Something crashed against the door hard enough to splinter wood.

"I might have known," Ignarp cried, leaping up. "Sold out by the vested interests!"

Retief came to his feet, looking around the small, dim-lit room. The only visible opening was a small ventilator grill.

"So long, Retief!" Ignarp yelled. "I'll be in touch. . . ."

With a rending crash, the door burst inward. The creature which bounded through the opening was seven feet tall, with sour yellowish skin blotched with black and purple. Three gaunt, bristly, knob-kneed legs terminating in broad rubbery webbed feet made up two thirds of its height. Four left and two right arms of graduated lengths sprang from the hunched shoulders, protected by a carapace resembling the shell of a turtle adorned with twisted spikes. Atop a short, thick, tendon-corded neck rested a pointed head given over largely to a foot-wide, purple-lipped mouth crowded with needlelike fangs, below a pair of wide-set eyes the size of tennis balls, a bloodshot yellowish white except for the off-centered metallic black pupils. A thick, powerful prehensile tail ending in a three-fingered hand waved a gnarled steelwood club aloft.

With a bellow, the monstrosity charged. Retief spun the table into its path, ducked a wild swing as the giant crashed into the obstacle with a plank-splintering impact. At the open door he turned; the intruder was threshing its way clear of the remains of the boards, but of the GRAB member there was no sign. Retief had time only to notice that the grill was missing from the register before the monster tossed aside a shattered timber and leaped toward him. Retief stepped through and slammed the door, dropping the heavy bar in place as the armored alien crashed against it.

In the gloom of the outer room, the squat figure of the landlord was dimly visible, scrambling for cover. Retief reached him in two strides, caught the back of his coarse-weave tunic, lifted him to tippy-toes.

"A slight double cross, eh, Fudsot? Who paid you?" he inquired genially, as the door behind him resounded to the berserker's blows.

"Leave me go, Terry, or I'll see to it you're broken down into surgical spares—"

"What was the idea? Were you out to get me, or was it Ignarp you were after—or both?"

"You know so much—you tell me," Fudsot grunted.

"But Ignarp fooled you," Retief said. "He separated into subassemblies of a convenient size and went out the ventilator, right?"

"You Terries aren't supposed to know about that," Fudsot muttered. "A lousy fate, even for a troublemaker like Ignarp."

"So that's the last of Ignarp, eh?"

"As Ignarp, yeah. His sweetbreads and tonsils are back where they started ages ago—free-living Freebies looking around for a partner to start up a new tenner." Fudsot wagged his head mournfully.

"A sad end for a social reformer of his zeal," Retief said. "Still, there's much to be said for the carefree life of an adenoid. I'll be on my way now, Fudsot, but before I go—just what was that that broke up our drinking party? I've gotten accustomed to a certain pleasing variety in the local citizenry, but that chap was in an entirely new category."

"I heard rumors, but—" Fudsot broke off.

"But what?"

"But it would be bad for my health to spread 'em. How's about getting him outa my back room now, Terry? I got to set the place to rights for the pre-dawn dustup crowd."

"No thanks, I can't use him."

"You mean—you're leaving that monstrosity on my hands?"

"Certainly. Mind if I use the back entrance?"

"No! That's where . . . I mean, there isn't one," the landlord finished sullenly.

"That's where they're waiting to make the pickup, eh? Thanks for the tip." Retief pushed through a greasy door behind the bar, crossed a kitchen reeking of stale fat, slipped out into a narrow alleyway decorated with neglected garbage containers. There was a soft rustling from a dense patch of shadow. A small, spindle-legged figure swathed in a dark cloak stepped forth. From the folds of the garment a gloved grasping member protruded, gripping a small power gun.

"So—success attends my efforts! The moose has taken the bait, and sprung the trap!"

"Mouse, I think you mean, Wilth," Retief corrected. "What brings you out in the damp night air?"

"Drat," the Groaci hissed. "Who informed you of my identity?"

"Don't you remember? The ambassador introduced us last week, at the Mother-in-Law's Day Pepsi bust."

"I refer to the treacher who betrayed my disguise."

"Oh, he's the same fellow who's standing behind you now with a crater gun aimed at your dorsal suture."

Wilth started violently, causing one of his government-issue eye shields to clatter to the cobbles. "Undone!" he keened, as Retief stepped forward to relieve him of his weapon. "Unhappy Wilth! I rue the day the mound burst to expose me to the harsh external world!"

"By the way, what did you have in mind doing with this?" Retief inquired, aiming the gun negligently at its former owner.

"My instructions—I assure you, my dear Retief, nothing personal was intended—were to intimidate you with the firearm, thereby causing you to accompany me to a designated place for an uninhibited interview with a Most Highly Placed Person."

"Most highly placed in the Groaci hierarchy, I assume?"

"But of course. Do you imagine I'm in the habit of trepanning fellow diplomats—even Soft Ones—for the convenience of members of lesser races?"

"I shouldn't have asked. And what was to be the subject of this conference?"

"Do you further imagine I am privy to the machinations of MHPP's?" Wilth glanced nervously behind him. "As a courtesy to a colleague, would you kindly instruct your toady to point his piece elsewhere. . . ." His faint voice faded. "Wh-where is the creature?"

"He couldn't make it," Retief said. "Liquor inventory, you know—but the intention was there. Now—"

"Hoaxed!" Wilth whistled. "Hoodwinked by vile Terran duplicity!"

"Don't take it so hard, Wilth. No harm done; it's always a rewarding experience to make the acquaintance of an MHPP of whatever persuasion. I'll go with you."

"You'll . . . ah . . . accompany me to the rendezvous as planned?" Wilth goggled all five eyestalks at Retief.

"Why not? The evening is still young." Retief snapped open the butt of the power gun and removed the energy cell, handed the disarmed weapon back to the Groaci.

"Why, this is quite decent of you, Retief," Wilth whispered breathlessly. "What a pity all Groaci-Terran relations can't be conducted in the same spirit of amity."

"They are, Wilth, they are," Retief said soothingly. "Shall we go? I wouldn't like to keep the MHPP waiting."

"Good notion. But no tricks, Retief. I trusted you once, to my sorrow. . . ."

"Don't worry, Wilth. I wouldn't want to miss an opportunity to hobnob with the great."

"I wasn't aware you were a climber, Retief," Wilth said as he motioned the Terran ahead. "Luckily your social aspirations coincide with my own plans for career advancement, to our mutual advantage. Straight ahead; I'll follow with the gun, for the sake of appearances."

It was a brisk ten-minute walk through the tortuously winding streets—hardly more than tunnels threading through the monumental jumble of Lumbagan architecture. Wilth halted at a small but massive door set in a deeply recessed niche, pounded stealthily on the dark panels. Weak grayish light leaked out as the door opened. A Groaci in the uniform of a peacekeeper peered out.

"Inside, Soft One," Wilth ordered curtly. Retief preceded his putative captor along a cramped passage papered in a pattern of puce and mustard lozenges to a highly varnished bile-green door that reflected the watery glow of the ceiling dim-strip. The guard rapped. At a faint response, he thrust the door wide and motioned Retief through.

A Groaci in jeweled eye shields was seated behind a wide desk. He waved a negligent three-fingered hand at Retief, indicating a stool.

"Any difficulties?" he inquired of his underling in Terran.

"Your Excellency would be amazed at how easy it was," Wilth replied glumly. "I was even astonished myself."

"To not accept the legends of Terry invincibility," the senior alien snapped, switching to the Groacian tongue, "lest you predispose yourself to quail in the breech!" He turned three eyes on Retief while holding the glare of the other two on Wilth. "I," he announced, "am Hivemaster Shlush. You, I believe, are the fellow Retief?"

"A pleasure, Your Excellency." Retief acknowledged his identity with a nod and seated himself.

"You," Shlush continued ominously, "are not unknown to me by repute."

"I'm flattered."

"Don't be," Shlush hissed. "Your name, Soft One, is a byword for the Terran duplicity and meddling that have plagued Groaci foreign policy since the first intimations of our manifest Galactic destiny!"

"That's a rather uncharitable description of Corps policy, Hivemaster," Retief commented. "By the way, what brings you here? I don't recall seeing your name on the last embassy list—"

"Not to pry into matters of no concern to foreigners!" Shlush hissed.

"In fact," Retief went on, "I seem to recall that you were rather suddenly retired to civilian life after that fiasco on Grabnark IV—"

Shlush jabbed a digit at Retief, all five eyes canted alertly in his guest's direction now. "Your role in the humbling of the great is not forgotten, Retief! But now the era of Terry domination comes to an end! No more will we Groaci suffer graciously the intolerable interposition of foreigners between ourselves and the objects of our desires!"

"Go on." Retief puffed a cigar to life, blew aromatic smoke across the desk.

"You," Shlush hissed, "have the honor of being

the first Terry to learn the fate of all inferiors who seek to impede the path of Groaci expansion!"

"I hope I prove worthy of the distinction," Retief said pleasantly.

"Ah, you have done so long since, my Retief—on the first occasion when you laid violent hands on the person of an Exalted One! And as soon as certain specialty devices I have caused to be installed in the vaults beneath my present humble quarters reach operating rpm, you shall reap your reward!"

"In the meantime," Retief suggested mildly, "I take it you'd like to have a little talk."

"Indeed yes," Shlush whispered. "How perceptive of you, Retief."

"Not at all," the Terran demurred. "Wilth told me."

"To have babbled of state secrets littermate of drones?" The hivemaster hissed the question at his underling.

"Whom, I, Excellency? Why, to have but hinted he'd best be on his metacarpals—"

"To commit another indiscretion, and to find yourself trussed by the policies alongside the Soft One!" Shlush turned back to Retief. "But I'm slighting my hostly obligations," he said smoothly. "Would you care for a little something whilst we chat?"

"Brandy, thanks," Retief said comfortably.

"You," Shlush addressed the guard still hovering by the door. "To fetch brandy at once. Black Bacchus will do."

"To congratulate Your Excellency on Your Excellency's taste," the peacekeeper hissed unctiously. "But to wonder if Your Excellency would amplify Your Excellency's instructions to include data as to where I'm supposed to fetch it from."

"The usual source, hivefellow of defectives!"

"To do as commanded, Exalted One—but don't you inkthay the errytay ightmay recognize the abellay?"

"To assume you have itway enough to ourpay it in the itchenkay!" Shlush favored Retief with the Groaci equivalent of a sour smile. "I've instructed the fellow to serve our refreshments in a VIP decanter reserved for important guests," he translated.

"I'm sensible of the honor," Retief said. "Now, what was it you wanted to tell me?"

"Tell you? My dear Terry, you fail to grasp the full implications of the situation. It is you who are going to tell me!"

"What would you like to know first?" Retief said promptly.

"You may begin with full details of secret Terran armament schemes, overall invasion strategy, D-day tactical plans, and close-support logistical arrangements," Shlush said crisply.

"I can cover that in a very few words," Retief said. "There aren't any."

"Pah! You expect me to believe that an organization of the sophistication of the CDT intends to play it by ear?"

"Play what by ear?" Retief inquired interestedly.

"The take-over. What else?"

"The take-over?" Retief tipped an inch of cigar ash onto Shlush's polished desk top. "What of?"

"Of this plague spot known as Lumbaga, naturally!"

"Who's taking it over?" Retief inquired interestedly.

"We are! That is to say, you are! I mean to say, of course, having gotten wind of the perfidious schemes laid by you treacherous Soft Ones under the cynical guise of pretended participation in bogus peace talks, we Groaci have naturally been compelled to take appropriate steps to safeguard the endangered lives, property, and sacred self-determination of the indigenous autochthones."

"Remarkable," Retief said. "And I suppose that to properly protect the Lumbagans, it will be necessary for Groac to temporarily garrison a few troops here. And perhaps to take over a certain number of islands for official use. And possibly to requisition a modest percentage of the planetary production and manpower for the fight against foreign exploitation. And a reasonable tax levy to support a portion of the expense of this selfless action is to be expected."

"I see you have a grasp of the realities of interplanetary do-goodism," Shlush acknowledged. "Now, as beings of the world, why not just give me a brief rundown on your own development plans? Don't bother going into detail; I have specialists on my staff who'll assist you later in dredging up the odd unremembered trifle from the depths of the subconscious. For now, just limit your exposition to the high points."

"You're too shrewd for me, Hivemaster," Retief conceded. "Did you think up this scheme yourself?"

"Ah-ah," Shlush chided his prisoner. "No prying, Retief. Not that it matters, of course, inasmuch as you'll soon be occupying a shallow excavation under the dungeon floor—but it's bad form tipping one's opponents off to the details of one's operations, particularly as I have no time to waste. Now—"

"On a tight schedule, eh? Tell me, Hivemaster, is Ambassador Jith in on the plan?"

"Jith is a dependable civil servant of considerable seniority," Shlush said smoothly. "It was deemed unwise to burden him with excessive detail regarding operations outside the sphere of his immediate concerns."

"Just who is your boss in this operation, Shlush?"

"Ah-ah—mustn't pry, Retief," the Groaci wagged an admonitory digit at the Terran. "Suffice it to say he's a most unusual chap, a virtual super-Groaci of most uncompromising kidney, not the sort, as he himself declares, to stand idly by while Groac is cheated of her Lumbagan patrimony! You'll meet him soon enough."

"Let me see," Retief mused aloud. "As I recall, it was a Terry tramp captain who first put Lumbaga on the star maps. He stayed long enough to peddle a few gross of glass beads and take on a cargo of salted glimp eggs; oddly enough, his report made no mention of the natives' warlike tendencies."

"Doubtless he fortuitously happened along between massacres," Shlush said tersely. "But—"

"The next time Lumbaga cropped up in an official dispatch, ten years later, was on the occasion of a run-in between a Terry survey crew and a Groaci gunboat. It appears your people were well-established here by then."

"Yes, yes—and naturally enough, they took appropriate action to discourage unauthorized tourism. Now—"

"Shooting up an unarmed survey craft was the wrong way to go about it, I'm afraid," Retief said philosophically. "Our sociological teams couldn't pass up a challenge like that. They came swarming in—with suitable escorts of Peace Enforcers, of course—to ferret out the unhappy incidents in the collective Groaci childhood that were responsible for your aggressions, and—"

"I well recall the incident; an unexampled instance of Groaci restraint in the face of Terran provocation—"

". . . and found a planetwide riot in progress," Retief continued. "They also turned up the fact that your boys were running a rather dubious traffic in hearts, lungs, and other negotiable commodities—"

"Specimens destined for Groaci zoos," Shlush snapped. "Our Groacian interest in exotic wildlife is well-known—"

"—which raised certain questions among the coarse-minded. There was even a theory afoot that you were disassembling the natives, shipping them out as Freebies, and putting them back together for use in the sand mines."

"A baseless allegation! Besides which, the practice was at once discontinued out of deference to the prejudices of the unenlightened."

"A far-sighted move, in view of the number of guns lined up on you at the time. The Interplanetary Tribunal for the Curtailment of Hostilities moved in then, and war has raged ever since."

"I am not in need of a toenail sketch of recent Lumbagan history!" Shlush hissed. "The manifold iniquities of the CDT are well known to me!" The excited hivemaster broke off as the door opened abruptly.

"To forgive this intrusion, Exalted One," the underling who had gone to fetch brandy hissed. "But—"

"To better have an explanation of surpassing eloquence," Shlush screeched, "or to dangle inverted from a torture frame ere tiffin time!"

"The best, Excellency," the unfortunate fellow whispered, advancing into the room, closely followed by a hulking Lumbagan with a single eye, three legs, an immense grin, and a large, primitive needle gun in his fist.

"To shoot him down!" Shlush hissed in his native tongue to Wilth, who stood frozen against the wall.

"To . . . to . . . have apparently forgotten to load my piece," the latter whispered, and let the impotent weapon fall with a clatter.

"Which one of you aliens is the head Groaci around here?" the newcomer demanded.

Wilth's eyestalks tilted toward his chief. The latter scronched back in his chair, eyeing the aimed pistol. "Ah—why do you ask?" he inquired cautiously.

"On account of there's a big shot that wants to see him," the Lumbagan stated, studying the four foreigners in turn.

"Better hurry; I don't know what assorted innards are bringing in the open market, but it will be less if they're full of steel splinters."

"Merely a, er, social call, I assume?" Shlush said hopefully.

"Assume whatever you like—only snap it up.

The big boy don't like to be kept waiting." The caller glanced at the Dale Evans watch strapped to his lower left wrist. "Anyway, I change sides in half an hour, and I don't like unfinished business hanging around."

"Well, I suppose one must observe the amenities," Shlush said with a certain lack of conviction, rising slowly.

"It's all right, Shlush," Retief spoke up. "It's noble of you to cover for me, but we can't fool this fellow. I'll go quietly."

"Ha! Trying to pull a fast one, hah?" The Lumbagan pointed the gun at the hivemaster's head and squinted his lone eye along the barrel. "I've got a good mind to plug you for that. But to heck with it. I got to make my own loads for this popper, so why waste one?" He motioned with the bulky weapon at Retief.

"Let's go, big boy." He paused. "Hey, you aliens all look alike to me, but it seems like you got a little different look to you, somehow." He studied Retief, comparing him with Wilth and the guard with quick-side-glances.

"Two legs," he muttered. "One torso, one head—ah! Got it! They got five eyes each, and you only got two, kind of sunk-in ones. How come?"

"Birth defect," Retief said.

"Oh, excuse me all to heck, pal. No offense. OK, pick 'em up. We got a brisk walk ahead, and the streets are full of footpads."

7

TWO OF LUMBAGA'S small pink moons were in the sky when Retief and his captor, after traversing a passage hollowed in the thick walls of the pile housing secret Groaci Headquarters, emerged into the street.

"This seems to be my night for meeting the local civic leaders," Retief commented as they turned west, toward the waterfront. "Who is it you're taking me to?"

"You'll find out," his guide said shortly, swiveling his asymmetrical head from side to side so as to bring his single eye to bear first on one side of the route ahead, then the other. "If anybody jumps us, it's every guy for hisself," he notified the Terran.

"You expecting to be attacked?" Retief inquired easily.

The alien nodded. "Naturally," he said glumly. "Why should tonight be any different than any other time?"

"I understand street battles are the Lumbagan national pastime," Retief commented. "You sound a little unenthusiastic."

"Oh, a little rumble now and then, a friendly fight in a bar, a neighborly clash in the alley, sure. I'm as normal as the next guy. But the pace is getting me down. Frankly, Mr.—what was that handle again?"

"Retief."

"I'm Gloot. Like I was saying, Retief, between you and me I'd as lief take a break—a long break—from the fray. I got enough lumps to last me, you know? And there's plenty others feel the same."

"Then why do you go on squabbling?"

"That's kind of hard to explain, to a foreigner. I'm just sashaying along, minding my own business, and all of sudden—zop! The old fighting frenzy hits me, you know what I mean?"

"I'm striving to grasp it," Retief said. "By the way, does that gun work?"

Gloot looked at the heavy pistol. "Sure. Don't worry, the first guy that jumps us will be out shopping in the morning for a new navel and a few other accessories." He shook his head mournfully. "Unfortunately, I can't say the same for the second guy."

"Single shot, eh? How's your aim?"

"Well, I ain't bragging, but I usually hit what I shoot at."

"Five xots you can't hit that sign," Retief challenged, pointing to a board swinging in the wind ahead.

"You kidding? I could drill it dead center with one eye closed—at least I could up to last week when I misplaced my best eye."

"Phooey. I heard you Lumbagans couldn't shoot your way out of a greenhouse."

"Oh, yeah?" Gloot brought the gun up, took his stance, squeezed. . . .

The *Boom* echoed along the canyonlike street like a bomb burst. As the reverberations faded, a voice somewhere ahead shouted an angry inquiry; a door slammed. Feet clattered, approaching from both directions.

"Now look what you made me go and do!" Gloot wailed. "Come on, let's get out of here!" He turned and galloped back the way they had come, ducked down an intersecting alley as a party of mismatched vigilantes in red cloaks surged into view around a turn.

"There they go!" a hoarse voice yelled. "Get the disturbance-creating rascals!"

Retief followed the sprinting Lumbagan along

the noisome way, skidded to a stop as the other's dark bulk loomed ahead.ahead.

"Up there!" Gloot croaked. "Make it quick!"

Retief found the rungs of a ladder mounting the rough masonry wall; he went up it swiftly, negotiated an overhanging cornice, pulled himself up on a slanted roof of curled tiles. A moment later Gloot scrambled up beside him. Seconds later, their pursuers blundered past below in full cry.

"Wow, that was close," Gloot breathed as silence descended again. "Those boys are the City Guard. They don't mess around."

"Permanent cadre?" Retief asked.

"Right. Eight on, eight off. Of course, most of 'em got off-duty jobs with the major mobs; but when shift time arrives they fall in for duty, even if the mob happens to be in the middle of a shoot-out with the guard at the time."

"That could be a trifle confusing."

"Yeah, but they got ground rules. When the whistle blows, there's a five-minute time-out while the cops and robbers change sides."

"A civilized system," Retief conceded.

"I guess the coast is clear—but—" Gloot looked at his watch and uttered a coarse expletive. "Now looky what you made me do, Retief! I've run over shift-end! And I would of scored a nice bonus if I would of brought you in in one major piece!"

"You could explain you were unavoidably detained—"

"What—and hand a negotiable piece of merchandise like you over to the bums I used to be teamed up with? Besides, if they saw me now they'd set on me in a trice!"

"Don't your former associates change sides at the same time you do?"

"Sure—but they go their way, I go mine. I got to agree, it's enough to confuse a foreigner. Heck, even I get mixed up sometimes." Gloot sighed as he crawled up the sloping roof to scan the view beyond. "Seems like things are getting kind of out of hand," he said sadly. "A fellow can't hardly keep track of his own affiliations these days."

"What about us aliens?" Retief asked. "How do we fit into the hostility pattern?"

"You don't. My grabbing you was strictly business. Now that I've changed sides, all bets are off. It was nice meeting you, Retief. Frankly, I'd heard you Groaci were kind of creepy little characters, but you seem like a pretty good sport. Well, cheers, I've got to try to make it down to the port now without getting my sweetbreads scrambled. Time-out's almost over, and I'll be fair game."

"Who were you taking me to, Gloot?"

"Some bum over on Groo-groo Island. Why?"

"I'd like to meet him."

"No dice. I got a previous engagement. I'm part of a harbor hijack crew now and we've got a big heist scheduled."

"Suppose I go with you?"

"Sorry, I got no time to show tourists the sights," Gloot rose and started over the ridgepole; as he did, three figures in the red cloak of the City Guard appeared, clambering over the parapet opposite.

"There they are!" a muffled voice barked. "Get 'em!" Without hesitation, Gloot charged downslope, dealt one of the three a terrific buffet on the side of the head, sending him sprawling;

but before he could regain his balance, the other two cops had grappled him and wrestled him toward the edge. Thus occupied, they failed to notice Retief until he had secured a firm grip on both capes, and with a vigorous pull, tumbled their owners backwards. Recovering quickly, Gloot upended the nearer guardsman over the parapet. The last of the three dived for Retief, met a knee under the jaw, and collapsed in a limp heap.

"Say," Gloot said, breathing hard, "that was real friendly of you, Retief."

"Or unfriendly, depending on the viewpoint," Retief pointed out.

"Right. And from my viewpoint right now you came through like a champ. Well, so long, Retief. See you across the barricades." Gloot swung over the side of the roof; Retief followed him to the ground, clambering down the rough-laid masonry to the dark street below.

"Maybe you'll reconsider that invitation to come along and meet your friends," he suggested.

"Nope. We've got a full crew already."

"Just as a diplomatic observer," Retief reassured the local. "Naturally, I couldn't participate in anything violent."

Gloot shook his head. "Those boys upstairs are going to be kind of irritated when they come to. Us hijackers have got enough troubles without taking on a foreigner, with or without a police record. If I was you, I'd kind of drop out of sight for a few hours."

"Good idea. Aboard your boat would be a good place to be inconspicuous."

Gloot lifted his gun from its holster and

thumbed back the hammer. "I ain't going to have to get rough, I hope?" he said, rather sadly.

"Not with that," Retief said. "Single-shot, remember?"

"Oh, barfberries," Gloot exclaimed, eyeing the bulky weapon in irritation. "I should of known you didn't gull me into shooting it off for nothing." He studied Retief appraisingly. "I don't feel like tangling with you, not after the way you handled those bums on the roof. And besides, I'm short an arm right now, on account of a chum asked me to lend him a hand and forgot to return it. Why not just go your way and I'll go mine."

"I want to know who's been trying to kidnap me, Gloot. You can still take me along to this big shot, and demand a nice ransom for me."

"Hey—the idea ain't without merit. . . ." Gloot said with cautious enthusiasm. "But don't look for any favors. The boys play rough, and this is their night to chew stones and spit gravel."

"I'll try to stay out of harm's way."

"A sixty-foot pirate sloop's kind of a funny place for that," Gloot said. "But—that's your problem, not mine—just so you stay alive long enough for me to collect."

8

AN ODOR OF ripe seafood and rotting wood rose from the lateen-rigged junk wallowing as it half

sunk at the sagging wharf. A bulky Lumbagan
with the usual random placement of facial features stepped out of the shadows to bar Gloot's
way as he approached.

"Hi, Snult," the latter called in guarded tones.
"This here is Retief. He came along to get an
alien's-eye view of the operation."

"Yeah?" Snult replied without detectable enthusiasm. He barked a command over his shoulder; two large locals with exceptional tricep
development stepped forward.

"Dump this spy in the drink," Snult grunted,
pointing to Retief. "And then hang Gloot to the
yardarm for half an hour for reporting in late." He
turned his back and sauntered off. The two
bullyboys advanced, reaching for Retief in a busi-
nesslike way. He leaned aside, caught the proffered arm of the nearer and gave it a half twist,
causing its owner to spin around and bow from
the waist, at which point an accurately placed foot
propelled the unfortunate chap off the pier. The
second enforcer lunged, met a chop to the neck,
followed by a set of stiffened fingers to the midriff.
As he doubled over, Retief turned him gently by
the elbow and assisted him over the side, where
his splash mingled with that of his partner. Ten
feet away, Snult paused.

"Quick work," he said over his shoulder.
"But . . . two splashes . . . ?"

Gloot stepped to his departing chief, seized him
by the back of the neck and unceremoniously
pitched him into the water.

"Three," he corrected, and thrust out a large,
six-fingered hand to Retief. "The cruise is off to a
good start. We've been needing a change of ad-
ministration around here. Come on, let's hoist an-

chor before a platoon of cops come pelting down
the dock looking for you." He swaggered down
the gangplank bawling orders.

There were a few questions from the crew who,
however, quickly adjusted to the change in management, assisted by a number of sharp blows
from a belaying pin wielded by the new captain.
In a matter of minutes the ancient vessel had cast
off and was threading her way out across the
garbage-strewn waters of the bay.

"The target for tonight is a shipment of *foof*
bark," Gloot advised his guest as they relaxed on
the high poop deck at the stern an hour later,
quaffing large mugs of native ale and admiring the
view of the moonlit jungle isle past which they
were sailing. "It comes from Delerion, another
few islands to the west. Potent stuff, too. A pinch
of *foof* in your hookah and you're cruising at fifty
thousand feet without oxygen."

"Dope traffic, eh? Is that legal?"

"No law on the high seas," Gloot said. "And
damn little on land. I guess you'd call the *foof*
trade semilegit. They pay taxes—if the free-lance
customs boys are sharp enough to collect 'em.
And they place a few bribes here and there. However, they overlooked the good ship *Peccadillo*
and her merry crew, which makes 'em fair game."
He peered across the oily ripples. "She ought to
be rounding the point of that next island
and weathering right into your trap any minute
now."

"You seem to know a lot about the opposition's
movements," Retief commented.

"I ought to—I heard all about it last week when
I was a *foof*-gatherer."

"I didn't know you Lumbagans changed islands as well as affiliations."

"I was a prisoner of war down there. I managed an escape during the changing of the guard. By the way, keep a few sharp eyes out for a low-slung boat with a big carbon arc light on deck. Inter-island Police. They're supposed to be up at the other end of the line now, but you never can tell."

"I can see you've done your homework, Gloot."

"Sure; I got the schedules down pat last time I was on the force."

"Don't these rapid changes of allegiance get confusing?" Retief inquired. "I'd think you'd run the risk of accidentally shooting yourself under the impression you were on the opposite side."

"I guess you can get used to anything," Gloot said philosophically.

"There's Groo-groo coming up on the starboard bow," Retief said. "Isn't it about time to start tacking in?"

Gloot yawned. "Later, maybe," he said. "I decided maybe it's too much trouble trying to ransom you. I prefer life on the briny deep to floundering around in the creepers—" He was interrupted by a shout from the masthead; jumping up, he aimed a spyglass toward a dimly seen shape gliding closer across the dark water.

"Oh-oh—get set. That looks like . . . yep—it's them! Hey, Blump!" Gloot sprang to the companionway. "Hard aport! And keep it quiet!"

As the unwieldy craft came sluggishly about, a dazzling yard-wide shaft of smoky blue light lanced across the water, etching the privateer's crew in chalky white against the velvet black of shadows.

"Heave to, you bilge scum!" an amplified voice bellowed from the direction of the light, "before I put a solid shot into your waterline!"

"We're in trouble," Gloot rapped. "That's old Funge on the bullhorn; I'd know his voice anywhere. One of the best pirate captains around, when he's working the other side of the street."

"Do we strike, Cap'n?" a crewman cried from amidships.

"Remind me to keelhaul you when this is over!" Gloot roared. "Strike nothing! Swing our stern chaser around and run it out over the port rail!" He charged across the deck, sharply canted by the abrupt maneuver in which the elderly tub was engaged, as the sailors dragged the small wheeled cannon into position.

"Load with cannister; double-charge!" he yelled. "Get a firepot up here! Hold her steady on a coarse of one-eight-oh, and stand by to come about fast!" He turned to Retief who was standing nearby, observing the preparations for action.

"Better get below, Mister," he snapped. "This is no place for noncombatants!"

"If you don't mind, I'll stick around on deck. And if I may make a suggestion, it might be a good idea to steer for shore."

"For shore? You must be hysterical with panic! Everybody knows Groo-groo is swarming with carnivores that are all stomach and teeth, with just enough legs to let 'em leap on their prey from forty feet away."

"In that case, I hope you're a strong swimmer."

"Don't worry, Retief, those revenue agents are lousy shots—" Gloot's reassurances were interrupted by a flash and a *Boom!* and the whistling passage of a projectile that sailed high overhead to raise a column of water a hundred yards to starboard.

"I see what you mean," Retief said. "Nevertheless, I think you're about to lose your command." He pointed with his cigar at the water sluicing across the buckled planks of the deck. "We're sinking."

As he spoke, cries rose from the crew, who suddenly found themselves ankle-deep in seawater. Gloot groaned.

"I guess I took that last corner too fast; she's opened her seams!"

A breaker rolled across the deck. A crewman, swept off his feet, went under with a despairing cry. As the vessel wallowed, the waters surged, rushed back across the half-submerged planking, swirling around Retief's shins. The crewman was no longer in evidence; instead, a swarm of disassociated parts splashed in the brine, as the Lumbagan's formerly independent components resumed their free-swimming status, making instinctively for shore.

"Well, so long, Retief," Gloot cried. "Maybe our various limbs and organs will meet up again in some future arrangement—" he broke off. "Ah—sorry, I forgot your hookup is a one-time deal. Tough lines, Retief. Take a last look around, here we go. . . ."

"Let's swim for it, it's not far."

"Well, I guess you could do that if you want to prolong the process. As for me, I'd as soon get it over with—"

"And miss finding out if the superstitions are true? Come on, Gloot, last one ashore's an amputated leg." Retief dived over the side. He stroked hard against the suction created by the sinking hulk, surfaced in time to see the tip of the mast descend slowly from sight amid a vigorous boiling of water strewn with flotsam from the ill-fated *Peccadillo*. Multitudes of Singletons which had formerly constituted the privateer's complement churned the waves, heading instinctively for shore. A ragged cheer went up from the revenue cutter.

Gloot bobbed up a few yards away. "She was my first command," he said sadly. "I guess maybe she was put together a little too much like us Lumbagans."

"A melancholy moment," Retief acknowledged. He shrugged out of his jacket, pulled off his shoes and thrust them into his side pockets and set off at an easy crawl, Gloot dog-paddling beside him. It was a cool evening, but the water was pleasantly warm, mildly saline. Groo-groo congealed from the darkness ahead, resolving itself into a cluster of rhubarb-shaped trees above a pale streak which widened into a curving beach. They rode the breakers in, grounding on coarse coral sand, and waded in through tidal pools to shore. Ahead dark jungle loomed, impenetrable in the dim light of the moons, now obscured by ragged clouds.

The Lumbagan tested the wind, all ears angled to attitudes of total alertness.

"Hear something?" Retief asked.

"Yeah," the Lumbagan breathed. "Kind of a stealthy slosh."

"That's just the water running out of your boots," Retief pointed out.

"Huh? Oh, yeah."

The lesser moon emerged from behind the clouds. Retief scanned the beach, noted a small keg half-buried in the pink sand, the word RUM stenciled on the end.

"At least we won't want for basic supplies," he commented as he extricated the container. "You're about to sample Terry booze, Gloot."

"Not bad," the local commented five minutes later, after the puncheon had been broached with a lump of coral and the contents sampled. "It kind of burns, but my stomach kind of likes it. In fact"—he paused to hiccup—"I like it all over. Actually, I just suddenly realized life is just a bowl of bloopberries, now that my vision has improved—"

"I see you're one of those affectionate drunks," Retief said as Gloot flung an arm about his shoulders. "Better take it easy, Gloot. You may need all your faculties intact for the evening ahead."

"Take it easy? I only had one li'l old swallow. And what's scheduled for the evening? Fun? Gaiety? Wine, song, and crossword puzzles?"

"More of a cross-track puzzle," Retief corrected. "Look." He pointed to a three-toed footprint deeply impressed in the sand.

Gloot studied the impressions. "Ha! I've got it!" he caroled. "Terries—just like my old buddy Shlush!"

"I doubt it," Retief said. "Aside from the fact that they're eighteen inches long—"

"So they're big Terries!" Gloot held a large, flat hand over his head. "This high!" He glanced up at the hand and seemed to sober abruptly. "This high?"

"That's a little high for a Terry, especially the kind you have in mind," Retief said. He followed the tracks, which led up across the wet sand to the edge of the forest.

"Let's go find the big Terries and have a li'l party," Gloot proposed cheerfully. "All palsies together."

"I understood you didn't care for Terries, Gloot."

"That was then," Gloot cried gaily. "This is now. Terries are my pals, the Groaci are my pals—everybody's my pals, even this little fellow," he added as a small free-flying pineal gland fluttered about his head. "Kootchie-koo—ain't it cute, Retief?" he added as it landed on his head.

"A most appealing organ," Retief agreed. "But I think you'd better lower your voice."

"What for? Somebody snoozing?" Gloot stood, weaving slightly. "Tell the little guys with the hammers to go away," he mumbled, groping at his scalp; there was a sudden flutter as the visitor departed hurriedly. Gloot sat down hard on the sand.

"Tell 'em to turn off the sireens and the bright lights," he moaned, "and take the stewed gym shoes out of my mouth. . . ."

"Congratulations, Gloot," Retief said. "I think you broke the galactic speed record for hangovers."

"Wha? Oh, it's you, Retief. Lucky you happened along. I just been set upon by a strong-arm mob and worked over with lead pipes. Which way'd they go?" Gloot staggered to his feet.

"You were too much for them," Retief reassured his companion. "They fled in various directions."

"Yah, the yellowbellies," Gloot muttered. "Oh, my skull."

"Where on the island does this big shot hang out?" Retief asked.

"Beats me. I was to of been met on the beach."

"Let's take a look around," Retief suggested, studying the looming woods above them. "You check that way"—he pointed to the south—"and I'll have a look up here."

Gloot grunted assent and moved off. Retief followed the curve of the shore for a distance of a hundred yards before the beach narrowed and was pinched out by a rocky ridge extending down from the forest-clad slope above. There were no tracks, no empty beer bottles, no signs of animate life. He returned to the starting point. Gloot was nowhere in sight. He followed the Lumbagan's bootprints as they wove unsteadily across the sand, then turned toward the nearest tongue of forest. Directly under a stout branch extending from the mass of foliage, the trail ended. Above, barely visible among the obscuring leaves, was the freshly cut end of a coarsely woven rope.

9

RETIEF STUDIED THE ground. Other footprints were visible here, but Gloot's were not among them. The marks leading away from the spot, he noted, were deeply impressed in the sand, as if the

owners had been burdened by a heavy weight—
presumably that of the Lumbagan.

Retief started off along the clearly marked spoor
leading up into the deep woods. The darkness
here was almost total. Creatures of the night
creaked, chirred, and wailed in the treetops. An
intermittent wind made groaning sounds among
the boughs. Nearer at hand, something creaked
faintly. Retief halted, faded back against the
knobby-barked bole of a giant tree.

A minute passed in silence. Just ahead, a small
figure emerged cautiously from the underbrush; a
curiously truncated Lumbagan, advancing in a
stealthy crouch. Gripping a stout club in a cluster
of fists, the native advanced cautiously, peering
under bushes and behind trees as he came. Retief
silently circled the sheltering trunk, stepped out
behind the stranger and cleared his throat. With a
thin yell, the native sprang straight into the air
and struck the ground running, but with a quick
grab Retief snared him by the garland of teeth
encircling his neck.

"I'm looking for a friend of mine," Retief said in
the native tongue. "I don't suppose you've seen
him."

"Him monster like you?" the terrified captive
squeaked, hooking a finger under his necklace to
ease the strain.

"Another type of monster entirely," Retief said;
he gave a succinct description of his traveling
companion.

"Negative, Sahib. Tribe belong me not nab
monster fitting that description. By the way, how
about letting go ceremonial collar before I suffer
embarrassment of bite own head off."

"You'd be more comfortable if you'd stop tugging," Retief pointed out.

"Against instinct not try get away from monster," the native explained.

"Curious; a moment ago I had the distinct impression you were trying to get closer to me."

"Iron maiden on other foot now. You eat now, or save for snack?"

"I'll wait, thanks. Is your village near here?"

"Usually don't stop to chat with stranger," the captive muttered, "but in this case looks like best bet to increase longevity. Monster right, I citizen of modest town half mile up trail."

"I'd like to pay it a visit. How about acting as guide?"

"I got choice in matter?"

"Certainly," Retief said. "You can either lead me there or take the consequences."

"Most likely lead monster there and take consequences. Chief Boobooboo not like stranger poking around."

"In that case you can introduce me. Retief's the name. What's yours?"

"Zoof; but probably change to Mud, once chief get eyeful of humiliating circumstances attending surprise visit."

"Actually, Zoof, it's not absolutely necessary that I lead you there by the neck, if you'll promise not to run out on me."

"Got funny feeling monster run faster than me anyway. OK, it's deal. I lead you to village; when you get there, you look over menu, maybe pick choicer specimen."

"It's a promise." Retief said. "Nice teeth," he added as he disengaged his hand from the necklace. "Local product?"

"Nope, fancy imported, guaranteed solid plastic." Zoof started through the dense woods, Retief close behind. "No catchum real tooth these days. Life in woods going to hell in handcart. Monsters ruin hunting, lucky make deal with Five-eyes monster for steady supply grits and gravy."

"The Five-eyes you refer to wouldn't by any chance be Groaci?"

"Could be. Shiny-leg city slicker, same big like me, all time whisper, like offer deal on hot canoe."

"That's Ambassador Jith to the life. But I wasn't aware his interests extended this far back into the brush."

"Sure, small monster go everywhere, do everything. All time ride giant bird, make stink, noise, pile up stone, while big monster trample underbrush, rig net, hunt, eat—"

"What do these big monsters look like?" Retief inquired.

"Take look in mirror sometime, see for self."

"They're Terrans—like me?"

Zoof twisted his head to study Retief. "Nope, not exact same, maybe. Not so much eyes. Some got more. Some two time so big like you, tear head off, eat one bite—"

"Have you seen the monsters yourself?"

"You bet; see you, see Five-eyes, hear plenty rumor fill in gaps in information."

"Are there any Groaci at your village now?"

"We find out," Zoof said. "Home town just ahead." He led the way another fifty feet and halted.

"Well, what monster think of place?"

Retief studied the gloomy forest around him, insofar as he could see in no way different from the previous half mile of woods.

"It's unspoiled, I'll say that for it," he commented. "Is this Main Street?"

"Monster kidding? Is snazzy residential section, plenty tight zoning, you bet. Come on, we find chief and boys over at favorite hangout, Old Log."

"A bar?"

"Nope, just swell place root for grubs."

"I take it the Grubs aren't a ball team?"

"More of hors d'oeuvre," Zoof corrected. He led the way through a dense stand of forest patriarchs, emerged in a small, open glade where half a dozen Lumbagans, differing wildly in detail, wandered apparently aimlessly, gazing at the ground. With a sharp cry, one pounced, came up with a wriggling creature which he thrust into a sack at his waist.

"My grasp of Lumbagan zoology is somewhat hazy," Retief said. "How do these grubs fit into the general biological picture?"

"Play essential role," Zoof replied. "Grub grow up be kidney, jawbone, kneecap, you name it."

"So much for future generations. Still, it's no worse than eating eggs, I suppose."

"Not eat 'em," Zoof corrected. "Collect, sell to skinny-leg monster, get plenty Colonel Sanders fried chicken and other exotic chow, you bet."

The grub hunters had interrupted their search to stare inhospitably at Retief.

"Hey, Chief," Zoof greeted his leader, "this monster name Retief, express desire meet jungle big shot. Retief, shake grasping member of Chief Boobooboo, son of Chief Booboo, son of Chief Boob."

"Grandpa name Boo, not Boob," the chief corrected sternly. "Why you want me, monster? Zoof not look tender?"

"Actually I was looking for a friend—"

"Hmm, neat switch. Usual custom eat enemy, but after all, why be prejudice? Eat chum too, get varied diet." Boobooboo looked appraisingly at Zoof.

"As it happens, I've already eaten," Retief said. "The friend I'm looking for seems to have been involved in an incident involving a rope."

"Monster bark up wrong flagpole," the Chief stated. "Unsophisticated aborigine unequal to technical challenge of make rope."

"Any idea who might have snared him?"

"Sure."

"Possibly you'd confide in me."

"Why?"

"I don't suppose the simple desire to do a good turn would be sufficient motivation?"

"Not *that* unsophisticated," Boobooboo said flatly. "Good time remember ancient folk wisdom embodied in old tribal saying: What's In It For Me?"

"What about a firm promise of a year's supply of pizza pies?"

"Not much nourishment in promise," the Chief pointed out. "Got better idea. . . ." Boobooboo lowered his voice. "Know where big supply eatables located; you help collect, maybe I get bighearted and tell all."

"I think I'd prefer a more definite commitment," Retief said. "Strike out the 'maybe' and we might be able to get together."

"Sure; just stuck 'maybe' in so have something to concede."

"I see I'm dealing with a pro," Retief acknowledged. "*En passant,* where is this food supply located?"

"Half mile that direction." The chief pointed. "Enough chow for whole tribe from now to next St. Swithin's Day."

"I take it you've actually seen the groceries for yourself?"

"Sure, same time deliver."

"I see: you plan to hijack the supplies you've been selling to the Graoci."

"Hijack loaded word. Just say decide to share wealth with underprivileged. Monsters got wealth, we got underprivilege."

"At the present rate, Chief, I predict your supply of unsophistication won't last out the winter. But why do you need my help? You have enough troops to stage a raid on your own."

"Monster not get big picture. Skinny-legs spoilsport hide comestibles away inside magic cave, patrol perimeter with plenty fearsome monster, tear a simple tribesman apart with two hands while hunt fleas with rest."

"And you think I can penetrate this fortress?"

"Maybe not; but better you than me and boys; we just simple pastoral types; hunt, fish, steal, not go in for heavy work."

"On the whole, Chief Boobooboo, the proposition doesn't sound overwhelmingly attractive."

"I figure maybe you feel that way; so save snapper for end: you come here ask about missing buddy? Monster in luck; get economical combination deal. Kidnapped pal same place victuals. Get two for price of one."

"I think," Retief said, "I've been outmaneuvered."

A quarter of an hour later, Retief and Chief

Boobooboo, attended by Zoof and the bulk of the truncated tribesmen, stood in the shelter of a giant mumble tree, the soft mutterings of its foliage covering the sound of their conversation.

"Straight ahead, can't miss it," Boobooboo was saying. "But watch snares; you get caught same way absent chum, deal off."

"Understood, Chief. And you'll keep your people posted in position to create a diversion in the event I have to leave the vicinity in haste."

"Correct; we stand by, catch any wandering grub come galloping past."

"It's been a pleasure dealing with you, Chief. If you ever decide to give up the rural way of life, drop me a line. The Corps could use your talents instructing a course in naïveté."

"Thanks, Retief. Keep offer in mind in case present caper not pan out."

The forest was silent as Retief made his way along the dimly marked trail, but for a stealthy rustling in the undergrowth which ceased when he halted, began again when he went on. He had covered perhaps a hundred and fifty yards when he rounded an abrupt turn and was face to face with twelve feet of tusked nightmare.

10

FOR A MOMENT Retief stood unmoving, studying the monstrosity looming gigantic ten feet away. Its bleary, pinkish eyes, three in number, stared unwinking at him from a lumpy face equipped with tufted whiskers placed at random around a vast, loose-lipped mouth and a scattering of gaping nostrils. From its massive shoulders, immense arms hung almost to the ground; three bowed legs supported the weight of a powerfully muscled torso. The big fellow's generous pedal extremities were housed in gigantic sneakers with round black reinforcing patches over the anklebones. A long tail curled up over one clavicle, ending in a seven-fingered hand with which the creature was exploring the interior of a large, pointed ear. Other hands gripped a naked two-edged sword at least nine feet in length.

Retief took a hand-rolled Jorgenson's cigar from an inside pocket, puffed it alight, blew out pale violet smoke.

"Nice night," he said.

The monster drew a deep breath. "AHHHrrrghhh!" it bellowed.

"Sorry," Retief said, "I didn't quite catch that remark."

"AHHHrrrghhh!" the creature repeated.

Retief shook his head. "You're still not getting through."

"Ahhrrgh?"

"You do it well," Retief said. "Exceptionally nice timbre. Real feeling."

"You really like it?" the giant said in a surprisingly high-pitched voice. "Gee, thanks a lot."

"I don't know when I've seen it done better. But is that all there is?"

"You mean it ain't enough?"

"I'm perfectly satisfied," Retief assured his new acquaintance. "I just wanted to be sure there wasn't an encore."

"I practiced it plenty," the oversized Lumbagan said. "I wouldn't of wanted to of did it wrong."

"Certainly not. By the way, what does it mean?"

"How do I know? Who tells me anything? I'm just old Smelch, which everybody pushes me around on account of I'm easygoing, you know?"

"I think I met a relative of yours in town, Smelch. Unfortunately I had to rush away before we really had a chance to chat."

"Yeah? Well, I heard a few of the boys was to of been took for a glom at the bright lights. But not me. No such luck."

"You don't happen to know who's been down for a barefoot stroll on the shore do you, Smelch?" the Terran inquired casually. "A party with three-toed feet."

"Three? Lessee." Smelch's tail-mounted hand scratched at his mottled scalp with a sound reminiscent of a spade striking marl. "That'd be more'n one, and less than nine, right?"

"You're narrowing the field," Retief said encouragingly.

"If I just knew how many nine was, I'd be in business," Smelch muttered. "That ain't nothing like say, six, fer example?"

"Close, but no dope stick. Skip that point, Smelch, I didn't mean to get technical. Were you waiting for anything special when I came along?"

"You bet: my relief."

"When's he due?"

"Well, lessee: I come out here a while back, and been here for quite a time, so what does that leave? Say—half a hour?"

"More like a jiffy and a half, give or take a few shakes of a lamb's tail. What's up at the top of the trail?"

"That's what nobody ain't supposed to know."

"Why not?"

"On account of it's like a secret, see?"

"I'm beginning to get a glimmering. Who says it's a secret?"

Smelch's fingernail abraded his chin with a loud roaching sound.

"That's supposed to be another secret." Smelch's features rearranged themselves in what might have been a puzzled frown. "What I can't figure is—if it's a secret, how come you know about it?"

"Word gets around," Retief said reassuringly. "OK if I go up and have a look?"

"Maybe you ought to identify yourself first. Not that I don't trust you, but you know how it is."

"Certainly. I'm Retief, Smelch." He shook the hand at the end of the tail, which returned the grip firmly.

"Sorry about the routine, Retief, but these days a guy can't be too careful."

"What about?"

Smelch blinked all three eyes in rotation, a vertiginous effect.

"I get it," he said, "that's what you call a joke, right? I'm nuts about jokes; only the trouble is usually nobody tells me about 'em in time to laugh."

"It's a problem that often plagues ambassadors, Smelch. But don't worry; I'll be sure to tip you off in advance next time."

"Gee, you're a all-right guy, Retief, even if you are kind of a runt and all, no offense."

The sound of heavy feet came from uptrail; a squat, five-foot figure lumbered into view, as solidly built as Smelch but less beautiful, his various arms, legs, and ears having been arranged with a fine disregard for standard patterns. One of his five hands gripped a fifteen-foot harpoon; his four eyes, on six-inch stalks, goggled atop a flattened skull which gave the appearance of having been matured inside a hot-water bottle.

"About time, Flunt," Smelch greeted the newcomer. "You're a shake and a half late."

"Spare me any carping criticisms," Flunt replied in a tone of long-suffering weariness. "I've just come from an interview with that bossy little—" He broke off, looking Retief up and down. "Well, you might at least offer an introduction," he said sharply to Smelch, extending a hand to the diplomat. "I'm Flunt. Pardon my appearance—" He indicated two uncombed fringes of purplish-blue filaments springing from just below his cheekbones. "But I just washed my hide and I can't do a *thing* with it."

"Not at all," Retief said ambiguously, giving Flunt's feet a quick glance: they were bare, and remarkably human-looking. "My name's Retief."

"Goodness, I hope I'm not interrupting anything," Flunt said, looking questioningly from one to the other.

"Not at all. Smelch and I were just passing the time of night. Interesting little island, Flunt. See many strangers here?"

"Gracious, I hope not. I'm supposed to do dreadful things if I do—" Flunt broke off, gave Retief a startled look. "Ah, you aren't by any chance a stranger . . . ?"

"Are you kidding?" Smelch spoke up. "He's Retief, like I told you."

"Just so you're sure. Little Sir Nasty-nice wouldn't like it a bit if any outsiders sneaked a peek at his precious whatever-it-is. Really, for this job one needs eyes in the back of one's head!"

"Yeah," Smelch said. "Lucky you got 'em."

"Flunt, do you know anyone with three-toed feet in these parts?" Retief asked.

"Three-toed feet? Hmmm. They're a bit passé this season, of course—but I think I've seen a few around. Why?" His voice lowered confidentially. "If you're interested in picking up half a dozen at a bargain price, I think I may be able to put you onto a good thing."

"I might be," Retief said. "When could I meet the owners?"

"Oh, I don't think you'd like that," Flunt said soberly. "No, I don't think you'd like that at all, at all. And neither would little Mr. Sticky-fingers, now that I reflect on it. Actually, I shouldn't have mentioned the matter. My blunder. Forget I said anything about it."

"Come on, Retief," Smelch said loudly. "Me and you'll just take a little ankle up the trail, which I'll point out the points of interest and like that." He gave the Terran an elaborate three-eyed wink.

"Capital idea, Smelch," Retief agreed.

"Look here, Smelch," Flunt said nervously, "you're not going to go sneaking around you-know-where and getting you-know-who all upset about you-know-what?"

"I do?" Smelch looked pleased.

"Maybe you don't; it's been dinned into your head hourly all your life, but then you've only been around for a week. . . ." Flunt turned to Retief.

"I hate to sound finicky, Retief, but if this um-myday tries to ipslay you into, well, anyplace you shouldn't eebay, well . . . one has one's job to do." He fingered the barbed head of his harpoon meaningfully.

"I can give you a definite tentative hypothetical assurance on that," Retief said crisply. "But don't hold me to it."

"Well, in that case. . . ." Retief felt Flunt's eyes on him as he and Smelch moved up the trail toward whatever lay above.

11

FOR THE FIRST hundred yards, nothing untoward disturbed the silence of the forest at night—nothing other than the normal quota of chirps, squeaks, and scuttlings that attested to the activities of the abundant wildlife of the region.

Then, without warning, a gigantic shape charged from the underbrush. Smelch, in the lead, late in swinging his broad-headed spear around, took the brunt of the charge solidly against his chest. His explosive grunt was almost drowned in the sound of the collision, not unlike that of an enraged rhino charging a Good Humor wagon. The antagonists surged to and fro, trampling shrubbery, shaking trees, grunting like beached walruses. Suddenly the stranger bent his knees, rammed his head into Smelch's midriff, and rose, Smelch spread-eagled across his shoulders. He pivoted sharply, went into a dizzying twirl, and hurled the unfortunate victim from him to hurtle into the undergrowth, snapping off a medium-sized tree in the process. The victor paused only long enough to beat out a rapid tattoo on his chest and wait until a brief coughing fit passed before whirling on Retief. The Terran sidestepped the dimly seen monster's first rush, which carried the latter well into the thicket beside the path. As he threshed about there, roaring, Smelch reemerged from the opposite side of the route, shaking his head and muttering. The stranger came crashing back onto the scene only to be met by two lefts and a right haymaker that halted him in his tracks.

"Sorry about that, Retief," Smelch said contritely, as his antagonist toppled like a felled oak. "But the mug got my dander up, which he shouldn't ought to of come out leading with his chin anyways."

"A neat one-two-three," Retief commented, blowing a plume of smoke toward the fallen fighter. "Let's take a closer look." He parted the brush to look down at the casualty who lay

sprawled on his back, out cold. The ten-foot-tall
figure was remarkably conservative for a Lumbagan, he thought: only two legs and arms, a single
narrow head with close-set paired eyes, a lone
nose and mouth, an unimpressive chin. The feet,
clearly outlined inside rawhide buskins, featured
five toes each, matching the hands' ten fingers.

"What's the matter?" Smelch said. "You know
the mug?"

"No, but he bears a certain resemblance to a
colleague of mine."

"Jeez, the poor guy. Well, beauty ain't everything. Anyways, here's your chance to pick up a
set of dogs at a steal, if you know what I mean." He
rammed an elbow toward Retief's ribs, a com-
radely gesture capable of collapsing a lung had it
landed.

"I think I'll pass up the opportunity this time,"
Retief said, stepping forward to investigate a
strand of barbed wire vaguely discernible in the
gloom. It was one of three, he discovered, running
parallel to the trail, firmly attached to stout posts.

"Retief, we better blow," Smelch said. "Like
Flunt said, nobody but nobody don't want to poke
his noses and stuff in too close around you-
know-where."

"Actually, I don't think I do," Retief corrected
his massive acquaintance. "Know where, I
mean."

"Good," Smelch said in a relieved tone. "You're
safer that way."

"Not afraid, are you?"

"Yeah." Smelch nodded his head vigorously. "I
hear they got ways of making a guy regret the day
his left leg met up with his right."

"Who says so?"

"Everybody, Retief! All the boys been warned to stay clear, once they was outside. . . ."

"You mean you've been inside?"

"Sure." Smelch looked puzzled, an expression involving a rapid twitching of his ears. "How could I of not been?"

"Flunt's been there too?"

"Natch. You don't figure the moomy-bird brung him, do you? That's a little joke, Retief. I know you know the moomy-bird didn't bring him."

"How about this fellow?" Retief indicated the unconscious Lumbagan stretched at his feet. "He came from inside too?"

Smelch clucked sympathetically. "I guess they must of left out some o' your marbles, Retief. Where else would Zung of come from? In fact"— he lowered his voice confidentially—"he ain't never graduated, poor sucker."

"Maybe you'd care to amplify that remark a little, Smelch."

"Zung is one of the boys which they ain't been allowed out in the big, wonderful world like you and me." Smelch spread several hands expansively. "Except only maybe a few feet to clobber anybody that comes along. What I figure is. . . ." He lowered his voice to a solemn hush. "Him and the other ones, they ain't all there, you know? Rejects, like."

"Rejects from what, Smelch?"

"Shhh." Smelch looked around worriedly. "I don't like the trend of the conversation, which we're treading on shaky ground, especially this close to you-know-what."

"No, but I think it's time I found out."

"Hey—you ain't planning on climbing the fence?"

"Unless you know where the gate is."

"Sure—right up the trail about a hundred yards, or maybe ten. I ain't too precise on the fine detail work."

"Then I'll be off, Smelch; give my regards to Flunt when you see him."

"You're really going to sneak back into you-know-where and grab a peek at you-know-what? Boy oh boy, if you-know-who sees you—"

"I know. Thanks for clarifying matters. By the way, if you should run into a fellow with three legs who answers to the name of Gloot, I'd appreciate any help you could give him."

"Sure; you let me know if we see him."

"We?"

"Heck, yes. You don't think I'm going in there alone, do you? And we better get moving. Zung's starting to twitch."

As they proceeded silently up the path, Retief was again aware of the soft rustlings and snufflings he had noted on and off since his arrival on the island. Through a gap in the shrubbery he caught a fleeting glimpse of a stealthy figure which ducked out of sight as he paused. He went on; the rustling progress of his shadower resumed.

The gate—a wide construction of aluminum panels and barbed wire—blocked the trail a hundred feet above the point where they had encountered Zung. A green-shaded spotlight outlined it starkly against the foliage. A padlock the size of an alarm clock dangled from a massive hasp.

"Any more guards hidden out around the area?" Retief asked.

"Naw—with Flunt and me doing a tight security job down below, and the other bum working in close, who needs it?"

"An incisive point." Retief conceded. They walked boldly up to the gate. Smelch tried it, seemed surprised when it failed to swing open.

"Looks like it's stuck," he commented, and ripped it from its hinges, lock and all, tossing the crumpled panels aside with a metallic crash.

"Nothing like direct action," Retief said admiringly. "But from this point on I suggest we observe a trifle more caution, just in case there's anyone up there whose suspicions might be aroused by the sound of a three-car collision this far from the nearest highway."

"Say, pretty shrewd," Smelch said admiringly. "I always wanted to team up with a guy which he could figure the angles."

Beyond the former gate, the path continued a few yards before debouching into a wide cleared strip adjoining a high board fence that extended for some distance in each direction.

"Home, sweet home," Smelch said nostalgically. "The old place sure has changed since I ventured out into the great world."

"Has it?"

"Sure. After all, that was a couple hours ago."

"This is where you were born and raised, in other words."

"Yeah—inside the fence is where I spent my happy childhood, all four days of it."

"I'd like to see the old place."

"Well, old Sneakyfeet won't like it—but to heck

with him and his dumb rules. Who but a alumnus
would want to look inside anyways? Come on,
Retief." Smelch led the way to an inconspicuous
gate which yielded to his efforts, not without a
certain amount of splintering. Retief propped the
door back in place and turned to regard an exten-
sive array of ranked cages stacked in long aisles
that led away in the moonlight to the far line of the
fence. A dispirited yammering chorus of sound
started up nearby, reminiscent of visiting day at a
pet hospital. A vaguely zoolike odor hung in the
air.

Retief approached the nearest row of cages. In
the first, a creature resembling a rubber rutabaga
with spidery legs slumped dolefully against the
bars. Adjacent, a pair of apprehensive-looking
ankles huddled together for warmth.

"Freebies," Smelch said. "Just in from the
jungle. Little do the poor little fellers dream what
a high class destiny's in store for 'em."

"What destiny *is* in store for them, Smelch?"

"Right this way," the Lumbagan invited, indicating the next rank of cages. These were somewhat larger than those in the first section, each
containing a creature giving the appearance of
having been assembled from spare parts. Here a
spindly leg drummed the fingers of a lone hand
springing from where a foot might have been expected; there a bored-looking lower lip, flanked
by a pair of generous ears, sprang directly from an
unmistakable elbow. In the next echelon, the
cages were still larger, occupied by specimens of a
more sophisticated appearance. A well-
developed paunch with a trio of staring brown
eyes at the top squatted on four three-toed feet,

watching the visitors incuriously. A remarkably human-looking head with a full beard swung from the roof of its prison by the muscular arm that was its sole appendage.

"Uh, some o' the boys look a little weird," Smelch said apologetically, "but in the end they mostly turn out handsome devils, like me."

"Someone seems to have gone to considerable trouble to set up this lonelyhearts farm," Retief commented. "In the natural state, I understand, matches among Freebies take place at rare intervals. This looks like mass production. Any idea why, Smelch?"

"Nope. I ain't one of them guys which he asts questions all the time, you know what I mean? I mean, why poke the old nostrils in and maybe get 'em stuffed full of lint, right?"

"It's a philosophy without which bureaucracy as we know it would soon wither away," Retief conceded. "What was your job when you were here, Smelch?"

"Well, lessee, there was eating. That took a lot o' my time. Then there was sleeping. I like that pretty good. Then . . . lessee . . . I guess that just about wraps it up. Why?"

"You must have a strong union," Retief said. "Why were you here?"

"Jeez, you know that's a question which a guy could wonder about it a long time if he wouldn't drop off to sleep first. Personally, I got like a theory that before we can attack the problem of transcendentalism, we got to examine the nature of knowledge and its limitations, making a appropriate distinction between noumena and phenomena. I figure by coordinating perceptions by means of rationally evolved concepts of understanding we can proceed to the analysis of experience and arrive at the categorical imperative, with its implicit concomitants. Get what I mean?"

"I think possibly I've been underestimating you, Smelch. I didn't know you read Kant."

"Can't read, you mean," Smelch corrected. "Nope, I never had the time for no idle pursuits, what with that heavy schedule I told you about."

"Quite understandable, Smelch. By the way, Flunt mentioned you'd only been here a week. Where were you before that?"

"Well, now we're getting into the area o' the metaphysical, Retief, which when you examine material phenomena by inductive processes you arrive at a philosophical materialism, not to exclude ontological and epistemological considerations, which in general could be assumed to deny metaphysics any validity in the context o' Aristotelian logic. Or am I just spinning my wheels?"

"Did you work that out for yourself, Smelch, or did somebody tip you off?"

"Never mind. I don't think I'd grasp the full significance of the answer anyway."

They passed the last of the cages, these occupied by a bewildering variety of Lumbagan life forms in a wide range of colors and shapes, and displaying a remarkably diverse endowment of limbs, sensory equipment, and other somatic elements.

"They look vigorous enough," Retief commented as one hefty specimen gripped the bars and drooled at him. "But I get an impression they're not too bright."

"Well, sure, first they got to go through the indoctrination center. You can't except a agglomeration which last week it was grubbing roots in the woods to be a instant intellectual. That takes a couple days."

"I see. Where do we go from here, Smelch?"

"How about the cafeteria? I got a yen for some good old home cooking."

"Let's save that until after I've met you-know-who," Retief suggested.

"Mondays they usually got mud-on-a-mortarboard," Smelch said nostalgically, testing the air through his multiple nostrils. "Also on Wednesday, Saturday, and all the other days. Lucky it's my favorite. But I guess you're right, Retief. We got to make our courtesy calls before we chow down. I guess old Sneaky-feet. . . ." Smelch paused. "Hey, talking about sneaky feet, old you-know-who has got three toes on each foot; I barged in on him once when he was climbing out of a tub of hot sand. Wow, if language was skinning hooks, I'd of been flayed to the ribs in no time. That's when I seen 'em. His feet, I mean. . . ."

He broke off as a faint, rhythmic sound became audible, swiftly growing louder. The running lights of a copter appeared above the treetops, winking in a complicated pattern. The machine sank out of sight beyond the fence.

"What do you know, Retief—that's old Whatzis himself," Smelch cried delightedly. "But now that it's time to make the introductions," he added with sudden doubt, "I kind of wonder if it's a good idea. If he's in a bad mood he could maybe interpret it as me not doing my job of keeping outsiders on the outside."

"Let's hope he doesn't take a narrow-minded approach," Retief said encouragingly. He had reached the section of fence opposite the point where the copter had descended. He jumped, caught the top, pulled himself up in time to see a hurrying figure in a dark cloak and pale headgear disappear into a small structure at the edge of the clearing.

He pulled himself over and dropped to the ground. A moment later Smelch joined him.

"That copter's been busy tonight," Retief said. "What's in the building?"

"All kinds of neat stuff, like the cafeteria," Smelch said. "Did I mention they got mud-on-a-mortarboard?"

"You did. Let's go take a closer look."

They reached the door through which the heli's passenger had disappeared. It opened, and they stepped into a brightly lit corridor. At the far end, light gleamed through a glass-paneled door. When they reached it, muffled sounds were audible from the room beyond.

Retief took a small button-shaped object from his pocket, pressed it to the door, put his ear to it.

". . . you still hesitate?" a suave voice said. "Possibly you are deterred by ethical considerations, a reluctance to betray those who have placed their trust in you. Dismiss the thought, fellow! What harm to honor if nobody blabs, eh?"

Snorting and threshing sounds followed.

"Ah . . . Exalted One," a breathy Groaci voice whispered, "to offer a suggestion: the removal of the gag to facilitate compliance with instructions."

"Um. I was just about to order. Guard!"

Heavy footsteps sounded, followed by a ripping sound and a hoarse yell, then a shuddering sigh.

"Just one," Gloot's voice said yearningly. "Just one little old ocular, right by the roots. . . ."

A faint buzz sounded, eliciting a grunt of annoyance.

"Cretin!" the Groaci hissed. "The unwarranted interruption of His Unutterableness' virtuoso performance!"

"To regret—but to report untoward circumstances without," a second Groaci whispered in agitation.

"Begone, imbecile. This taciturn wretch is just on the point of divulging all!"

"Ah—Eminent One—the desirability of completing my report."

"What report?"

"The one which prompted this lowly one to intrude on Your Loftiness' deliberations: namely and to wit: the discovery that the security of this installation has been breached."

"Indeed?" the Groaci hissed. "To imply you failed to see to the complete combustion of file copies of certain special requisitions? To attend to it at once, thus forestalling any possible criticism by the small-minded—"

"To entreat your pardon, Your Greatness—but to correct a misapprehension: the breach to which I had reference is the unauthorized presence inside the station of certain intruders—"

"Intruders! Why wasn't I notified at once!" the non-Groaci voice barked.

"To have sought in vain to get a word in edgeways—"

"To skip the apologies! To dispose of the interlopers instanter!"

"To regretfully report their precise whereabouts is not yet known!"

"To find them at once and to dispatch them out of hand!"

"I don't like this," the order voice said in Lumbagan. "Flabby security is something I can't afford at this point. I'm off to Omega Station, Nith. Carry on with the interrogation."

Retief tried the doorknob, found it locked. He quickly extracted a small but complicated device from an inner pocket, applied it to the latch. There was a soft click. The door opened silently on a small dark room lined with coat hooks; beyond was a second room, clinically furnished in white. Under a ceiling glare panel, Gloot sat in a steel chair, strapped in position by heavy bands of wire mesh. An elaborate network of color-coded wires led from a cap-like device clamped to his head to a gray steel cabinet resembling a ground-car tune-up console.

A Lumbagan, if anything larger and more baroque than Smelch, leaned against the wall. A uniformed Groaci stood by a door in the opposite wall. Before the captive stood a slight figure nattily attired in bile-green Bermuda shorts, an aloha shirt in clashing pinks, and orange and violet Argyles.

"Well, my old friend Nith, formerly of the Groaci Secret Police," Retief said softly to Smelch. "I wasn't aware his duties had brought him to these shores."

"Hey—for a couple minutes I thought that was Whatchamacallit," the Lumbagan whispered. "But I guess not . . . he ain't yelling."

"He looks like him, does he?"

"Who?"

"You know."

"Oh, him."

"You didn't answer the question."

"Uh—what was the question?"

"On second thought I withdraw it."

"Now," the Groaci addressed Gloot eagerly, "there are none here but you and I and Leftenant Chish, and a lone guard unequipped with the higher cerebral centers, so there can be no thought of repercussions arising from your master's misinterpretation of events. Now, speak up, fellow. Tell all!"

Gloot struggled against his bonds, "Oh boy oh boy oh boy," he said. "If I just had a couple hands free, or maybe a prehensile tail, if I *had* a prehensile tail—"

"Bah! My lone chance to acquire glory in the absence of his Pushiness—"

"You mean his Puissance?"

"You heard me. Now, whilst he's absent, quickly spill the legumes, fellow! I'll see to it you're awarded the Order of Groac, *with* bladder!"

"Go soak your organ cluster in concentrated sulphuric acid."

"I have no time now for such indulgences, reticent one! You force me to extreme measures, entered into the more reluctantly in the light of certain prohibitions promulgated by His Extremeness regarding unauthorized use of equipment! But you leave me no choice, if I'm to score a badly needed point or two!" Nith turned to the knob-studded console, twiddled controls. "Now to administer a stimulus which will unlock your mandibles, producing a veritable torrent of data. . . ." He pushed a button; Gloot leaped against his restraints, yodeling enthusiastically. Nith pushed another button. Gloot slumped in his chair.

"Ah, you see?" Nith whispered. "Already you feel better: the cathartic effect of unburdening oneself of baseless hostilities. Now, you may begin with the designation of your employers. Whose hireling are you, fellow?"

"Nobody's," Gloot muttered.

"Shall I be forced to consign you to the parts bins after all?" Nith hissed ominously.

"Ah . . . Uplifted One," the bystanding Groaci officer offered diffidently, "to note that the veracitometer indicates the inferior one is speaking the truth."

"Eh? Impossible!" Nith whipped his eyestalks around to focus on the panel. "The impossibility, that is, that you should imagine me to be unaware of that circumstance." He twiddled knobs on the panel, then addressed himself again to Gloot:

"Who sent you here!"

"Nobody sent me; me and a chum came together."

"Aha! This chum! What power does he represent?"

"He's a Groaci," Gloot said sullenly.

"A . . . Groaci?"

"You heard me, Five-eyes! And a big wheel at that!"

"The indication of the instruments," the lesser Groaci whispered. "The possibility of a malfunction?"

"To not descend to the fatuous, Leftenant Chish! I myself to have overseen the installation! The acceptance of the preposterous: the hobbledehoy's truthfulness!"

"Amplified One!" Chish hissed. "To begin to
see the light! Lackaday! To have accidentally abducted a member of the personal staff of a Groacian MHPP!"

Nith waggled his eyes at Gloot playfully. "In
your report to your superior, I'm sure you won't
find it necessary to mention this little contretemps, eh? Just look upon it as a slight misun-
derstanding easily mended—"

"Upthrust One," Lt. Chish interrupted. The
possibility that though this one's companion is of
the noble Groacian stock, he himself might yet be
in the pay of inferior races—"

"To be sure, Leftenant," Nith said smoothly.
"To have been about to raise precisely that issue."
He faced Gloot. "Confess all, unfortunate dupe!
You were the prisoner of the Groacian noblebeing,
correct?"

"Well—technically he was my prisoner. But between you and me, Five-eyes, I was beginning to
wonder who was in charge."

"You dared impede the freedom of a High Born
One? You abducted him here against his will?"

"Naw, it wasn't that way," Gloot said. "It was
kind of a joint venture, like."

"Joint venture? I fail to postulate any conceiva-
ble circumstance under which the interests of
Groac and of an aboriginal would coincide!"

"Dough," Gloot said succinctly. "Mazoola.
Bread. You know."

"You shared an interest in gourmet cookery?"

"Cripes, how'd you know that?"

"Further association with us Groaci will accus-
tom you to such casual displays of omniscience,"
Nith said smoothly.

"But—to have implied that it occupied the status of coequal with its Groaci companion," Chish objected.

"To have spoken allegorically, as is customary with artists! To have implied only His Supernalness' shared interest in matters gastronomic. But now to wonder—what brings Groaci brass to this dismal backwater, checking up unannounced? The possibility that Supreme HQ is checking up on me."

"The possibility of inquiring subtly of His Supremacy's cook," Chish whispered.

"To try to curb your tendency to get into the act, Leftenant," Nith hissed. "Tell me, fellow," he addressed Gloot, "what was the purpose of your Groaci master's visit to these remote environs?"

"To see what was cooking, what else?"

"Yes, yes, of course—a clever cover story. But in addition to his culinary researches, what was the mission of the High Born?"

"If he had one, he never told me," Gloot said.

"To be expected that His Grandeur would not confide in an underling," Nith murmured.

"Estimable Broodmaster," the Leftenant hissed. "To hypothesize: Might not these same intruders be a veritable inspection team, dispatched by Ambassador Jith, who, jealous of his prerogatives, may have introduced them here by devious means, the better to check up on your operation unheralded?"

"Exactly what I had deduced!" Nith whispered and started for the door. "Certain reactionary elements have long desired my downfall. What better time than now to bring long schemes to naught by meddlesome probing, thereafter to cry me culpable! Forewarned, I'll see to certain matters regarding the voucher files; meantime, dispatch the prisoner instanter, lest he level feckless charges against my person!" Nith skittered through the door and was gone. The Leftenant made a rude gesture at the closed door and turned to Gloot, drawing his pistol.

"No violence, now," he cautioned the Lumbagan as he removed the cranial attachments of the veracitometer. "And remember to mention my name in glowing terms to your master. That's Chish: C-H-I-S-H, by a gross miscarriage of justice a mere leftenant—" He broke off as Retief stepped through the door, Smelch behind him. Uttering a faint cry, the officer whirled toward the door by which his superior had just departed. The Terran reached it first.

"Guard! To me!" Chish keened, but as the Lumbagan behemoth lumbered into action, Smelch stepped behind him, gripped hands with himself, raised the resultant picnic-ham-size aggregation of bone and muscle overhead and brought it down atop the fellow's cranium with a resounding thump, felling him in his tracks.

"Poor old Vump, he always had a glass head," Smelch commented.

"Nice one!" Gloot yelled. "But save old Nith for me!"

"Unhand me, Terran!" Chish whispered, trying unsuccessfully to dodge past Retief, "To have important business requiring my urgent attention!"

"You're confused, Leftenant," Retief said. "It was Broodmaster Nith who had the pressing appointment."

"Indeed? To have never heard of him."

"Too bad. I was hoping you could tell me who he works for."

"Never, vile Soft One!"

"I'd avoid those long-term predictions if I were you, Chish. They have a tendency to unravel at the edges." Retief looked past the Groaci to Gloot, busily freeing himself from the last of his entanglements.

"Don't break anything, Gloot; we wouldn't want to short the leftenant's wiring."

"What's this?" Chish hissed. "My w-wiring?"

"Where'd the other one go?" Gloot demanded. "That's the one I want. I want to pluck those eyes one at a time, like picking ripe froomfruit! How about it, you?" he glowered at Chish, who recoiled from the menacing figure towering over him. "Where's the other Terry?"

"The . . . the other Terry?" the Groaci hissed in agitation. "What other Terry?"

"You know what other Terry!" Gloot roared.

"Oh, that Terry," Chish said hurriedly. "Why, I do believe he's occupying the, er, guest suite, just across the passage."

"Yeah!" Gloot looked baffled. "What's he doing there?"

"He was, ah, assisting me in certain experimental activities," Chish replied. "Which reminds me, I'm overdue for my saline infusion, so if you'll kindly unhand me. . . ."

Gloot pushed the Groaci away and went across the room and into the passage. He paused before the door across the hall and rapped. A faint, uncertain cry answered him.

"Whattya know?" he said. "He's in there." He tried the knob, then stepped back and kicked the stout panel; the plastic cracked. A second kick shattered the lock, and the door banged inward. A slight figure appeared in the opening, checked at the sight of the Lumbagan.

"Hey," Gloot said weakly as Retief came up behind him. "That's not—"

"Well, there you are at last, Retief," First Secretary Magnan gasped. "Heavens, I thought you'd never turn up!"

12

"I DON'T GET it," Gloot said, looking from Magnan to Retief. "Another Graoci with only two eyes, just like you, Retief—and I just noticed that Terry you're holding onto is wearing three fakes, just like that other Terry, Chish. What gives?"

"Duplicity on a vast scale," Retief said. "It's creeping in everywhere these days."

"You labor under a misappreheninsion, dull-witted bucolic!" the Groaci began, subsiding in midword at a minatory tweak.

"What's this person referring to?" Magnan inquired, favoring Gloot with a distasteful look. "Is he somehow under the impression—"

"He's a great admirer of the Groaci, Mr. Magnan. Naturally, he leaped to the conclusion that you enjoyed that status, since you resemble me so closely." Retief gave Chish's collar an extra half-twist as the latter attempted to speak.

"I resemble you?" Magnan echoed. "Oh, really?

Well, actually, the press of other duties has precluded undue emphasis in my case on gross muscular development, but I fancy I cut a rather imposing figure in any case. But I fail to see the connection—"

"How come," Gloot asked bluntly, "this Groaci's got the same shortage of eyes as you, Retief?"

"Quite simple, Gloot. He's a relative; we're both members of the ape family."

"Oh. But what's he doing here, palling around with these foreigners?"

"Simplicity itself," Magnan said. "Though I was far from palling around, as you so crudely put it. I was seized by a brace of brigands and whisked here for some obscure purpose unconnected with normal diplomatic procedures." The first secretary looked severely at Chish. "Perhaps you have some explanation?"

"I'm sure he does." Retief assisted the struggling Groaci to the chair, and with Gloot's enthusiastic aid strapped him in position, fitting the cranial attachments in place atop his cartilaginous skull amid his eyestalks, which drooped dejectedly now.

"Alas for lost opportunities," the officer mourned. "Had I but known of the imminence of my downfall, I might at least have had the pleasure of making plain to the abominable Nith my true assessment of his worth!"

"Too bad, Chish. Maybe I'll find a chance to make it up to you," Retief said. "Now, I believe this model has the automatic prevarication-suppressor, which shoots a nice jolt through your trigeminal nerve if you accidentally stray into inaccuracy. Just set it at max, Gloot, to save time."

"Base alien, thus to serve an innocent official, harmlessly engaged in the performance of his duties—"

"Later, Chish. Who was the big shot?"

"One Swarmmaster Ussh, a most prestigious official. You'll rue the day—"

"Probably. Where's Omega Station?"

"I haven't the faintest—yip! the faintest intention of lying, I was about to say—eek! On a desert isle some leagues from here, drat all Soft Ones!"

"Which one?" Gloot demanded. "Rumboogy? Delerion?"

"Sprook!" Chish whispered. "I could wish you no more dolorous fate than to set foot in its miasmic swamps!"

"The needles say he's telling the truth," Gloot said.

"As he sees it," Retief said. "Unfortunately, false information doesn't register as long as he believes it. I have a feeling his boss wasn't keeping him fully informed."

"It is you, vile counterfeit—" Chish started, and broke off, listening. Faintly from afar a clattering sounded. "Ha!" the Groaci hissed in triumph. "In instants a squad of peacekeepers will be upon you, to put an end to your presumptuous invasion of sacred Groacian symbolic soil, as well as to your grotesque imposture!"

"What's he talking about?" Gloot demanded.

"I refer to the understandable aspirations of lesser races to the lofty status of Groacihood—"

"He also means the cops will be here any minute," Retief cut in. "I wonder if you'd be kind enough, Chish, to direct us to the nearest exit."

"A door—at the end of the passage there. A passage leads thence to a hidden egress—and good riddance to you!"

"Well, we'll have to be saying good night now, Leftenant. When Vump comes to perhaps he'll unstrap you. In the meantime, you can while away the time by planning what you should have said to Nith when you had the chance."

"True," Chish whispered. "Gone are my dreams of early advancement. But I may yet get a crack at that lousy civilian."

"Let that thought sustain you in your hour of trial," Retief said.

Ten minutes later, after carefully skirting the spot where Flunt guarded the trail, humming tunelessly to himself in the moonlight, the party reached the rendezvous where Boobooboo and his villagers had lain in wait. A long-legged native materialized from the mist.

"Well, you got one," Zoof said, eyeing Smelch appraisingly. "Two if you count skinny one." He prodded Magnan. "Hey—this one inedible like you, Retief. Not count!"

"These are just samples," Retief said. "The main course is right behind us."

In the pause in the conversation, faint cries were audible from the rear.

"Well, delivery to figurative door, real deluxe service, Retief," Chief Boobooboo said. "Maybe you not bad monster deal with after all."

"Nothing like a satisfied customer, Chief. And now I think we'd better be off and leave you to your celebration. Which way to Sprook Island?"

"Funny time decide end it all," Boobooboo said. "But to each his own. Just head for river, follow down to shore. Sprook just across way, nice swim, give time to reflect on misspent life before end. But look out for monsters, patrol river mouth every hour on hour in magic fish."

"What's a magic fish?" Gloot demanded.

"Local name for light-weight straked dory with V transom."

"Boy, you natives sure talk funny," Gloot commented.

The hue and cry had drawn near by the time the refugees found the stream. They followed its course as it wound across mud flats to the north shore of the island. A mile across the water, the low shape of the next land mass was barely visible in the pink moonlight.

"Surely you aren't thinking of going there?" Magnan said querulously. "At this hour of the night?"

"Just long enough to keep an appointment with a MHPP," Retief reassured his superior.

"Well, in that case—but how will we get there?"

"I expect our transportation will be along soon."

"Hey, I just remembered," Smelch said. "Sprook Island is where the wizards hang out. Guys which they can be in two places at once—or so the older boys told me."

"Nuts," Gloot scoffed. "Everybody knows Sprook is where the walking dead get their exercise."

"H-how do you know that?" Magnan said.

"I got a uncle that's an eye, ear, nose, and throat man over there."

"He cures them?"

"Naw, he sells 'em."

"I understood you Lumbagans didn't die in an ordinary sense," Retief said.

"Yeah—but when spare parts go west, Sprook is where they get together and make new friends. Picture it, Retief: phantom Lumbagans, made out of the odd ectoplasmic leg and the discarded ghostly elbow, prowling around in the mist looking for a spectral pancreas to make up a complete set."

"A curious superstition," Magnan commented with a shudder. "One might almost wonder if it's home-grown or imported."

"Superstition nothing," Smelch said. "I know a guy who saw a familiar face peeking out of the stranglemoss one time when a squall blew him aground off Sprook. It was a face he wouldn't likely forget, he said, on account of he chopped it off a stranger in a barroom brawl the week before."

"Maybe it was lucky enough to strike up a new friendship with a lonely head—"

"It don't work that way, Retief. Once a Four-Decker breaks up, it's all the way back to Freebies: eyes, ears, cerebellum, the works—and the whole lousy job to do over again."

"Presumably Nith's alien components won't interest the local haunts."

"Yeah—it's OK for you foreigners," Gloot said. "But us Lumbagans are fair game."

"Then it looks as if Mr. Magnan and I will be going alone," Retief said. "Thanks for your help, fellows—"

"Hey—what's the idea? What about my investment?" Gloot protested. "Besides, I got no particular hankering to hang around this place for those five-eyed little devils and their overgrown hatchetmen to beat the brush for, come sunup!''

"Gosh, I'd sure like to go on a sea voyage," Smelch said. "I always wanted to see the bright lights and all. But I got a feeling if I don't get back to my post my career as a alert sentry is at a end."

"The brightest light we're likely to see on Sprook is a will-o'-the-wisp, or maybe a little burning swamp gas," Gloot said gloomily. "But I guess even that's better'n the one Chish'll put you under when he gets his mitts on you."

"Yeah," Smelch sighed. "Well, so long, fellers. I hope you enjoyed your stay. Drop in again sometime."

"It was a pleasure, Smelch," Retief said. "I don't know when I've been as efficiently guarded."

"Gee, thanks, Retief. If you'd drop a line to my boss, I might get a pay raise out of it."

"I'll keep that thought in mind, Smelch."

As the oversized Lumbagan moved off, Retief, Magnan and Gloot made their way out through a dense stand of reeds sprouting from the mud to a hummock giving a clear view of the creek mouth. Ten slow minutes passed.

"Get set, gentlemen—here it comes," Retief said. A dark shape came into view downstream: a boat, crowded with oversized Lumbagans sliding silently toward them across the black water.

Retief moved quietly forward, wading out into the stream until the waters rose neck-deep, the reeds rising well above his head. Through the thickly scattered stems he could catch only glimpses of the approaching craft. Quite suddenly it was directly above him, sliding past. He ducked under water, rose noiselessly just aft the rowers' station, grasped the gunwale of the overloaded skiff, and heaved hard. With startled yells, the near-side passengers grabbed for support, missed, and struck the water with resounding splashes. On the return oscillation, Retief thrust upward, sending the remaining passengers over the far side. Bubbling sounds rose all around him; abruptly a swarm of Freebies were making for shore. Half a minute later, the refugees were aboard the craft, Gloot manning the sweeps, Retief in the bow scanning the open sea ahead, Magnan crouched shivering in the sterm.

"Heavens, I'm sure I've caught a chill," the First Secretary said. "Can't this appointment wait, Retief? As you know, I'm a stickler for punctuality, but. . . ."

"So is our host, I suspect," Retief said. "And we wouldn't want him to start without us."

Twenty minutes' brisk effort brought the boat within a hundred yards of the light surf breaking on Sprook's windward shore.

"We'll take her around to the far side," Retief said. "No use making it too easy for the leftenant."

Gloot eyed the dark shore without pleasure. "In there, a guy would be lucky to find his head with both hands—if he once happened to drop it, I mean. How're we supposed to get a line on which way the bum went?"

"I suspect we'll encounter a clue," Retief said.

"Gracious!" Magnan said excitedly. "I see the bright lights, way up in the middle of the air!"

"Yeah—there's a lone peak sticking up from the middle of the island," Gloot said gloomily, turning to stare at the faint glow shining through the mist. "According to rumor, that's ghost headquarters."

They rounded a low headland, saw a shallow bay ahead. At Retief's suggestion, they steered for shore at a point where the mangrovelike water trees seemed thinnest. Rubbery stems bent and snapped with damp popping sounds as they forced the boat through. When it grounded on mud, the three passengers stepped out, waded through ankle-deep water to shore.

"Well," Gloot said dubiously, "we could sure use that clue about now . . ."

A sharp click sounded from the darkness ahead.

"All right, just stand still until the moon comes out," a coarse voice ordered from the shadows, "so I can see to shoot you."

13

"WELL, THERE'S OUR clue, right on schedule," Gloot said in an undertone to Retief. "But I never heard of a zombie needing a gun." He raised his voice: "What do you mean, shoot us? How do you know we're not friends?"

"Easy. We don't have any."

"You're likely to get yourself in a peck of trouble," Gloot said, edging closer to the source of the voice. "I happen to be a pretty influential fellow—"

"One more teeny little step and you'll influence me to blaze away ready or not. With the spread I get with this sawed-off, there won't be a piece of you that'll survive long enough to stomp on."

With dramatic suddenness, the larger moon swam clear of the obscuring cumulonimbus. The Lumbagan who stood twenty feet away, aiming a large and efficient-looking gun, was of medium height, equipped with four arms, two legs, two eyes, a single mouth of modest dimensions. Behind him stood a second Lumbagan of identical aspect, clothed in an identical tunic of dun and chicle drab, differing only in its simple ornamentation.

"Jeez—old Smelch said you wizards could be in two places at once," Gloot muttered. " But I didn't expect it to be the same place."

"Don't bother your misshapen head," the gunner snapped. "Stand closer together, no use wasting a round." He gestured impatiently with the gun.

"Now, just a minute," Gloot temporized, pointing to Retief and Magnan. "You don't want to shoot these foreigners here. They got diplomatic immunity."

"Does that mean bullets won't punch holes in them?"

"It means anybody that tries it gets the whole Groaci Navy landing on him with a barge-load of chopped liver!"

"Did you say—Groaci?"

"Right. This here one is, ah, Superhivemaster Retief, head Yumpity-yump of the whole Groaci show!"

"Well, that's different." The receptionist lowered the brak-gun. "Why didn't you say so? We've been expecting a MHHP visit—"

"Because it's a secret, Dum-dum!" Gloot explained.

"Oh. Well then, why'd you tell me?" the captain challenged.

"If you shot us it would spoil the surprise."

"Yeah—that figures. I guess you want to see Colonel Suash, eh, sir?" the Lumbagan inquired of Retief.

"I couldn't have phrased it better myself," Retief said. "How is the colonel these days?"

"Just like me," the greeter replied. "How else?"

"And naturally, I got to go along as interpreter," Gloot said.

"What for? The Groaci gent speaks pretty fair Lumbagan."

"He only speaks the diplomatic dialect. Everything he says means something else."

"Oh, well, in that case I guess you better come too." The local stepped back and motioned them past. A narrow trail became visible ahead, a raised causeway between dark pools thick with rank growth. Two more identical Lumbagans emerged into view, fell in at the rear of the column.

"Weirdest thing I ever saw," Gloot muttered to Retief. "Boy, it must be confusing, having everybody in sight with the same number of everything. A guy could get mixed up and wander into the wrong bedroom even."

"It happens," Retief confirmed.

"Say, that's right, you Groaci come all of a pattern too," Gloot said. "Except for you getting a little short-changed on eyes, of course. Funny, I keep forgetting you're a foreigner and an alien, Retief; you seem just like a regular fellow."

"Thanks, Gloot. I take it twins are a rarity on Lumbaga, to say nothing of octuplets?"

"Hey, no more talking," the officer barked.

"Trying to figure out what's the opposite of everything the Groaci says is giving me a swift pain in the parietal lobes."

"Don't even try, rube," Gloot said callously "Decoding diplomatic conversations is a job for experts—and even they can't do it."

The trail debouched into a wide clearing, lined with neatly pitched tents, before one of which, larger than the others, a gay-colored banner hung limp in the still air. In the ruddy glow of a campfire were gathered a dozen more soldiers, all carbon copies of the reception committee.

"Wow!" Gloot exclaimed, "I heard of putting troops in uniforms, but this is fantastic!"

"Retief!" Magnan said behind his hand. "We've had no reports of any organized native militia here on Lumbaga! Heavens, I shudder to contemplate what effect this development might have, law-and-orderwise!"

"A thought-provoking spectacle," Retief agreed.

"Wait here," their captor ordered, and stepped inside the oversized tent. A moment later he reemerged, followed by still another duplicate of himself, this one wearing a gaudy cummerbund and braided shoulder tabs. The newcomer stared at the Terran, then jerked a power gun of foreign manufacture from a holster at his hip.

"What's this, a hoax?" he demanded sharply. "You're not Swarmmaster Ussh!"

"Of course not," Retief said briskly. "For a mission of this importance I thought I'd better come personally."

"You don't even look like the other ones," the officer barked. "Not enough eyes—"

"Lay off," Gloot spoke up sharply. "The poor guy was born that way."

"Born? Born? What's that?"

"It's kind of hard to explain," Gloot said. "It's kind of like you start from scratch, and one day— bloop! There you are. Get the idea?"

"Hmmphfff, do you take me for a nincompoop? I've heard rumors that foreigners come into existence in some such miraculous fashion, but I don't believe in spontaneous generation! Now: what did you expect to accomplish here? Sabotage? Espionage? Assassinations?"

"Keep going," Gloot muttered. "You'll hit something yet."

"I'm afraid we're wasting time, Colonel," Retief said. "Shall we go inside? What I have is confidential."

"Well," the commander started, but Retief had already brushed past him, Gloot at his heels, Magnan bringing up the rear. The interior of the headquarters tent was spacious, comfortably furnished with chairs, tables, straw cushions, beaded hangings.

"Pretty plush," Gloot commented to Retief. "You Groaci do all right by your chums."

"Lots of people would be surprised to know just how far Groaci chumship has penetrated into the jungle," Retief commented.

Their host bustled past, waved them to seats, rang for an orderly who quickly produced drinks all around.

"Now, what's all this about a confidential mission?" Suash said ill-temperedly. "I thought all that was settled."

"It's a matter of adjusting to fluctuating conditions," Retief advised the officer coolly.

"You mean — the Terries are getting suspicious?"

"There is that possibility."

"But I was assured they were a pack of self-serving incompetents, who wouldn't realize what was going on until they found themselves stacked in a parts bin."

"A slight exaggeration, Colonel," Magnan said icily. "Not that we Groaci care one way or another what sort of base canards you spread," he added quickly as the officer frowned.

"I don't like that." The colonel shifted in his chair. "Do they know *we're* here?"

"They just found out."

"That's bad! But surely they're not aware of the secret installation in the interior?"

"The word is out," Retief admitted.

"This is terrible!" Colonel Suash cried. "Do they know our role on D-day?"

"Not yet," Retief said. "But they're hoping to learn any time now."

"How?" Suash flapped his arms in agitation. "It's the most closely guarded military secret in Lumbagan history. In fact, it's the *only* military secret in Lumbagan history!"

"Simple," Gloot spoke up. "You got a spy in your midst."

"A spy. Impossible!"

"Oh, yeah? Nothing easier. After all, all you birds look alike. All a spy has to do is disguise himself to look like one of you—and zingo, he's invisible."

"Diabolical!"

"It's just the old needle-in-a-froomstack principle," Gloot said carelessly. "With a new twist."

"No wonder you were sent to warn me." Suash groaned. "What can I do?"

"Easy," Gloot volunteered. "Stage a showdown inspection."

"How . . . how do you mean?"

"Call your troops in one at a time, and order 'em to disassemble. The one that's a Terry in disguise won't be able to do it."

"What? Order my lads to destroy themselves?"

"Got any better ideas, Suash? Anyway, the odds are you won't work more'n halfway through the roster before you hit paydirt."

"You concur?" Suash looked anxiously at Retief.

"It ought to be interesting to see what happens."

"I . . . I suppose I haven't any choice. Not after the demonstration Shlush gave me of the fate in store for failures." The colonel tinkled his bell again. An orderly promptly appeared.

"Ah—Private Spub. I have, er, to inform you that your nation, ah, requires of you the, er, supreme sacrifice."

"You're not cancelling my furlough?" Spub said aggrievedly.

"By no means. As a matter of fact, you're about to enjoy a type of freedom you've not known for some time—"

"You mean—my discharge came through? Yipeeee!"

"Private Spub! You're at attention! I suppose in a sense one might say you're about to be discharged. At any rate, after tonight you'll no longer be a member of my command. I'd like to say that you've been a satisfactory soldier, except for a slight tendency toward insubordination, goldbricking, and slovenliness in dress—"

"I get it," Spub said. "You're resigning. Can't say that I blame you, Suash—"

"*Colonel* Suash, Private!"

"Not if you've resigned. Make up your mind," Spub said sullenly.

"Spub, I order you to . . . to . . . disassemble yourself."

"You mean—?"

"I mean disassociate! Into Freebies!"

Spub took a step backward, whirled, and darted from the tent.

"Head for the tall timber, boys!" he yelled. "Old Suash has finally blown his rug! He's on a suicide-pact kick!"

"Here, fall in for inspection!" Suash roared, plunging through the tent fly. "Sergeant! Come back here. . . ."

"It appears the colonel has a slight discipline problem," Magnan sniffed as he and Retief followed their host outside. The encampment was already deserted but for the irate officer and a lone private who loitered near the campfire, staring into the woods where his comrades had disappeared.

"Well, I'm glad to see I have one loyal subordinate," Suash cried. "Fall in, you!"

"I wonder why he didn't depart with the others," Magnan said.

"Maybe because he had reason to stick around," Retief conjectured.

"Well, Private," Suash addressed the fellow, "it was a pleasure to have you in my outfit."

"Was?" the private inquired in a shy whisper.

"It's now my sad duty to order you to disincorporate," Suash went on. "Seems a shame, with you the only loyal trooper in the group. But such are the fortunes of war."

"Ah . . . I'm afraid that won't be convenient," the soldier demurred feebly.

"What's this, mutiny?"

"Aha!" Gloot said to Retief. "We're on to something. Watch this." He stepped forward, shouldered Suash aside, and rammed a stiffened finger into the private's midsection. The latter doubled over, emitting hoarse wheezing sounds.

"I told you so!" Gloot cried. "Grab him!" he added as the assaulted private ducked suddenly and sprang past him, only to be brought down in a flying tackle by the colonel.

"A dead giveaway, Retief," Gloot explained happily. "Any genuine Lumbagan will break down into Freebies if you land a solid poke in his lunar plexus."

"So," Suash growled, dusting himself off and glaring down at the unfortunate impostor. "A Terry spy, eh?"

"By no means," the bogus private gasped, tottering to his feet.

"I happen to know better!" Suash barked. "Luckily, this Groaci civilian, Mr. Retief, tipped me off—"

"Retief? Groaci?" the accused spy fumbled at his head, stripped away a rubber mask to reveal five stalked oculars in a pale gray visage.

"I happen to be one Pilth, Groaci observer assigned to undercover surveillance duty!" he hissed. There" — he pointed at Retief — "is the Terry spy!"

Suash looked uncertainly from Retief to the Groaci, gave Gloot a sharp look as the latter guffawed.

"Nice try, Terry," Gloot said. "But it so happens I can vouch for Retief. I collected him personally from Groaci secret HQ in Dacoit Street. He and Shlush were just like that."

"Cretins! Assassins! Dumbbells! Are you so ignorant of aesthetics as to be unaware of the characteristics defining the noble Groaci race? Where, may I ask, are this impostor's handsome stemmed oculars, five in number? And—"

"*That* again," Gloot said wearily. "OK, so the guy's deformed, but in spite of the handicap he does OK. How about you, Terry? I got a hunch about three o' those eyeballs you're waggling at me are phonies. . . ." He reached for Pilth's twitching eyestalks, but with a sharp cry, the Groaci dodged aside.

"Unhand me, vile aborigine!" he keened.

"I'll just give 'em an easy yank or two," Gloot assured the terrified captive, making another grab for his eyes.

"I confess!" Pilth squeaked, cowering behind Suash. "I throw myself on your mercy! Just don't let that great uncouth bruiser lay hands on me!"

"The effrontery of it!" Suash exclaimed. "Trying to pass yourself off as one of my good friends, the Groaci—as if you could fool me—while spying on my operation!"

"Better find out how much he's learned," Retief suggested.

Suash glowered at the culprit. "How many of our secrets have you ferreted out?"

"Colonel—might I have a word with you in

private," Pilth entreated earnestly, "ere a gross miscarriage of justice takes place, as well as a disaster to the common cause?"

"Don't listen to him, Colonel," Gloot urged. "Anything this Terry has got to say he can say in front of us Groaci.""You're claiming to be a Groaci *too* now?" Suash exclaimed in startlement.

"Well, an honorary one, sort of. On account of me and Retief being pals and all."

Suash grunted, turned back to Pilth. "Start talking."

"And reveal Groacian state secrets to this vile Terry who has the audacity to bogusly claim Groacihood?"

"Back to that, huh?" Gloot said, and reached for an eye. Pilth screeched breathily and dived for cover behind Retief.

"I know nothing!" he whispered frantically. "Actually, I slept through the orientation lectures—"

"He's lying!" Suash cried. "I'll bet you know about the secret recognition signal, two long and three short—and the reinforcements we're expecting from Rumboogie and Hylerica and Slovenger—and—"

"Very well, I confess, all that and more," Pilth confirmed hastily. "No need to spell out the particulars—"

"But surely you haven't yet tipped them off about the plan for a coordinated police action a week from Tuesday, under cover of the Spring Rites?"

"Assume the worst!" Pilth hissed.

"This is a disaster!" Suash cried, clapping various hands to his forehead. "The pernicious little sneak has blown the operation wide open!"

"I wonder how he got the word back?" Gloot inquired. "Him still being here and all."

"Yes—how *did* you get the word back to your Terran masters?" Suash echoed. "No one's left this island for weeks!"

"Ah . . . I employed a variety of clever ruses, no need to burden you with such trivia," Pilth temporized.

"I'll bet the little villain has spilled the beans about our Galactic Ultimate Top Secret weapon, too!" Suash yelped. "Let me at him!" Retief restrained the outraged officer as he lunged for the trembling spy.

"Colonel," he said soothingly. "We may be able to turn this situation to advantage."

"How? The rascally knave has probably reported everything to the Terran ambassador! He must have sent off his dispatches via the bakery man, now that I think of it! He calls every morning in a sampan that's probably a fast courier boat in disguise!" Suash groaned. "And while I was dunking jelly doughnuts, news of every move I made was being whisked off under my very noses!"

"Well, what are we going to do about it?" Gloot demanded. "Call the whole thing off?"

"There's only one thing we *can* do," Suash declared, and smacked several fists into an appropriate number of palms. "Move D-day forward! We attack at once! Now! Today!"

"Impossible!" Pilth screeched. "We're not ready!"

"All the better!" Suash barked. "I'll catch you Terries off-balance, and—"

"I mean you're not ready! Your noble Groaci allies have not yet completed all arrangements necessary to bring off the coup with the flawless timing that will leave no treacherous Terran alive to carry exaggerated tales of perfidy and betrayal!"

"That's their lookout!"

"Then, too," Pilth whispered acidly, "there is the problem of your loyal troops, now dispersed through the woods like so many strayed kine, aquiver with apprehension lest their beloved commandant run amok amongst them!"

"Hmm. You've put your finger on a problem area," Suash conceded. "But forget those shirkers! There are plenty more where they come from—and you and I know where that is, eh, Retief?"

"One of us does," the Terran agreed.

"Oh, you think I'm not in on the top-level planning, eh?" the colonel bridled. "Well, as it happens I'm well aware that the location of the repo depot is—" he broke off. "But I won't mention the name in front of the Terry spy, just in case he doesn't already know. Not that it matters much." Suash drew his pistol. "Stand aside, Retief, and I'll finish off the sly little devil before we go."

"Wait!" Pilth whispered in Groaci. "Retief! To appeal to you as a fellow alien, to stay the hand of the barbarian ere he commits a tactical error of incalculable dimensions!"

"To propose a deal," Retief replied in the same tongue. "To give me details of the secret weapon, and then to put in a good word for you."

"To suggest that I, a trusted minion of the Groacian autonomy, would divulge information bearing a GUTS classification? Fie, Terran! To do your worst!"

"I was afraid you'd feel that way," Retief said.

"Here, what are you aliens gossiping about?" Suash demanded suspiciously. "Speak plain Lumbagan!"

"Pilth was just saying a few last words," Retief explained.

"But on the other hand," Pilth added quickly, "why make an issue of a few dry data? The supply of cannon fodder will be adequate to compensate for any modest foreknowledge that might leak to the enemy camp—"

"Hey," Gloot cut in, "do you hear something, Retief?" He cocked a pair of ears toward the forest trail.

"Yes, but I hesitated to interrupt at this point. You were saying, Pilth?"

"Wait a minute," Suash barked. "I'll bet that's my boys coming back to report for company punishment and then back into harness with no hard feelings!"

"Ha! Doubtless succor approaches!" Pilth hissed. "Now will your crimes be visited on your head, insidious Terry impostor!"

There was a flash of blue light from the darkness, a simultaneous sharp report; Suash yelled as the gun flew from his grasp.

"Keep your hands in sight and don't make a move," an authoritative voice barked. "I'm Ensign Yubb of the Harbor Patrol, and all you smugglers are under arrest!"

14

"WELL, QUITE A haul," the Lumbagan, neat in a dark blue uniform, commented as his variegated detachment of marines closed in, aiming guns of unmistakable Terran design. He was of medium height and unexceptional appearance, having three arms, four legs, and a random distribution of other members. "A couple of renegades, I see, plus a pair of foreigners."

"See here, fellow," Pilth hissed, "if you will employ your good offices to eliminate the Terry and his toady, as well as their dupe, Colonel Suash, you will find the Groacian Autonomy not ungrateful."

"Don't let this trickster delude you, Admiral," Suash spoke up, "for some reason he's trying to pose as a Groaci—"

"A Groaci, you say? Is that a fact?" Yubb looked Pilth up and down. "Got any proof?"

"Proof? I invite you, Ensign, to observe for yourself! I exhibit in classic form those characteristics which alone endow the owner with the peculiar beauty of Groacihood!"

"Peculiar is right," Gloot commented. "Just grab his eyes and pull. They're plastic, stuck on with rubber cement. I spotted 'em the minute I saw 'em. This here"—he indicated Retief—"is the genuine article."

"Then I guess that makes *this* one a Terry," the officer deduced, eyeing Pilth unenthusiastically. "Not too impressive looking, but what the heck.

Mine not to reason why, mine but to shoot the guy."

"Wouldst cut down a helpless prisoner on the strength of a mere literary allusion?" Pilth screeched. "And a garbled allusion at that."

"I don't have much choice," Yubb assured the alien. "I've got orders to drill at Groaci on sight."

"Unconscionable!" Pilth hissed. "I warn you, sir, any such thoughtless act will earn you a regrettable fate at the hands of vengeful Groaci hordes, soon to sweep clean the infected real estate of this pestilential world!"

"For a Terry, you come on kind of ambiguous," Yubb said. "You'd think I was about to plug you"—he swiveled to cover Retief with the gun—"Instead of *him*."

"Ah . . . to be sure," Pilth recovered. "It was merely my kindly instinct at work at the prospect of seeing a fellow alien dispatched before my eyes. However, in the interest of interplanetary amity, I withdraw my objection."

"Gee, the sentiment does you credit," Yubb said. "In fact, out of deference to the nobility of the gesture, I'll spare the Groaci scoundrel for the nonce." He gave Retief a look designed to intimidate. "But don't let it go to your head, fellow. I've heard about you Groaci, always on the lookout for a way to repay a charitable act with a knife in the ribs."

"An exaggeration," Pilth snapped. "There are occasions, of course, when expediency requires the sacrifice of the softer principles, but I can assure you that there are compensating virtues in the Groaci makeup, not the least of which is a commendable tenacity in the avenging of affronts."

"Sure, don't get carried away," Yubb said. "You'd think the Groaci were you Terries' best pals. Don't worry, I'll watch him. Now let's get moving. If I can get this Groaci and these two smugglers back to port before shift change, I'll net a nice bonus—"

"One moment," Pilth interrupted hastily. "I must protest your apparent intention to include my person in your party. As it happens, I have urgent business here, rudely interrupted when these miscreant locals, assisted by their, ah, Groaci henchmen, set upon me."

"What business?"

"That," Pilth whispered, "is my affair."

"For a foreigner you're throwing a lot of weight around, Terry," Yubb retorted. "My orders were to chase down these *foof* smugglers and clean out their base of operations. Maybe you're just an innocent bystander, but that's for higher authority to figure out. Let's go; we're wasting time."

"If you're after smugglers, you're scaling the wrong molehill," Colonel Suash demurred. "I happen to be a legitimate rebel leader, and my work is here. Beside which, I outrank you."

Yubb cocked his pistol. "I hate these jurisdictional disputes," he sighed. "But fortunately for the triumph of democratic processes, I happen to have the firepower. So—"

"I wouldn't if I were you, Ensign," Retief said as Yubb's finger tightened on the trigger.

"Why not?" the officer inquired.

"Because if you do," a new voice explained from the underbrush, "then I will."

"My loyal lads, back on duty!" Suash cried. "Yubb, surrender instantly and I'll try to prevent them from committing any excesses!"

"At the first sign of an excess, they'll be looking for a new boss." Yubb held the pistol firm on Suash's cummerbund.

"Hold your fire!" Suash yelped to his troops.

"You bet we will," the reply came from the darkness. "We're not letting this stranger plug you, Colonel; we want to do the job ourselves!"

"The rot's struck deeper than I thought," Suash muttered. "Well, Ensign, it looks like a standoff. Just give me and my Groaci advisors a modest head start over my chaps, and—"

"The Groaci are my prisoners," Yubb cut in curtly. "You can have the Terry."

"Who wants him?" Suash exploded. "The creepy little spy's already blown my security sky-high!"

One of Yubb's patrolmen edged forward. "Why don't we draw straws?" he suggested with a glance over his shoulder at the shrubbery concealing the rebel troops. "We wouldn't want any unfortunate incident to take place—"

"At the first shot, rake the woods with fire!" Yubb yelled. "I'm taking the Groaci, and that's that!"

"I'm keeping him, and that's *that!*" Suash shouted.

"Just my luck," Gloot said lugubriously. "Square in the middle of the crossfire."

"By the way, which one's the Groaci?" Yubb's second-in-command wondered aloud.

"The little one with the five wiggly eyes," someone called from the darkness.

"Wrong, it's the big ones with only two arms," someone else contradicted.

"Are you nuts? Everybody knows Groaci have got five eyes—"

"They're fakes! I heard—"

"I happen to know—"

"My brother-in-law had it on good authority—"

"Your brother-in-law wears ankle socks!"

"Oh, yeah?" One of Suash's mutinous troops emerged from concealment to confront his verbal adversary. A second rebel followed; a trio of Yubb's marines drew together to confront them. A sailor pushed a soldier; a soldier shoved a sailor.

"Now, lads, no fighting, it's unmilitary," Suash called.

"Sink the Navy!" someone shouted, a proposal followed instantly by the smack of a fist on leathery hide; at once, the underbrush erupted into a free-for-all; fists flew, some, Retief noted, well into the woods. Yubb and Suash danced about the periphery of the fray, bellowing orders, then fell on each other with flailing arms. Unnoticed by the combatants, Pilth whirled and scuttled off down the trail leading to the interior.

"Nice night for a riot," Retief said over the clamor. "I suppose they'll be happily occupied for some time, so we may as well be on our way."

"Jeez, I'd sure like to join in," Gloot sighed, eyeing the battle enviously and massaging a number of lumpy fists. "But I guess you're right: We better steal down to the beach while the stealing's good."

"A splendid notion," Magnan said quickly. "Speaking of stealing, if we hurry we might be able to borrow the patrol boat; much faster than rowing, and far less conducive to blisters."

"On the other hand," Retief pointed out, "I suspect Colonel Suash and his troops are stationed here for a reason—presumably guard duty. If we knew what he was guarding, it would spice up our report on our field trip."

"Yes, but in this wilderness. . . ." Magnan said indecisively.

"I'm curious as to where Pilth was headed in such haste. If we follow him, we might find answers to both questions."

"He's gone nuts is all," Gloot explained. "He panicked and headed for the deep swamp. Forget the Terry; we can still make it back to town in time to get in on the Midnight Melee."

"I have a feeling a somewhat larger melee is in the making, nearer at hand."

"A rumble in town is worth two in the bushes, as the old saying goes," Gloot said. "On the other hand, I kind of like your style, Retief. You don't say much, but where you are is where stuff seems to happen. I'm with you!"

Together, Retief, Magnan, and Gloot set off in the wake of the Groaci *agent provocateur*. The path, while narrow, was high and dry, twisting and turning to avoid the boles of giant, moss-hung trees rising from the dark water, skirting the deeper pools. In a small, open patch of spongy ground the trail ended abruptly. There was no sign of Pilth.

"Well, whattaya know," Gloot commented, peering into the surrounding darkness. "Who would of thought the little Terry was that fast on his feet? He's gone and got clean away, so I guess we might as well get started back—"

"Listen," Retief said softly. From somewhere ahead, a faint cry rang out. He started off at a run, picking a route from one root-clump to another. A hundred feet farther on, he emerged into the open to witness a curious sight; from a sturdy bough

overhanging the path, Pilth dangled by one leg in
midair, supported in an inverted position by a
length of stout rope.

"Good of you to wait, Pilth," Retief said. "An
excellent spot for a confidential talk."

"To cut me down at once and to enjoy the eter-
nal gratitude of the Groacian state, renewable an-
nually at a modest fee," the snared alien whispered.

"Stumbled over one of your own trip wires,
eh?" Retief said sympathetically. "It's one of the
hazards of the diplomatic way of life."

"What is this talk of diplomatic wiles? As it
happens, I am a simple scientist, here to observe
the nest-building habits of the Lesser Tufted
Adam's Apple—"

"Sorry, Pilth, an ingenious cover, but blown,
I'm afraid. We met a few years back, when you
were number two to General Fiss, the time he tried
to take over Yalc."

"Tour Director Fiss and I were interested only
in the excavation of artifacts of the Yalcan culture!" Pilth protested.

"You Groaci have pioneered the science of instant archaeology, true," Retief conceded, "but
good form requires that you wait until the owners
aren't using the bones any longer before you try to
wire them together in a glass case. However, we
have more immediate matters to discuss at the
moment. Let's begin with where you were headed
in such haste."

"I find it singularly difficult to marshal my rec-
ollective faculties while suspended in this un-
seemly position," the Groaci hissed.

"You'd find it even more difficult if the point of

attachment were your third thoracic vertebra," Retief pointed out.

"Long will this day live in infamy," Pilth wailed. "Very well, Terry, I'll reveal my destination, but only under protest. As it happens, I maintain a modest retreat in the foothills above, to which I retire on occasion to meditate. Now cut me down promptly and in my report I'll do my best to minimize the shabby role you played in this sorry contretemps!"

"Too late for secrecy now," Retief said as Gloot and Magnan arrived panting, splashed with mud and festooned with algae.

"Well," the first secretary said as he spied the dangling alien, "at least he had the decency to attempt suicide—though one might have known he'd bungle it."

"You speak of suicide, Soft One?" Pilth keened. "Such indeed is the fate of those who would invade the sacrosanct precincts of, ah, my bucolic hideaway," he finished weakly.

"Don't imagine for a moment that your threats intimidate me," Magnan replied loftily. "It's just that we happen to be leaving now anyway. Come, Retief, suitably padded—discussed in adequate detail, that is—my report of the disasters we've encountered up to this point will serve adequately to impress the ambassador with my zeal."

"An inspiring thought, Mr. Magnan. Just picture his expression when you tell him you've discovered there may be a plot afoot to take over Lumbaga, and that you hurried back to let him know what, without wasting time finding out when, where, why, and how."

"But, as I was about to say," Magnan said quickly, "why dash off just when we're on the

verge of achieving a coup of such stunning proportions?"

"Now, just how would one go about finding this
weekend cottage of yours?" Retief queried Pilth.

"You imagine, presumptuous alien, that I
would reveal details of my personal affairs to such
as you?"

"My mistake, Pilth." Retief turned to Magnan
and Gloot. "It seems we'll have to find it on our
own. Shall we go, gentlemen?"

"What—and leave me here suspended, prey to
any passing appetite, to say nothing of the risk of
incipient apoplexy?" Pilth shrilled in protest.

"Yeah, that would be cruel," Gloot said and
drew his knife. "I'll just slit the sucker's throat—"

"Oh, I don't think that will be necessary," Magnan said judiciously, as Pilth uttered a yelp of
dismay. "Just cut him down, truss him securely,
and tuck him under a bush well out of sight."

"There to starve, assuming the unlikely eventu-
ality that I'm overlooked by predators?"

"We'll leave the details to you, chum," Gloot
said callously.

"I capitulate!" the Groaci hissed. "Proceed
northeast by east to a lone *foof* tree, take a right,
proceed another hundred paces upslope, and you
will confront my confidential lair. I appeal to your
better natures to pry then no more, but to betake
yourselves in haste to more congenial surround-
ings, there to report favorably on this concrete
evidence of the importance of the reflective life in
the philosophy of the benign Groaci!"

"I don't get it," Gloot said. "How come this
Terry's all the time putting in a plug for you
Groaci?"

"Conscience," Magnan said crisply. "I suppose

you may as well cut him loose now—provided he promises not to go scuttling ahead and spoil our surprise."

"I assure you I will scuttle in another direction entirely," Pilth whispered as Gloot slashed the rope, allowing him to drop to the ground with a painful impact. He sprang up and disappeared along the backtrail.

"I'm not sure that was the best move we've made all evening," Retief said. "But I suspect we'll know for sure very soon. Meanwhile, let's go take a look."

15

A DIM LIGHT glowed from a point high above, shining down through the trees dotting the steeply rising slope.

"Well, whattaya know," Gloot said. "I thought the little runt was lying, but here's his meditation parlor, just like he said."

"Why, the very idea," Magnan whispered. "Ambassador Jith never mentioned funding any R and R facilities in the hustlings."

They emerged onto a talus slope. From here they were able to make out the silhouette of a cluster of towers rising from the crest of the peak. The lighted window went dark; a moment later a glow sprang up at another.

"Apparently Pilth doesn't do his thinking alone," Retief said.

"If the place is full o' Terries," Gloot said, "what's supposed to keep 'em from blasting us into Freebies before you can say 'oops'?"

"Nothing much; accordingly, I recommend extreme stealth from this point on."

Twenty feet higher, they encountered a flight of narrow steps cut into the stone. Retief climbed over the handrail, beaded with moisture in the damp air, and led the way upward, Gloot and Magnan close behind him. At a landing twenty feet higher the steps took a right-angled turn. The drop below was vertical now; the tops of trees rustled in the faint breeze. Far below a cluster of lanterns moved on the shore. Far across the water, the lights of the capital floated on blackness.

"Hey, Retief," Gloot whispered, "I get dizzy when I get this high. I would have told you sooner, only I never got this high before."

"Compared with the roofs we were negotiating a few hours ago, this is nothing," Retief said.

Gloot groaned. "Was that this year? It seems like something out of my early youth."

Gloot started to speak, then changed his mind. "Never mind," he muttered. "The more I know, the less I like it. I'm even beginning to get a funny feeling it was your idea and not mine to grab you from Groaci HQ."

At the next landing, by leaning far out over the rail to look up, Retief was able to see a row of shuttered windows set in a squat, thick-walled structure of a bilious ocher color. The building appeared to consist of several wings, set at slightly different levels in accommodation to the contours of the rugged peak on which it was built.

"Quite a layout," Gloot started, and broke off as feet clacked above. A spindly figure in a flaring helmet and a spined hip-cloak leaned over the railing of a terrace, peering down the barrel of a blast-rifle with five alertly canted oculars.

"Hssst! To advance and give the password!" a thin voice whispered sibilantly.

"To contain yourself in patience, hivemate of brood foulers," Retief whispered sharply in Groaci. "To have had a brisk trot to report the failure of the incompetent Nith! To require a moment in which to respire!" He motioned to Gloot. "You go first," he whispered softly. "Pretend to be scared."

"Pretend?" The Lumbagan choked. "I'm petrified! But what the heck, I don't aim to show the purple glimp feather. Here goes."

"The impropriety of your nattering—and my curiosity as to whom you natter with!" the Groaci peacekeeper hissed.

"The prompt satisfaction of your curiosity," Retief whispered back, motioning Gloot past. He followed up the final flight of steps. As the Lumbagan reached the sentry's terrace, the latter hissed and swung the gun to cover him.

"The impropriety of taking hasty action," Retief said sharply. The guard swiveled a pair of eyes toward him, and uttered a faint Groaci yelp of dismay.

"A Soft One—" he started, but his feeble cry was cut off abruptly by a smart rap to the side of the jaw delivered by Gloot. Retief deftly caught the victim's helmet as he collapsed.

Retief quickly scouted the narrow gallery on

which they now found themselves. From the platform at the end, a complicated system of rods was visible atop a tower.

"Curious," Magnan whispered. "Trideo antennae here? I wasn't aware Lumbaga boasted transmission facilities."

"I have an idea the transmitter hasn't gone into full service yet," Retief said. Further discussion was interrupted by a faint *whop-whop-whop* which grew swiftly louder. A copter came sweeping in low over the treetops, made a sliding turn, and came back to hover for a moment before settling gently to the roof of the building. Before the rotors had stopped, the pilot—a small, thin-legged individual wrapped in a black cloak and wearing a solar topi—hopped down and disappeared into the shadows. A moment later, light shone from an opened hatch in the roof, into which the new arrival descended, closing the panel behind him.

"I believe that was the same chap we just missed meeting back on Groo-groo," Retief said. "An omission I'd like to correct."

"Too bad it's impossible," Magnan said crisply. "Still, if we hasten back now, we may be able to see the ambassador and persuade him to request departmental approval for authorizing an inquiry into the possibility of considering the appointment of a committee to look into a proposal for asking Jith some rather pointed questions."

"A dynamic program, Mr. Magnan," Retief said. "But we might save a little time by some judicious eavesdropping right here on the spot."

"Hmmm. An interesting theoretical point. A pity we didn't bring snoop gear, but who would have imagined any occasion for diplomatic activities this far from the nearest cocktail party?"

"An unfortunate oversight; but possibly we can rectify it by shinnying up the drain pipe."

"Drat it, Retief, I'm beginning to suspect that the hazards of being rescued by you exceed those threatened by the kidnappers!"

"Give me a leg up, Gloot," Retief said.

"Anything for you, pal," the local said dubiously, grasping his shin firmly. "But are you sure you can use it?"

"On second thought, just a boost will do," Retief amended. Gloot offered linked hands as a stirrup; Retief went up the pipe. The roof was deserted but for the silent copter squatting inside a yellow-painted circle. He leaned back to lend a hand to Magnan, then to Gloot. Together they crossed to the trapdoor. It opened soundlessly. Steep steps led down into deep gloom.

"I dunno," Gloot said, looking dubiously down into the dark recess below. "What if it's booby-trapped? What if they're waiting down there with skinning knives? What if the whole thing is a fancy scheme to feed fresh spares into the black market? What if—"

"If so, it's working perfectly," Retief said, and started down the steps. At the bottom, he used his pocket flash to quickly check the room; it was empty but for stacked crates and cartons bearng stenciled markings.

"Electronic gear," Retief said. "And surgical supplies."

"Here's one labeled *Acme Theatrical Services*," Magnan whispered. "Curious; I never suspected the Groaci had an interest in amateur dramatics."

"I suspect they may have entered the field at a professional level," Retief said.

The storeroom opened into a narrow, dimly lit passage. Faint murmurings sounded from behind a door along the way. Retief went to it, put his ear against the panel:

". . . to have come within an ace of discovery!" hissed a breathy Groaci voice. "To make all haste now—"

"The inadvisability of rushing the cadence!" another voice replied. "To not louse up the triumphant culmination of my researches!"

"Yes, yes, to get on with it. To have a tight schedule."

A muted humming sound started up; a faint odor of ozone filtered past the closed door.

"Sounds like an illegal transmitter," Retief said.

"What's illegal about a transmitter?" Gloot demanded.

"Let's find out." Retief turned the doorknob silently, eased the door open an inch. Two Groaci, one in bile-green shorts and orange and violet Argyles, the other in a stained white laboratory smock, and holding a clipboard, stood before a wide panel with a puce crackle finish thickly set with dials, switches, oscilloscope tubes, and blinking indicator lights. One side of the room was given over to stacked cages in which eyeballs, kidneys, adenoids, and other forms of Lumbagan wildlife perched disconsolately on twigs moped glumly in corners amid scattered straw.

". . . the completion of preliminary testing," the technician was whispering, "to be ready now to conduct field trials of limited range, after which, on to the final stage in the fulfilment of selfless Groaci objectives with all deliberate haste!"

"To spare me the propaganda," the other snapped. "To have read the official handouts. To now tellingly demonstrate the effectiveness of the device without further procrastination."

"The eagerness with which I confirm the accuracy of my theoretical predictions," the white-smocked Groaci hissed sharply. "To anticipate the prompt material gratitude of our government."

"To deliver the goods in accordance with specs, or to promptly adorn the Wall of Hooks as an example to other boasters!" the other whispered harshly.

The technician wiggled his oculars in expression of righteous fury courteously restrained, and turned to the control panel, began setting dials in a complicated sequence, referring frequently to the clipboard.

"Haste, haste," the other Graoci muttered. "To not procrastinate in the eye of the metaphorical cannon—or is it the mouth of the needle?"

"To be unfamiliar with Terry saws," the white-smocked alien hissed, continuing with the check list. The observer watched for a moment in sour silence; then: "Pah!" he burst out. "To reject out of hand this transparent hoax! To perceive that you stall the proceedings in order to extort even more golden promises of future emoluments!"

"To commit a wrong of vast proportions, thus to accuse me!" the technician cried. "To underestimate the insidious sublety of the mechanism—"

"To have penetrated your deception—and to remind you of the redundance of mere technical personnel after completion of their function!"

"The inadvisability of threats to my person! My indispensability to the scheme—"

"Is at an end! To point out that even a cretinous underling is fully capable of closing a switch!" The Groaci stepped forward and before the other could intercept him, pushed the largest button on the panel.

With a hoarse bellow, Gloot plunged past Retief into the room. The two Groaci whirled, uttered shrill yelps and dived in opposite directions. The small creatures in their cages had gone into a flurry of activity, Retief noted peripherally, hurling themselves against the wire mesh as if frantic to come to grips with their neighbors. The momentum of Gloot's charge carried him full tilt against the button-studded console. Lights flashed; harsh buzzings sounded, ending in a crackle of arcing electricity. Gloot staggered back and sat down hard. The lab animals subsided as abruptly as they had leaped into motion. Retief jumped forward in time to nab the technician as he dithered, unsure which way to run. A door slammed at the back of the room.

"Retief! What in the world . . . ?" Magnan quavered, peering into the room.

"Oh boy," Gloot muttered, fingering his head with all three hands as he sat weaving in the middle of the room. "Oh boy oh boy oh boy. . . ."

"Would you care to amplify that remark?" Retief said, holding the struggling Groaci.

"I guess I blew it, huh?" the Lumbagan said blurrily. "I don't know what come over me, Retief. It was like festival time and spring rites and the fall offensive all hit me at once! All of a sudden I was raring to go! Too bad that Terry got away, I would have liked to field-strip the little rascal, just to see what color juice ran out of him." He eyed Retief's prisoner wistfully. "The fit's passed—but I still got kind of a lingering urge to pull that Terry apart, one skinny leg at a time."

"I thought you Lumbagans saved all your hostilities for each other, with none left over for tourists," Retief said.

"Yeah—me too. But somehow, all of a sudden it was open season on Terries. Funny, huh? I never been nuts about 'em, but this is the first time I appreciated to the full what a really swell sensation it would be to rip 'em to shreds—"

Far away, an alarm bell clanged harshly.

"Now are you undone, abominable intruders," the Groaci hissed. "In moments my well-trained bullies will fall upon you, your misshapen members to distribute over the immediate landscape!"

"Retief, we have to get out of here at once!" Magnan yelped. "If a platoon of peacekeepers should get their nasty little digits on us . . . !"

"Yeah, let's blow," Gloot agreed. "Me and cops never did get on too good together."

Retief released the Groaci, who at once darted for cover behind the nearest rank of cages. The hall was empty; a lone peacekeeper appeared at the far end of the corridor and set up a weak shout as they dashed for the storeroom. Inside, Retief and Gloot paused long enough to stack half a dozen crates against the door before ascending to the roof. Magnan was at the parapet, staring down into the darkness.

"Trapped!" he hissed. "Retief—the grounds are swarming with them! And—" he uttered a stifled exclamation. "Retief! Look!"

In the gloom below, Retief could discern the forms of several dozen armed troops in flaring helmets, polished greaves, and spined hip-cloaks moving efficiently out to surround the building.

"Retief! What does it mean? This laboratory, hidden in the wilds; that insane monster farm, and that horrible little Nith—and his obscure experiments—and now Groaci troops secretly garrisoned in the boondocks!"

"It means we know enough now for a preliminary report. If you'll give Ambassador Pounce-trifle the details of what we've learned—"

"But—Retief—what *have* we learned?"

"That the Groaci have worked out a method of controlling Lumbagan evolution, plus a method of selectively stimulating the natives' natural love of hostilities."

"But—whatever for?"

"You'd better get going now, Mr. Magnan; I seem to hear the sounds of a posse pounding on the door down below."

"Get going? You sp-speak as though I we-were expected to descend alone into that lion's den!"

"Not descend; ascend. The copter is a standard Groaci export model—"

"Yes, but—but I don't have my driver's license with me!"

A loud thumping sound from below as the stacked cases toppled. Gloot slammed the trap door and stood on it.

"Better hurry, Mr. Magnan," Retief said. "Head due west, and stay clear of the peaks."

Magnan made vague sounds of protest, but scrambled awkwardly into the copter. He pressed the starter; the rotors turned, spun quickly up to speed.

"It seems a trifle irresponsible, dashing off and leaving you here alone, Retief," he said, and winced as thunderous pounding shook the trap-door.

"I hope them Terries don't take a notion to send a few rounds of explosive slugs through this hatch," Gloot said, struggling for balance as it heaved under him.

"—but as you point out, duty calls," Magnan added quickly, and with a hasty wave, lifted off into the night.

"I don't get it," Gloot said as the sound of the machine faded. "You said Ambassador Pounce-trifle? I thought he was the head Terry."

"I think it's time for me to clear up a slight missapprehension you've been laboring under, Gloot," Retief said. "Those aren't actually Terries down there; they're Groaci."

"Huh? But they look just like what's-his-face, Nith, only bigger!"

"Correct. That's because Nith is a Groaci, too."

"But if he's a Groaci—then what about whozis—the one that just ran out on us?"

"Mr. Magnan," Retief confided, "is actually a Terry."

"Aha! I should have known! Talk about masters of disguise! Pretty slick, the way you got rid of him. . . ." Gloot paused reflectively. "But—if they're Groaci down there, how come we don't just open up, and shake hands all around?"

"They think I'm a Terry."

"Oh, boy, that complicates things. How come you don't tell 'em who you really are, and—"

"Undercover operation."

"Oh, I get it. Or do I?"Gloot said vaguely. "But I guess I can worry about that later, after we get out of this mess. What nifty trick are you going to pull out of the hat now? Frankly, if I didn't have lots of confidence in you, Retief, I'd be getting worried about now."

"I think you may as well go ahead and worry, Gloot," Retief said. "On this occasion, I'm fresh out of hats."

"You mean . . . ?" At the words, the hatch gave a tremendous lurch, sending the Lumbagan staggering. It flew open, and a Groaci warrior bounded forth, power gun aimed, his fellows crowding out behind him.

"He means, nocuous encroacher, that now indeed is your fate upon you!" the white-jacketed Groaci technician hissed, thrusting forward.

"How about it, Retief," Gloot said from the corner of his mouth. "We could jump 'em—but what I say is, why give 'em the fun of blowing us into sausage?"

"Wait!" a piercing, yet curiously timbreless voice called from the rear. The Groaci soldiery fell back, came to rigid attention. In the sudden silence, the technician ducked his head servilely, stepping aside as an impressive figure wrapped in a black cloak with a twist of gold braid adorning the stiff collar strode forward. Typically Groacian except for his near six-foot height, the newcomer stared Retief up and down, ignoring Gloot.

"So, impetuous Terry," he rasped in a voice surprisingly vigorous for a Groaci. "We meet at last."

"Swarmmaster Ussh, I presume?" Retief said. "Your Ultimateness has led us an interesting chase."

"And one pursued to your indescribable sorrow," Ussh grated.

"I agree it's saddening to see so much effort wasted," Retief agreed. "Yours, I mean—not ours."

"Wasted effort is for lesser creatures, Terran!" Ussh waggled his oculars in token of amusement. "For all the diligence of your prying, you have failed, naturally, to correctly assess the full scope of my genius."

"Possibly," Retief said. "But I think you've failed to correctly assess CDT policy on sensitive issues like genocide, slavery, and vivisection—"

"Pah—what care I for a gaggle of diplomats? I happen to be the forerunner of a superrace, to whom ordinary values have no application!"

"I've seen your experimental monster farm," Retief said. "The woods seemed to be full of unsuccessful experiments in forced evolution—"

"True, there were a certain number of failures before I was able to reproduce the precise forms needed in the Great Plan, but even those had their uses—"

"And I've seen your matched sets of garrison troops. Not bad, except that they didn't seem to be a great deal brighter than armies usually are—"

"As I suspected, the true implications of their existence were lost on your limited imagination. Soon, however—"

"I think I got it. Manipulating Lumbagans at random is all very well, but it would be a bit difficult to stage anything more organized than a free-for-all unless you could elicit uniform responses. *Ergo*—uniform puppets."

"You've correctly gauged the more pedestrian

portions of my plot, Terran dupe! But you've failed utterly to grasp the incredible scope of my true greatness! While you dashed hither and thither, assembling your trifling clues, my giant intellect has been coolly completing the final detail work. And now—tonight!—the New Age dawns, ushered in by the successor to all previous life forms, namely myself!"

"What is this guy, nuts or something?" Gloot muttered. "If he's so busy, why's he standing around making speeches?"

"He's trying to find out how much we know," Retief said.

Swarmmaster Ussh waved a negligent hand. "Petty minds can but ascribe petty motives," he hissed. "What you may or may not know is a matter of supreme indifference—and I include any fragmentary facts in the possession of your flown accomplice, for whose absence from this cozy group certain incompetents will suffer. In fact, I freely confide in you: Tonight, I assume planetary rule. Tomorrow, I issue my ultimatum to the Galaxy. Next week—but contain yourself in patience. You yourself—in chains, of course— shall serve as my emissary to carry the terms to your former masters! As for the Untouchable, you may retain him as your personal menial."

"I assumed you had a reason for not shooting us immediately," Retief said.

"I do nothing without a supremely practical motive," Ussh stated flatly. "And now—will you go to your durance peacefully, or will it be necessary for me to have you dragged by the heels, a most undignified progress for a future Slave Ambassador."

"I think a period of quiet contemplation may be just what we need at this point," Retief said.

16

THE DUNGEON INTO which Retief and Gloot were conducted, cut deep into the rock beneath the secret Groaci lab, was a damp chamber six feet by eight, without lights, furniture, or other amenities. The narrow portal through which they had entered was barred by a foot-thick door of solid iron. The ceiling was a seamless surface of rough-hewn stone, as were the walls and floor.

"At least we got a drain hole," Gloot commented after they had conducted an examination of their prison by the light of Retief's cigar lighter. "If worst gets to worst, I can always flush myself down the sewer; but don't worry, pal, I'll stick around and keep you company until you starve to death before I split—and I do mean split."

"That's thoughtful, Gloot; but maybe it won't come to that."

"Aha! So you *have* got a couple aces up your sleeve! I figured; come on, Retief: Let me in on the scheme! How are we going to hoist these Terries—"

"Groaci."

"Whatever you call 'em, I still don't like 'em. What dramatic stroke are we going to bring off now, which they'll be caught by surprise with their kilts up?"

"First we find a comfortable spot on the floor," Retief said.

"Yeah? OK, I'm with you so far."

"Then we wait."

"I'll be frank with you, Retief: Somehow the program don't sound too promising."

"It's all I have to offer at the moment."

"Oh." There was a pause. "Are we, ah, waiting for anything in particular?"

"I'd be inclined to jump at anything that comes along."

"You must be joshing, Retief. How can anything come along to jump at, seeing that we're locked up in an underground dungeon with only one hole in it, namely the one the bilge runs out of?"

"That narrows it down," Retief conceded.

"You mean . . . ?"

"Shhh . . . listen!"

In the utter silence, a faint rustling sound was audible. Retief thumbed his lighter; the pale flame cast a feeble glow across the slimy floor.

Below the four-inch drain orifice, something stirred.

An eyeball crept into view on spidery legs, swiveling to look around the cell before emerging onto the floor. Behind it, an ear fluttered up the shaft, circled the chamber, came to rest in a far corner. A hand crawled into view, paused to hold up two fingers in a V, then turned to assist a couple of gallbladders over the coping.

"Cripes," Gloot muttered as more and more Freebies swarmed into the cell. "What is this, a convention? The place is crawling with vermin!"

"Steady, Gloot," Retief cautioned. "When I said jump, I didn't mean literally."

"It figures the crumbums would stick us in a hole infested with parasites!"

"Keep your voice down, Gloot. If our jailors suspect we have guests, they'll soon be along to break up the party."

"Yeah—even a bunch o' Terries—or Groaci—foreigners, anyway—ought to have the decency to fumigate the place if we put up a howl—" Gloot broke off, his mouth hanging open in an expression of horrified outrage. "Why, the lousy, dirty, obscene little buggers!" he gasped. "Right out in public, too."

Under the feeble beam of the lighter, the eyeball had edged close to a generously proportioned nose which waited coyly for its advance. They touched, groped—and melted into a close embrace. A second eye appeared from the drain, glanced around, rushed to the conjoining couple and promptly took up a position on the opposite side of the nose. An upper lip linked with them, as other candidates crowded around, while more and more streamed up from the depths.

"It's—it's a regular orgy, like I heard about but never got in on!" Gloot blurted, and raised a large, booted foot to stamp out the objectionable spectacle; Retief caught his ankle barely in time, dumped him on his back.

"Easy, Gloot," he said. "It's time you faced up to the facts of life."

"Just wait until I get my other lung in place," a breathy voice squeaked from the direction of the congregating singletons, "and I'll give that big hypocrite a piece of my mind! Maybe that'll raise his IQ to the moron level so he can understand me when I tell him what I think of him!"

"I thought maybe it was you who's been dogging my footsteps," Retief said. "Welcome aboard, Ignarp. You couldn't have come at a better time."

17

"SO THAT'S OUR Big Secret, Retief," Ignarp said five minutes later. He was completely reassembled now, his component parts having settled into position and accommodated themselves so perfectly that the lines of juncture were barely visible. "Being able to reassemble gives us a big advantage; that's why the rest of 'em are out to get us."

"The reasons normal Lumbagans got no use for these degenerates," Gloot stated with contempt, "is on account of they got no finer feelings. When they put theirselves together thataway, they as good as admit all us Lumbagans evolved from lower forms!"

"Ontogeny recapitulates philogeny," Ignarp said smugly. "Everybody knows that."

"Sure—but decent folks don't admit it!"

"Which brings us to the question of why you trailed me here," Retief said.

"I told you I'd keep an eye on you—"

"Yes, I saw it fluttering in the middle distance."

"And it looks to me like maybe things are even worse than we thought. And you're the only one that maybe can do something about it. Ergo—here I am. What can I do? Get you some light reading matter? Take last messages to loved ones?"

"Better yet, you can get us out of here."

"I don't know, Retief," Ignarp said, eyeing Gloot, who stood at the far side of the cell, arms folded, a sullen expression on his face. "Why should I go to the trouble to bail this clod out of stir?"

"Because without him, I'm afraid my plan won't work out," Retief said.

"Who needs him?" Ignarp challenged. "All I have to do is slide back out the way I came in—"

"I still don't believe it," Gloot muttered. "Me—associating with this degenerate. Having to stand here and listen to him talk about it."

"—infiltrate the building and reassemble inside. Then, when you pound on the door and yell and the guard comes to work you over with the rubber hoses, I jump out and nail him."

"I got a better idea," Gloot said. "Retief, you lend your coat to this deviate; we set up a yell, and when the bums come running, they open the door and see the two of you up against the wall thumbing your noses. Naturally, they come charging in, and I jump out behind 'em and lay 'em low."

"Some plan," Ignarp commented. "They see Retief without his coat and a total stranger wearing it, and that's supposed to lull their suspicions?"

"Ok, then I borrow his coat—"

"So they see *him* without a coat, and me naked—and they figure I'm you, only two feet shorter and better looking—"

"No, I got it: Retief borrows *my* coat—"

"You're not wearing one, dummy."

"So he keeps his coat! You get back of the door—"

"Don't tell me what to do, tall, spotted, and grotesque!"

"You got a nerve, short, blotchy, and depraved! I got a good mind—"

"Want to bet? We do it my way.. See you later, Retief—"

"How about waiting long enough to hear my proposal, Ignarp?"

"Well—OK. Who wears your coat?"

"I do. It's you two fellows who have some changes to make."

"Huh?" Gloot said uneasily.

"What you got in mind?" Ignarp said suspiciously.

"Something far worse than you think," Retief said. "Tell me, Ignarp, how would you like to see Lumbaga pacified by a dictator?"

"You kidding? We like to fight amongst ourselves. Having all the fat in the hands of the exploiting classes is bad enough, without some spoilsport depriving us of our national pastime. Forget it, Retief—"

"I'd be glad to, but I'm afraid a fellow named Ussh has a more tenacious memory. Unless we do something to stop it, by this time tomorrow, Lumbaga will be at peace—permanently."

"Well, what are we hanging around here for?" Ignarp demanded. "Let's try my plan, and—"

"All the more reason to get going on my plan!" Gloot cut in.

"Gentlemen," Retief interrupted, "there comes a time in any friendly fight when it's wise to pause and give a thought to consequences. At this moment, the opposition is busy putting the finishing touches on a plan that's been years in the making. The occupying armies are already on the march for the capital—and we're sealed in a vault forty feet underground, engaged in a jurisdictional dispute."

"Oh . . . well . . ." Gloot said.

"It doesn't look good, does it?" Ignarp said soberly.

"The proposals now before us," Retief said, "would afford a few satisfying cracks at the heads of our captors, and might even get us as far as the end of the hall before the inevitable end. What's required is a plan with sufficient scope to carry us through to a successful conclusion."

"I'll buy that," Gloot said. "But—"

"Out with it, Retief," Ignarp said. "I've got a funny feeling I'm not going to like this."

"Probably not," Retief agreed. In a few brief words, he outlined his proposal.

A stunned silence followed.

"Retief! And I thought you were a fine, upstanding fellow—for a foreigner!" Ignarp said weakly.

"If I wouldn't of heard it, I wouldn't of believed it," Gloot said in a choked voice.

"Well, how about it, gentlemen?" Retief said. "We don't have much time."

"You expect me to lend countenance to a thing like that?" Ignarp protested. "It's enough to make your eyebrows crawl!"

"What if my friends heard about it?" Gloot muttered.

"It's not traditional!" Ignarp complained.

"It's against nature!"

"Mongrelization!"

"I'll be dragged down to his level!"

"It'll never work!"

"Couldn't we talk about it first? For a few years,

say—or maybe a century or so?"

"It's now or never, fellows," Retief said. "After tomorrow, every Lumbagan on the planet will be herded into a Freeby farm and integrated forcibly, regardless of his sensitivities."

"Me?" Gloot said. "And that . . . that . . . dilettante?"

"That . . . that oaf—and *me*?" Ignarp wailed.

"It's that—or something worse," Retief said with finality.

"Could you at least . . . douse the light?" Ignarp said.

"I need a shot o' rum," Gloot said.

"Of course." Retief handed over his flask and switched off; the dim glow faded. In the darkness there were soft, tentative scufflings, faint mutterings; Retief paced the cell, three paces, back three paces, whistling softly to himself. Time passed. . . .

Silence fell. Retief paused.

"Ready, gentlemen?"

"We . . . I . . . guess so," a curiously mellow voice answered. Then, more strongly: "Yes, ready, Retief."

He flicked on the lighter. In its glow stood not the dumpy Ignarp nor the lanky Gloot, but a tall, superbly muscled figure, brawny arms folded over a mighty chest, four golden eyes glowing from a broad and noble brow alight with intellect.

18

"How do I . . . we look?" the idealized Lumbagan inquired.

"Ready for anything," Retief said. "By the way, what do I call you now? Somehow neither Ignoop nor Glarp seems to fit the new you."

"What about . . . Lucael?"

"It's better than Michifer. Now, Luke—if you'll pardon the familiarity—I think we'd best go on with the next phase without delay."

"The next phase being . . . ?"

"As the first Octuple Lumbagan in history, I assume you have unique abilities. Let's find out what they are."

"Yes—I see. The conclusion is logical. By introspection, I note that I have, of course, enhanced physical strength and endurance, exceptionally keen hearing and vision. . . ." Lucael paused. "A most interesting effect," he said. "By bringing either pair of eyes to bear on an object, I of course achieve the familiar stereoscopic effect: three-dimensional sight—a vast improvement over the monocular vision of the former Gloot identity. But when I bring both pairs into play simultaneously, channeling the impression through my compound occipital lobes, there is an exponential improvement. I can clearly perceive nine dimensions: five spatial, two temporal, and two more the nature of which will require careful analysis. . . ." The resonant baritone faded off as Lucael stared, somewhat crosseyed, at the corner of the room.

"You'll have plenty of time later for research in depth, Luke. For the moment we'd better stick to the practical applications."

"Of course. The first order of business, clearly, is to adjust spatial coordinates in such fashion that our *loci* lie external to the enclosure by which we are at present circumscribed."

"Unequivocally, if not succinctly put. Any suggestions?"

"Hmmm." Lucael glanced at each of the four walls in turn. "Solid rock to a depth of several hundred feet on all sides." He stared at the floor. "Twenty-five miles of rock, underlain by a viscous fluid at high temperature and pressure. Fascinating!"

"That leaves the ceiling," Retief prompted.

"To be sure," Lucael glanced up. "Yes, this is the simplest route." He glanced at Retief. "Shall we go?"

"After you."

The super-Lumbagan nodded, folded his arms—both pairs—and rose gently from the floor. In the moment before his head would have contacted the ceiling, the rocky surface seemd to shimmer, fading suddenly to invisibility. Without pausing, Lucael rose steadily up, waist, knees, ankles, to disappear from sight. A moment later, a sharp, breathy cry sounded, followed by a dull thump.

Retief crouched, jumped, caught the edge of the circular opening now miraculously existing in the stone slab, and pulled himself up into what appeared to be a guardroom. A lone Groaci lay stretched on the floor, peacefully snoring.

"It was necessary to numb his cortical synapses—temporarily, of course," Lucael said apologetically. "Poor little creature, so full of vain plans and misconceptions."

"Aren't we all," Retief said. "Luke, let's see how good you are at finding things at a distance. We need fast transportation."

"Let me see. . . . Hmmm. I detect a boat at a distance of three hundred yards on an azimuth of 181° 24°."

"What kind of boat?"

"A hand-hewn canoe sunk in four fathoms of water. There's a large hole in the bottom."

"Skip that one, Luke. How about a nice two-man copter?"

"No . . . nothing like that. However, I note a modest power launch lying at anchor some two miles to the east."

"Ensign Yubb must still be busy pacifying the army. I believe his boat was powered by a small fusion jet. I don't suppose . . . ?"

"I've already started it," Lucael said. "Just a moment while I lift the anchor . . . there. Now, let me see: Which is reverse? Oh, yes. Now, all ahead, half speed until she's past the bar. . . ."

"Nice work, Luke. While you're bringing her around to this side of the island, take a quick scan of the building."

"Very well. . . . A guard or two dozing in the keep. . . .Two Groaci in sick bay with contusions. . . . Half a dozen unfortunates lodged in the brig. Ussh seems to be gone. Yes, I detect his aura—a most powerful one—some ten miles to the east, traveling fast."

"It's time we emulated him. Let's go, Luke; we

don't want to miss all the excitement."

"You refer to the moment when Ussh announces his assumption of power and his program of Galactic conquest?"

"No," Retief said. "I mean the moment when he discovers that Newton's Third Law applies to politicians as well as ping-pong balls."

They met no opposition as they left the now almost-deserted building. Lucael picked a route down the hill through the dense woods to emerge on the beach just as the unmanned power launch rounded the curve of the shore and headed in toward the beach. They splashed out through the shallows as the engine cut; the boat glided silently up to them. Aboard, Lucael restarted the engines, and Retief took the helm.

"Ussh's first column has just entered the city from the west," Lucael announced. "He himself is at this moment leading a procession along Brigand Street toward the palace. Rioting seems to be proceeding as usual."

"Let's be grateful for His Ultimateness's fondness for dramatic gestures," Retief said. "If he'll occupy himself with his victory parade for an hour or so, we may be in time."

"In time to thwart his coup?"

"Probably not. But with luck, in time to stage a small coup of our own." He opened the throttles and the powerful boat surged ahead across the dark water toward the city lights fifteen miles to the east.

The shadowy shapes of Groo-groo and Delerion and Rumboogie rose in turn from the darkness, slid past on the port side, dwindled astern, none showing any signs of life with the exception of a

few small campfires glowing high on their
forested slopes. Ahead, the lights of Thieves' Harbor spread wider, reaching out to enclose them as
they passed the breakwater. The wharves were
deserted as the sleek craft nosed up to the Munic-
ipal Pier.

Retief cut the power, tossed a line around a
piling and jumped down onto the wharf.

"The place looks strange without at least one
small street fight in progress," he said. "Apparently it takes a war to bring peace to Lumbaga."

"The crowds have gathered near the Castle
complex," Lucael said. "A cordon of armed troops
surround the area. Ussh is in the ballroom, in
company with a number of off-worlders."

"Is Ambassador Pouncetrifle among those present?" Retief described the Terran Plenipotentiary.
Lucael confirmed that he was included in the
group.

"They seemed to be linked together," the
super-Lumbagan added, "by means of a chain attached to a series of metal collars which in turn
encircle their necks."

"Apparently Ussh intends to establish a no-
nonsense foreign policy," Retief commented.
"The idea has merit, but in the present case we'll
have to try to introduce a little nonsense after all."

"Interference may prove difficult. All entrances
are blocked by the crowd. I can of course levitate
myself to any desired point within the atmosphere, but the amount of extra weight I'm capable
of carrying is limited."

"Piggyback is out, then. Let's try the back door
where your Ignarp segment and I first met."

Retief led the way across the plaza and down

Dacoit Street, poorly lit by the widely spaced gas lamps, deserted now, littered with the forlorn trash crowds leave behind. They were within a hundred feet of the inconspicuous door when a small party of helmeted and greaved Groaci soldiers emerged suddenly from a narrow cross street ahead. The officer in charge hissed an order; his troops spread out to block the way, then one by one crumpled to the cobblestones. The officer, the last on his feet, stared uncomprehendingly at his collapsing command, then belatedly jerked his pistol from its sequinned holster only to drop it, totter two steps, and fall.

Lucael staggered back against the wall of the building beside them, his face working like yeast.

"Jeez . . . I just had the screwiest nightmare," he muttered, almost in Gloot's voice. "Another . . . lousy trick by . . . unprincipled exploiters, I'll wager," he added in Ignarp's petulant tones.

"Luke! Pull yourself together!" Retief snapped. "You can't afford to go to pieces now!"

Lucael's features twitched and subsided. The four golden eyes settled back into position.

"I . . . find that . . . there are limitations to my power output," he said weakly.

"Come on, Luke. Just a little farther." They covered the remaining yards to the doorway. The heavy door opened on the musty passage.

"From now on, save your strength for emergencies," Retief said. "I think I can guarantee there'll be a steady supply."

They threaded the route through the dusty passages, ascended the stairs to the kitchens, which they found deserted, showing signs of rapid evacuation. A cramped spiral service stair led from an alcove beside the dumbwaiter to the upper stories. At the top, faint voices muttered beyond the door which opened into the private apartment wing.

"A party of minor Groaci officials," Lucael said, speaking with his eyes closed. "They seem to be placing wagers as to whether Terra will be granted colony status, or merely regarded as conquered territory." He paused. "They're gone now."

Retief eased the door open half an inch; crimson carpet led to a pair of massive, carved purplewood doors, just closing behind the bet-laying aliens. Retief went swiftly forward, got a foot in it before it closed. The anteroom beyond was empty; through a low, arched opening the barbarically splendid ballroom was visible, crowded with a mixed throng of locals and aliens. In an elaborately carved chair at the far end of the room sat a towering Lumbagan draped in a robe of Imperial purple, flanked on one side by Colonel Suash at the head of an honor guard of matched native troops in shining cuirasses and polished helms, power guns at present arms, impressive in spite of a number of black eyes and Band-Aids in evidence. At the other side of the throne stood a detachment of Groaci peacekeepers in full uniform. A gaggle of Groaci functionaires, including Ambassador Jith, stood nearby. Ambassador Pouncetrifle, leaning sideways due to the weight of the chain on his neck, stood before the throne; a dozen or so members of his staff huddled behind him in a tight group, none apparently craving the honor of sharing the front rank with the Chief of Mission.

". . . sensible of the honor and all that, Your

Imperial Highness," the Terran Ambassador was saying, "but see here, I can't simply offer Terran recognition of your regime on my own authority!"

"Let's simplify the proposition," a deep bass voice boomed from the Imperial chair. "Acknowledge our divine right, and sign the treaty, and we'll allow you to linger to observe our coronation before being whipped back to your kennels!"

"Ah ... if I might venture an observation. . . ." A faint voice spoke up from the Groaci delegation. It was Ambassador Jith who stepped forward. "While one fully appreciates the eminent propriety of the installation of a native Lumbagan regime entertaining kindly sentiments toward the Groacian state—"

"Yes, yes, get on with it!" the enthroned Lumbagan rumbled.

"To be sure, Your Imperial Highness—I merely meant to suggest that perhaps a less precipitate approach to the question of recognition—"

"Our photograph, hand-tinted by skilled coolies, will be distributed to every village, hamlet, and town in the Eastern Arm! Recognition-wise, we'll be better known that that fellow Whatzizname who won the noodle-knitting contest on TV!"

"Doubtless, sire, your fame will be quickly spread abroad—

"No broads! As an asexual race, we Lumbagans look with disfavor on any sport we can't get on on! Now, that's enough of the subject! On with the formalities!" His Highness favored Pouncetrifle with a scowl involving three eyes and four eyebrows.

"Well, what about it, Terran? Do you want to acknowledge the legitimacy of our gracious rule and receive an exequatur allowing you to go on using up our Lumbagan air, or would you prefer to play a stellar role in the first death sentence we hand down from our newly established throne?"

"Apparently Your Imperial Highness is having his little jape," Jith hissed in apparent dismay. "As Grocian Plenipotentiary, I must advise that the Groacian state would look with extreme disfavor on the establishment of any unfortunate precedent with regard to informal methods of diplomat disposal. A simple declaration of *persona non grata*—"

"Nope. Italian food gives us heartburn," the Imperial figure decreed. "And if we hear any more static from aliens of any persuasion, we might just revise our whole plan for Galactic enlightenment to include you Groaci out!"

An unusually tall and robust Groaci stepped forward from the rear rank.

"Ussh!" Lucael whispered.

"I'm sure that matters need not come to that," Ussh said unctuously. "Doubtless His Excellency, on further consideration, will wish to withdraw his objection."

The Emperor-elect, who had slumped rather vaguely on his throne as the Groaci spoke, sat up alertly.

"Very well; on with the executions. We'll make a note to send for a fresh set of Terries more amenable to reason—"

"To protest this unwarranted assumption of authority," Jith whispered urgently in his own language to Ussh. "To remind you—Special Appointee or otherwise—that I am ranking Groacian official here!"

"I see no reason to coddle Terran spies," the other replied in Lumbagan. "This is Groac's opportunity to get in on the ground floor; why annoy His Imperial Highness with minor quibbles on technical points?"

"To point out that once these natives begin lopping alien heads, Groaci organ clusters may be next to roll!"

Retief's companion was staring at nothing with his eyes half closed. Ussh stirred uneasily, looked around the ornate room.

"It appears that I now confront an intellect equal or superior to my own," Lucael murmured. "He sensed my touch and instantly erected barriers, the strength of which I cannot assess."

"Enough!" the enthroned Lumbagan spoke up abruptly, as if returning from a reverie. "Captain!" He pointed a limber digit at the guard chief. "Escort the condemned to the courtyard, and give your marksmen some unscheduled target practice! No need to finish them off in a hurry; just keep peppering away until they stop twitching."

"Time to move," Retief said. "Luke—stay out of sight and keep an eye on Ussh. No matter what happens, stay tuned to him—and don't tip your hand prematurely."

"What's your plan, Retief? I'm not at all sure I can control him—"

"No time for plans; we'll have to play it by ear," Retief said, and thrust the door wide.

"Hold everything gentlemen," he said as all

eyes turned toward him. "There are new dispatches just in from the home front that cast a different complexion on matters."

19

FOR A MOMENT, a total silence gripped the chamber. Then:

"Seize him!" Ussh snarled. When the guards failed to move, he repeated the order, in a shout this time.

"Don't slip out of character, Ussh," Retief said. "You're just a Groaci MHHP, remember? The troops work for His Putative Highness the Emperor-to-be."

"Retief!" Pouncetrifle blurted hastily in Terran, "Run for it, man! The official comset is in my quarters, at the back of the wardrobe under my golf clubs? Send out a code three-oh-two—"

"Silence!" the Imperial candidate yelled, and hesitated.

"Uh—what about it, Your Highness?" Colonel Suash said hesitantly, still standing fast. "Is it your Imperial command to nab this foreigner?"

The would-be emperor's mouth sagged slightly open. His expression was that of someone lost in thought.

"His Highness," Ussh said, and paused. He seemed to be struggling silently with himself.

"Looking for just the right word, Ussh?" Retief inquired amiably. He turned to the colonel. "Relax, Suash," he said. "As you can see, His Highness is having second thoughts on a number of matters."

"Take. . . ." the Emperor said. Retief took a swift step toward Ussh, who recoiled.

"Stand back, Terran!" he hissed.

"Your Highness?" said Colonel Suash, staring up at the musing figure on the throne.

"Ughhrrr," the royal claimant said, gazing vacantly into space.

"Ah—Your Highness?" Suash repeated. "In the, uh, absence of any new orders, I presume I carry out the executions?"

"Just a minute, Colonel," Retief said. "You Lumbagans don't take orders from foreigners, do you?"

"Not on your second-best toupee I don't," the officer snapped. "So don't try to give me any!"

"By no means, Colonel. I'm referring to Swarmmaster Ussh, who represents himself as a Special Appointee of the Groacian High Council."

"I don't take orders from him either!"

"No," Retief said, and pointed to the throne, "but His Would-be Highness does."

"Wha—?" The officer half drew his dress sword and turned to the emperor-elect. "Do you mind if I chop this foreigner down right here, Your Highness, for that crack he just made about you?"

"Ungunggunggg," the enthroned Lumbagan mumbled. His head lolled on his shoulder; his mouth hung slackly open. Abruptly, he closed it, pulled himself upright.

"We were just, ah, pondering our next pronouncement," he said briskly, as Retief took another step toward Ussh, who stood frozen, two eyes canted tautly toward the throne, the other three hanging limp. At the Terran's advance, he spun to face him.

"Now, Colonel. . . ." The emperor-to-be paused, mouth open.

"Yes, Your Highness?" The Colonel watched in dismay as his ruler-presumptive's expression relaxed into vacuity.

"You might as well address your remarks to Ussh," Retief advised the officer. "He's the brains of the operation."

"See here, Retief," Pouncetrifle spoke up. "The intellectual prowess of the emperor is no concern of ours—"

"It's the intellectual prowess of Ussh I'm thinking of at the moment, Mr. Ambassador. He has a number of rather unusual capabilities."

"Lies!" Ussh shouted. "Fantasies! The ravings of a disordered imagination! I'll see you all hanged for disrespect to His Imperial Highness! It's all a plot to discredit the people's choice, elevated by acclamation to the Lumbagan throne!" He was interrupted by a slithering sound, followed by a heavy thump as the Emperor slid from the elaborate chair and sprawled full length on the dais, snoring gently.

"It's a plot, all right, Ussh—but you're the one behind it," Retief said. "It wasn't His Imperial Highness who mobilized the troops and took the capital by storm; it was you."

"Guards! Shoot them down in their tracks for aggravated lèse-majesté!" Ussh shouted.

"What about it, Colonel?" Retief addressed the guard chief. "Was it our slumbering host who gave the order to march on the capital?"

"Well—not personally, of course. General Ussh

notified me—but he was simply relaying His Imperial Highness' commands—"

"Wasn't it also Ussh who passed along the instructions that organized your unit in the first place, and handed out the orders regarding the secret laboratory?"

"Here, that's GUTS classification material you're discussing!"

"Not any more. You've been taken in, Colonel. Those were all Ussh's ideas—"

"Mr. Retief!" Ambassador Jith spoke up. "May I remind you that *I* am principal officer here, and that *I* have given no such instructions to any member of the Groaci delegation—"

"I'm sure you haven't, Mr. Ambassador," Retief said. "But Ussh seems to have taken it upon himself to use your name."

"Very well!" Ussh hissed suddenly, wheeling to face the irate Groaci, who shrank back. "Perhaps I *have* employed unconventional methods! But clearly it's to Groac's advantage to go along with the *fait accompli!* As soon as the emperor is safely ensconced on his throne, I'm in a position to assure you that Groac will be the object of very special attentions by His Imperial Majesty!"

"What's that?" Colonel Suash roared. "Are you suggesting that the Emperor of Lumbaga is nothing but a tool of foreign interests?"

"Not at all, Suash," Ussh hastened to reassure the officer. "Merely that the new Lumbagan government can rely on the full support of Groac." He turned back to Jith. "What about it, Your Excellency?" he said urgently. "You'll agree that it's clearly your duty to support his Highness' claim—"

"Don't listen to him, Jith," Pouncetrifle blurted. "You're quite right, Groac has no business whatever sticking its olfactory organ into Lumbaga's affairs, especially when I was right on the verge of proposing a well-rounded scheme for installing a provisional governing committee under Terran sponsorship—"

"You presume to tell me my duties, Harvey?" Jith cut in chillingly. "As my subordinate Swarmmaster Ussh so cogently points out, Groacian obligations in support of formerly exploited peoples require that I put aside ordinary protocols for the nonce, and—"

"I don't like it," Suash spoke up. "It sounds to me as if you aliens are getting ready to slice Lumbaga up among yourselves! Accordingly, as senior Lumbagan national present, I'm assuming temporary command! And my first act will be to order the lot of you to the port to embark inside of thirty minutes, with or without your suitcases!"

"Fool!" Ussh snarled. "Do you imagine your feeble native regime can survive for a moment without the sponsorship of Groac? If it weren't for His Highness' temporary indisposition, he'd have your head off for this!"

"And I might add, my dear Colonel," Jith whispered piercingly, "that at a word from me, units of the Groacian Grand Battle Fleet are prepared, if necessary, to land and restore order here!"

"You wouldn't dare!" Pouncetrifle quavered, jowls aquiver.

"Would I not?" Jith contradicted. "I see a great Groacian triumph in the offing! And now, Colonel," he addressed the officer, "you and your chaps may withdraw. I'm sure that His Highness will be himself in a moment—"

The Emperor stirred, sat up.

"Well, just felt a short nap coming on," he mumbled as he scrambled to his feet. "Now, you just run along as Jith suggested, Suash, and—"

"How do you know what he suggested?" Suash snapped back. "You were stone cold out on the floor!"

"Yes, well, as to that—"

"He knows," Retief said, "because Ussh is feeding him his lines."

"Have you taken leave of your senses, Terran meddler?" Ussh yelled. "Everyone in the room heard His Imperial Whatsit's cogent comments!"

"Uh-huh—but you were doing his thinking for him—what there was of it. Unhappily for the future of empire, you can't think of two things at once. Right now, for example, you're busy being indignant with me—and your candidate for the crown is relaxing on the job."

Every head but those of Ussh and Retief swiveled to regard the figure slumped again on the throne.

"Heavens!" Magnan gasped from the sidelines. "You mean we were about to offer our credentials to a ventriloquist's dummy?"

"Not quite. He's alive—but when Ussh assembled him, he carefully left out the more useful portions of the brain."

Suash stared uncertainly from his potential sovereign to Ussh, who stood with canted eyestalks in a pose of total concentration.

"If that's true. . . ."

"Nonsense, Colonel," the Lumbagan emperor-elect said firmly. "I repose the fullest confidence in Ussh, a marvelous fellow and my most trusted advisor. Now I think you'd better run along, as we have matters of high state policy to discuss."

"Don't go!" Pouncetrifle cried. "Colonel Suash, I call on you in the name of humanity to remain present! There's no telling what might happen in the absence of witnesses!"

"I take orders from His Highness, Terry," Suash snapped. "And he said go. Accordingly, we're going!" The colonel barked a command. His troops right-shouldered arms and marched away across the polished floor.

"Retief—do something!" Pouncetrifle wailed.

"Do what, Mr. Ambassador?" Ussh inquired in tones of triumph. "His Highness has spoken! And now—" he paused until the last of the Lumbagan soldiers filed from the room and the tall doors shut behind them—"and now, with those trouble-makers out of earshot, on to the disposition of the Terran spies!" With an abrupt motion, he drew a power pistol from inside his ornate jacket. "A pity they should happen to be shot down by accident as they led an attempted assault on His Highness' person, but such are the tribulations that beset those who would stand in the path of empire."

"You wouldn't!" Pouncetrifle gasped.

"See here, Ussh," Ambassador Jith whispered. "You don't actually mean to commit violence on the persons of the Terrans, I trust? To deport them in restraining fetters, yes. But I forbid you to do away with them entirely."

"It will be our little secret, Your Excellency," Ussh cut in curtly. "His Imperial Highness has matters under complete control."

"Are you quite certain of that?" Jith asked, eye-

ing the presumptive ruler, who now stood swaying slightly, gazing into the middle distance.
"Candidly, he presents the appearance of an unsuccessful lobotomy case."

"Why not tell him the rest of the secrets, Ussh?"
Retief said. "Let him know how clever you really
are. Describe your discovery of a sure-fire method
for assembling Lumbagans to order, according to
any genetic code desired. Tell him about your
experiments, which produced some rather unusual types, some of whom proved useful for special purposes, such as terrorizing the populace.
Describe your soldier farm, and let him in on the
secret of the lab on Sprook where you worked out
the details of your hostility transmitter—"

"Silence, spy!" Ussh shouted.

"Don't be modest," Retief urged. "Give the ambassador full details on how you plan to manufacture a few million soldiers, modeled after himself
and equipped by Groac, and use them to set up a
modest empire in this end of the Arm, after which
you'll no doubt establish ranches on all the likely
planets to raise spares for the army. With forced
feeding, you can produce a fully equipped infan-
tryman in a little under three weeks, gun and
all—"

"Ha ha," Ussh said. "You *will* have your little
jest, eh? Gallows humor, I believe it's called."

"You made your big mistake, of course, Ussh,
when you let Suash and his boys leave," Retief said. "He was your only chance to make it
stick—"

"So you imagine!" Ussh spun to face Jith. "The
time has come for the carrying out of His Highness' commands! If you would like to do the job
personally it would be a gracious touch, in keep-

ing with the close relations existing between
Lumbaga and Groac!"

"Wouldn't it though?" Retief said. "If you could
con Ambassador Jith into committing himself to
the murder of a covey of Terries, he'd have no
choice but to back your play. Fortunately, he
won't be so foolish—"

"You think not!" Ussh snarled. "Jith—order
them shot—now!"

"Don't you dare, Jith!" Pouncetrifle yelped. "I
absolutely forbid it!"

"Forbid, you say?" Jith whispered. "You go too
far, Harvey—" The Groaci ambassador faced
Ussh. "If you're quite sure the Terrans planned the
murder of His Highness, it of course becomes my
duty to—"

"To listen to the rest of the story," Retief said.
"There are a couple more things Ussh forgot to
mention—"

"Details, details!" Ussh yelled. "The important
fact is that I, at the head of an army of dedicated
troops, will lead the way to the conquest of vast
new territories, eliminating or enslaving inferior
peoples along the way, and in the end organizing
the entire Galaxy as a single empire under a single
rule!"

"A glowing picture," Retief said. "But of course
Ambassador Jith has no reason to lend support to
the scheme."

"Have I not, Mr. Retief?" Jith whispered. "I
admit Swarmmaster Ussh has employed unor-
thodox methods—but if the end result is a Galactic Empire under Groac—"

"Correction, Mr. Ambassador. Groac will be
among the first victims."

"Victim? Of her own troops, under her own general Ussh? Preposterous!"

"It's true Ussh and his army will be in position to cut quite a swath, with Groaci backing and Groaci materiel. And no doubt in the end the CDT would come to what's known as an accommodation with the *de facto* situation. But you're forgetting an important datum. The troops who'll be doing the conquering won't be Groaci; they'll be Lumbagans, no matter how many eyes they happen to have."

"Well—as to that," Jith stalled, looking to Ussh for counsel. "I assume that as honorary Groaci, true to their exalted somatype, we may rely on General Ussh to keep the interests of his motherworld in the forefront of his mind."

"Exactly," Retief said. "And his motherworld is Lumbaga."

"Clearly, he's taken leave of his senses," Ussh grated.

"Granted, he's a most unusual Lumbagan," Retief went on. "Normally, once an accretion of Freebies reaches the four-decker stage—at which point intelligence appears—their finer sensibilities prevent them from carrying evolution any farther. But it appears that General Ussh broke the taboo."

"What vile allegation is this?" Ussh yelled.

"Careful, Ussh, you'll give yourself away," Retief said. "It doesn't seem vile to anybody but a Lumbagan."

"This is all nonsense, of course," Ambassador Jith purred. "But out of curiosity—go on, Mr. Retief."

"Ussh—or whoever the original Lumbagan

personality was who had the idea—overcame his scruples and integrated himself with another individual—possibly a Trip; a subintelligent creature, but of course the combination has capabilities that exceed those of either of the original components. Unfortunately, he used his enhanced mental powers to concoct a scheme to take over first Lumbaga, then the rest of the material universe. Naturally, he needed help; he made a study of the foreigners present on his world, and picked the Groaci as the likeliest partners. With his abilities, it wasn't hard to readjust his external appearance to match yours, Mr. Ambassador—"

"He's raving!" Ussh yelled. "How could anyone possibly—"

"It wasn't easy, at first—but you figured it out. Some of your practice models are still running around in the woods, making Groaci tracks to confuse the trail. But in the end you were able to palm yourself off on a few malcontents as a Groacian MHPP, and enlist some behind-the-scenes help in setting things up for your coup—"

"That, Terry, is your final error!" Ussh grated, and aimed the gun at Retief's ribs.

"Ussh! Control yourself!" Jith keened. "What simpler than to give the lie to this fantastic allegation!"

"Is it?" Retief said. "Ussh, deny you're a Lumbagan—but do it in Groaci, just to be certain your fellow countrybeings don't miss any of the finer nuances."

"Bah! Prepare to die, witless Terran!"

"Ussh! If you expect my aid and support—do as he says!" Jith hissed.

Ussh hesitated, then turned to include the

Groaci delegation in his field of fire.

"Think what you like, Jith! You'll do as I bid, or die with the Terrans! I'll explain to your successor how you and they slaughtered each other, only myself surviving; then I'll enlist his support and on to empire!"

"Why—why, Retief's right," Pouncetrifle gasped. "Jith—he won't speak Groaci—because he can't! He's an impostor!"

"Duped!" Jith wailed. "Undone by my credulity! Faked out of position and into unwitting support of a non-Groaci conquest by an underling, and a bogus one at that!"

"Don't feel too badly," Retief said. "He only intended to use you Groaci to finance his first few local take-overs. As soon as he'd consolidated his gains, Groaci would have been quietly consolidated into his empire, with the help of a number of pseudo-Groaci agents who would have infiltrated Groac by then."

"Rave on, Retief!" Ussh invited. "Familiarize these fools with the scope of their folly—and then—" Ussh whirled as the tall double doors burst wide. Lucael strode forward, his golden eyes gleaming.

"Yes? What is it?" Ussh barked uncertainly. "You have dispatches from the field? Or—" He staggered suddenly, as if struck a heavy blow between the eyes.

"Treachery!" Ussh gasped—and Lucael stopped in his tracks, stood swaying. Face to face the two super-Lumbagans stood, locked in mortal—though invisible—conflict.

"Ussh!" Retief called. The imitation Groaci half-turned—and in the momentary distraction,

Lucael struck. Ussh gave a hoarse cry, stood dithering for a moment. . . .

Like a tree struck by lightning, the false Groaci's body shivered and split. For a moment there was a wild scramble of parts as the former superbeing's components, like a mob of troops falling in on command, regrouped themselves into two separate entities, arms and legs and ears scuttling for their assigned places. In a moment, two short, sullen individuals stood where Ussh had been, staring apprehensively around at their astounded audience.

"Why—it's Difnog and Gnudf, the Lumbagan observers!" Pouncetrifle gasped.

"And apparently," Jith whispered, "they were more observant than we suspected!"

20

IT WAS HALF an hour later. The Terran diplomats, freed of their shackles, had huddled with their Groaci colleagues for an impromptu meeting.

"Well, then," Ambassador Pouncetrifle said crisply, "since General Ussh seems to have opted for a return to civilian life, and His Highness is permanently catatonic, it appears we're left with the administrative problem of setting up a pro tem housekeeping government. As Terran emissary, I'll reluctantly assume the chief role in affairs—"

"Hardly, my dear Harvey," Jith interjected. "Inasmuch as the present contretemps was produced in part by Groacian efforts—"

"Pseudo-Groacian efforts, need I remind you!"

"A mere quibble, Mr. Ambassador. Groac will ⸱rtake to set up a caretaker government, with the ᴣsistance of Colonel Suash and his native constabulary—"

"Gentlemen," Retief said. "Aren't you forgetting the Emperor?"

"Eh?"

"What's that?" Both plenipotentiaries turned to survey the imperial figurehead, who stood erect now, gazing sternly at the assembled foreigners.

"You need not trouble yourselves, gentlebeings," he said curtly. "I'll handle the government of Lumbaga—to the extent that Lumbaga needs governing." He turned, stepped up on the dais, and seated himself on the throne.

"Item number one," he said impressively, "Any foreigner found meddling in Lumbagan affairs will be shipped home in a plain wrapper. Item number two—"

"If we could go back for a moment to item one, Your Highness—"

"Make that 'Majesty', Pouncetrifle. I've just assumed Imperial dignities for the duration of the emergency."

"To be sure, Your Majesty. I'm certain that on reflection you'll want to rescind the restriction on Terran participation in Lumbagan national life, inasmuch as, as worded, it would tend to somewhat restrict the free play of diplomacy—"

"Precisely. Item number two: Since that government governs best which governs least, I intend to provide only the best for my people. Accordingly, all laws are declared illegal, including this one."

"Hmm," Pouncetrifle mused, "since His Majesty seems clearly to be non compos mentis, Jith, it's clear that duty requires that responsible authorities step in, in the interest of the welfare of the Lumbagan people. I trust you're with me?"

"Assuredly, Harvey," Jith whispered. "I suggest we find quieter quarters for His Majesty; possibly space could be found in the former root cellar—whilst you and I proceed to arrange matters in consonance with the principle of the greatest good for the greatest number; and inasmuch as we Groaci breed like flies, I suppose you'll concede the obvious primacy of Groaci interests."

"No need for dispute," the emperor cut in decisively. "Inasmuch as neither of you will have anything to say about Lumbagan affairs from now on."

"He's raving," Pouncetrifle stated flatly. "Jith, I call you to witness that His Majesty was babbling incoherently at the time I was forced to have him restrained. Retief—assist the poor fellow down from his chair. . . ."

"Curious acoustics in this room," Retief said blandly. "I thought for a moment your Excellency was proposing that we lay hands on a foreign Chief of State."

"Mutiny, eh?" Colonel Warbutton barked. "Well, fortunately for democracy, I'm here to carry out the wishes of the people as interpreted by regs and expressed via appropriate channels!" He advanced on the throne. Ten feet from it, he found himself floating an inch off the floor, his feet paddling vigorously. A brace of underlings sprang to his side, found themselves adrift, rising lightly as balloons toward the ceiling. Pounce-trifle uttered a bellow as he floated up from the floor, followed by Magnan and the rest of the staff. Jith uttered a faint cry and drifted upward, attanded by his staff. Only Retief and Lucael remained on their feet.

"Now that you've heard the details of the new constitution," the Emperor advised the levitating bureaucrats, "I declare the audience to be at an end. Don't bother backing from the presence; just disappear."

At his words, there were a series of sharp *plop!*s as air imploded to fill the vacancies created by the suddenly absent dignitaries.

"I hope you didn't throw them completely away," Retief said. "Once they get their feet on the ground, I have an idea they'll take a realistic view of the proper role of diplomacy in the development of Lumbaga."

"They're sorting themselves from among the tubers in the subbasement," His Majesty said. "And now . . . I declare Parliament dissolved . . . until . . . the next time . . ." He slumped on the throne and snored. Retief turned quickly to Lucael.

"Well done, Luke. I was wondering how long you could hold out."

"If anybody asks," the super-Lumbagan said in a failing voice, "tell them . . . their emperor . . . will return . . . whenever the situation demands. And now . . . farewell, Retief . . ."

There was a final sharp implosion, and Retief was alone in the throne room.

21

"HEAVENS, RETIEF," FIRST Secretary Magnan said, "now that the excitement is over, one wonders if the entire affair weren't merely the product of group hysteria." They were sitting at a long plank table in the Imperial Feast Hall, dining somewhat meagerly on CDT emergency banquet rations in company with a cosmopolitan crowd of Terrans, Groaci, and Lumbagans.

"Frankly, I'd be tempted to dismiss the incident involving the rutabagas as sheer delirium," Colonel Warbotton put in glumly, spooning in caviar, "if it weren't for the fact that I've suffered a virulent recurrence of an old potato blight." His expression brightened. "Of course, the condition will necessitate my being invalided out home for a few months' convalescent leave, which time I might spend quite profitably penning a memoir of recent events, possibly titled: *The Importance of Mass Hallucination in Military Affairs*."

"How about *The Hallucinatory Importance of the Military in Mass Affairs*?" Magnan proposed tartly.

"Gosh, Retief," Gloot said as the men of war and peace sparred verbally. "So you were really a Terry all along. Makes me feel kind of dumb to of been chumming around with the enemy. Lucky I changed sides."

"You claim there's two kinds of Terries, male

and female," Ignarp said. "Frankly, you all look alike to me."

"Oh, there's a *vas deferens* between us," Retief assured his guest.

"And I never got my ransom dough," Gloot said glumly. "On the other hand, I found out running things ain't all a bowl of cherries."

"One taste of government was enough for me," Ignarp agreed. "I'll settle for good old anarchy any time."

"Umm," Magnan smiled loftily. "But of course you chaps know nothing of the intricacies of politics. Now," he indicated the head of the table, where Jith and Pouncetrifle huddled, tête-à-tête. "Notice the resilience with which the ambassadors are coming to grips with the new realities, or whatever they are, of the situation, working out the rather complex protocols of establishing formal relations with a nonexistent government."

"As long as they stick to shooting dispatches back to headquarters and putting on charades for visiting politicos, OK," Gloot said. "But the first time they step out o' line—whammo! The Legendary Magical Emperor will be back on the job—and next time they're liable to wind up digging their way into the root cellar from below."

"I hardly think the Lumbagan in the street is in a position to criticize matters of Imperial policy, Mr. Gloot," Magnan said coolly. "I hope your association with Mr. Retief on his expedition up-country hasn't given you a false sense of involvement in matters over your head."

"You must be kidding, Terry," Ignarp said. "Gloot here is Minister of Imaginary Affairs in the Lumbagan government-in-exile."

"Government-in-exile?" Magnan frowned.

"The only place for a government to be," Ignarp confirmed. "And I just accepted a post with the Department of Education as Commissioner of Superstitions."

"You're stamping them out?" Magnan queried confusedly.

"Heck no. I'm starting new ones, in keeping with a fine old tradition dating back almost twenty-four hours."

"Speaking of superstitions," Warbutton said behind his hand to Magnam, "I think we'd do well to initiate a few of our own devising. For example, a carefully tailored myth to the effect that Terrans can work miracles—like turning water into vintage Pepsi, for example. . . ." He broke off, staring in horror at the glass before him which rose gracefully into the air, its contents darkening to deep purplish red. The colonel followed it with his eyes as it took up a position directly over his head and inverted itself, discharging a cooling stream of effervescent fluid over the officer's startled features.

After the colonel had left the table—a departure noted by all present, accompanied as it was by a well-directed jet of liquid emanating apparently from thin air—Magnan dipped a trembling finger in the puddle on the table and tasted it.

"Pepsi?" Retief inquired.

"Burgundy," Magnan choked. "Romanée-Conti, '24, I believe." He rose hastily. "I think I'd best add a number of emendations to my preliminary report," he muttered, "lest it appear that I was so shortsighted as to doubt the existence of magic." He hurried away.

"I thought you fellows had gone out of the miracle business pending the next crisis," Retief addressed Gloot and Ignarp as the two locals gripped hands across the table. "But since you haven't, try that last one again. Only this time don't spill any." A moment later, they raised three paper-thin goblets of purple wine, touched them together with a musical clink. At the far end of the table, Ambassador Jith caught the gesture, raised his glass in response.

"To a new era in interplanetary relations," he whispered cheerfully. "To peace and plenty for almost all, within reasonable limits!"

"That reminds me," Ignarp said, "The boys in GRAB are going to be wondering why I didn't redivide the loot along more practical lines while I was emperor."

"While you were emperor," Gloot retorted. "While I was letting you go along for the ride, you mean—"

"You big slob, I was the brains of the outfit!"

"You little creep, I handled all the tricky parts—"

"Gentlemen," Retief interjected, "we were about to propose a toast, remember?"

Gloot lifted his glass. "To our friends, the good guys," he said.

"And to our enemies, the bad guys," Ignarp added.

"And to the hope," Retief said, "that someday we'll be able to tell which are which."

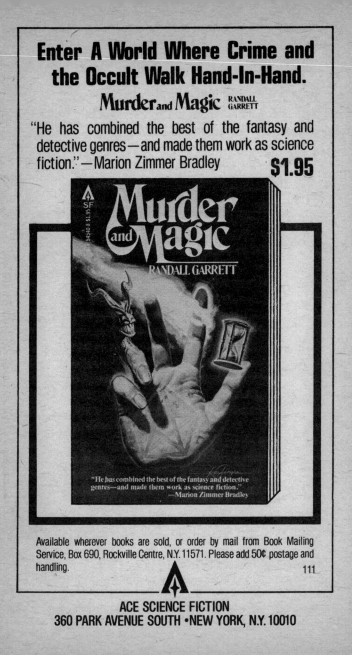

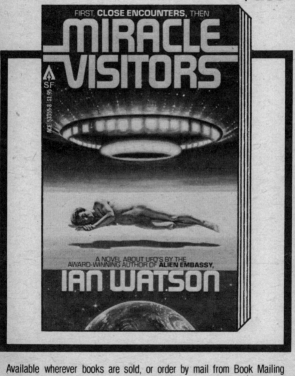

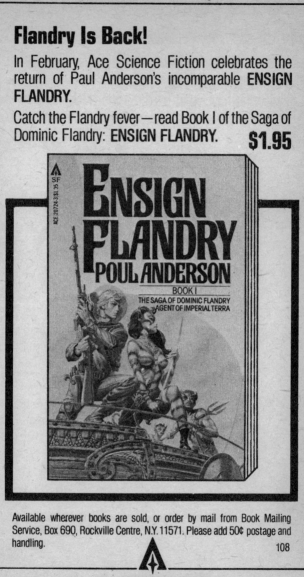